LEVINSON of HARVARD

A novel

Also by L. M. Vincent

Novels

Final Dictation
Pas de Death
Saving Dr. Block
Reception

Nonfiction

The Dancer's Book of Health
Competing with the Sylph
In Search of Motif No. 1
A Theft of Privilege

L.M.Vincent

For Alexander (Eliyohu) Margolis
1887-1967

No doubt the past can be a place for drowning.
But without it, where are you? What's love or war?
You wouldn't think he knew where he was going
In all that glare, alone, the scholar rowing.

—RICHARD DEY
(from "Scholar, Rowing")

A Reunion Conversation

Cambridge, Massachusetts
Spring, 2008

I scanned the overcrowded Quincy Dining Hall and spotted Rebecca Appleton Wyatt chatting with overdressed alumni. The gathering was ostensibly casual; more of the reunion allotment was earmarked for the buffet luncheon and formal dinner dance with live music the next day, super fancy and no holds barred. I wasn't sticking around for those. I had been asked to participate in that afternoon's symposium, had come up from Philly to perform my duty, and would return in the morning. I hadn't noticed her that afternoon, and hadn't seen her since college. Before Becca, I hadn't known anyone who went by three names. But naturally her lineage from both the Appleton and Wyatt sides deserved recognition. If any name were to be dropped, it should be her fourth, her adopted married one. Which, most improbably, was Rosenberg.

I wasn't a reunion person. A few old friends and acquaintances had buttonholed me after the panel discussion, which was pleasant enough, but aside from accepting the invitation from the Thirty-fifth reunion committee, I wasn't a gung-ho alumnus. Not that I wasn't grateful for my Harvard education, I just hadn't always been in sync with the place—our relationship was badly timed. I blamed Harvard for the angst of those years when I could have attributed it to family, a stressful adjustment, and even the social and political upheaval created by the Vietnam War. When and if I ever responded to fundraising requests, I'd know I'd come to terms with the place.

Becca had kept her slim figure, shown to advantage with a slinky sparkled black cocktail dress with an audacious knee slit for a woman her age, and a body desirable enough to stop an underclassman in his tracks. She tossed her head back with a burst of laughter that years before would have produced a tantalizing aftershock through long dark hair, worn loose. But now barely a ripple, her hair in a short and stylish pixie. The color was salt and pepper, feigning the old Yankee disposition for naturalness, but likely out of bottles. Her face also evidenced some work. A lift, or fillers, or both—it was hard to tell from a distance—but clearly a job well done.

I took a sip of Cabernet and continued watching Becca as she again thrust back her head and levitated a slender arm in an ethereal *porte de bras*. Such delicacy was a stark contrast to her being wound tighter than an unpredictable thoroughbred. Unpredictable and uninhibited. In the summers her custom was naked nocturnal swims at Singing Beach. And during the school year she had been a regular at the Adams House pool, where she also swam naked. Living in Dunster house, I never saw this for myself, but the rumors were confirmed by a buddy who had the good fortune to work as a lifeguard. That he was actually paid to watch Rebecca Appleton Wyatt swim nude was a frequent topic of conversation among sex-starved males, who fantasized of either swimming or lifeguarding themselves.

Only later did I recognize that her edginess revealed the precarious stranglehold by which life held her. Her impulsiveness was ominous—instead of jumping into a fountain to wade in winter, could she fling herself from a window? Or, at Singing Beach some starless night, instead of shedding her clothes for a dip, might she fill her coat pockets with stones and walk resolutely toward Great Egg Rock?

A wealthy, well-traveled prep school girl, sophisticated and highly sexed, naturally had this self-confessed rube more than intimidated. The young and reckless beauty I had known had been unapproachable and out of my league. Our first meeting was the only time in our relationship I ever took the initiative, and only then prompted by an extraordinary coincidence. Without that coincidence it was unlikely that I would have known her at all.

Catching my eye, she wasted little time leaving her coterie of admirers and walked toward me with those long athletic strides of hers. I was surprised. We had barely associated after freshman year. Seeing her from a distance was an image burned into my consciousness, remaining an expectation after decades. With each step closer, the shock and strangeness of seeing her aged dissipated, the young woman I had known returning like a spirit unleashed.

So what did Becca Appleton Wyatt see as she approached, head tilted to one side as if yielding to a wind gust, and with a restrained smile as seductive as the strap of a slip falling off an irresistible shoulder? A late middle-aged man, substantially graying but still reasonably fit, wearing—for Christssake, was I subconsciously trying to make some sort of "I don't give a fuck" statement at a Harvard reunion?—a corduroy sport jacket with patches at the elbows, a pair of dress jeans, and black cross-trainers. In short, she also was seeing a cliché. We were who we were, then as now, and some things could never be expected to change.

"You look wonderful, Mark," she said, kissing me on both cheeks as I inhaled her fragrance.

"You look . . . even better," I said, unable to return a compliment without hesitation. I was wishing the room brighter so I could see the sapphire blue of her eyes.

"I don't believe you for a second," she replied, a stab at false modesty she knew utterly ridiculous. "After a total hysterectomy and breast cancer, I'm hardly a trophy wife."

A typical Becca Wyatt response, and I reacted with a restrained smile. She had no filters and of course I had no reply. Who did? So I stood dumbly with a frozen look on my face, confident she would pick up the slack.

"You'd heard, I suppose," she said, "that I married a Jew." Another zinger, put out there with no additional pleasantries. "Rebecca Appleton Wyatt Rosenberg. More than a few bodies in graves at the Old Granary are rolling, I can assure you. And on top of that, I converted a number of years ago. Irv and I raised both of our kids Jewish. I'm a Jewish mother, Mark, imagine that."

"I need a moment to wrap my head around that, Becca," I said. "And I suppose you know that I married—"

"—a shiksa," she finished, using the Yiddish term that I had commonly used growing up but abandoned once I married out of the faith and realized how derogatory it was.

"Episcopalian," I corrected her.

"Ironic, isn't it? Back in the day, neither one of us would have considered it very likely."

"Not even remotely possible." Becca had been unobtainable for any number of reasons, religion being only one of them.

"I never even got far enough to meet the parents," I said.

"You wouldn't have liked them," replied Becca, "and I'm sorry to admit that they probably wouldn't have thought very much of you, either." She put on an exaggerated mid-Atlantic accent. "'He's a nice enough boy, but REALLY, Becca?'"

"You always did what your parents expected of you?" I had no idea where that sarcasm came from, perhaps the Cabernet was supercharged. "I thought you might at least have brought me home as an act of rebellion." I was stunned by my own venom, as if a long buried carbuncle had been lanced at the sight of her and was oozing pus.

I needed to back off, steer the conversation in a more benign direction. Then I realized the awkwardness was one-sided. Becca was unfazed.

"Don't think I didn't consider it . . ." she responded, "but that wouldn't have been very fair to you." She tossed back her head and threw both arms upwards as if they had been jerked by a puppet master, transporting herself away from the subject. "But just *look* at you . . . the famous historian of our class! I can't tell you how many times people—finding out you graduated in my year—have asked me if I knew you . . ."

I smiled and shrugged in an expression of humility.

". . . and of course, I tell them that, not only did I know you, but that we had sex."

My smile tightened into a grimace. "Aren't there some rules about what can and cannot be said in polite conversation at reunions?" I finally asked.

"You mean, aren't some things sacred?"

"Yes, you might put it that way."

"Of course not, as long as the spouses aren't present. But don't worry about the sex revelation, I don't go into any details in distinguished company." She smiled and pursed her lips.

I responded non-verbally. She read my face.

"Oh, I do believe I've made you uncomfortable, Mark." She flung back her head and let loose her familiar laugh. Still captivating, but now in a bit lower register and betraying a long history of cigarettes.

No doubt she had not been joking. She would freely reveal our sexual escapade freshman year with as little compunction as talk of hysterectomies or lumpectomies. Maybe the entire class knew by now. It occurred to me to Google our names together to see if any hits involved a sexual nature.

On my part, I got my secretive nature from my grandfather. Being in the rarified although not exceptionally exclusive company of those who had been bedded by Rebecca Appleton Wyatt would have been worth boasting about. But I hadn't told anyone about it then, including my roommates. And later, not even my wife Sue knew. Sue incorrectly assumed that my mention of any woman from my college past implied that we had slept together; after all, it had been the early seventies. The assumption was usually as incorrect as it was flattering. But I had never mentioned Becca, so there were no assumptions to be made.

"All these years have gone by and I still wish there had been some sort of . . . resolution." I said. "A bang, not a whimper."

Becca's sudden change of expression suggested a mime practicing facial transformations in front of a mirror.

"You could have made more of an effort," she said.

I couldn't hide my incredulity.

"No, no, don't pull that," I protested. "It was obvious you were avoiding me. You wouldn't even look at me. I could take a hint. Besides, you intimidated the shit out of me anyway. I didn't even feel worthy enough to hang around you. You of all people knew that."

"It wasn't that at all, Mark. And you're right. I shut you out. But I was a real mess then, for a whole variety of reasons, and for many years after. I probably saved you a lot of time and trouble."

"I would have liked to have had a say in that at the time."

I took a breath in to continue, but she interrupted with a firmness I hadn't heard before. "You made me feel guilty for one thing, Mark. I was ashamed.

It was something I just couldn't deal with, and I told you, I was a mess, a total head case. You deserved better than me. Actually, I had a bit of a breakdown . . . or at least enough of an upset to get a couple weeks R&R at McLean. Most of it didn't have anything to do with you at all. Think about it and you'll understand. You were always better at understanding things than I was, you were just unaware that you were."

"It was just about my *grandfather*," I said, unable to hide my exasperation. "It had nothing to do with you or your family at all. I made no judgments, I was just trying to find out who I was and where I came from."

She visibly regained her composure. "There was more to it than that. You WERE your grandfather. And we were deluded, so sixties and thinking things had really changed. Perhaps you're right about things that one shouldn't talk about at college reunions."

I nodded, suddenly feeling very tired.

"I was expecting idle chit chat," I said.

"So was I," she said.

"Actually, I wasn't expecting any chat at all."

"No need for apologies. There may be something to be said for intensely catching up. It's grand to see you. You've done well. I always knew you would. I admired you. You had your head on straight. I was a fuck-up."

The admission gave her a moment's pause, but she recovered into a smile. "I had a feeling you might turn up tonight," she continued, "so I brought something for you." She took me by the hand and led me through the crowd to the far end of the room, where some people had placed their coats over chairs against the wall. She picked up a crimson and white plastic Coop bag from the top of one of the folding chairs. The package inside was rectangular and about three inches thick, wrapped in brown paper and heavily taped.

She handed me the bag. I set my wine glass down on the dining table within reach and started to remove the package when she stopped me.

"Not now. Take the bag."

"What is it?"

"A surprise. A couple of things. But don't open it now. Take it home. Open it with your family."

"My girls are out of the house. One in college, the other in med school."
I couldn't help bragging. To boot, they were both Ivy educated, following in
the old man's footsteps. Generically, at least. Specifically, both had turned
down Harvard, suggesting either my failure as a role model or the influence
of my deep-seated ambivalence.

"I know. I read your Red Book entries," she confessed, referring to the
class reports published every five years.

I didn't need to similarly confess that I read hers, it being so obvious.

"Give me a hint," I pressed, lifting the bag upwards.

"Okay. One is something you've already seen," she relented after pausing
to think. "The other is something I came across a few years ago when I was
going through my father's things after he died. My mother didn't want to stay
in the house on Masconomo, so we had to clear out a lot of stuff. I'd always
meant to send it to you, but I rather think I enjoyed keeping it for myself. But
it's rightfully yours."

"You sold the house on Masconomo?"

"Irv and I lived there for a while, when the kids were little. Then I inherited
the family cottage from Aunt Lillian, which is where we live now. That old
bird lived forever."

"You mean you moved into Longneck Cove?"

"I couldn't exactly let the family estate go, could I?"

"I suppose not."

"Well, it looks exactly the same, despite pouring money into it. It's a bitch
to heat—we still need to close half of it off in the winter. In any case, I came
across . . ." she indicated the contents of the bag with a nod of her head, "and
I hung it in my grandfather's library for a while. But it belongs to you."

"Thank you. I'm more than intrigued."

"And maybe you could drop me a line after you've opened it," she said,
and again became serious. "Don't be a stranger, Mark," she said, and kissed
me on the cheek.

Becca turned, and without a remorseful glance back like in the movies,
returned to her cluster of classmates. Our reunion was over.

More than partied out, I found myself hurrying to the dining room exit, the bag bumping against the outside of my leg. And then I became aware of a tear running down my cheek, as the floods of the past hurled me into a churning surf of memories.

Wait-listed

My grandfather Michael Levinson told me his Harvard stories one summer when I was ten. I spent a lot of alone time with him then. My mother would drop me off when she picked up my grandmother to take her shopping or to the hairdressers, or anywhere to get her out of the house. My mother was a good sport to assume responsibility for her in-laws—my father's two sisters and their families lived in St. Louis and seldom visited—but she had lost both of her own parents by then and was a dutiful fifties wife to a fifties doctor. Grandpa—Poppa as I called him—was ailing, and acting weird.

My parents whispered about "dementia" and "tiny strokes." His difficult and even abusive behavior was a strain on my grandmother, particularly since Poppa refused assistance of any kind and insisted he could stay alone. The house off Ward Parkway was too much for them under the best of circumstances—they were in their late seventies—but Poppa resisted moving to a sensible apartment or allowing a live-in maid. He was adamant about not employing help, which led to frequent and intense arguments. With me in earshot, my parents and Grandma Manya railed away in Yiddish, but my grandfather never reverted to the language of the Old World. He would only speak English, whatever the circumstances. I always found that a strange contrast, those bilingual arguments. Naturally I knew what was going on regardless of language, and I always found myself silently on Poppa's side.

Poppa, according to my father, had never shown his temper, even while a strict disciplinarian with high expectations for his son. And as a law professor at the University of Missouri he had been known as soft-spoken and thoughtful, possessing a near-legendary saint-like patience with law students. But the rage must have always been there somewhere, bubbling like a pot of oatmeal, only now surfacing due to diminished ability to filter. My father took him on half-heartedly, and was often at work when many of the arguments occurred. Even so, with my mother's reenactments and constant badgering him at dinnertime, he was forced to participate vicariously as penance. The fights about personal supervision lasted for a year or two, until Poppa died. But that particular summer, pretending to acquiesce, they obliged him to baby-sit me. If he knew the opposite was the case—that I was the caretaker—he never let on. We always had a special relationship and he doted on me. His only grandchild living in town and the youngest, I would have been his favorite in any case.

Poppa had been tall, but all my memories of him are of a frail, stooped-over man, walking hesitantly with a cane. He usually wore a plaid long-sleeve sport shirt buttoned to the neck, covered by a thin cardigan sweater that was too big. His favorite slacks, once complemented by a suit jacket, were high quality and years earlier tailored for a taller and heavier man. They were cinched tightly at the waist by a belt and bagged throughout the legs. The trouser legs needed to be rolled so he wouldn't catch a heel on them and trip. Since he wouldn't let grandma hem them, she would roll up the pantlegs every morning, with him complaining the whole time. But she had her way—he was no fool—his protestations more for show and dignity's sake.

Despite his haphazard attire, Poppa was never disheveled; his thin silver hair was always neatly combed back, revealing his prominent widow's peak. And not a morning passed without him shaving with his Gillette single-edged razor. He tended to nick himself, though, so he was often clean-shaven at the expense of being blood-speckled or with white crusty streaks from a styptic pencil. Bloodied or not he had a refinement about him, and an articulateness that always confounded me. Every other family member of his generation, including Grandma, spoke with a Russian accent—some more pronounced than others—but Poppa didn't have one. If anything, he sounded more British in his inflections than American. It was hard to imagine that he spent the early years of his life in the Pale of Settlement. And this man would become a distinguished attorney, a specialist in Civil Rights Law, and an iconic professor at the law school in Columbia, Missouri. How could Poppa not have stories to tell?

Some stories, but not the Harvard ones, I had already heard from him or grandma or my parents, bits and pieces that hovered above my full comprehension. How could they not? I had little knowledge of pre-Revolutionary Russia, and what I did know was from the perspective of a child. There were only images, incidents without meaningful context. I knew about antisemitism and heard stories about the czar, pogroms, the May Laws. His bare bones family history I could understand. Poppa came from a fairly prosperous family; his father was a land owner and sugar beet farmer. I knew they farmed land that was beside a river, and that as a child Poppa had a row boat. I knew that he traveled by steamer to Ellis Island with relatives, and that both of his parents had died of diphtheria. He was raised by his aunt and uncle among other Jewish immigrants in the north end of Boston. His cousin, my great Uncle Sam, also called Shmuel, was a few years older. I had met Sam a couple of times, so those details became reinforced. He was so unlike Poppa, a short and stocky man with a heavy accent and bad breath, who had gone into the rag business successfully and stayed in New England, where he had owned a garment manufacturing business until his retirement. I knew that my grandfather was very smart, and had been at the top of his law school class. Why in the world he decided to settle in Missouri, I had no idea. But things had turned out well, after all, so what did it matter?

Poppa's refusal to employ household help was less a manifestation of clinging to his independence than the emergence of a paranoia. He had occasional delusions, convinced that someone was trying to poison him, that he was being mistaken for some other person. Once I saw him rolling imaginary pills in his hands so convincingly that I almost thought they were real. Scared to admit Poppa was hallucinating, but still fascinated, I leaned in closer to watch him rubbing his fingers together, almost expecting to see the tainted tablets. Then when he opened his empty hand and asked "See these?" I nodded, wide-eyed. Then he violently flung them into space and my eyes automatically went to the floor, looking for the invisible tablets. When I looked back up at him he had calmed, rubbing his forehead just over the mole on the left side with his fingers, as if the pressure would resettle the thoughts that had temporarily scattered like buckshot. Then he casually picked up his cigar from his ashtray.

That one summer Poppa sat, cane resting in his lap, in the corner of the floral-printed sofa. He would only get up to pee or go to the kitchen table to eat sandwiches that Grandma had prepared for us. The TV was on but we never really watched; we just talked about all sorts of things from the Athletics' predictably lousy season to politics. He was a dyed in the wool Democrat and a Kennedy admirer, while my Dad was a Nixon man. Time was marked not by the clock, but by the lighting and relighting of his cigar, which defined some mysterious temporal rhythm. Poppa handed me the matches so I could light the cigar for him, which he knew I enjoyed. Sometimes he would intentionally direct the initial puffs into my face and smile, as I flinched and my eyes watered. By that time, I already had the cigar ring on my finger.

I had a cigar ring on my finger when Poppa gave me the antique dark purple velvet case that contained the tefillin his own grandfather had used. They held many secrets, he told me, as he slowly, ceremonially, opened the worn cloth bag to reveal its contents. But by then I knew I was his special grandson, and could keep a secret, so I didn't question him when he told me not to repeat his Harvard stories to anyone. At the time, I thought he was being paranoid, since he had been going on about his imaginary poison pills right before he gave me the tefillin. But I would obey him in any case; that he trusted me with his secrets made me even more special. I also decided, while wearing Poppa's cigar band on my finger, that one day I would go to Harvard also.

On April 15, 1969, the letter with the embossed Crimson logo arrived at our house. I was waiting outside for the mailman and knew as soon as the envelope was handed to me. It was as thin as a malnourished child. Not an outright rejection; I had been waitlisted but I knew my prospects for admission were bleak. I was crushed. After poring over the single page letter again and again, I was also confused. My parents took the news very well, especially my Dad, which made me angry and even more devastated. He hadn't wanted me to even apply, nor attend if I were accepted. The news was good in his estimation, and I would get over it eventually.

"It's a lot of money," he told me before, "and over-rated. Both your mother and I would prefer you stayed closer to home. The University of Missouri is an excellent school."

"Does that mean you won't pay if I get in?" I asked him, bristling.

"If that's what you really want . . . and IF you get in . . ." my mother said, "we'll pay for it, won't we, Hal? We can afford it." She looked over at my father, who nodded reluctantly and looked like he was holding a fart.

But my high school counselor Mrs. Riley had encouraged me, particularly when I let it slip that I was a legacy of sorts. Mrs. Riley helped me with the application and gave me suggestions and feedback about my essay. I asked my Mom to write me a check for the fee, and sent the application off without showing it to either her or my Dad.

"It was a long shot, anyway," my father said later, trying to console me and tamp down his satisfaction. "Very tough to get into, particularly if you don't have a close relative who went there."

"But Poppa went there!" I yelled, unable to keep my knowledge from gushing out.

There was a heavy silence. My Mom and Dad looked at each other, puzzled, then sad. They were thinking, I suspect, about how Poppa had deteriorated near the end of his life, how he hallucinated. Dementia. Tiny strokes. And I had just been a kid, and clearly impacted in a much more traumatic way.

Dad was the one to speak.

"Where in the world did you get that idea?" he asked in a soft voice.

"Poppa told me," I answered with defiance.

"You must have misunderstood him."

"I didn't misunderstand him. He told me all sorts of stories about Harvard."

"You're mistaken," said my Dad. "Your grandfather never went to Harvard. That was your Uncle Shmuel."

"But he knew everything," I protested, and tried to order the jumble of things Poppa told me that came to mind, about the Harvard-Yale regatta, and the president with the big birthmark on his face, and . . .

Rather than convincing him with the addition of these details, the more I blathered, the unhappier my parents looked, both shaking their heads and silent.

Their reaction, doubting me, was too much for me to take.

"He told me!" I finally screamed, breaking down.

My mother came over to hug me, and my father came just close enough to pat me on the shoulder with his right hand, still holding his pipe in his left.

I broke away and bolted upstairs to my bedroom. The ancient tefillin bag was in the bottom drawer of my bureau, buried under sweaters. I reached in and felt the wooden blocks with the wound leather straps. The inner lining was a printed cotton and thinned to tearing in places. I moved my fingers until I came across a narrow firmness of cloth, and pulled out the satin crimson "H." With physical proof in hand, I ran back downstairs and waved it in front of my parents' uncomprehending faces.

"Do you know what THIS is?" I raged, continuing to flap the "H" in the air like a banner, tears streaming down my cheeks.

Neither answered, so I told them that it was a Harvard Varsity letter, from the Varsity Eight. I knew that term for the crew squad, because that's how Poppa spoke of it.

'NOW do you believe me?" I shouted, defiantly resting my case.

They didn't. The atmosphere of gloom was relentless and unremitting.

"Maybe it belonged to Uncle Shmuel," my Dad offered.

"Uncle Shmuel, a varsity letterman at Harvard?" I was flabbergasted, and had I not been so enraged and indignant, I might have laughed, or at least snorted, since the image was ludicrous indeed.

"Mark . . ." my Dad began, looking shell-shocked with sympathy for his only child, "I'm no expert, but I can't imagine ANY Jew at Harvard in those days being a varsity sportsman. Maybe he picked it up at a pawn shop . . ."

Reconciled that further discussion was hopeless, I holed up in my bedroom and didn't come down for dinner. Eventually I calmed myself and transported myself back in time, sitting beside Poppa on his couch, picturing him in my mind so I would again hear his words. But the things I heard were filtered through the perceptions of a ten-year-old child. I could only conjure a non-cohesive chain of scenes and images, fragments from a jumbled newsreel. But some words I remembered so distinctly—how could the memories not be true?

The time in my memory had folded upon itself. Did I hear those stories only one time, or on multiple occasions during that summer? Could they have remained so vivid in my memory with just one telling on a single summer afternoon? I associated them with Poppa rolling imaginary pills in his hand, an understandably indelible recollection. But did I only watch him rolling those pills in his hand that single time, when he gave me the tefillin? And when did he tell me that the stories were a secret that bonded us together, that he had never told anyone except me, and not even my father or grandmother? Was I imagining that?

I made a list on a notepad of all the things I could remember that Poppa had talked about. He told me that I was smart and should attend Harvard, just like he had. At first all I knew was that it was a famous school in Boston and that John Kennedy had gone there. I knew there were old brick buildings that were much older than the buildings on the Mizzou campus, because it was the first and oldest college in the entire country. He told me about the President who would ride his bicycle around campus, a man with a large red birthmark on the right side of his face, and that all the pictures of him only showed his good side. There were other characters he talked about. A fruit vendor who had a cart pulled by a donkey. A man who made it his business to buy old clothes; another who lent students money. And he told me about the man who did nothing but ring the bells to announce class, and how students always tried to lock him out of the belfry or steal the clapper from the bell.

He told me about luxurious apartments with marble swimming pools in the basement, and taking a streetcar to attend parties and dances in Boston.

He told me about rowing on the Charles River with his best friend, and how he had made what he called the Varsity Eight. He explained that there were eight men in a rowing crew, and the varsity men would get a red "H" for their sweater if they rowed against Yale, a rival school. He spoke of big football games between Harvard and Yale, and how folks would dress up and come on special trains from New York and even farther away.

But two stories stuck out more than any others, because they involved famous people I had heard of. Poppa told me about working one summer at a hotel that was owned by the brother of John Wilkes Booth, the man who killed Abraham Lincoln. And he told me about seeing the great Harry Houdini escape from being tied up and handcuffed. He had actually met the great escape artist and gotten his autograph! How could my parents not know any of this?

Gradually I allowed the anger toward my parents to dissipate. But who could blame me for being mad at them? They didn't want me to go to Harvard anyway, so they were glad that I wasn't admitted. But that they didn't believe me was much harder to take. I couldn't be angry at Poppa, because I still believed he had told me the truth. But I kept coming back to the actual wait-list letter from Harvard, which was unsettling. I hadn't shown it to my parents, and had taken the precaution of bringing it upstairs with me so they couldn't see it, even if they had wanted to.

I took the letter from the envelope and read it over one more time. Beneath the boilerplate typewritten text, Dean of Admissions Chase Peterson had written a brief personal note in pen.

"Incidentally," the communique stated, "for your information we have been unable to find any record of your grandfather, Michael Levinson, having attended any of the schools of Harvard University during the time period in question."

The nagging thought was inescapable. My parents had given me the benefit of the doubt. But Harvard had wait-listed me because they thought I was a liar.

Mizzou

Being the obedient son, I felt guilty about misleading my father. At the beginning it wasn't intentional. Why need I mention that I sent Dean Peterson a profuse apology for confusing my grandfather with my great-Uncle Sam? Couldn't a seventeen-year-old have some secrets from his parents, particularly concerning a personal matter of honor? There were precedents; for example, when my Dad had asked me about my date with Rachel Feingold, the daughter of one of his patients. I resorted to the mundane generality of, "It was fun," without mentioning that I had felt her up. Certainly that was no lie, at worse a minor sin of omission.

Similarly, there was no need to reveal that I held out hope for Harvard. To the folks—after that initial rough night—I rebounded from my disappointment, accepting the inevitability of Mizzou in good spirits. Hiding my feelings wasn't lying per se and it was all for a good cause: they were spared feeling bad on my account and I was spared their sympathy, a win-win if there ever were one. In contrast, my letter to Peterson was total bullshit. I confessed to unfathomable embarrassment, detailing how an honest mistake had occurred, and how my distraught and mortified parents had confirmed to me that I had harbored the misunderstanding. I was earnest and Midwestern, the letter handwritten and with the subtext that I was not a psychopathic liar and Harvard could always use an admission from Kansas to fulfill their geographic distribution requirement. Peterson was undoubtedly touched and moved by my supplications—in retrospect, knowing Harvard as I do, he possibly saw through the whole thing and was impressed by my guile. In any case, soon thereafter I was notified of my acceptance from the Wait List. That much should be obvious by now, but I get ahead of myself.

Shortly after mailing my letter, I telephoned the Missouri University Archives to enquire about information on former professors. Records of faculty were only in the university's possession if they had been officially transferred by the individual or the family, and luckily the files of Professor Michael Levinson had been bequeathed to the university after he died. While I held the line, a cordial archivist summarized the catalogue listings for my grandfather's entries. As an Emeritus Professor, the holdings were extensive. I wasn't much concerned with his legal writings or academic accolades, but my ears perked up like a junk yard dog when she mentioned personal correspondences.

"Three boxes of personal correspondences, organized by groupings of years," she said, her voice effusing efficiency.

"I'm his grandson," I explained, "so I'm mostly interested in the personal stuff."

"There's a lot of that in here," she replied. "Eulogies from his funeral in 1962 . . . sympathy cards to your grandmother . . . information about the opening and dedication of the Levinson Room . . ."

"I was, you know, more interested in earlier, when he was young."

"Oh, I see . . . I'm afraid these just start with his admission to the law school in the fall of 1907."

"Are there admissions files, you know, like his application?"

"That isn't the type of thing that he would have had in his possession," she answered, a tinge of genuine regret in her voice. "The Registrar's office would have ledgers for registration going back to 1860, but that wouldn't provide much information. Of course, there's some student registration information in the University Catalogues published each year, which we have here. As far as the actual catalogued files go, they're kept off-site, and you need to give us a couple of days advance notice to retrieve them."

"Wow." Pay dirt. There was a good chance the registry listings would include his college information. It didn't occur to me to ask her to check the 1907-08 University Catalogue then and there.

"Wow," I repeated, too stunned to think of much else to say. I hadn't expected things to be so easy.

"You had a pretty well-known grandfather, you should be proud."

"Right. I am."

"Are you going to be a lawyer too?"

"I'm pre-med, I mean, I'll be pre-med when I start at Mizzou in the fall."

"That's wonderful," she said. "Once you're here you can come to the Archives anytime and I'll help you with your search. My name's Roberta, and I'm the lead librarian here."

"I was thinking of coming up earlier, before the beginning of classes. You know, things will get busy pretty quickly, I imagine."

"Would you like to set up an appointment?"

"Are you open on Saturdays?"

"Afraid not. Weekdays only, ten to five."

"How soon could you get the files?" I was emboldened, reflected in the all-business tone of my voice.

"I assume, from what you've been saying, that you'd be most interested in the box of personal correspondence . . ."

"Today's Tuesday," I reminded her.

"Thursday morning I can have them here, if you want me to—" The archivist assumed it was a school day for me, and clearly slightly distracted by the thought, offered "—but we have summer hours, if it's more convenient."

"Thursday's fine," I said quickly.

"Then I look forward to seeing you on Thursday . . ." she trailed off while still intoning the day of the week, providing my prompt.

"Mark. Mark Levinson."

"Mark. And again, I'm Roberta. I look forward to seeing you. The reading room is 703 Lewis Hall," she concluded the deal, no doubt wondering how I was going to manage the excursion on a school day.

Coincidentally, I was wondering the same thing.

At this juncture, it became harder to justify misleading my parents. I could come up with a myriad of reasons for wanting to hop up to MU for the afternoon. As one anticipating an upcoming four-year residency—and perhaps eight if I went to med school—I would want to check out the dorms, the classroom buildings, the frat houses, the beer joints, and all the other campus highlights. That, of course, could be accomplished on a weekend visit or anytime in the summer. And from what I had been told, I might soon expect invites from the Jewish fraternities to come down for weekend recruitment parties. But, let's say I wanted to really get a feel for the place by sitting in on a lecture, perhaps biochemistry... maybe if I had an acquaintance who was already a student, and pre-med, who could take me with him to class. For sure that would be reason enough to skip a day of school, and my parents could not object. In fact, they would encourage me, my interest being a further sign that I had come around to the notion of being a Tiger.

Swept along with the realm of possibilities of this finagling, I realized I only knew a single pre-med at Missouri, that being Rachel Feingold's brother, who hadn't been a big fan of mine since I dumped his sister after one date. All efforts toward honesty were out the window; I had become a liar and was accommodating to it. First to Dean Peterson, then my parents. My only option was to get in my Chevy Nova, graciously accept my mother's wishes to have a good day at school—Dad would have left already for hospital rounds—head off in the direction of Shawnee Mission East, then detour to haul my ass over to I-70 toward Columbia. My parents would never find out that I skipped school for a trip to the University Archives on what they believed a fool's errand. My grandfather, long gone, was a bad influence on me. While no longer the obedient son, I felt certain that Poppa, Professor Michael Levinson, would be proud of me and happy to play a seminal role in my liberation, if only from the grave.

Roberta the archivist was as pleasant and accommodating as she had been on the telephone. I had a fairly negative stereotype of librarians from elementary school days, when school bookmeisters were apparently selected from the primary school teachers who didn't like children very much. In addition to obsessiveness being a dominant personality trait—directing them into a field where both guardianship and organization were at a premium—they manifested a perverse possessiveness regarding bound reading matter, like an ancient auntie afraid someone would chip the good china. Of course, I based all of these prejudices upon one Miss McGowan, school librarian at Belinder Elementary, who in less enlightened times would be labeled a spinster. From continual harpings on book etiquette, I still look upon anyone who bends down a page corner as fundamentally lacking in morals.

But Roberta broke the mold; perhaps she made such a strong first impression owing to her uncanny resemblance to Shirley Jones as Marian the Librarian in the movie version of *The Music Man*, except, of course, that she wore no make-up. She had already placed three large gray files boxes and a book on one of four small round tables and had thoughtfully chosen the table closest to her work counter. The room was unexpectedly small, a few square feet more than cozy, but feeling larger given its lack of any humankind besides the two of us. She hovered over me expectantly for a couple of minutes as I settled myself in the hard-back chair. I filled out a registration form and was cordially instructed that I could only use pencils and blue sheets of paper that were also provided on each desk. She placed my spiral notebook and three pens into a small cubby behind her counter.

"I think I'll go for the university catalogue first," I said, reaching for the single dog-eared and faded volume that was on the desk, set directedly in front of my chair. She had led a horse to water.

"That's a very good idea," she said amiably, nodding in affirmation. "Let me know if you need anything," she added, walking in clattering pumps around her desk counter to her stool on the other side, directly opposite from me.

The University Catalogue for 1907-08 was a bust. I found my grandfather listed in the first-year law school class, but only by name, "post office," and county.

When I turned toward Roberta's counter, the expression on my face clearly one of supplication, she was already looking directly at me.

"I thought this would include information about where he went to college," I said, sighing.

"Unfortunately not. Just home town." Roberta straightened up on her stool. "And in 1907, not all the law students had a university undergraduate degree as a pre-requisite as it is today. It was possible to just test into the law and medical schools in those days, without going to college first."

I glanced down at the entry, considering what she had told me.

"This has my grandfather's home town as Columbia, in Boone County. Right here. But he was from Boston."

"Well," she explained, "they made a lot of errors in those catalogues." The answer seemed to satisfy her all right, but not me.

That was the first of many disappointments. Poring over communications in the files was tedious, the contents overwhelmingly mundane with handwriting often difficult to decipher. But I was fortunate that the material was contained in just three boxes. Poppa, to be honest, didn't seem to have much in the way of personal friends compared with all the business and professional communications. Roberta informed me that the latter were so extensive that to transport them on a cart would require multiple trips, since there were over sixteen linear feet, or more than twenty of the large file boxes. The realization made me feel sorry for him—I had never thought of Poppa as all work and no play—but now I had some insight into how driven he must have been professionally, and how he neglected his family as a result. It also helped to explain the distant and somewhat cold relationship between him and my own father that was hard to hide. Perhaps my grandmother and my aunt and my father had held on to some of the personal letters, which might account for their overall scarcity in the archives. But I didn't have time to reflect. I needed to plow through and had allotted myself until 2 p.m. at the latest to finish, needing to be on the road before rush hour to arrive home at approximately the same time I would get back from my classes at East.

At the end of the day I had only dug up three items of interest, enough to entice me even if they raised more questions than they answered. Roberta xeroxed these for me—five pages in all—without charging me the customary twenty-five cents per sheet. She handed me back the copies, with the originals to be returned to the files. I had marked their places in two different folders with the yellow bookmarks provided for the purpose.

The first item was an elongated postcard, folded lengthwise, an advertisement for a hotel called "The Masconomo House," an impressive-looking resort pictured on the front. The other three sides of the card contained promotional copy with specifics about the place. The second item was another postcard—specifically a "cabinet card"—of an attractive young woman leaning against an ornately carved wooden hearth, exposing mainly her side and backside, her head turned in profile. A theatrical pose compared with a standard portrait, and as the flip side revealed, a scene from the play "An English Beauty" was depicted. Brown cursive text surrounded by printer's embellishments identified a run at the Tremont Theater in Boston, the year 1904, and the actress as Emma Conghlan. The inscription in black ink was as follows:

> C—(I must me discreet!)
> Look how far we have come!
>
> An Irish lass and a—!
> Fondly,
> Emma

"This wasn't mailed," I said to Roberta, pointing to the absence of a stamp, "I wonder how it got in here."

Always an explanation for everything. "When materials are being catalogued, there are always the strays, things that don't have a specific place, so we just do our best. Perhaps it was something your grandfather had put in a letter file himself, or maybe it was in a desk drawer, no way of knowing . . ."

"And it's from before he even entered the law school . . . so maybe it was given to him personally in Boston . . ."

"Or it could have been something picked up in a shop. A collectible. Look how it's addressed to 'C,' not 'M.' Initialed instead of written out, for discretion's sake. Was it to a Charles? Or a Colin? What was your grandfather's middle name?"

"He didn't have one," I said.

"Definitely not an 'M,'" she mentioned more softly, as if lowering her volume wouldn't let me down as much.

I looked closely at the ingenue. She was a beauty. A straight nose, full lips, and flawless skin. And her hair—even from the sepia print—had to be a fiery red, the mane of a beautiful Irish lass. It was combed back off the forehead and behind her ears, culminating in long curled lockets that extended well into the middle of her back. She wore a light-colored canoe-shaped bonnet with flowers lining the top and a dangling ribbon from the back end, like the Glengarry hat of a Scottish bagpiper. Her dress was long-sleeved, with a high collar, ruffles at the elbow, and a narrow bustle. It was a solid color for the most part, except from the bustle downwards, a different fabric with a leaflike geometric pattern. The same fabric surrounded the lower part of her upper arm as a decorative band.

"She's beautiful," said Roberta.

"A redhead, I think," I said.

"I agree."

"And I bet the dress is a pale green, because of the leaves."

"I think so, too."

The photo, which sparked our separate imaginations, entranced us both. Roberta's sudden wistful expression revealed her reverence for the past, an obvious requirement for an archivist. And I suppose the inchoate historian in me could not help but reveal itself under the circumstances.

"An Irish girl and . . . a gentleman?" Roberta prompted.

"Could be," I answered. But what I was already thinking was left unsaid.

The third item, a handwritten letter, didn't elicit any particular attention from Roberta. A show of interest for something of a personal nature could come across as nosiness. Scholars were secretive, intensely paranoid about their research, because even the most minor-appearing of discoveries could be an historical jewel appropriated by competitors if unguarded. Loose lips could sink academic careers. So Roberta, averting her eyes, showed herself a dispassionate and trustworthy guardian on my behalf, no matter that I had yet to graduate from high school.

Not that she would have held back her professional impression had I asked. But I didn't want her opinion. Instead, I hurriedly replaced the possible treasure into the CORRESPONDENCE 1930-1940 folder, as if burying it in a motley collection of paper communications would prevent anyone from ever finding it again. The piece of stationary, about half the size of a normal sheet of paper, was the only personal communication I found that couldn't be dismissed. It screamed, actually, with a phrase that sent a shiver through me.

The stationery was fancy, a thick cream-colored stock with a linen-like texture. At the top was an embossed black ink representation of a grand house, a shingle style mansion with multiple peaks and protrusions. Underneath in a raised cursive was written: "Longneck Cove, Manchester by the Sea." The text itself, penned in an upright script, was dated Friday, April 19, 1935, and read as follows:

Michael—You could not keep your light under a bushel, old chap. Word of your accomplishments has traveled as far as these rocky eastern shores and I was able to track you down. It has been far too long.

No reason on earth to stay a stranger. Time has faded it all. They are gone. Hurlbut. Briggs. And old stain face, who threatened to live forever, departed from this world over a decade ago. So the only people around will have nothing but good memories and will want to see you. You would be welcomed.

I think of you often, Michael, you have informed my life. I wish things had ended differently.

Sometimes I only aspire to be your chum from Claverly again.

Come to the Tercentenary. Stay here with us at Longneck Cove.

Yours, ever,

As is generally the case, signatures disdain legibility. Regardless of the care one takes while writing the message—painstakingly not allowing the letters to clump, trying to keep each line from slanting downwards, making sure the dots don't stray too far afield from the "i's" and the crosses of the "t" aren't thrust into space like an arrow propelled from its bow—the signature is free and unfettered, muscle memory in display, full speed ahead. As was this one, but thankfully short. I struggled for a few seconds, then settled on "Hal," not knowing too many three letter names beginning, as I convinced myself, with the eighth letter of the alphabet.

It was the pejorative "stain face" that stopped me in my tracks. Poppa had told me about the Harvard President with the large birthmark on his face. It couldn't be coincidence; this had to be whom Hal was referencing. Which made the letter about Harvard, and linked Poppa to it.

After the initial excitement, the discovery of the letter calmed me down. By dinnertime with my parents I had returned to my usual laconic self, completely capable of containing my news and certain that it would spare all of us aggravation if I did. A simple document from over three decades earlier gave me all the confidence and reassurance I needed. Of course I was naïve, at the very least drunk on wishful thinking. While there were names and places that didn't mean much to me at the moment, I could investigate. I had something tangible to go on. And better yet, there was no rush or sense of urgency.

Perhaps I felt comfortable proceeding with deliberateness because of a premonition. Roberta, with only the resources in Columbia, Missouri at her disposal, could only do so much for me. I assumed—not exactly a wild guess—that the Archives at Harvard would have the answers. No point in barking up the wrong tree when I could be at the source. Would be at the source, I just felt it, as if Poppa would have a hand in it. My groveling missive had no doubt already come to the attention of Dean Peterson. In less than three weeks I received another communication from him, this time in a much thicker envelope and bearing considerably better news. Your truly, Mark Levinson, had been admitted to the Class of 1973.

Harvard University Archives

Cambridge, Massachusetts
October, 1969

My breaking-in period that first year was a bit rocky. I shared a suite in Weld Hall with two decent roommates, Aaron from Newton High outside of Boston, and Jeff from a private school in Philadelphia. Aaron had an actual beard, dark black and curly. When he answered my knock on the door—I was the last one to show up, not being local and also getting lost—I was stunned at the sight of him, thinking I had come to the wrong room, or that he was a visiting proctor. Aaron also smoked a pipe and didn't look foolish doing so. Jeff drank Scotch, on the rocks with just a splash of water, which equally shocked me. None of my Shawnee Mission contemporaries had facial hair, and no one, other than parents, drank anything other than 3.2 beer. Recalling now that I knocked on my own door rather than using the key that had just been given to me speaks to my befuddlement.

The three of us had all been editors of our respective high school newspapers, but otherwise I could not match them in a single regard. They were both National Merit finalists, had advanced placement credit (which SM East didn't offer, not to mention I had never heard of AP classes), were fluent in French (Aaron also in German), had taken Latin in high school, and been to Europe (Aaron, who was Jewish, had also spent time on a kibbutz in Israel). I had never attended a symphony, a ballet, or a Broadway show—in fact, I had never been to New York City. My travel destinations, aside from Columbia and St. Louis, Missouri, included Colorado Springs and San Antonio, where my father had medical meetings and dragged my mother and me along. There had been, however, an actual family vacation to Disneyland when I was thirteen—the extravagance being justified as a special Bar Mitzvah present—which I didn't mention in the "getting to know you" conversation. By the time the three of us walked across the Yard to the basement of Matthews Hall for the first weekly ration of clean sheets and towels, I had already decided I would never, under any circumstances, mention Disneyland.

Having been at the top of my high school class, it was a shock that I found myself in the academic minor leagues, with serious question as to whether I could make it to the majors. Other than knowing I was pre-med, I was lost and overwhelmed. Aaron planned to concentrate in Economics, and Jeff, when the time came, would declare in Philosophy. It only took minutes for me to realize that I could never dream of attempting such rigor. I was clearly second tier, sharing the company of many other public school boys, scholarship kids from the inner city, and jocks.

"I think I'll just try to get as many pre-med requirements and general education requirements out of the way for starters," I said, relieved that I wouldn't have to declare a major until the beginning of sophomore year—I would have to rethink Biochemistry and perhaps dumb down to Biology. Both Jeff and Aaron were aware of my anxieties and tried to provide paternal advice. Academically, the former stellar student from the Sunflower State was a project. The three of us sat on the used corduroy couch we had jointly purchased, which was shedding its stuffing on the side shoved against the wall. We all had our own copies of the red college catalogue and were flipping through it. I sat in the middle, trying to hide my despondence.

"You should take Finley's course on the classics for your humanities requirement," suggested Jeff. "He's a legend here."

"Isn't that the one where you have to write a paper every week?"

"Yes. And you'll really know how to write by the end of the term," Aaron added.

I couldn't mask my insecurity about writing papers, especially being concerned about keeping my grades up to get into med school. Objective tests were my preference, with perhaps a single paper at the end. A "B" in a course, or heaven forbid lower, could knock me out of med school running, a chance I couldn't afford to take. My college course selection was not determined by interests, but fear-based.

"Maybe something with not so much writing," I said.

"All right," said Jeff. "Hum 9. Oral and Early Literature. Much less rigorous, paper-wise."

And so it went, ever more discouraging as we ran down the list. "I need to take a year of math, a year of chemistry—"

"—Wait," interrupted Jeff. "You didn't quiz out of math or have AP credits?"

"Uh . . . no."

"Too bad. Which will you be taking?"

"Math 1a, first semester. And then, you know . . ." It was painful to express. "Math 1b second semester."

Aaron nodded, expressionless. He was planning on taking Math 155, just for the fun of it. Which meant he had quizzed out of Math 1, Math 6, Math 23, and Math 55 on the placement tests. He thumbed through the catalogue, stopped, and hurriedly turned a few pages. "Okay," he went on, plopping an index finger down. "The ground level chemistry course is Chem 6, Quantum Mechanics. Professor Leonard K. Nash. Another big shot, and a really entertaining lecturer, according to the *Confi Guide*."

"Big lecture course," added Jeff. "All the pre-meds take it. Very popular."

"Didn't do well enough on the placement test," I mumbled, aware that my lower lip was starting to quiver. "I'll have to take a Natural Science course from the Gen. Ed. Courses, but that will still fulfill the medical school requirement."

"That's great, then," said Jeff, trying to appear enthusiastic about a schedule that was beyond boring and, frankly, a waste of Harvard, where course offerings were abundant, diverse, and hopefully even interesting. For this schedule I could have gone to Johnson County Community College.

"You've nearly got it covered, then," Jeff continued. Math 1, Hum 9, maybe Nat Sci 3—that's a good one that non-science types take and isn't super hard—Expos, of course . . . and then you can take anything you want for fun."

"Maybe a freshman seminar," offered Aaron, who had been chosen for one of the coveted slots in famed psychologist Eric Erikson's small group study.

"I need a year of Spanish," I confessed, revealing that I hadn't even quizzed out of a language at which I had allegedly excelled all through high school. What would people say about SME's former "Spanish Student of the Year"? There was nothing to be said, unless I cared to make up a story about a serious head injury I had sustained in a car accident, my forehead breaking the windshield. That would explain things. Perhaps on a road trip to Disneyland which, by the way, I was never able to experience because of the wreck, subsequent long hospitalization, and rehab.

"I think I'll walk over to the Coop and look around for supplies," I said, pushing myself up from the sofa like an old man.

Thus my explanation for what, I could even admit at the time, was overstudying. And also why my trip to the Archives was shelved. Aside from breaks for requirements, like passing the swimming test, and rushed meals at the Union, I was the king of grind-dom, reviewing and even rewriting class notes, reading and re-reading course materials, agonizing over written assignments and exercises, spending hours with headphones making my ears sweat in the language lab in Boylston Hall.

Not that I was totally without social interaction. Usually arriving early to Nat Sci 3, my first morning class, I took time to engage in friendly conversation before the lecture began. Many of those with whom I had become cordial were on the football and hockey teams. Not exactly bearded, pipe-smoking or Scotch-drinking intellectuals, and when they confided concern that class time and study commitments were getting in the way of their gym workouts and team practices, I began to recognize my slight academic advantage and a glimmer that I might pass my courses after all. Magnanimously, I even let them copy my notes, legible and organized, the original chicken scratches meticulously transcribed every night. I had not managed a conversation with any of the relatively few females—outnumbered by males by about four to one—partly due to availability but primarily due to the intimidation factor. On occasion I would accompany Aaron and Jeff to Hazens or Elsie's for a ten o'clock study break, but it took some cajoling.

Frequently I just gave them my order for take-out, not wanting to disrupt my momentum.

On the weekends I let myself blow off steam, contingent upon study goals that I consistently met. Several parties were simultaneously held in suites scattered in the Yard dormitories, and because of the noise it was difficult to study even for those who didn't participate. The sources of the marijuana were not clear to me, but the booze was from a locally well-known liquor store in Somerville. The party organizers would scrape together bills and change, decide on how much and what could be acquired with the funds, and place a phone order. No questions asked, a delivery person would wheel boxes and bags of the stuff directly into the Yard on two-wheelers, unloaded from a van parked outside the gates. That all the freshman were underage and could not legally purchase alcohol—common knowledge—did not apply to those of us in our cocoon of privilege. No attempt at concealment or surreptitious behavior, no consciousness of guilt, no fear of the authorities. The transactions were under the full view of the Harvard cops. Short of helping to deliver the orders themselves, they couldn't have been more accommodating.

At the pre-determined time, the hosts would move all furniture against the walls, open the windows, turn the stereo up to maximum volume, and like carnival barkers, stick their heads out the windows and yell "Pah-ty! Pah-ty!" at the bands of co-eds—from Leslie, Simmons, Emerson, Pine Manor, Endicott and other local institutions of higher learning—meandering along the pathways of the Yard below waiting for invitations. These events were spontaneous, crowded, noisy, and fluid, since party-goers of both sexes could travel around and check out all the offerings. There was thus an ebb and flow at each individual locale, times of social boom and bust, but ultimately, they were all desperate affairs, with many contestants but few among them who would consider themselves winners. The aftermaths, when the guests had departed and the hosts dared to turn on the lights, were a sight to behold. Each suite a dump site of cans, bottles and plastic cups, and the stench of beer often comingling with the odor of vomit. No wonder Radcliffe women were conspicuously absent from the shenanigans, being far too adult to participate in such crass and sophomoric goings-on with drunkard children. Besides, most by this time had already found themselves objects of attention by upper classmen, the closest thing at hand to men in any real sense.

It took a few parties for me to realize that I was accomplishing little besides drinking too much and dealing with hangovers. Attempts at meeting any suitable, eligible females up to that point had been fruitless, when not embarrassing. Neither roommate was a participant or enabler either, Aaron being faithful to his high school flame who was at Bryn Mawr, and Jeff pursuing one of his home town Philly girls enrolled at Wellesley. So I arranged a bargain with myself, a workaround for the inconvenient fact that the Harvard Archives was only open between 10:30 a.m. and 4:30 p.m. and closed on weekends. I would justify losing a study afternoon by promising myself to forgo either a Friday or Saturday night fete, instead holing up in Lamont Library for the duration, all night if need be. It was time to expand my horizons and develop some extracurricular activities at Harvard, even if that meant only trying to track down my grandfather.

The Archives Reading room was a rectangular room in Widener Library with a checkerboard linoleum floor, six simple oak library desks—each with four spindle back chairs—and bookcases along most of the available wall space. Not quite reaching the ceiling, the case tops were lined with a variety of old prints of the college and other framed ephemera, propped against the wall, too small and too high up to be clearly seen or appreciated. An eighteenth-century portrait of an austere woman was the only piece of art hung properly on a wall. Despite the nearsightedness betrayed by a squint, she coldly surveyed her domain from above the card catalogue, ready to sound the alarm for the slightest transgression. The dominant color of the center of the room was the golden oak brown of the desks and chair, but the shelves were a mass of red. The volumes—class books and secretary's reports for generations of Harvard men—displayed covers of varying hues of crimson, a procession of passing time indicated by increased fading and fraying of the spines. The more recent volumes were gaudy in their bright and uniform saturation, and as firm as the bodies of young athletes. These were boastful showoffs proclaiming

"Some of us inside are still alive!" but they too would eventually fade.

I was not surprised to find myself the only patron. The librarian was older and more reserved than Roberta; she also wore no make-up but had graying hair pulled into a bun at the nape of her neck. She had been a beauty and still was one, despite a half-century of lines configuring the terrain of her face into an unnavigable landscape. I found myself looking down when we spoke, breaking eye contact, embarrassed by how drawn I was to the clarity and tropical ocean blueness of her irises, magnified by her eyeglasses. Predictably efficient and by the book, she was aloof but pleasant, guiding me through the registration process and informing me of the rules and procedures of the collection with a distinct mid-Atlantic accent. Soon enough I would learn that her name was Eleanor, and she would become a valued and trusted guide. Long afterwards, we would keep in touch through letters and Christmas cards until her passing. But at the moment, I felt like I had been dropped into a movie scene with Katherine Hepburn, having been cast in a minor role as a fool.

I guardedly told her only that I was looking up information about my grandfather, whom I thought to have been in the Class of 1906 or 1907, and set out searching the pertinent alumni materials. It didn't take me long to discover that Michael Levinson was not to be found anywhere in the Quinquennial Catalogue of university graduates from 1636 through 1930. Similarly, I couldn't find a listing for him in any of the Secretary's class reports for the relevant years, which began the first-year post graduation and continued to the fiftieth anniversary report. I perused every senior photo in the Class Album for those two years, which I should have assumed to be a fruitless task, given he was not catalogued as a college graduate. I also looked at the group crew photographs, paying particular attention to the lists of names below the photographs. Again, my grandfather never came up. The earliest photograph I had ever seen of him was when he was already a young lawyer, bespectacled and looking distinguished and mature for his years. But he had a mole above his left eyebrow, large enough to usually be seen in photographs.

Tired of coming up empty-handed, I decided to check out Uncle Shmuel.

He was represented both in the composite alumni catalogue as well as in the Class Reports for his class of 1903 as Samuel Rabinowitz. In early class reports the only entries concerning him were "Has not responded to the Secretary's notices." By the twenty-fifth report the Alumni Association had tracked down his location and occupation, and knew of his marriage and the birth of his children, but Shmuel himself never contributed a personal narrative of his life. Maybe he was ashamed of being in the schmatta business, albeit successfully, or perhaps he just had never cared enough about his experience at Harvard to bother filling out the class secretary's questionnaire. Shmuel hadn't made it easier for any future biographers, but who would want to write anything about him, anyway?

But more striking was glancing through the photographs of his senior class album. There were only a handful of Jews in Shmuel's class, and even fewer Blacks. Both stood out from their classmates of predominantly well-groomed lads with smoothed-back blond or brown hair and straight noses. Sam Rabinowitz's hair was thick and midnight black, and obdurately wavy. His features were coarse and oversized, his nose an exaggerated aquiline. The Blacks, mostly light-skinned and from the upper echelons of black society and prepped at Andover or Exeter academies, were at least decently dressed. The Jewish students looked shabby, their otherness leaping from the pages as if a different species.

"I can't find him . . . my grandfather, I mean," I finally confessed to the librarian after re-shelving my uncle's class album, trying not to sound forlorn.

"The Quinquennial Catalogue only includes graduates, so your grandfather might not have graduated, but still attended."

"And he wouldn't be listed anywhere?"

"First check the College Catalogue for . . . you say he was in the Class of 1906 or 1907?" She stroked the inside of her left eye, briefly displacing her readers from the bridge of her nose.

I nodded. "I think so, or thereabouts. I know for sure he started law school in the fall of 1907."

"Check the 1902-03 class catalogue to begin with. It lists the names of all undergraduate class members for the four years, including the Special

Students. He should be listed as a freshman if he were admitted to the graduating class of 1906. Check the upperclassman listings as well, in case he came in with advanced standing or was admitted to a class prior to 1906. And then check out the catalogue for 1903-04 for the freshman members of the Class of 1907." She pointed to a section of shelving. "Over there in the corner."

The search was half-hearted and unsuccessful.

"Sorry I can't be of more help," Eleanor said, "but I'm out of suggestions. If he's not listed in any of the senior class albums for the relevant years, and you can't find his name in any of the catalogues, it would be extremely unlikely that there would be a student file for him. I'll be happy to request it anyway, but those files are kept off-site, and in case there is one, we can't get it for a day or two."

I nodded, hiding my sullen spirits so as to show I appreciated her efforts. But my work at the Archives appeared done. After an awkward pause, not wanting to admit total defeat by leaving, and despite having announced my intentions by putting on my jacket, I reached into my back pocket for the copy of the letter I had found in Poppa's correspondence file from Mizzou. I couldn't bear the thought of yet another person considering me a liar. And so I unfolded it and held it out with a neutral expression, like trying to get into a bar with a fake ID.

Eleanor didn't take the paper, only lifted her chin and glanced through the lower part of her lenses. "Longneck Cove," she said, matter-of-factly.

"What?"

"The stationery is from Longneck Cove, Manchester-by-the-Sea."

"It says that. But do you know it?"

"Better than most," she said, "because I grew up on the North Shore. The estate sits on a hill above Longneck Cove, hence the name. And it's well-known—a landmark of sorts—belonging to the Wyatt family. And particularly well-known around here, since the Wyatts have been major benefactors of the university since the mid-nineteenth century. Surely, you're familiar with Wyatt Hall, the Wyatt Fellowship, the Wyatt Chair?"

I hadn't heard of any of them, but didn't bother to admit my ignorance.

Instead I said, "Someone in that family was friends of my grandfather."

"I'd say you have a significant lead, then," she said.

"I think his name was Harold, like my father, and he went by Hal," I ventured. "Like my father."

Eleanor gave me a puzzled look. "There was no Harold," she said as definitively as a school marm. "May I?" She placed a hand on the paper to steady it and leaned forward to see the signature at the bottom. I found myself still gripping the other end.

"That's not Hal," she said, non-judgmentally, despite the fact that I must have seemed a nincompoop. I looked directly into Eleanor's eyes, and for the first time that afternoon I saw her lips rearrange themselves into a rather sly, if not provocative smile. I would learn that solving mysteries, even the tiniest of ones, would make her smile.

"It's 'Hol.' H-O-L. For Hollis." And then she said the name very slowly, so I would be sure to understand her, obviously needing all the help I could get.

"Hollis. Appleton. Wyatt. Class of 1906."

I was straining to take everything in. Remarkably, I wasn't entirely unfamiliar with the name. Still, I was at a loss as to how to respond.

She was holding the copy in both hands now, with me not remembering that I gave it up.

"May I read the whole thing?" she asked.

I nodded dumbly and watched her.

"He's inviting your grandfather to come for the three hundred year celebration of Harvard's founding, which was held in the spring of 1936. And quite the shin-dig."

It was clear that I would need to return to the Archives. And if it meant all-nighters at Lamont, so be it.

Where I came from, rich boys went to Pembroke Country Day School, but that was the extent of my class consciousness. The notion of social stratification operating in any real sense in modern day United States didn't register with me. Two generations away from the old country, I naively assumed a ubiquitous meritocracy. And I knew nothing of the old New England families, the merchants and privateers who spawned generations of bankers and financiers and businessmen. Their descendants, those who had not squandered inherited fortunes and those who had made good on their own with a substantial head start, would send their progeny to Harvard, as had the generations before them.

And thus, essentially from scratch, I had acquainted myself with the legacies of the famous and moneyed families. Not coming from a preparatory or elite private school, I was disadvantaged and poorly connected in that regard. My learning didn't come from reading the society pages of the *Boston Globe* or by hanging out with the more privileged kids themselves. Rather, I developed a familiarity by spending an inordinate amount of time—out of a mixture of boredom and fascination—perusing the Radcliffe Freshman Register, known as the Facebook, for potential dates. That I considered any of the faces in that freshman register achievable girlfriend material at all revealed the extent of my naiveté. Which is beside the point, since I only mean to explain how the name of Hollis Appleton Wyatt sounded familiar to me when Eleanor mentioned Longneck Cove in the Archives Reading Room.

The high school graduation photographs in the soft-bound catalogue were of extremely smart women of all ethnicities and backgrounds, and far from a random sampling of humanity. Clearly over-represented were daughters of business, political, and literary heavyweights, social register surnames reflecting East Coast pedigrees, achievement, wealth, and high society. The indicators of money and class were obvious: the schools attended, for starters, with names like Brearley, Concord Academy, Milton, and Cranbrook. Other not so subtle indicators were the hometown listings from communities like Greenwich, Connecticut, or Bloomfield Hills, Michigan, or Manhattan's Upper East Side. A total glaring giveaway was a house absent a street name or number, with only a descriptor, such as Hill House or Beaux Park or Longneck Cove.

Her home address had a number, though, on Masconomo Street in Manchester-by-the-Sea, the same town on the letter that had been mailed to

Poppa from the man I had known then only as "Hal." Her photograph was one I had admired for weeks. Frequently when I had a spare moment, needing a respite from a math problem set or an essay for Expos, I would ritualistically thumb through the book and savor reaching her picture at the end, a reward of sorts, and the last photo I would look at. In those moments I fantasized about meeting her, or more impossibly, her seeing beyond my immature Midwestern shell and discovering I possessed something of value. That she was obviously not taking pre-med courses, and not in any of my classes, was the least of my obstacles to an introduction. But I had spotted her in person on a couple of occasions, once outside the Fogg and another time walking down the steps of Emerson Hall, both times laughing and accompanied by upperclassmen.

I had stared long and hard at the photo of Rebecca Appleton Wyatt in the register, not because her name meant anything to me at that time, but because she was so beautiful. I had deemed her, in my private internal competition—being both Bert Parks and the panel of judges—the fairest and most desirable of the entire class of freshman women, blessed with the trifecta of looks, brains, and money. Admittedly, a disproportionate number of contestants would not have made the competition at all were it not for aptitude in science or high SAT scores. But winnowed down, the finalists came down to a dozen or so notables that stood out from all the other faces as boldly as Uncle Shmuel stood out from all those Arrow Shirt men.

And so I knew immediately, before leaving the Archives reading room that first time and even before getting back to my dorm room in Weld to confirm, that Rebecca Appleton Wyatt from Manchester-by-the-Sea had to be the granddaughter of Poppa's good friend Hol.

Pickled Herring

"Pickled herring! And three pounds of it!" Abe Rabinovitz said in his Old World accent, chuckling as he sopped off the gravy from the kishka left on his plate. He looked over at Esther, who had finally sat down herself at the table to eat, assured that the three men were already settled. She adjusted the headscarf she still wore out of habit on the Shabbos. The Shabbat candles were in the menorah on the counter next to the soapstone sink, halfway burnt down. The silver-plated wine cup, emptied earlier by Abe without sharing, was aligned beside it, along with a basket holding the remains of a challah. Americans for nearly a decade, they were getting a bit lax about observances. For Esther the transitioning had been the hardest, but the men in her life were more sanguine about the loosening of their orthodoxy.

"Why do we have to keep acting so different?" Abe once reasoned to Esther. "We'll always be Jews to everybody else whether or not we are observant. Why go to all he bother?" He had been joking, but the sacrilege had upset his wife. They still regularly went to shul, kept a kosher home, and Abe laid tefillin every morning. Still, he had become a free thinker. They could not let traditions and rituals keep them from moving ahead in the new country, a country with so many possibilities. Not as much for him, perhaps, but here he was, the father of a boy attending Harvard, the finest university in the world. Religion was a desirous thing, but it shouldn't hold people back.

"We'll make the best of any new customers, who CARES from where they come? *A goldener shlisk efnt ale tirn.*" Abe mostly spoke English upstairs, but couldn't resist the occasional Yiddish expression. *A golden key opens all doors.* In his shop on the ground floor on Salem Street, he almost always spoke Yiddish. The neighborhood teemed with immigrants of all nationalities, including Irish, Italians, and even some Portuguese, but most of his customers were fellow Jews from the Pale of Settlement.

"So these two hoity-toity boys came by . . . starched collars they were wearing with silk ties . . . and these beautiful jackets . . ." Abe, who enjoyed telling stories and could be relied upon to have a joke or two for his patrons at the delicatessen, looked over at his son and nephew. Shmuel—who had begun going by "Sam" outside of the family once he started college, was his characteristic glum, moving his fork along the plate, making streaks in the gravy. Moishe, a strong, sinewy youth of eighteen and nearly a head taller than Shmuel, always had a hearty appetite, and continued to eat eagerly while keeping his eyes fixed on his uncle.

"Why would a Harvard club need to order pickled herring?" Shmuel was skeptical. He was finishing his senior year as a scholarship student and still having to grab any job that came his way to help make ends meet, in addition to working for his father. He was currently worried about not having the money he owed in order to graduate. In his estimation, neither his parents nor his cousin had any concept of Harvard or any college. Maybe no one did, aside from the privileged who attended and the others like him who were invisible. The invisible ones were the scholars, of course, the real students, while the spoiled rich fellows—the swells—were do-nothings and know-nothings, just passing time until getting set up in banking or the long established *goyishe* family businesses. The Jews and the other hard-working poor kids, the greasy grinds, would win out in the end, though. For Shmuel, the pejorative was a badge of honor, and a greasy grind he would remain until he got his diploma, no matter what hardships it entailed.

"Why would they need pickled herring?" Abe was setting up his own joke. "Because they're having a fancy dinner party! Why else? And wait until they get to taste your Momma's chopped liver! We'll have regular repeat customers, of that you can be assured!"

"Three pounds of pickled herring. That's a lot of herring." Shmuel shook his head. "Something's fishy."

"Of course it's fishy . . . it's herring!" Abe finished chewing the challah and looked at his wife enquiringly, then down at his plate. His desires silently communicated, Esther stood up to take his plate. Yes, there was more kishka.

"So," Abe continued, "naturally we were closing early because of Shabbos and these fellows come in the store, and I didn't HAVE three pounds of pickled herring on hand. But I wasn't going to lose a sale like that—they could be repeat customers for certain, and what that would do for business!—so I told them I would have it special and could deliver it tomorrow—"

"—On the Shabbos," said Esther, setting down the replenished plate in front of him with more force than necessary.

"—and I offered to give them a sample for free of your wonderful chopped liver on some fresh pumpernickel, Esther, loaded with schmaltz . . ."

"Did they like it?" Moishe asked, captivated by the story. How could anyone not love Aunt Esther's chopped liver?

Shmuel was shaking his head.

"Well, they had already just eaten, as they explained it to me, had a big meal at some fancy-schmancy hotel restaurant on Charles Street, so they had no appetite . . ."

Shmuel snorted, then set his elbow on the table and plopped his forehead into his open palm hard enough to make a slapping sound.

"On the Shabbos," Esther repeated.

"What do they know from Shabbos, Esther? And I'm a businessman. Besides, I figured the house goy could deliver it for me . . ." He smiled and looked over at his nephew. The designation was a running joke.

Moishe Levinson was the son of Esther's sister Molka and brother-in-law Ephraim, who had both died in the diphtheria epidemic shortly prior to the family's decision to emigrate. Her nephew had been eight at the time and there had been no choice but for her and Abe to bring him to America with Shmuel and raise him as their own. Moey was a good boy, Esther knew, but had been difficult at times, much more of a challenge than Shmuel. But he had good reason. Orphaned and angry, he had been taken away from the only world he knew by relative strangers from a neighboring village. Moey had always had problems with his temper; he was rebellious and had a chip on his shoulder. He would get into fights with the Irish boys because they called him a sheeny, but Esther always suspected that the anti-Semitic slur was prompted by Moey calling them micks.

Moey had refused to have a Bar Mitzvah—what gossip that had caused in the congregation!—and went out of his way to flaunt non-observance, at times causing her and her husband considerable embarrassment. Abe and Esther saw no recourse but to shrug and make excuses for him. So they came to terms with indulging him, Abe in a less threatening and more jovial fashion. Thus, Moey became the house goy, who would turn the lights on, tear the toilet paper, and do any other activities that would be considered work on the holy day. Abe joked that no one in the neighborhood could afford the luxury of a house goy, and they had one for free.

As the years passed, the family conceded to pulling light chains and tearing toilet paper on their own, along with other compromises. And Shmuel, upon becoming a Harvard student, had taken to studying and writing homework assignments on Friday nights and Saturdays without hesitation. As the family assimilated, Moey had paradoxically become more tolerant of the faith, and would occasionally attend Shabbat and high holidays services at their synagogue. The family had mellowed from both sides of the religious spectrum. Moey had less and less to bristle against, and by now the neighbors didn't seem bothered or pay much attention. What did anyone expect from Moey Levinson, anyway? He was a troublemaker, no better than a *shaygetz.*

"I'll be happy to do the delivery, Uncle Abe," said Moey.

"I want you to wear your nicest clothes," his Uncle replied. "We have to make an impression. These Harvard people could become regular customers, and look at the size of this order!"

Shmuel gave a loud sigh, but looked back down at his plate when his uncle flashed him a dirty look.

"Where is this place, anyway?" Shmuel asked without hiding some aggression. He was peeved by the whole situation. Besides, wasn't it HIS territory, even if he couldn't actually lay claim to it in any fashion?

Abe had written down the address on a piece of butcher paper, and had left it in his apron pocket. After dinner and some schnapps, he would walk down the stairs and retrieve it from the store. How fortunate he had been to be able to rent both the storefront and the four-room apartment above it in the same tenement.

"It's on Linden Street, as I recall, I can't remember the number, but it's near Mt. Auburn Street, as they told me. It's an Institute of some kind, an important place, by the sound of it." Abe turned to Shmuel. "You know this Institute?" he asked.

Sam was puzzled, trying to determine to which Institute his father was referring. His Harvard was a small and highly circumscribed one. He took the streetcar into Harvard Square, then headed to classroom buildings near the yard. He knew the landmarks like Memorial Hall and Harvard and University Halls, several of the main buildings where he had lectures—Boylston, Emerson, and Sever—and the Gore Library, of course, the enormous Gothic structure where he spent most of his time when not in class, having nowhere else to go. A few of his Jewish friends from Dorchester and Roxbury were in the habit of all sitting at the same table in Gore to study. After they had occupied it several times, the table remained conveniently empty, designated by the high bred majority as the "Kike" or "Jerusalem" table. None of the gentiles would sit at it again. He had been to the Sargent gymnasium once, but only to take the required muscle and strength test, at which he didn't score very well. He knew Appleton Chapel and the Philips Brooks House by sight, but hadn't been inside either one of them.

Shmuel bit his lip and felt shame. Truth be known, he wasn't even familiar with the eateries and shops along Massachusetts Avenue and Brattle Street, since he couldn't afford to buy anything anyway, but always brought his lunch and sometimes his dinner from home. In this regard, being the son of a delicatessen owner had distinct advantages; many of his friends went hungry while pretending they had no appetite. Even the tobacco store, Leavitt and Peirce, seemed impenetrable. He had never needed to check on the sports team scores in the window, or wait in line to purchase football game tickets. He felt self-conscious about entering the shop, even though it was known to be collegiate friendly, where jovial young men laughed and played pool, the air thick with the smoke from Cake box tobacco and the walls crowded with memorabilia.

Those students without the social status to gain admission to a club or fraternity used Leavitt's as a communal meeting ground. The un-clubbed, a majority of the student body, occupied the lower rungs of a very tall social ladder. They might be public school boys, or relatively well-heeled migrants from outside Boston or New York—even young gentlemen from the Midwest or the Far West arrived in Cambridge only to find Boston society impenetrable. Still, they had a ladder, with some expectations they could climb it through achievement in sports or activities. For the Jews and colored students, even the first rung was too steep a reach. Shmuel was an outsider who would never belong. They would stare at him if he dared to enter Leavitt's, and then ignore him. Fortunately, he had no need of the place, since he didn't smoke and didn't know how to play pool or care to learn.

"I'm not all that familiar with that part of the campus," he said, after feigned reflection. "There's generally no call for me to go towards the river from Massachusetts Avenue." Part of the area, he knew quite well, was known as the Gold Coast.

"I'll find it, cousin," said Moey cheerfully, always savoring any opportunity to be dismissive to the young man and elder with whom he had shared a bed since they had arrived in America.

"I need to study for mid-term exams," Shmuel replied, pushing his plate forward, concluding his Sabbath meal. It had not come to rest before being swooped up by his mother's hands. Abe was going nowhere, but would stay put for rugelach and tea.

"You want I should go over some things from your notes for your test?" Moey asked his cousin, who was making his way to their bedroom. Going over Shmuel's notes and even reading classroom materials had become a routine. Moey could ask him questions, test Shmuel on events and dates, check the faithfulness of his recitations. The kid was smart and quick, studies came easy for him, and yet he had not considered any formal education past high school. Perhaps another thing for him to rebel against. Shmuel would never admit that working with Moey was a big help.

"Sure, why not," replied Shmuel, shrugging. "You don't have anything else worthwhile to do."

The Institute

They were tired from the prior night's activities, but this undergraduate threesome had awoken, attired themselves appropriately, and finished their hearty breakfast early, all in preparation for a less than ambitious settle in the club's den, *dolce far niente*. A number of their junior cohorts, stragglers who had managed to drag themselves out of bed—including six of the previous night's ten initiates—were still at table in the large adjacent dining room, reliving the details of their recent adventure in hushed tones punctuated by bursts of hilarity. The colored waiters Ben and Marcus attended their needs in a distant background, their presence as assumed as the clattering of utensils and clicking of teacups. The civility at table betrayed the sanctioned ungentlemanly rowdiness of the evening before. The colored staff had been up most of the night cleaning the mess and setting things back in order, a task that had become their own parallel tradition. None could complain that it wasn't a job well done, as no one could detect the slightest whiff of vomit.

In the den, a bit sick at stomach, Bobsy Baxter was already smoking a cigarette, sitting at the library table and reading the *Transcript*. He and his two other chums in the room had gone through the post-initiation re-hashing already and were bored by the retelling of the exploits, the unruly behavior, the drunken re-enactments of Shakespeare in the basement using bananas and punch bowls as props—in this case, inebriated interpretations of Brutus's stabbing of Caesar and the Three Wicked Sisters and their intoxicating brew.

Wilcox had staked out the longest and most comfortable of the leather divans for his lanky frame to stretch out upon, feet crossed at the ankles, head propped up by interwoven fingers behind his neck. He gazed, unseeing, at the ornate plastered crown molding wrapping itself around the periphery of the Institute's sitting room and beneath it the wall of bookshelves displaying leather-bound volumes, donations or legacies from the personal libraries of former club members. For the moment he would daydream about next year's Varsity Eleven. With Tricksy Benton graduating—it seemed to have taken forever—Teddy Wilcox would finally have the starting left guard position all to himself.

The third established Institute man, Weatherhill, who excelled at track, relaxed in a Morris chair, plucking at the club banjo that he had taken from its stand in the corner of the room. It was a battered old thing and missing a string, more of a prop than anything else, providing a semblance of informality to the elegantly-appointed room, all brown leather and mahogany paneling and oriental rugs. All three had ensconced themselves in the club earlier than they might have done otherwise, since a delivery was expected that morning.

"Wyatt's running on Monday should be an absolute corker," said Weatherhill, grinning at the thought as he arpeggiated a four string cord. He and Bobsy were orchestrating the stunt as they would for any hapless initiate, and had undertaken the adventurous and admittedly distasteful duty of venturing into Boston's underbelly for some of the needed props, since local Harvard Square ragmen couldn't provide the required outfit. The two found an authentic ragtag outfit from the Salvation Army on Chelsea Street to procure, but had second thoughts upon reflection, fearful of vermin. Wyatt was a good sport, but perhaps less so if he contracted lice. Ultimately they found what they needed—along with a suitable fake long black beard—from the Hasty Pudding's theatrical storeroom.

Hollis Wyatt in the flesh was the antithesis of hapless. The scion of a Boston banking family dating back to the *Arbella*, he had been "the First of the First Ten" sophomores from the Class of 1906 selected the past evening. He and the nine other classmates would select another ten, and those twenty would select yet another, and so on, until before Christmas of that year, the membership of the Institute of 1770 would be filled with one-hundred sophomores, the social elite of the class, and ranked accordingly. Many had prepped at St. Mark's or St. Paul's—or like Hollis, at Groton, where he had been a top oarsman his last two years. The youths had come up together from the top "fitting" schools in the country, all New England institutions, and would continue their social ascent through their undergraduate years at Harvard and then the rest of their lives.

But the social winnowing was only beginning, the Institute being merely a preliminary stamp of social acceptability from which further classification would commence. The stratification, reflecting the social order of Boston if not an amplification of it, was ingrained, closed, and inviolable. The ultimate social goal was selection into one of the final clubs, tightly bound associations of generally no more than ten members of the senior class, providing a social identity for life. And of these, only two clubs—the Porcellian and the A.D.— really mattered as a determinate of the smart set. Young Hollis, as first man elected to the Institute, would undoubtedly achieve his social destiny as a member of the former, the more prestigious of the two and the pinnacle of Harvard social achievement.

At that very moment, Hollis Wyatt, immaculately dressed in stiff collars, four-in-hand tie and sack jacket and trousers with matching waistcoat, was in the Institute's dining room finishing up poached eggs on toast and drinking his second cup of Darjeeling tea. Unbeknownst to him, the trio lounging in the den—all technically a year ahead of Wyatt had they not been "dropped" from the Class of 1905 for academic reasons—were making big plans for him. All the initiates would undergo a ritual hazing over the coming days and weeks—the "runnings"—being subjected to public displays and ridicule, and Hollis would be the first. For those instigating and witnessing the forced indignities and antics—be it a fit thrown in a crowded theater or an outlandish scene in a restaurant over an alleged fly in one's soup—it was a jolly time indeed, good collegiate fun. Besides, when in their lifetimes—if not during their carefree years at Harvard—would they have the opportunity to see a filthy rich Brahmin like Hollis Appleton Wyatt dressed up as an old Jew, peddling pickled herring right in front of the gold dome of the State House on Charles Street?

Moishe Levinson found the entrance for servants and deliveries in the alleyway behind the building; he knew enough not to approach from the front. The building was not particularly large but was grand, with a brick and marble façade and an entry bracketed by two fluted columns. The rear was more utilitarian and familiar to him—a narrow, somewhat grungy alley, with uneven cobblestones and wafts of unpleasant rotting smells from refuse-filled trashcans.

The delivery boy wore a brown gabardine jacket over a collarless shirt. His trousers were a mismatch, being gray and a heavy wool. The choice was too hot for the unseasonably warm autumn day, but it was all he had that weren't work clothes, and his uncle had insisted he not look like a common tradesman. Worse, he was told to wear his cap. The herring was in a large glass jar with a screw-on lid, wrapped in brown paper and tied with string. Not that heavy but cumbersome, the only safe way to carry it was to cradle the load in both arms. And thus he had transported the order, guarding it like a precious gift, traveling by streetcar from Salem Street and transferring at Park Street. Once in Harvard Square, he had asked someone for directions to Mt. Auburn Street, but after that had navigated the Cambridge streets on his own. He was perspiring and itchy, a small price to pay for getting to roam the environs of Harvard University. Moishe, wide-eyed, had enjoyed gazing at the buildings and hubbub around him.

It was after eleven a.m.; the trip had taken longer than anticipated. Moishe wrapped his left arm around the jar and tucked it securely in the crook of his elbow, squeezing it against his chest, and reached for the buzzer with his right arm.

Baxter and Weatherhill leaped to their feet upon hearing the back door buzzer. They hurried through the club kitchen into the back receiving area, breezing past the gray-haired cook Willie and two other colored servants who were washing breakfast dishes. Willie had already been informed about a special delivery and told that the members would handle things themselves. The cook had passed on the news to his waiters, and all thus forewarned, he and the kitchen boys had dawdled. Normally long finished cleaning, they knew when something was cooking and were curious to see what it was.

By then all the late breakfasters had made their way to the den, and speculation and excitement had begun in earnest. Baxter and Weatherhill couldn't keep a secret, and gossipy whispers had made their way around the room. Even Hollis Wyatt had learned of the plans in store for him, and since the fuss and preparations involved him specifically, he considered his own participation unseemly. Unpresuming and sanguine, he lounged in a wing-back chair in the corner of the den, legs comfortably crossed, smoking his pipe with a self-assured smile, amused by the nature of his upcoming assignment.

"Come in, come in," said the taller of the two youths standing in the doorway. Given their manner of dress, they appeared to Moishe to have just stepped out of an illustration in a *Saturday Evening Post* college story, or even one of the advertisements. Both had hair slicked back with crisp off-center parts. The shorter one, with a fairer complexion, was pimply, but both had straight noses and light-colored eyes. They were both good-looking and presentable, high-class *goyim*, and while close to him in age, they seemed more adult. How did that illusion come about? Was it simply the clothes they wore, or something deeper and more impenetrable, the confidence and assurance of a privileged place in the world?

The delivery boy stepped over the threshold and peered around the entry. The vestibule was a generous open space with a worn dark wood floor, erratically scraped and stained from numerous encounters with crates and spills. A wide cement staircase led to the basement; shelves along one wall held a variety of non-perishables and kitchen staples, as well as general supplies for the clubhouse: rolls of toilet paper, bars of soap, and cleaning supplies.

"I brought the herring," he said, holding out the cylindrical package as if it weren't obvious. Even the utilitarian entrance was awe-inspiring, an enticing gateway into a world that he could not even imagine in real life. Beyond that room, he suspected, was something straight out of the library book he had recently read, "Brewster's Millions," that had made such an impression on him.

"Excellent," said Weatherhill, taking the package. "We didn't see you at the shop yesterday when we placed our order. I'm Mr. Weatherhill and this is *Monsieur* Baxter. Can I call you Abie?" He cast a coy glance at Baxter, who was grinning.

Instantly shown his place, Moishe bristled but was determined to control his temper. He didn't want to spoil possible future business for his uncle, who taught him that the customer was always right. A smart mouth or worse were bad manners and belonged somewhere else; here it was uncouth. How strange to enter the back entrance of a club at Harvard and liken it to being in shul, Moishe thought.

"The name is Moishe, and the amount due is one dollar seventy-five."

"That's a good deal of money for such a common aquatic creature," said Baxter, looking quite serious.

Moishe, puzzled, didn't respond. He assumed his uncle had already discussed the price.

"Why don't you wait here while we take this into the kitchen and make sure things are copacetic." said Weatherhill, a directive and not a request, and both lads exited to the adjacent room and closed the door behind them. Moishe stood in place, looked again at his surroundings, and fidgeted. He felt in his pants pocket to confirm the invoice was still there, and strained to make some sense of the murmurings from the other side of the door. What could be so complicated about an order of herring?

There was hushed but spirited activity in the kitchen, which now contained all the newly minted initiates except for Wyatt, as well as Wilcox, who had abandoned his position of comfort on the leather divan. They gathered around the counter next to the large utility sink as Weatherhill painstakingly, dramatically, removed the string and brown wrapping paper to reveal the glass jar with its mixture of liquid and chunky contents. He then unscrewed the lid and moved his face close to smell. With expressions and gestures of humor and disgust, all the others crowded in for a turn at closer examination, while Willie and the other colored workers silently observed, lined up against the back wall.

"Abie the delivery boy's still out there," said Weatherhill, "awaiting our judgment."

"I think it stinks," said Wilcox, straightening up and twisting away in revulsion.

"I agree," said Baxter, squeezing his nostrils between thumb and index finger. "We should inquire about this smell. I'm not sure it's *kosher*." The response to the remark was one of delight. A high premium was bestowed on cleverness, and Baxter was fully into the spirit of the affair.

"Indeed, we must bring the herring lad in here to speak to the quality of this pickling," said Weatherhill, his tone reflecting sober good sense and gravitas.

Since humor and conviviality harkened to the prior night's festivities, it was no surprise that one of the newbies by the name of Cabot rushed unprompted from the kitchen, only to return seconds later with a glass lamp pipe. He shouted "Hey!" to get everyone's attention, and held up the cylinder. Familiarity with the game attained the night before, several of the new members reached into their pockets. A nearby grinning cohort was the first to come up with a shiny quarter, which he handed over to Cabot. Baxter and Wilcox had been the instigators the night before, with hilarious effect, and they watched with pride as the newbies, already old hands, demonstrate what they had learned.

The set-up was spontaneous and unrehearsed, everyone on board—the kitchen staff unwittingly—with no spoken communication necessary. The members hastily assumed their places. When Moishe Levinson was finally brought into the Institute's large and fully equipped modern kitchen, the sights and sounds were overwhelming. A spectator at a three-ring circus, he wasn't certain where to look. On his left was the least interesting tableaux, but one which momentarily drew the eye nonetheless. Five colored men, three in kitchen attire and the two others in crisp white high-necked jackets, were lined attentively, backs straight, against a row of floor to ceiling white painted cabinetry. Nearby on the counter next to a deep double porcelain sink sat the large opened jar of pickled herring, with four or five young men solemnly considering it as a scientific exhibit. Finally, and most distracting was the grouping of youths in the room's central open portion, boisterously engaged in a game that involved attempting to drop a coin from a player's forehead into glass lamp pipe tucked in the front of his trousers. The target being a circular zone of only about a three-inch diameter, success evidently required some skill. Moishe witnessed two failed attempts amidst cajoling, advice, taunting, and laughter of the surrounding youths, each of whom seemed more than eager to have a turn of his own—before Weatherhill directed him to the matter at hand.

"This appears to smell strange," he said, leading Moishe to the jar. The observers in that particular circus ring moved aside.

Moishe looked around warily before sticking his nose closer.

"That is the way it is intended to smell," he said. "My uncle sampled it before he packed it. I saw him."

"It also seems awfully watery to me," added Baxter. "All the excess liquid, I should think, which accounts for less of the actual fish, which is what we are paying for. We don't want to be cheated."

"But you need the brine for the pickling, otherwise . . ." began Moishe, unable to squelch the defensiveness in his voice. But he was interrupted from one of the players.

"Hey!" offered Cabot, "perhaps our visitor wants a try at the coin drop! He looks like a capable sportsman!"

Weatherhill and Baxter appeared intent on pursuing the herring discussion, finally acceding to the requests and shouts of encouragement spontaneously coming from their colleagues.

"I'll wager he can't come close!" shouted someone.

"You're on!" responded another.

"Who's in on this?"

Moishe stood by the herring mutely as the group continued to discuss him and lay odds on his abilities, an unknown but promising-looking prospect. As the betting, enthusiasm, and noise level increased, Moishe began shaking his head adamantly, despite confidence that he could succeed. The game didn't look that difficult, all that was required was coordination and concentration.

"I just need to get paid for the herring and return to my uncle's shop," he said futilely, now the center of attention of the entire room, which was protesting and trying to convince him to play among a chorus of supplications and arguments.

"Wait! We'll provide some inducement!" offered the chap who had suggested Moishe try in the first place, making himself heard over the other voices. "I'll give you fifty cents if you get it on the first attempt . . . you have only three chances . . ."

Two comrades offered to double that amount, all sweetening the pot. The conversation turned in a different direction, as new bets, new odds, were arranged. From what sense he could make of things, at the culmination of the monetary proceedings, Moishe would get three dollars if he made it on the first try, and a dollar fifty if he succeeded at all, and this with nothing for him to put up himself. He had no skin in the game, and everything to win.

The inducement of money made Moishe less than more likely to relent. He wanted to show his own skill, to demonstrate he was their equal, not acquiesce as a money hungry Jew, overly tempted at the prospects of lucre. But, he rationalized he would give the extra money to Uncle Abe. And besides, he wanted to show these *machers* what a street kid from Salem Street was capable of.

He was familiarized with the rules and handed the quarter. He was allowed to position the glass lamp pipe into the front of his trousers by himself, angling the target somewhat by how much of the pipe was exposed and how much was tucked down his pants. The crowd quieted as he took his position in the center of a half circle, although a few of the onlookers, trying to be helpful, offered advice.

"Take your time, make sure the coin is perfectly balanced before you move your head forward . . ."

"Don't move your head forward too fast . . ."

"Arch your back a bit for a better angle . . ."

"A lot of money is riding on this one . . ."

Moishe nodded his head, signaling his readiness for the first attempt, and made a final adjustment to the position of the lamp pipe. He removed his cap and flicked it to the floor, brushed his hair back with his hand, and slowly tilted his head back to balance the quarter on his forehead. The room, captive to suspense, was totally silent.

And while Moishe stood motionless, neck craned back and looking at the ceiling, brow furrowed in concentration as he balanced the quarter in preparation for the drop, the semicircle of youths separated as if by some unforeseen hand. They were making room for Baxter, who had stealthily approached and penetrated the line of observers. And before Moishe had the chance to drop the quarter, to lower his head to realize what was happening, Baxter had poured a large tumbler of pickled herring juice down the opening of the lamp glass, into the depths of Moishe Levinson's pants.

Moishe Levinson stood on the pavement and gave the door a final, futile kick. His *tuchis* hurt from landing on the cobblestones when shoved from the threshold. The sides of his fists were sore and scraped from his pounding on the door, and now his foot pained him as well. If he didn't give up, he could break a toe. Defeated, he picked up his cap—someone had tossed it out during the fracas when they were manhandling him out the door—and put it on. Without an outlet to express his rage, Moishe couldn't hold back the tears. He sobbed, then wailed. Agitated, he started to walk away but then paced back, not knowing what to do or where to go. He stank and looked like he had peed himself. More than his humiliation, he had let down his uncle. And worse, Shmuel the know-it-all would be smug, and mock the both of them for being so naïve. He sat down on the curb beside the Institute's back door to think things through.

He was surprised that he hadn't put up a fight. Of course, he was shocked when he first felt the cascading wetness in his pants and knew he had been duped. Instinctively he had pulled out the lamp piping and furiously cast it to the ground, shattering the glass. And then he had been disoriented by the noise and laughter, bodies blurred, sound amplified, a mob with hands pushing at him from all directions. He still could have bloodied a few of them, had he the presence of mind. But it all happened so fast. He resisted being pushed out the door, that was all, more to keep his balance so not as to fall than to defend himself.

The club boys themselves had reacted instinctively and by now, rather subdued, had returned to the lounge as if nothing had happened, or nothing they cared to talk about. For as long as it lasted, they pretended not to hear the pounding sounds coming from the kitchen, where Ben and Marcus were cleaning up the glass and mopping the floor. Quiet conversations eventually surfaced from various quarters of the room, strained punctuations of the silence. Things had gotten out of hand, their behavior had been ungentlemanly. Among their set, the reaction to being played the fool was uniformly good natured, no one would think to respond angrily. Just the opposite, as the attention reflected well on the chosen victim, signaling acceptance into the group. Pranks were part of the college experience and a means for masculine expression and bonding. The substitution of cold water with herring juice had been off-script, however, a spontaneous alternative. Baxter, empty tumbler in his hand, was reaching to turn on the water tap, and without thinking things through, succumbed to meanness mistaken for originality.

Even as the charade was progressing, some of them sensed a vague disconnectedness. The Hebrew was not one with whom they shared or would ever share a tradition. Nor had they any real experience with Jews; the ones who were disturbingly a visible population at Harvard traveled in their own circles and their presence wasn't acknowledged. A Jew bringing pickled herring to the Institute was laughable in itself, but this delivery boy ran counter to stereotype. He was no pathetic creature or weakling, but of strong build, like a workman, and possibly capable of physical menace. Subconsciously they made the calculation that with their large numbers, he was no threat. What did it matter if he were unpredictable and wouldn't respond in customary fashion?

But once done, an actual provocation, how could things return to the normal aftermath of horseplay among friends? They had no choice but to act the mob, transform laughter into ridicule, and forcibly expel him. No other scenario made sense. No one could say, "That was fun, sport. Now here's your money and you can go back to wherever you come from." Baxter had intended to pay Moishe for the herring, but how could he do so given the way events had transpired? He had misjudged things, but what was done was done, and he had the rest of the day to look forward to. He would not fret over some humiliated Jew. If there had been a mistake, it was letting him in the kitchen in the first place.

Hearing footsteps on the cobblestones, the devastated Moishe, cheeks tear-streaked, looked up to see a tall well-dressed young man walking toward him.

Moishe did not recognize him as part of the throng in the club's kitchen, but knew immediately that he had come around the corner from the club front entrance. He was an Institute man, and alone. Moishe jumped to his feet and stood up straight, wiping the snot from his nose with the back of his forearm. Determined to pound the *shagetz* to a pulp, he waited, preparing to introduce himself by throwing the first punch as soon as the well-heeled Harvard man came within arm's reach. Moishe, with cold staring eyes, filled his chest with a deep breath, the calm before the storm of his fists.

The swell approached without hesitation or evidence of concern, meeting the stare with his own piercing blue eyes. Moishe, for the second time that morning, surprised himself. He was paralyzed, a cobra hypnotized by a snake charmer.

"My name is Hollis Appleton Wyatt," said the young man, extending his arm. "I just heard what happened and I'm terribly sorry for it. My lodgings are just across the street, and I'd be most appreciative if you'd accept my offer to take you there so you can clean yourself up."

Moishe did not shake the proffered hand nor remove his cap. Not averting his gaze, he saw the man passively drop the extended arm to his side without the least sign of rebuff or insult.

They looked at one another with intensity for several seconds.

Moishe Levinson surprised himself yet again. He gave a barely perceptible nod, and then followed Hollis Appleton Wyatt out of the alleyway.

At Claverly

Moishe arched his neck back and let the cascading rivulets begin their downward journey from mid-chest. Elbows out, he raised both hands to caress his forehead, then passed them backwards to squeeze the wet from his hair. The water was hot, and remarkably a temperature of his own choosing through control by taps. Moishe had never experienced a cleansing like this. He had bathed in hot water, of course, but never with a faucet from above his head; instead, he would curl up in a tub of sheeted zinc, water brought to a tolerable temperature by replenishment from Aunt Esther's kettle.

And such a bathroom! Moishe was standing in a tub made of marble, enclosed by a curtain threaded onto an elliptical copper rod. The washstand—with hot and cold taps like the shower—was of a matching marble, and the floor was composed of small black and white marble octagons with a patterned border. The toilet was only porcelain—did they even make them from marble?—but who was to complain since it was inside? He had availed himself of the toilet before showering—carefully lifting the finely burnished walnut seat as if it were a piece of fine crystal—in spite of no urge to pee. For a few moments he stood over the toilet bowl, patiently waiting for a stream, rejoicing in his surroundings as if standing on a mountain top.

The luxuriousness of Claverly had overwhelmed Moishe the instant he went through the mahogany door into the vestibule, Hollis holding it open for him. In passing, Moishe allowed his hand to brush the brass doorknob—a gesture of affection. Hollis gave the delivery boy a wary glance, then continued to lead him into the massive entryway and up the staircase. Moishe had followed the club man silently, but now he was speechless—he gazed up and around, unable to focus on anything in particular, such was the assault on his senses. He had entered a phantasmagoric world of marble flooring and antique oak wainscoting and dark flocked wallpaper. And Hollis' personal suite was even more of a visual feast: the antique dark oak-lined walls now extended from floor to ceiling. A large fireplace was bordered by carved oak pillars and an ornately carved mantlepiece. A semi-circular window seat bounded by curved plate glass gave an expansive view upon Mt. Auburn Street.

Hollis closed the door behind him and appraised his guest, allowing the latter's eyes to acclimate, as if he had entered a dark room. Moishe absorbed the dominating brass chandelier in the center of the room, the various oriental rugs strewn across the floor, the bookcase filled with haphazardly arranged books and knick-knacks, the desk with a brass double-globed Harvard lamp, and the paraphernalia more revealing of personality: a Harvard pennant, medallions and trophies, framed photos and posters suspended on the walls by wire from picture rails along the ceiling. Moishe felt himself in a museum, under the professional scrutiny of museum guard Hollis. Moishe wondered, was some sort of comment in order? Perhaps a compliment? Would praise have any purpose or worth, coming from a poor Jew who lived in a tenement in the North End?

Having taken in as much of the room as he politely could, Moishe settled his gaze onto his host—to him another museum piece of sorts—and both looked at each other with now softened stares. An immigrant and a swell in a face-off in a deluxe suite in Claverly was an unlikely situation to which both were unaccustomed.

Eventually, Hollis was saved by his reflexive good manners, responding as he would at the arrival of any other guest. "Let me take your jacket," he said, extending an arm.

Moishe complied. And still they both stood, in silence as before, except that Hollis was holding a well-worn brown gabardine jacket. Uncertain as to where to set it, he kept it loosely in his grasp. "I don't believe you've told me your name," he finally said.

"Moishe . . . Moishe Levinson."

Good manners could only go so far, as ordinary follow-ups did not apply. Not available were such standard polite inquiries such as "Are you related to the Levinsons from Newport?" or "Did you know the Derby boys at Groton?" or "Didn't we meet at the Bancroft wedding?" There was simply nowhere to go, other than apologize once again for what had happened.

"It wasn't your fault," said Moishe. Equally uncomfortable, he wanted to move things along. He pointed at the radiator along the wall, which he had fortunately identified as such despite being housed in the ubiquitous antique oak, its utilitarian purpose betrayed by decorative metal circulation grating at the top and along the sides.

"If I set my clothes on that, I think they will dry very quickly and I can leave you to your business," he said.

Hollis nodded agreeably and pointed in a contrary direction. "And the bath is through that door and to the right. There should be clean towels. Please make yourself at home."

Moishe walked to the radiator, hesitating before removing his trousers, his underpants, and his shirt, all under the watchful eye of Hollis. Naked but for his dingy singlet—stripping completely would have made him feel too vulnerable—Moishe strode across the room toward the door to the toilet. Hollis couldn't contain his curiosity and was unable to resist a glance at a circumcised penis. Exposed, and feeling at a disadvantage, Moishe kept his eyes downward and was not aware of any looks that could be misconstrued as prurience, although Hollis was more self-conscious. The notion of being caught out comparing—or heaven forbid, admiring—the genitals of such an inferior gave him a flash of considerable unease.

"There are only three suites with marble bathrooms in the entire building," he commented, a covering pleasantry, as Moishe made his way to the threshold. "The others are just porcelain," he clarified in a slightly raised voice to Moishe's departing back.

Hollis shook his head. That was a stupid and pointless thing to say. Who was he trying to impress, anyway? Hollis was confused by this peculiar Jew. Still shaking his head, and deciding not to place the garment among the foul smelling items warming above the radiator, he draped the gabardine jacket over the back of the sofa—there was no need to bother hanging it in the closet. His good deed and display of civility had unsettled him.

Levinson emerged from the bath shirtless, with a large plush white bath towel wrapped around his waist. He carried his grimy and stained singlet, to postpone putting it on for as long as possible. Placing the fabric against his clean skin, which now smelled of Pear's soap, seemed a sacrilege. Hollis was relaxing on the Morris chair beside his desk, crossed legs on top of an ottoman. He was smoking a cigar. The familiarity of a customary posture was soothing to him. Hollis Wyatt, after all, was known for being calm and unflappable. He stood up politely at the sight of Levinson, struck by the latter's physique. Levinson was lean, but his broad chest, delineated arm musculature, and washer-board abdomen rivaled any of boys on the varsity eight; he was practically a Bernarr Macfadden, as far as Wyatt could tell. To his dismay, Wyatt realized he was again appraising the Jew's physicality, but wasn't it only natural to size up the stranger?

"Can I offer you a smoke?" Wyatt asked.

Levinson shook his head,

"I believe I owe you an explanation," Wyatt continued, glad to embark on directed conversation, however delicate the topic. "It's all very silly, really, and difficult to explain, but the reason for the herring order . . . you see, I am about to be initiated into my club, and my upper classman chums thought it would be amusing to see me dressed up as a . . . as a peddler. A peddler selling pickled herring on the street. All just for amusement, really, and they had procured these ragged clothes, and a long black beard for me, to keep in character . . ."

"You mean you were going to dress up as a Yid," Levinson interrupted. There was an assertiveness, a sharpness to his tone, the intimidation of his surroundings having dissolved into the ether. He could have been on Hanover Street in the North End, standing up to an Irish kid.

"I'll confess it was play acting . . ."

"Mockery you mean . . ."

"I'll confess to that as well," said a contrite Wyatt, "and I'm truly sorry for it. As far as the herring liquid, that trick was something the boys had been playing on one another last night. Everyone was a bit in their cups. With water, of course, but perhaps if herring brine had been accessible . . . in any event, things got carried away and . . . and I've spoken to them and everyone is truly embarrassed and repentant for what happened."

Levinson stood silently as Wyatt waited for a response, hopefully one that would defuse things.

"I accept your apology," Levinson finally said, sounding as if he meant it.

"Excellent. Then can I offer you a drink, perhaps? No? Well, at least have a seat and we can chat for a moment."

Levinson was not reluctant to stay. How many chances would he have to inhabit this world, to be lounging amidst it after a hot shower? He chose the sofa, upholstered in a dark brown velvet fabric with an undulating rim of wood carved into leaves and clusters of grapes. His coat was hanging over the back in the middle, but also a man's outfit was now laid out at the far end. He pretended not to see it.

"I can't help but notice," Wyatt began hesitantly, "that you're quite . . . quite . . . fit. I myself try to make it to the Hemenway Gymnasium at least three times a week. Dr. Sargent has set up all the modern apparatuses there. It's really quite astounding."

"I know of it," said Levinson, "but I've never seen it. I work for a blacksmith in the North End, on Cooper Street. Mainly tending to carriages and wagons, but some farrier work. I'm good with horses and O'Rourke, the Irishman I work for, is scared of them, but pretends like he isn't, so I make shoes, mostly. My apparatus is a hammer."

"Oh . . . I thought you worked for a fish monger."

"My uncle owns a delicatessen. Sometimes I help him out. Such as today."

"Well, it certainly must be good exercise, because you look like someone who spends all day in the tank."

Levinson gave a look of non-comprehension.

"The rowing tank, in the boathouse, where an oarsman can practice when the weather's bad," Wyatt clarified. "Of course, Sargent also has rowing machines in Hemenway, but they're not in water. It isn't the same, you see . . . the feel of it is quite different, I mean."

Levinson nodded. Oarsmanship of this type was not in his conversational boathouse, but he was reminded of his rowboat back in Vinnytsia, his very own, a birthday gift from his *tate*. He vividly remembered the slapping sound of the oars against the water.

"But what occurs to me," Wyatt went on, becoming more comfortable, "is that the President of our esteemed University would be pleasantly surprised by your physique. He has been somewhat critical of the vitality and vigor of your people, despite having much respect for your race as a whole. But he has referred to a mode of life that is not hardy enough . . . not enough time spent out of doors."

"That big stain on your President Eliot's face has crept up and penetrated his brain!" Levinson said with some bite. He was feeling his own creep, a hotness moving into his face, and couldn't help but lash out at the indignities suffered by his cousin. Shmuel the Schmekel wasn't mensch enough to do anything but lie down and take it. And sadly, Eliot could have been specifically referring to his cousin, a weakling, which made things all the worse.

Wyatt could not contain his astonishment. The Jew delivery boy was familiar with Charles William Eliot!

"My cousin attends Harvard," Levinson explained, not expecting Wyatt to ask his name. "You wouldn't know him," he pre-empted anyway.

"There are many different social circles at Harvard," Wyatt replied, a simple statement of fact.

"Social circle is one way to describe it. I have a better way: My cousin is invisible. You will walk right past him and not acknowledge or even see him. He can jump up and scream and wave his hands in front of your face and you still cannot see him!" Levinson had become animated again before settling down to his baseline. Wyatt was squirming in his seat.

"Harvard is just reflecting the society we live in . . . nothing more, nothing less. It's a social reality, not much more can be said about it."

Levinson quieted. "You are right. You would never see my cousin, at Harvard or anywhere else. But if you ever wanted to meet him, he can be found, when he's not in class, studying in Gore Library at what some people call the 'Kike table.'" That "some people" included Hollis Wyatt was implicit, which both of them knew without pursuing any further. "And I know much about Harvard, not just Eliot. I know about Briggs and Hurlbut, and Baker and Kittredge and Shaler and Copeland and that putz Coolidge . . ."

Wyatt broke out into laughter at the epithet linked with Archibald Coolidge; although he didn't know what the word meant, he knew the gist, as many derogatory terms were descriptors of the unpopular history professor. Once he stopped laughing, having been drawn in, he leaned up in his chair to ask "What's a putz?" and Levinson grinned, wagging his index finger at his groin.

Levinson went on to explain that he learned most about Harvard from his cousin Sam, who was a bit of a putz himself. And not only did he hear the gossip about the professors, but he was more than familiar with their course material also. He would read any of the texts that Shmuel could procure from the library to bring home, and for those he couldn't, Shmuel was a prodigious note-taker. Levinson not only studied the notes for pleasure, but was continually prepping his cousin for his examinations from them. So far, English 2, Kittredge's course on Shakespeare, was his favorite, although he also found Shaler's teachings on geology held his interest.

Wyatt listened in disbelief as Levinson became more and more excited describing the courses with which he had become acquainted over the previous four years, as Shmuel was now a senior. Wyatt was familiar with some—he was currently enrolled in English 2, and had taken introductory courses from Shaler and Coolidge his freshman year—but had found little in them of merit. For Wyatt's circle, academics was not a priority, since his chums were assured of prosperous futures regardless of academic efforts or achievement. Harvard was a place to come of age socially, to make contacts with the right sorts of people, to act out youthful exuberance, and to prove one's manhood in athletic competition. What mattered most of all was being a club man, and if one could be a varsity "H" man as well, all the better.

Wyatt was not surprised that the young man in front of him had a scholarly bent. Eliot had recognized this trait of his people, hadn't he? The kinsmen of Levinson who were enrolled and disturbingly growing in number were stellar book learners from public schools like Boston and Cambridge Latin. Of honor roll caliber, they managed to procure a goodly share of scholarship money, a fact producing considerable resentment among those with such concerns. But they did not belong within the gates of Harvard; they were outsiders, even outcasts, who kept to themselves. Naturally, they were beyond University life, excluded from virtually all sports teams, clubs, and organizations. Nothing more than greasy grinds, the lot of them. These progeny of stooped bearded men with head coverings, bent over books and scrolls in darkened, foul-smelling rooms, could never be Harvard men. They were an inferior race, and along with other immigrants, polluters of American society. Thankfully, true Harvard men were doing something about the situation, three of them having formed the Immigration Restriction League only a handful of years earlier. They were making progress.

But this Jew, the first he had ever spoken to, was an anomaly. He was disarming. Under ordinary circumstances Wyatt would have found his situation—brought upon himself—entirely absurd. A Jew in Claverly, wrapped only in a towel, casually conversing with him as if he were an equal. Normally Wyatt would have found this a display of unimaginable insolence. Yet equally confounding, Levinson appeared oblivious to the fact that he was comporting himself in a manner to suggest he was an equal. He manifested no consciousness of his proper place. Wyatt listened while Levinson discoursed on his reading preferences. Apparently when not wielding a hammer in front of a forge, Levinson was at the Boston Public Library. His reading range extended far beyond Harvard professors expounding on their knowledge; he was equally if not more enthusiastic about popular literature: novels and the short stories in popular magazines like the *Saturday Evening Post*, the *Popular Magazine*, and *Scribner's*. They had mutual tastes and interests, remarkably. And Wyatt continued to be distracted and baffled by Levinson's physicality.

Wyatt retreated into his accustomed mode. He had atoned for his clubmates' indiscretion, performed his act of charity, fulfilled his obligations. Enough was enough.

"I'm so sorry to cut this short, but I'm expected back at the club soon." Glancing at the clothes set out on the sofa, he was wondering why he had prepared such an expansive gesture, above and beyond, but it was too late. He had misgivings that the gesture might be misconstrued, but why should it be, and what did it matter? Was Levinson too prideful to accept the offering? Wyatt got up from his chair and walked to the radiator for Levinson's trousers, pincering them between thumb and index finger. The crotch seemed to be nearly dry, but still reeked.

"I've laid out some clothes for you to take," he said, indicating the clothes on the sofa. "You certainly can't get on a trolley wearing these things."

"I can't take these."

"Of course you can, Levinson. I was giving them away, anyway, along with a bagful of others. And there's no point in you just taking the trousers and leaving the rest. The waistcoat and jacket are matching, and I always wore the suit with that particular shirt and tie. And it must have a collar of some kind, that goes without saying."

Levinson was dubious. "Why would you give these away?" The suit looked brand new and perfectly fine to him. He had already reached over and was rubbing the high quality wool between his fingers.

"Why, just look at the cut of the lapel, man!" Wyatt exclaimed. "L. P. Hollander hasn't shown anything like that for two years or more!"

"And who would you give these to?" Levinson was questioning for truthfulness. From Shmuel he knew about Max Keester, who dealt in used apparel, and the less reputable Poco Bennett, whose procurement of hand-me-downs from the wealthy was more a front for his notorious money lending at usurious rates.

"I set my old clothes aside for Cram, the Recorder in the Dean's office. He distributes them to some of the poorer students here. Now, you must try these on to see if they fit. And if they do, you have no excuse but to take them."

It was clear to Hollis that Levinson would no longer protest. But while Levinson was already half-naked, and his genitals had been previously revealed, Wyatt felt the necessity of propriety.

"You can change in my bedroom," he said.

Standing in the doorway dressed in Hollis Wyatt's cast-off clothes, Moishe Levinson was unrecognizable. Apart from the worn and scuffed shoes, the peculiar Jew had disappeared and been replaced by an entirely presentable character, or as Levinson would have seen it, as someone "visible." The transformation was startling. Levinson seemed mildly embarrassed, standing stiffly like a schoolboy awaiting affirmation. Wyatt could not believe his eyes. Was there any possible improvement? Fascinated by the notion, he led Levinson into the bathroom and retrieved his bottle of Pinaud's *Tres Flores* Brilliantine from the cabinet above the washstand. He handed him the bottle along with a bristle brush.

"Why not complete the picture," he instructed, then watched as Levinson gingerly poured the liquid into one hand, set the bottle down, and rubbed his hands together. He hesitated for a moment before bringing his hands to his head and massaging his scalp. Silently checking himself in the mirror as Hollis watched, he slicked his hair straight back with the brush. Wyatt was still amazed by the transformation, but Moishe was more preoccupied by the masculine floral scent. He was delighted to realize that he didn't smell like a sissy. No one in the neighborhood, taking a whiff, would call him one, although they might not know how to react.

"There now," said Hollis, intending to bestow a compliment, "you could pass for a gentleman." He led a very different person from the one who had entered back into the living room and toward the door, picking up the gabardine jacket along the way. But now he was nagged by a thought: would he need to throw the hair brush away, or simply give it a good cleaning with lye soap?

Wyatt handed Levinson his jacket. "I'll have someone dispose of those garments," he said, referring to the remaining clothes still on the radiator housing.

"My aunt will wash them," said Moishe, detouring to the other side of the room to retrieve them. He laid out the jacket, layered his old shirt, trousers, and underwear on top, and rolled the clothes into a bundle that he could tuck under his arm.

"Goodbye, then," said Wyatt, surprised to find himself extending his hand and smiling.

Moishe's expression was somber. "The money owed to my uncle was never settled," he replied.

Wyatt was stunned beyond words. What gratitude was this! All appearances to the contrary, the well-dressed rogue in front of him was still a greedy, money-grubbing Jew underneath! He flushed and took a deep breath, preparing to unleash and put the ingrate in his place. Rarely if ever challenged, Wyatt was not accustomed to a situation that demanded an imperious tone.

"After all I've given you!" was all he could manage, an expression more of disappointment than rage.

"And I am most grateful, sir," Moishe spoke calmly. "You are a generous person. And you have done me a kindness because of my mistreatment. But this has nothing to do with my Uncle Abraham Rabinovitz, who is out for his herring. And, by the way, the biggest herring order he's ever had!"

Hollis shook his head, wanting to extricate himself from this stranger as quickly as possible.

"And a gentleman pays his debts, am I right?"

"How much?"

"A dollar and seventy-five cents."

Wyatt reached into an inside jacket pocket and pulled out the leather wallet that his mother had brought back from her recent trip to Italy. He took a two dollar bill and held it out.

"That is too much," said Moishe, "and the only change I have is for the trolley back home."

"Oh, for Christssake!" Wyatt shouted dismissively. "Just take it!"

Moishe didn't flinch. "My uncle would not want me to take advantage of a customer," he said, "especially a gentleman." It was now Levinson who was being dismissive, but he was smiling.

Wyatt shook his head, all the while thinking of where he could acquire change. Or perhaps he could write a check, a draw from his trust account at State Street. For pickled herring. Who could dream such a thing?

Moishe Levinson was now smiling more broadly.

"Perhaps you would like to arm wrestle for it," he said. "That would be fair, no one could argue."

By the time the two dollar bill had been changed hands, Wyatt, well-trained by Reverend Peabody at Groton in good sportsmanship, was gracious in defeat and breathing heavily.

Both men had taken off their jackets, and Wyatt had set up for the battle on his desk, dragging over an extra side chair for his opponent. Wyatt knew early on that it was never going to be a contest; Levinson was toying with him. Nonetheless, he gave it everything he had. Initially they were deadlocked in the center position for a number of seconds, then Hollis got the edge, Moishe yielding to a spot about halfway to defeat. And then Levinson slowly and evenly pushed back to the center and held for a few more seconds, before letting Wyatt regain advantage to roughly the same spot. This continued, as if Wyatt were reeling in a large marlin, but with no change in the length of the line. At one point, Hollis appeared just inches from victory—at the brink of exhaustion, arm aching and quivering—with Levinson not letting him move any further, face passive, revealing no sign of strain. Finally, Moishe showed him mercy and brought the contest to an end, the club man's arm forced to collapse back with a jolt, his knuckles rapping against the desk like a solitary urgent knock at a door.

Moishe eased his hand from the sweaty grip and wiped it against his new trousers before standing up to put on his jacket.

"You should go to Hemenway for Dr. Sargent's testing," Hollis conceded, unable to hide his admiration. He was not embarrassed by his loss; Levinson was formidable.

"That is only for Harvard students," said Moishe, as if Wyatt didn't know any better. All students were required to take the yearly physical examination devised by the innovative health authority and gymnasium director, a "total strength" score determined and documented on the basis of lung capacity, back, leg, and arm strength. Shmuel dreaded the testing every year, and predictably performed miserably, never ranking higher than the E group, and barely cracking that. But all was relative—a couple of his classmates from the Jerusalem table had never made it upwards from the G group of 200 to 300 points, which was as low as it went.

"I made the A group this year," Wyatt said, "and I would wager that you'd score much higher, even above a thousand. At least on the basis of your arms and back; more difficult to tell about your legs."

Levinson shrugged. "I'll tell O'Rourke. I'm sure he'd score over a thousand, if he cared, and he'll be sixty-seven. But do me a favor and mention the winner of our own little wager to your President Charles Eliot, if it should come up."

He was straight-faced when he delivered his quip, but Wyatt laughed.

"If it ever comes up, I will." Then, seriously, "Have you ever considered attending Harvard yourself, like your cousin? Surely you could meet the academic criteria, and maybe get a scholarship. You'd have to work, of course. Perhaps even earn money as a tutor."

Levinson tucked his clothes bundle under his arm and opened the door to exit Claverly 301. He allowed himself one final look around at the world of Hollis Wyatt. Hollis doubted he would ever see this strange and exceptional youth again.

"I don't want to be a Harvard student like my cousin. That is not for me," he said. "I want to be a *real* College Man."

Eleanor

The letter came to my room at Weld about a week after my initial visit, the envelope bearing the Harvard University Library letterhead. A handwritten note from Eleanor Hopkins—as I learned her surname to be—informed me that, as she had feared, no student files for Michael Levinson existed. She had taken the liberty, though, of requesting the student file for my great uncle Samuel Rabinowitz, which she would keep behind the counter for a few days if I wanted to drop by to peruse it. And if I wanted to approach my investigation from the Hollis Wyatt angle, there was a wealth of material, which could require a considerable time commitment. Narrowing things down, though, my best bet would be to start with Wyatt's personal correspondence. For the time period from his undergraduate years to his twenty-fifth reunion year of 1930, his letters filled six large boxes, or nearly four feet of shelf space, filed in manila folders.

I went to the Archives directly after the Nat Sci 3 lecture ended the following day, skipping lunch at the Union. Eleanor did not seem surprised to see me, and already had Shmuel's file in hand as I was signing in. Uncle Shmuel's transcript showed him to be a strong student, but the handful of letters in the file mainly dealt with money woes and his scholarship status. He continually received small checks from the Beneficiary fund, and nearly postponed graduating on schedule for the lack of twenty dollars owed, which somehow he managed to come up with through a bondsman and his father's intervention. His situation as a Russian Jewish immigrant at Harvard, I assumed, was not atypical. A recommendation from a professor was telling:

"I have had Samuel Rabinowitz this year in Philosophy 2 and he gets an A in the course. I do not know him personally but I should think that he is an exceedingly suitable person to receive a scholarship, partly because he seems extremely poor, partly in the hope that he may thereby be enabled to achieve some measure of personal cleanliness; an ambition which he has not yet attained."

Poor Uncle Shmuel! But of his cousin, my Poppa Levinson, there was no mention. Eleanor was fussing with some papers behind the counter when I returned with the file. I shook my head and shrugged. With an angled tilt of her head, peering over her glasses, she indicated two large gray boxes that rested on the end of the counter.

"I think you'll only need to go through the correspondences in these two boxes," she said, adjusting her glasses a bit up her nose. "I've gone over the index for this collection, which was catalogued a number of years ago. All the letters in the remaining boxes were sent to, or addressed from, specific individuals. Your grandfather Michael Levinson is not among them. But . . ." she tried to convey some encouragement, "individual letters from him might be included among the Miscellaneous communications, which are filed in groupings of years, rather than names, in one of these."

I nodded, but made no move for either of the boxes, and Eleanor sensed my discouragement.

"Perhaps," she began, "your grandfather never actually matriculated, but, you know, hung around. Regardless, from the letter you showed me, he certainly seems to have had a connection with Hollis Wyatt—what seems to have been a rather warm one—and relationships with other Harvard men as well. Think about it for a moment . . . how would a poor Jewish boy from the North End develop those sorts of acquaintances?"

"Maybe he was their tailor," I replied, only half-sarcastically, thinking of Shmuel's livelihood in the schmatta business, as well as Poppa's mention of the man who traded in used clothes. I had not conveyed my recollections of these stories to Eleanor on our first encounter, but I was beginning to feel that she was open to more personal revelations.

"My grandfather told me about a man around Harvard who dealt in used clothing."

"That would have been Max Keester," Eleanor replied without hesitation, "although Poco Bennett dealt in used clothing as well. But he was best known for lending money to students, with highly inflated rates of interest . . ."

"How to you know all this stuff?"

"Oh, it's all part of the common lore around here," said Eleanor with a dismissive wave of a hand. "There were a host of characters associated with Harvard for years and years. We have files here on all of them, in case you're interested. Billy the Postman, Angus Jones the bell ringer, John the Orangeman . . ."

"I remember hearing about two of them," I piped in, letting my voice rise in excitement, no one being in the room besides the two of us.

"Angus Jones rang the bell in Harvard Hall for fifty years, until 1908, and I believe he may have only missed ringing it one time, before the Civil War, when he was laid up with the measles. Billy Prentice, known as Billy the Postman, delivered mail for over thirty years. Both were around in . . . in Hollis Wyatt's time here."

"And John the Orangeman . . ."

"Of course," Eleanor said, "the most famous. But he was more than a fruit peddler, he was more a sort of—" she paused, "—he was a mascot, to be honest, a cheerleader at sporting events. An Irishman, John Lovett was. I always found it rather telling that Harvard men chose an actual human being as a mascot . . . someone of the lower social orders who was treated less like a man and more like a beloved pet." Eleanor was no longer making eye contact, but gazing off beyond the enclosing walls into the distance. "Unfortunate," she murmured.

I tried to change her mood by retrieving her from thoughts of an Irishman mascot.

"And the president, you know," I ventured, "with the large birthmark," I added needlessly.

Eleanor snapped out of her reverie and looked directly at me.

"Yes," she said, "now THAT was unfortunate as well, but couldn't be helped."

On that note I proceeded to tackle Hollis Wyatt's personal letters, wasting three hours with sifting and skimming, coming up empty. I was tired and hungry, but the Archives was open for another hour, and Eleanor suggested if I had any energy left I might look through the class albums again. I began with the Class of 1903, which I had already perused, to revisit my great Uncle Shmuel. I skimmed through the front matter—photographs of faculty and the main Harvard buildings of the time, group photographs of junior and senior athletic teams as well as college organizations, and a class history summarizing organizational activities and accomplishments. Then I revisited the single photograph of my great uncle among the rest of the graduating seniors in the final section of the album. Nothing accompanied his humble visage besides the barest essentials: his address on Salem Street in Boston and attendance at Roxbury Latin School. If that were any indication, as far as I could tell he had not participated in a single extracurricular activity. I mentioned this to Eleanor on my way to a bathroom break, wanting to relieve the pressure on my bladder before turning my attention next to Hollis Appleton Wyatt in the Class of 1906 Album.

"That is not surprising," said Eleanor. "He was a poor scholarship student, with no time for activities, since presumably he needed to work. And even if he had the time—"

"—He wasn't the kind of guy I expect would have played sports" I interrupted, "but he was a good student. I can tell from his transcript."

"I'm sure he was," said Eleanor, almost reassuringly, as if this somehow was a reflection on my own academic prowess. "But even had he had the time to participate in extracurriculars," she returned to her earlier train of thought, "he would have been shut out from most activities because of . . . of who he was." She paused. "After about 1880 or 1890 it would be nearly impossible for a Jew to be selected for the staff of the newspaper or literary journal, ability notwithstanding. And certainly not the clubs or most of the social organizations. It just wouldn't happen. Before that, there were hardly any Jewish students around, and virtually all of them were well-do-to, highly secular German Jews."

"I see. So all he did was study."

"But not necessarily by choice. There just weren't many other opportunities available."

"He was a grind," I said, employing the closest vernacular of which I was aware, and which hit close to home.

"Indeed. The term is still in parlance, but it was more derogatory then. More specifically, your uncle might have been referred to as a 'greasy grind,'" she elaborated.

"Never heard that. It certainly adds . . . a dimension."

"Yes, that particular expression has fortunately faded with the passage of time." Eleanor once again stared into the distance abstractedly. Her gaze, the way she held her head, and her brilliant blue eyes reflecting like a clear pool reminded me of Judy Collins' face on the "Who Knows Where the Time Goes" album cover.

"Harvard was an extremely socially stratified place," she finally went on. "The poor students were generally good students, because education gave them the possibility of a future. Some qualified for a number of honor societies, and certainly many received the bulk of academic scholarship awards. A few years later more activities would open up, although opportunities were still limited. There was the Menorah Society, of course, founded in 1906, in fact . . . and the Socialist Club." She chuckled at that, as if I were more than vaguely privy to the joke.

"Right." I nodded and grinned rather vacuously.

"But their overall college experience was quite narrow. Students like your uncle would have been looked down upon and isolated from the likes of—I regret to say—Hollis Wyatt and his society. Which is not meant to diminish the Wyatts." She took a deep breath and exhaled in a sigh. "The Brahmins possessed some less than desirable traits, anti-Semitism being one of them." Again she paused. "But to be fair," she went on, "the Brahmins were not unique in their prejudices, nor were those prejudices confined to Jews." Her gaze seemed to wander again, this time to an empty corner of the room. Yes, I thought, take off those glasses and Eleanor is an older version of Judy Collins.

With that sentiment seeming an appropriate closure, Eleanor temporarily lost in thought and with me having nothing to add—but wondering if she could sing—I nodded solemnly, just to myself, and headed off to the toilet.

Picking up with the Class of 1906 Album I went straight to the individual class portraits and thumbed toward the end of the alphabet. And there I came upon Hollis Appleton Wyatt, who could have modeled Arrow shirts. He was a refined handsome, manly without ruggedness or hardness of feature. Relatively light hair was straight and slicked back with a high, ruler-straight part on the left side. Full lips, a strong chin, and an enviable nose gave cause for a confident stare, from one whose carriage suggested athleticism and good health. All this revealed from a portrait encompassing little more than what would be included in a sculpted bust, cut off a hand's breadth below starched collar and the knot of his tie. Despite this, one assumed him to be tall, in the same way that, looking at a shoulder-up photograph of Samuel Rabinowitz, one knew him to be short.

But besides the address of Longneck Cove, Manchester-by-the-Sea, and preparation at Groton, the text accompanying Wyatt's picture was extensive, documenting a college life well-lived:

Porcellian Club; Hasty Pudding Club; Spee; D.K.E.; Institute of 1770; O.K. Club; Memorial Society; Political Club; Freshman baseball; Freshman team, Sophomore team, Football; Freshman, Sophomore Crew, Varsity Crew; Junior Class President; First Marshal; Class Day Officer.

I riffled back through the pages to locate him in the group of twenty or so Class Day Officers, all donning cap and gown. He was easy to identify, sitting cross-legged in dead center, front row. The clubs were not represented by group photographs, and his sports activities as an underclassman wouldn't be in the album. But Wyatt could again be seen front and center in the group photo of the 1906 University Crew, but this time sitting between two other crew members on a bench. Standing behind were five crewmates, and at his feet, comfortably situated on the floor in mermaid fashion and leaning on outstretched hand, was the coxswain, distinguished by being the sole wearer of long pants. The others were in white shorts, but all wore either jerseys with their class year or a long sleeved white high-necked sweater with a red band around the collar and a large red embroidered "H," indicating they had rowed in a Harvard-Yale Regatta. I perused the names in the caption under the picture. Though I subconsciously burned the image of that photograph of Hollis Wyatt in my memory, afterwards I could never look at it the same way, like an optical illusion that, once perceived, doesn't allow the unhidden to become hidden again

But at the time, my efforts appeared to be finished; I had run into a brick wall at the end of a blind alley. A queasy sensation in my head and stomach, a phantom lightheadedness and nausea from the let-down, I languidly re-shelved the book, put on my coat, and went up to the counter to thank Eleanor for her efforts and retrieve my green bookbag, empty except for a spiral notebook and a couple of pens.

"I'll let you know if I come up with any other ideas," she said, her own spirits seeming downcast with empathy. She handed me the bookbag over the counter; I clasped it by the draw sting and let my arm flop to my side. "There's absolutely nothing else you can think of?" she persisted.

There was the actress picture, of course, which I hadn't thought had anything to do with Harvard, and had not bothered to show her. But now I opened the cinched bag and removed the Harvard spiral notebook that I had purchased at the Coop specifically to keep track of notes and research about my grandfather. It was pretty much blank, although I had stored the postcard photo in a slot in the first of several manila divider pages. I retrieved it and handed it to Eleanor, who gave both sides what I thought was a cursory look.

"I assume your grandfather didn't have a middle name or a nickname that began with 'C'. . ."

"Nope."

"If you don't mind," she said, "let me make a photocopy of this. I can pass it along to my friend Eileen in the Theatre Collection."

"Okay."

"It's a longshot, but one never knows . . ."

As she turned and took a couple steps to the photocopier, I thought back to the list I had made that past April—things I remembered Poppa telling me. After Eleanor returned the card, and while I struggled to slip it back into its proper place in my notebook, I mentioned that Poppa had met Houdini. Eleanor responded that Houdini had once been dropped, in chains, from the Harvard Bridge for an obviously successful underwater escape in the Charles River. And even better, he had once given a private performance at Harvard.

"Either in Sanders Theatre or the Union, I can't remember which," said Eleanor, looking into the far distance with her recollecting, missing my amazed head shaking. "Around 1905 or 1906," she concluded, "but that's easy enough to check out."

And then I remembered that Poppa had worked in a hotel linked to John Wilkes Booth.

"Oh, now that's an easy one," said Eleanor. "The Masconomo House. Also, in Manchester-by-the-Sea. Or was. Burned down in the early twenties. But in its heyday, it was one of the finest resorts in New England. And it was built and owned by Junius Booth, elder brother to Edwin and John Wilkes—"

Excitedly, I interrupted her. "I have a postcard advertising the Masconomo House from my Grandfather's things! I have it right here! So that's where he worked!" I was frantically rummaging in the pockets of the spiral notebook in my book bag, and came up with it.

"Oh, yes," Eleanor continued, giving the promotional postcard a quick look. "That appears to be the case." Having seen that no additional clues were written on the advertisement, she didn't appear very interested in it, and, handed it back.

The excitement of the discovery of the place of Poppa's employment quickly evaporated. Eleanor had lifted my spirits to some degree by being her usual font of knowledge, but I was still convinced that my quest was at an end. So I was as sullen as I can ever remember being when I left the archives that afternoon, sullen being a euphemism for depression when one doesn't want to admit to it. Learning about my grandfather had become an obsession, and all else in my life seemed diminished. The newness of Harvard and my classes were wearing off. My courses held no allure nor could I even imagine other ones that might. The ideal of intellectual pursuits had collapsed into pre-med drudgery. From a broader perspective, I wasn't even so sure that I wanted to be a doctor anymore, so my entire future prospects required recalibrating. I was lost, clueless about everything except the emptiness I felt.

Perhaps it was time to give up the whole Poppa investigation. Which I might have, had not the last possible lead to the mystery—and perhaps my heart—been Becky Appleton Wyatt.

At Hilles

Over the ensuing weeks in Nat Sci 3 I had become chummy with a bunch of the freshman jocks—Fritz Magnussen among them. With my fear-based academic obsessiveness, copious note-taking, and willingness to help, I came to occupy the upper intellectual echelon among the lower one of other students who also couldn't qualify for Chem 6. A commonality brought us together: aside from taking the lowest level science course offered at the college, we shared an overwhelming interest in women, tempered by apprehension and self-doubt.

Our shared insecurities had different origins; mine have been adequately explained. For the athletes, exploits on the playing field offered no advantage with the opposite sex; it actually worked against them. Radcliffe women in general did not value their skills, and some even scorned them unfairly—what use were speed, strength and coordination for a true scholar? Thus no one could blame the boys if they neglected to mention, let alone boast, of being part of a squad, afraid of being stereotyped as a dumb jock. No doubt it was a humbling adjustment, when meeting a co-ed, to highlight a major in Government and entirely avoid the topic of scrimmages.

Only much later would I appreciate that none of us was spared the angst, all were engaged in formidable personal battles. For scholarship and poorer students, entering Harvard was an ear-shattering blast that resolved into a nagging and persistent tinnitus. Blacks and other minorities found themselves tokens in a privileged world that pretended to include them. Political conservatives found themselves in a sea of liberals, or worse, radicals, who in turn unnerved the liberals. The devout found themselves in a world of nonbelievers. The straight-laced found themselves among the sexually licentious. Some, particularly the privately schooled, were more adept at showcasing better fronts than others—more attuned to the bluff—but no one was immune from needing to adjust and reframe their vision of themselves. Even the most socially secure and privileged—the scions of Harvard past in its current incarnation—were forced to accommodate to the threats to their former stature, previously taken for granted.

Fritz was a public school boy from Kenosha, Wisconsin, who was the starting linebacker on the varsity football squad. A cheerful giant, he was a thinly-veneered tough city kid who could keep his aggressions in check, or at least confined to turf. We started sitting beside one another in the lectures, saving a seat for each other. Our relationship never reached the point where I could ask about the missing finger on his left hand, though, and I preferred to believe it bitten off during a street fight. For a while we met in Lamont, the Harvard undergraduate library, to study together, and for purely selfish reasons I enlisted him to join me for weeknight study sessions at Hilles, the library at Radcliffe. Radcliffe women tended to avoid Harvard libraries in the evenings, uncomfortable walking in the dark through or even past the Cambridge Common, the quickest route between Harvard and the Radcliffe Quad. So was I.

The Common was poorly lit and spooky to cross in the dark, being the site for serious drug dealing involving the locals and where muggings were not uncommon. But with the fearsome frosh football player beside me as a bodyguard I was untouchable. If his size weren't imposing enough, the sight of Fritz's missing finger would give pause to any druggie with ill intent, who might speculate that the other guy was probably lacking a hand, if not his entire arm. And so I strolled unhurriedly, fearless, across the Common to Hilles and back after its closing at midnight. The routine enabled us to breeze through Nat Sci 3, but my primary goal, realized thanks to Fritz, was to meet Rebecca Wyatt, which I managed to orchestrate one night in early November.

She always took an alcove on the second floor, while Fritz and I were on the third, a choice I made before discovering Becky's habit. I had taken to smoking a pipe bought from Leavitt and Peirce, using the famed Cake Box mixture as part of my sophistication makeover. Fritz wasn't particularly wild about the smoke or the smell, but he indulged me after realizing that the puffing didn't last long. It took time to pack the tobacco correctly and get a decent smoke going, but then the tobacco burnt hot, as did my tongue. The sensation not unlike gulping scalding tea, I eventually abandoned the pipe after a few puffs and Fritz would shift his chair closer to see my work more easily.

At ten o'clock, many studiers would take a break at the grill on the fourth floor, where the true socializing occurred. I would see Becky there, but always in a crowd, and I was too wussy to force my way in for an introduction. There was good reason for trepidation on those few tries of making friendly conversation with other females. My overtures, even timid and unthreatening, were unwelcome. Radcliffe women seemed hostile to small talk, and I couldn't think of anything interesting to say, leading to the depressing conviction that I had nothing interesting to say. At these times I envied Fritz for missing his finger, since at least he probably had a good story as a conversation starter. Apparently, I had grossly misinterpreted the social hour—the friendly chatter and unwinding was designated for pre-existing contacts, not making new friends. Any semblance of male hustling was gauche, the Hilles grille was not a singles bar. Or more to my own experience, it was not Shakey's Pizza in Overland Park.

I reminded myself that pursuit of Becky Wyatt was tied to the mystery of my grandfather, which made it a legitimate and non-prurient quest. That I viewed her as the most desirable woman on earth was beside the point. Granted, a homely Wyatt descendant would have made things easier, but I had to work with what I had. And thus I succeeded on the evening of November third. Predictably, the initial contact was clumsy and humiliating. Had I brought the stupid pipe with me, it would have been unimaginably worse.

Unable to find her on the second-floor after the social hour, I wandered around the library searching. Finally I spied her through a small window in a door on a third floor corridor of closely packed doors. The music listening cubicles, walls and ceiling soundproofed with acoustic tiles, were equipped only with a small desk with a turntable. The rectangle of thick glass was placed solely for determining if the enclosed private space were occupied. Peeking in from the side I saw her—headphones on, elbows on the desk, resting her head on outstretched hands and staring downward, immersed in a music assignment.

Heart-pounding pulsations audible deep to both my ears, I opened the door and walked in as if it were the toilet. Startled, Becky immediately looked up and swiped off her headphones, as if I had come to warn her of a fire and building evacuation. Her look, at first expectant, morphed into an inhospitable glare. As classical music streamed faintly from the earphones, I grasped for an opening line like a drowning sailor.

"Oh!" I blurted inanely, sinking below the surface "Is this a *private* room?"

"Jesus fucking Christ!" she blurted back. "Are you trying to pick me up?" Her eyes had done a quick roll before hardening into anger.

"No, no, no . . ." I protested. "But you're Becky Wyatt, right?"

"You're fucking trying to pick me up," she said, exasperated and shaking her head. "Can't you see I'm trying to work here?"

I shook my own head in earnest denial, while my eyes tracked the movement of her long dark hair, following the swaying as if it were a short tennis volley.

"No, no . . . I mean 'yes' I see you're working, but it isn't that at all. I'm not interested . . ."

She cut me off. "Then you're a liar," she said.

"No—it's about my grandfather . . . he . . . he knew *your* grandfather."

"Well, that's certainly unique . . . and *really* fascinating," she countered, sarcasm as thick as cold bacon grease. "My grandfather knew everyone in Boston worth knowing . . . and even some who weren't." That she didn't say "I don't give a fuck" signaled some progress and gave me momentary hope. I also had enough self-awareness to realize how hapless and pathetic I must have appeared.

"And whoever you are," she went on, "I really don't give a fuck."

And with that I was back on my rear end, struggling to regain my footing.

"But, but let me explain . . . I'm trying to figure out how they knew each other . . ." At this point I felt in my back pocket for a duplicate copy of the letter, freshly creased and twice folded, and dutifully carried like a condom in a wallet. I carefully unfolded it, made sure the correct side was up, and reached out to her with it.

Clearly put out, she pulled the stylus off the record to stop the music and set it down in its cradle. The turntable continued to rotate. She took the paper and I watched as she read it.

"So your grandfather was friends with him at Harvard," she stated when finished, no more curious than a public servant tasked with the filling out of a form based upon my answer.

"That's what I'm trying to figure out. There's no record of my grandfather ever having attended Harvard. He was a civil rights lawyer, a professor, at the University of Missouri. But that was later, not when your grandfather knew him."

"What was his name?"

"Michael Levinson."

Becky shrugged. "My grandfather's been dead a long time. I don't even remember him all that well. But he was, you know, quite the proper Bostonian. I'm sure we were all disappointments to him. Anyway, I don't see how I can help."

"I'm not sure exactly what I'm looking for myself," I admitted, "but it all seems very strange. My grandfather wasn't exactly well off back then, and he was a far cry from a proper Bostonian. In fact, he was . . . he was a Russian immigrant." Then I added, "And Jewish."

"Well, then . . ." Becky arched a single eyebrow, "all I can tell you is that they didn't meet at the Somerset Club."

I nodded, pretending to get the allusion. It was time to bow out.

"Well, sorry to bother you, you can get back to your . . ."

"Beethoven," she said. "For Critical Listening. Big mistake. And by the way, my great Aunt Lil, my grandfather's younger sister, still lives in Longneck Cove. I spent a lot of time there when I was growing up. It has this amazing salt-water swimming pool, filtered water pumped directly from the ocean, an absolute plumbing marvel." She handed the copy of the letter back to me.

"But in the winter . . . Shackleton couldn't have survived a winter in that house."

I nodded, refolded the paper, and returned it to my back pocket before turning to go.

"You know," she said, stopping me as I started to leave, "I wouldn't mind finding out a little something new about my family, particularly if it doesn't involve scandal or mental illness."

I stood motionless, absorbing her presence. Her eyes were an incredible blue.

"Meet me at the Pewter Pot at 10 o'clock Saturday morning," she ordered. "You can buy me a muffin."

I was too stunned to say anything, so she went on, filling the void.

"Orange Delight is my favorite."

"Right," I said, a neutral expression and admission that I had never been to the Pewter Pot.

"And I go by 'Becca,' not Becky. No one calls me 'Becky.'"

"Sorry. I didn't know."

She nodded, stone-faced, and put her earphones back on, a clear sign that I was excused, reinforced by her returning the stylus to the spinning record.

I had passed through the threshold and was about to close the door, when she spoke, too loudly because of the music playing through the headphones.

"Aunt Lil still uses the same damn stationary," she said. And with that she flashed me a benevolent smile as I gently secured the door.

She hadn't even asked my name.

A Date With Becca

The Pewter Pot was in the center of Harvard Square, on Brattle Street just around the corner from the Coop, Harvard Trust, and Brigham's, where I had my first "jimmies" on an ice cream cone. The small restaurant's dark beams were intended to give the place a Colonial feel, but it was a slapdash effort. There were corny menu references to "ye Sandwich bar" and "ye fountain," but that was as far as it went. The waitresses, known in some quarters as the "Pewter Pot Muffin Girls," were dressed in the standard white blouse, black skirt, and red vest, more barmaid attire than apparel evoking either Anne Bradstreet or Anne Hutchinson. Breakfast and lunch sandwiches could be had at modest cost, but the main business, at least for students, was in coffee and muffins—fifteen cents a mug for the former, and twenty-four varieties of the latter.

I cursed myself for my impatience, even though I had walked around Harvard Square for at least twenty minutes before relenting and letting myself enter. What if I waited much longer and no tables were available? I was still five minutes early, of course, but Becca would be nearly ten minutes late, and the wait seemed an eternity. The room was moderately full, but I found a two-top by the window. I had told the waitress that I was waiting on someone, and she brought two glasses of water to the table and asked if I wanted to go ahead and order something. I was in mid-order of an Orange Delight for Becca and a corn muffin for myself when I was interrupted.

"Do you want that split and heated?" she asked, smiling as if I had complimented her on her vest.

It seemed a complicated if not a trick question. If the muffin were split and warmed and arrived before Becca did, it could get cold. Plus, I didn't know for sure whether Becca liked her muffins split and heated or not. How did wealthy sophisticates generally take their muffins? She hadn't specified, and I was in no state to make assumptions as far as Rebecca Appleton Wyatt was concerned.

"Shall we wait on the order, then?" suggested the waitress, since I was still mulling things over in my mind and she had, after all, other tables with which to be concerned.

"How about coffee for you in the meantime?" she added.

Nearly forty years later I am almost idiot savant-like in my recollection of a roughly twenty minute snack, and the anxiety preceding it, as if it were a major life event. At the time, I suppose it was, and so I guess it still is. The memory could only be etched in my brain more indelibly, perhaps, had Kennedy been shot at the instant I was buttering my muffin.

I assented to the coffee and requested cream and sugar. Before the first Christmas break of 1969 I always took cream and sugar. I had not drunk coffee at all prior to freshman year, and becoming a coffee drinker had been one of the earliest responses to peer pressure. During my first return trip home and before coming back for reading period, I had resolved to learn to drink my coffee black, as a Harvard man should, much as I had earlier pledged to drink Scotch, which was equally difficult. At any opportunity to avail myself of hard alcohol, it would be Scotch, and by spring break, I had managed to acquire a taste, Bacardi and Coke a relic of misspent youth. The nonsense with the pipe was not really as much due to peer pressure, but more in the category of an affectation taken as an elective and then wisely dropped before being graded. I also incidentally resolved to become fluent in French and read "The Education of Henry Adams," neither of which I ever did.

To say I was anxious about the meet-up with Becca was an understatement. I couldn't think of any topics of possible conversation other than that associated with Poppa, which I would try to drag out. Hopefully we could avoid discussion of our respective class schedules, since a line-up of Math 1a, Nat Sci 3, Hum 9 and Spanish C was more than an embarrassment—I would come off as a total ignoramus. But my anxiety that morning was not entirely the result of perceived academic deficiencies, the shame of being a Midwesterner, or intimidation by a wealthy, sophisticated, and beautiful Rebecca Wyatt.

The subtext was sexual inexperience, given the presumption that Becca Wyatt had been around the block. Her vibe suggested more of a parade around the block, or even laps around the block at full sprint. Which made her a woman, and me a boy. How could I approach her on equal footing? My sexual worldliness was still expressed in terms of rounding bases on the diamond, and sticking with the metaphor, I was more a bunter than a power hitter. In fairness, I was not alone. For a first term freshman at Harvard to lose his virginity then was considerably more arduous than learning how to drink black coffee or Scotch or suck Cake Box tobacco smoke from a Leavitt and Peirce pipe. What made things even more disturbing was that a sexual revolution was raging around us. How did I miss the boat? And for that matter, where was the boat dock?

"I'm not late, am I," she asked?

"Oh no."

"Been waiting long?"

"Oh no."

She had breezed into the Pewter Pot and begun settling herself, sliding her purse off her shoulder and removing an expensive-looking white linen jacket, which she set over the back of her chair. The purse was thick and roughhewn, like something a hippie artisan would sell at a street fair. But the linen jacket would be seen on a window mannequin at Bergdorf's or Bonwit Teller (I had not heard of either then, so was thinking more along the line of Harzfelds or Emery Bird Thayer). Underneath, however, she looked a flower child, with a Mexican wedding shirt and low slung bell-bottom jeans. This much I had seen through the window upon her approach, along with slip-on shoes of a style unfamiliar to me. But now I was looking at her face, at those cerulean eyes and cold cream complexion and the full lips, movie starlet looks. And that straight nose, perfect in size and proportion, like the picture my cousin Barbara took to her plastic surgeon to show him exactly what she wanted for her nose job. I became aware of my muteness and the fact that I was staring. I hoped she hadn't noticed.

"Take a picture, it will last longer." she said without malice. "Have you ordered?"

I reacted with a stunned blink, as if a camera flash had just gone off in my face.

"Not yet," I said.

She flicked her head like a horse bothered by a fly, flinging back cascades of hair encroaching on her cheeks. Then, more definitively, she leaned her head back and ran both hands along the side of her head, using her ears as floodgates for her hair. It was a gesture she would repeat—she tended to lean forward and look one directly in the eye as she spoke, and her hair would spill forward. Eventually she pulled a hair band from her purse and tied most of the mass into a loose pony tail. Even then, she would still occasionally flick her head back, forgetting, perhaps, that there was no longer a need. The movement—which looked stupid when teenage boys did it—was remarkably provocative, purposeful or not.

"I called my Great Aunt Lil last night and she'd never heard of a Michael Levinson," she said. Just like that, Becca had completely dispensed with the matter at hand. She waited for my response, as I registered that she was a dead end as far as Poppa was concerned. Disappointment intensified my mental paralysis.

Becca never had patience for conversational pauses, and would always charge in. "So that's that," she concluded. "Sorry I couldn't be of any help." She paused, and as I didn't respond quickly enough to suit her, continued. "So should we forget about the muffins and call it a day?"

Somehow I managed to stammer "Um . . . well . . . uh . . . if you don't have any plans . . ."

"I was planning on having a muffin," she snapped, and raised her arm to signal for our waitress.

At first, I found a dialogue with Becca challenging and emotionally draining. Mostly I felt like a boxer, hunched over and pinned against the ropes, covering his face with both gloves and submitting to a barrage of body blows. Soon I would begin to feel like a high school foreign exchange student, perhaps from South America.

"So you're from Missouri, like your grandfather? Wait . . . maternal or paternal grandfather? Are you a Levinson?"

I nodded.

"And do they give people first names in Missouri?"

"Yes. It's Mark."

"A pleasure to meet you, Mark. So you are from Missouri?"

"Kansas. Kansas City."

"Kansas City, Kansas."

"No. Kansas City, Missouri."

Prompted, I went headlong into my oft-repeated explanation, one I felt obligated to give nearly every time I met someone new in Cambridge. The gist was that I lived a few houses on the Kansas side, where the boundary between the states was not demarcated by the Missouri River but by State Line Road. Metropolitan Kansas City, Kansas being significantly smaller than Metropolitan Kansas City, Missouri, my residence was more a suburb of the latter, and I identified as being from the dominant Kansas City. It only mattered because I was hesitant to admit being from the Sunflower State without qualification; I didn't want any new acquaintance to take me for some hayseed farmer. But I never had realized how inane and inconsequential the whole thing sounded until I embarked on explaining it to Becca.

She did not find the topic, let alone the particulars, very interesting, judging by her response. My discourse provoked an expression of both boredom and impatience in record setting time.

"Kansas . . . Missouri . . . not really all that much difference, is there?"

The interruption stopped me before I had finished my explanation. I considered. Aside from the border wars in the 1850s, she made a good point.

"I suppose not."

The waitress approached, and Becca asked what I was having.

"A corn muffin, I suppose."

"They grow a lot of corn in Kansas."

"Yes. And wheat."

"So they probably have a shitload of corn muffins in Kansas. A plain corn muffin when there are twenty-three other varieties to choose from?"

I was too taken aback to get defensive. Why was she browbeating me? And what was she thinking? Did she take me for some backwater rube who had just fallen off the turnip truck? They had blueberry muffins and banana muffins and pumpkin muffins and all sorts of varieties all over the place in Kansas City. And KC was the home of Wolferman's, where they made the best English muffins in the world. You could ask anyone. Besides, I happened to like corn muffins, as well as corn bread.

"Why are you busting my chops over a muffin?" I asked with a boldness that even surprised me.

Becca's lips compressed into a smile. And then the smile expanded, revealing her teeth. They were white and straight, as expected. But it was the first time I had ever seen her teeth through a smile and it was a thrill.

"Live a little, and spring to sunny Florida with an Orange Delight. Or maybe California."

I looked up at the waitress whose smile now seemed patronizing.

"Two orange delight muffins, please."

"Split and toasted?"

"Yes," Becca chimed in immediately. "And I'll have a mug of black coffee," she added.

The waitress looked over at me. "Another coffee, sir?"

I dreaded where this could lead. If yes, then I took it with cream and sugar. And I couldn't very well start drinking it black.

"Orange juice for me, thank you." I looked over at Becca. "You know, in keeping with the sunny Florida theme."

I had barely met the woman, and she was telling me what kind of muffin to order. And I obliged her. Thus began a pattern, with my first Orange Delight. She would later introduce me to quiche and Calvados at the Café Pamplona, and a noir film at the Orson Wells. She also would lead me into a hippie store to purchase my first pair of clogs. It occurred to me then that

Becca Wyatt saw me as a project, a Midwestern bumpkin, and felt called to show me the light, like some sort of Ivy League missionary.

"Speaking of sunny Florida, have you spent any time there?"

"Never been," I confessed.

"California?"

I looked at the butter knife in front of me on the table. I would commit hari-kari with it if Disneyland came up.

"No," I said.

"The parents have a place in Boca Raton. But I'm not much of a beach person. I mean, I can do beach up here in the summer. I'm more of a ski person. I suppose you don't ski."

"Skiing isn't one of the major tourist industries in Kansas."

"The parents have a chalet in Stowe. I try to spend most of my weekends there in the winter, but not sure I'll be able to so much with all the papers I'll have to write. I'm already underwater. I'm going to concentrate in History and Literature, so I'll be busy. Even the Music course—which was supposed to be my gut—is more time consuming than I expected."

History and Lit was the nervous breakdown major, and not a course of study I would ever possibly consider.

"How about you?"

"Pre-Med. Probably Biology. Maybe Biochemistry."

"So you must be smart . . . or else really obsessive-compulsive." Becca leaned back as our waitress transferred the plates of muffin and the beverages from a cork-surfaced round serving tray. "At least obsessive enough to get into this place. And you're not a legacy, apparently," which might have been construed as a dig but seemed inadvertent.

"No." I was ready for a consoling reply relating to my grandfather.

"But no doubt it's easier getting in from Kansas, anyway," she said instead, oblivious to causing any possible offense. "Harvard aspires to geographical diversity, and you certainly tick that box in spades."

I had no comment to make, taking another verbal punch to the gut. It was a relief to start eating. I was waiting to see if she would pick up a fork, but it was going to be hands. I followed suit.

"People must find you quiet," she said, taking her first bite.

I shrugged. "I assumed most people view me as obsessively thoughtful."

"Ha! You're cute, Mark Levinson. You're really cute. Anyone ever tell you that?"

"My cousin Celia," I said. I found it hard to smile at my own repartee, which would signify that I thought it clever, or at least the best I could do. What kind of question was that, anyway?

But Becca seemed amused and smiled. She picked up the recently delivered coffee and took a careful sip. I had sampled the Orange Delight and found it pretty tasty. She eyed me over the top of the mug.

"So. Mark Levinson." Becca put down the mug with resolve, as if she had come to a decision or had an announcement to make. "Tell me. Honestly. Are you afraid of me?"

She leaned back into her chair, a serious expression on her face. Clearly she would not take another bite of her muffin until I replied, so I considered. I knew that baring one's soul was not always advisable in matters of the heart, especially early on. But this time, there was no point in lying or trying to bluff.

"A little," I confessed.

"Well," said Becca Appleton Wyatt, picking up the same half of muffin, "at least you have THAT going for you."

Subsequently the conversation became easier—unburdened by a secret revealed, the confession somehow put me at ease. Besides, Becca had brought up her horse Winchester, stabled in Hamilton. Maybe in a nod to my Midwestern origins, Becca felt I could relate to horses, not knowing I was afraid of them and the closest I had come to one was on a junior high hayride. But I faked both interest in the mare as well as some equine knowledge, nodding intermittently as Becca provided a very lengthy account of the animal, including parentage, where "the parents" had acquired her, what her training routine was, eventual plans for breeding, and so on. Becca could not tarry much longer, since dressage was on her afternoon schedule, while I was heading to Lamont to work on math problem sets. I wasn't certain what dressage was, but when asked, readily admitted that I had never done it. Becca barely paused for my answer anyway, and only out of politeness had allowed me a word in edgewise before moving on to gossip about Winchester's trainer, who was apparently a lesbian.

Before we decided that we would split the check—after her first insisting on it being her treat—we talked about our upcoming plans for Thanksgiving break. For me, the break was not long enough to justify the expense of a trip to Kansas City. Becca was also staying local, spending as much time as she could with Winchester. Hamilton being more convenient to Manchester-by-the-Sea than Cambridge, she would be at her family home most of the time. Becca, I learned, had her own car that she garaged in Cambridge—I had never heard of anyone bringing their own car to Harvard—but the commute to Hamilton from Cambridge was a hassle, she told me, especially if there was going to be any snow. I tried to restrain myself to not ask what kind of car she had, but as I was about to anyway, she had jumped in and moved on.

"The parents will be at the villa in Vicchio, and they wanted me to join them and my great aunt—you know, Auntie Lil—but it's not worth me flying to Italy for such a short time."

"Yes, hardly worth it," I agreed, a bit actor reciting a single line of script. "No skiing?" I pivoted, reminding myself that I would have to look up Vicchio later. I wasn't sure how to spell it, and unless I came up with a convenient rhyme to jar my memory, I'd forget. Pinocchio? Daddy-O? Spaghetti-O?

"Maybe a couple of days on the slopes, but I hate the holiday crowds. And it depends on the weather."

"Another advantage of living in Kansas," I replied, my mind still racing for a memory aid. "No long lines at the lifts." I saw the waitress returning with our change.

"So where's Vicchio, anyway?" I relented, which was at least better than asking her the model of her car. I had a math problem set to do, and I wasn't about to spend valuable time in Lamont looking up about Italy. And I wasn't sure how to spell it.

"Tuscany. Not far from Florence."

"Your parents own that as well?"

"It's been in the family for generations. My great grandfather bought it in the 1880s—I suppose to break the monotony of Longneck Cove. Your granddad's friend Hollis spent his summers there growing up as a child. Some of the distant relations are even buried there. But yes, eventually it will belong to them—the parents. And me, I imagine." She was taking the band off her ponytail and letting her hair out of the barn.

Perhaps because my retreat to the gulag of problem sets was imminent, an algebra problem intruded to distract me. On one side, a place in Boca Raton; a chalet in Stowe, and a villa in Hi-ho the Derry Oh, Italia. So far, that is. On the other side of the equation, my mother's cousin Lee's cabin on the Lake of the Ozarks. We could stay there anytime we wanted, as long as Lee and his family weren't there. Otherwise, we'd get a room at Tan-Tar-A for a few days and meet up with them for dinner and go for a ride in their ski boat. The problem was much too advanced, and I feared it would never compute for me.

This time, Becca did not attempt to end the sound void. Instead she stood up, took her purse off the chair, put on her linen jacket, and flicked her head back with ferocity. She had ignored the change on the table, and so would I. I hoped the tip was enough, but emotionally taxed, I couldn't tackle that math calculation either.

A comment about the Italian villa—could I conceivably even come up with one—or asking about the car model were past their conversational expiry date. I was already standing up as well, required to say something. Like back in high school at the end of a date, standing awkwardly by the door and searching for some congenial parting comment, already having given up on a goodnight kiss. Something emboldened me.

"If I can find the time," I said, "I might make a day trip to the Historical Society in . . . in Manchester-by-the-Sea. Over the break. If I have time."

"Trask House, you mean."

I nodded—so that was apparently the name for it—and she advised me to make sure they were open before making the trip up on the train. And then she asked why, and I told her that I had good reason to believe that my grandfather had worked at the Masconomo House.

"Doing what?"

"No idea."

"There's nothing there anymore. Just the Brown's house, where the Booth's originally lived. The rest was torn down ages ago. Nothing else is on the old property except the Singing Beach Club."

"Maybe there are records of some sort somewhere . . ."

"Unlikely. Needle in a haystack."

She appreciated my look of disappointment. Which was real, and surprisingly heartfelt considering that my research excursion plan had only been hatched seconds earlier on the off-chance that I might see her there.

". . . but who am I to tell you what to do?" added the woman who only minutes earlier had shamed me into abandoning my Golden Corn muffin. She dug into her purse and pulled out a pen. "Give me your hand."

I obediently extended my right arm. She took my hand, turned it over to access the palm side, and wrote down her phone number.

"Call me if you decide to go," she said. "If I'm around and free, I can give you a tour of town. Got to run."

So far, the scheduled line-up for Becca Appleton Wyatt that Saturday had been me, followed by Winchester. She would no doubt return from Hamilton in time for an evening date with some upperclassman, probably a preppie. Maybe two dates, stacked in sequence—dinner with the first, and late drinks and a club with the second. This was not an uncommon practice among the more desirable Radcliffe women of the time, six dates in a weekend not unheard of. I knew this already, but still felt the sting before Christmas break when Becca went with me for dinner and the Jackson Brown-Joni Mitchell concert, a special event. Only in the subway afterwards, returning from the Music Hall and looking forward to a nightcap at the Casablanca, was I informed that she had another date at 11 p.m. with the senior tutor in Lowell House.

But before that I would get to know Becca Wyatt better, and even have the opportunity to see her on her home turf. And when with her, even at the Pewter Pot, I sometimes completely forgot about Poppa Levinson and his mystery.

I slung my green book back over my shoulder, stepped into Brattle Street, and headed to Lamont. The sky was blue and cloudless, but the sunshine was offset by a chilling breeze of a New England fall. I walked all the way with my right hand in my pocket to make sure my palm wouldn't rub against anything. Once in the library, the first thing I did was get out my pencil and write down Becca's number in my notebook. After I figured out the first math problem, I rewrote the number down in ink on the inside cover. I had the entire afternoon to plow through the Math 1a problem set, which was a good thing, since I was having difficulties concentrating.

Manchester-by-the-Sea

I looked out at the Atlantic, thinking that no one appreciated the ocean more than someone from Kansas. Singing Beach was deserted except for a couple of locals accompanied by hyperactive unleashed dogs. The beach was relatively small compared with Huntington Beach in California—the only other time or place I had seen an ocean—and was demarcated by rocky promontories that jutted into the water on either end: on the south was the projection of Ballarach Cove, and on the north the formation known as Eagle Head. It actually bore a stronger resemblance to a duck in flight or a goose laid out on a platter, but knowing its name, you tended to see it as such. The front portion of the eagle's "head" was unvegetated, but the back of it was capped with bushes and trees, which became denser and lusher and more complex as they extended back into the less rocky hill away from the shoreline. Unprejudiced, I thought the silhouette most resembled the cartoon character Jeckle, wearing a green yarmulke.

"What are you thinking about?" Becca asked. As I look back on that moment now, she might have been wishing that she could experience the joy and wonder that must have shown on my face. Were I to go back in time, I might have dwelled more on what Becca was thinking instead of just my own thoughts about her.

"This place is incredibly beautiful," I effused, taking a sudden chilling gust full in the face and zipping up my jacket. Which was true, but I was also thinking about a pair of talking magpies. Even in the midst of rapture, I was sometimes incapable of blocking wandering thoughts and associations. Jeckle was the one who spoke with the British accent, more appropriate for Manchester-by-the-Sea than the uncouth Heckle, from the Bronx. The yarmulke part crept up from my subconscious, a not so subtle reminder of my outsider status. To that extent, my joy was not pure, which might have disappointed Becca had she known. But nothing could completely distract from the specialness of the moment, made more abundantly so by her presence alone.

She led me a short distance down the beach and turned her back to the ocean, white linen jacket billowing, and pointed. "Can you make out that house way back there? That's what's left of the Booth's original cottage, before they built their hotel." The current inhabitants of that cottage were likely Becca's neighbors. Her family home was somewhere on Masconomo Street. I had not seen the house, but noted in passing the street name on a sign while walking down Beach Street to the oceanfront.

"And right there, occupying most of that property," she continued, vaguely sweeping her arm over a broad expanse, upslope of the shoreline with vegetation blocking much of the view, "was Masconomo House."

She could have pointed out the location earlier, to our right as we walked down Beach Street, since the Booth property extended from Masconomo Street to the shore, Beach Street being a boundary. But imagining the sea-facing end of the former three-story grand hotel conveyed a more impressive mental picture, and Becca had a flair for the dramatic. One could imagine the onlookers sitting on benches or leaning on the railings of the pavilion, the small sailboats, the row of wooden bath houses fronted by a boardwalk, the clusters of bathers, the children scrambling around or digging in the sand. One could almost hear them over the gentle pounding of the waves and the whistle of the wind—the men in their one-piece tank suits and the women in blouses and bloomers and long stockings, gay and laughing ghosts, frolicking and splashing in the surf.

A few days before I had heard from Eleanor with interesting information. Emma Conghlan, Agnes Booth's junior by forty years or so, had evidently held small roles in a couple of Boston stage performances in which Agnes had featured. The Masconomo House hosted theatrical performances during the season as a special treat for the prominent guests from all over the country, and Agnes would assemble a troupe of actors to form a pick-up repertory company. Eleanor had learned from her contact in the Theatre Collection that Emma Conghlan had been in residence there in the summer of 1904, at about the time of Poppa's possible hotel employment. There was not much in the way of details about Emma's time at the Masconomo, but afterwards she had gone on to have a respectable career on stage. Her first lead role was "An English Beauty" at the Tremont Theatre in 1905, and after that she was regularly featured in Boston theatres, as well as occasional bookings in New York. She was born in East Boston in 1874—which made her nine years older than Poppa, and died in Brookline, Massachusetts in 1937.

I hadn't needed the additional incentive to make plans to visit Manchester-by-the-Sea over the holiday break. After confirming that the historical society would have a volunteer on site the Friday after Thanksgiving, I called Becca on her home number in the late afternoon Thursday—which I hoped was after normal horsing hours with Winchester—and luckily reached her. She didn't seem surprised to hear from me, and as if already prepared, told me to meet her at the Beach Street Café at 11:30 a.m. the following day. No coffee, though, just a rendezvous point. She only had time to take me down to the beach and show me where the Masconomo House had once stood, needing to leave by noon for another appointment with Winchester in Hamilton.

I had taken an early morning train on the commuter rail from North Station, which got me to the Trask House just as it was opening at 10 a.m. A doddering but mentally sharp elderly woman was on duty; she had been notified of my arrival and interests, and immediately walked me to a cluttered back office off the central exhibit space.

The room was jammed, with the surfaces of two tables covered by seemingly random piles of documents, photographs, and folders. Framed maps and old photographs hung haphazardly on available walls, suggesting that only existing hooks already embedded in the plaster could be used, without being moved. Extending the length of one wall was a desktop with three armless wheeled secretary chairs demarcating work spaces. Above the work space, bookshelves were filled with tattered oversized volumes, local history books, and a myriad of thick loose-leaf notebooks, edges of paper protruding like gravy spilling from the sides of an overcooked chicken pot pie.

The woman pointed me to the middle swivel chair. In front of it, on a partially cleared piece of desk real estate, was a faded manila folder labeled "Masconomo House."

"Sorry for the mess," she said, leaving me alone to get back to her desk duty.

I could not fault the old woman for not being more gracious; I was amazed she had been able to find anything at all. Roberta and Eleanor had spoiled me. This place looked like it was organized and run by a family of hoarders. An all-volunteer staff of civic-minded senior citizens evidently ran the show and were overwhelmed. They appeared decades behind.

I had plenty of time to examine the materials in the file before my meeting with Becca. The folder included photos, advertising and promotional material, newspaper and magazine clippings, articles from historical journals, and handwritten and typed summaries written by members of the historical society. I learned that after the Civil War, Manchester-by-the-Sea became a desirable residence for Boston theater people, several building summer homes on Sea Street, soon known as Actor's Row. Three years after baby brother John Wilkes had killed the President, Junius Brutus Booth, Jr., the namesake and eldest of three sons of the famed English stage actor, bought his own large lot on Beach Street. He had recently married a much younger widowed actress, an Australian transplant who performed under the name of Agnes Land.

A decade after building their cottage in 1877, the theatrical power couple expanded their dwelling into a grand hotel, with over a hundred rooms and a dining room that could accommodate three hundred. A decade later, the twelve-acre complex was expanded to include detached guest houses, a bandstand, a concert hall, a bowling alley, tennis courts, a large stable, and living quarters for staff, including separate accommodations for colored workers. The Masconomo House became the Gilded Age gem of resort hotels on the North Shore of Boston, catering to heirs and heiresses, politicians, financiers, captains of industry, and diplomats. By then Junius had died, and Agnes had remarried John Schoeffel, the former manager of the Tremont Theatre, who brought his expertise to the management and expansion.

I was not surprised to find no mention of Emma Conghlan, a minor player who had once passed through the octagonal grand hall along with a hoard of others over nearly a third of a century of the hotel's operation. Only two theatrical productions were referenced in the filed materials, both widely publicized, large scale events that had occurred over a decade before my grandfather or Emma Conghlan would have been on site. The first was a "pastoral performance" of "As You Like It" on the resort grounds on August 8, 1887, and the second a production of "A Midsummers Night's Dream," again outside, but this time after dark, the stage and surrounds lit by calcium lights and railroad lamps. I had no clue as to what performances Emma might have been involved in, but I suspected nothing rivaling those two groundbreaking productions was held afterwards. Besides the grounds, a number of venues were available for a variety of entertainments: the bandstand, the concert hall, the ballroom, the dining hall, and even the octagonal hall—demarcated by its four enormous brick fireplaces—could have served as stages for full-length productions, dramatic readings, singing performances, or comedic sketches.

Automobile travel heralded a new type of tourism in America that doomed the grand hotels in New England. Extended stays in destination resorts, with wealthy tourists brought in by rail, was no longer a viable business model, as evidenced by a number of suspicious fires. Agnes died in 1910, but things had gone downhill before her death, with the property changing hands a couple of times before being destroyed by fire in 1919. I had hoped there might be surviving hotel records and documents, but apparently everything went up in flames, along with any confirmation that Michael Levinson had indeed worked there.

Becca and I made a circuit of the beach, me detailing the high points of what I had come across. Basically nothing about Emma Coghlan or my grandfather. Then we headed back up Beach Street toward town, since Becca had to go to her house to get her car for the drive to Hamilton.

"Do you have more work to do at the Trask House?" she asked. We had stopped at the corner of Masconomo and Beach, where she would turn off and I would continue the few blocks into town to catch the next commuter train to North Station.

"There are some old bound copies of *The Cricket* there," I said. "Maybe I could come across a newspaper reference to Emma." I very much doubted that. Eleanor's contact at the Theatre Collection probably had access to more information about Emma's career than I could ever find at the Trask House, and if anything had looked like a promising lead, Eleanor would have mentioned something.

"Well, if you're still here when I get back," Becca said, "we can have dinner together." Clearly there wasn't a queue of Harvard upperclassman in Manchester-by-the-Sea over the Thanksgiving weekend. It seemed I had made the short list by default.

"When will that be?"

"Around six."

Six hours was a long time, and the Trask House closed at four. We both knew that I would be willing to keep myself occupied until then. Perhaps Becca was more of a planner and less spontaneous than I had imagined her to be. Either way, I was flattered and beyond excited.

Becca didn't wait for my answer, and Winchester was waiting. She moved things along.

"I'm just a few houses down. If I'm not back when you arrive, walk around the back and wait on the porch. I'll unlock the gate and turn the alarm off. And I'll set out something for you to drink and nibble on."

She told me the house number, then repeated it, as if I were too dumbfounded or dense to remember it.

I nodded and repeated it back to her before she turned on her heels and walked away.

It was not humanly possible to stretch out my return trip to the Trask House to much more than two hours. By that time my eyes were burning and my brain felt too large for my skull. I had initially thumbed through and examined every page of the bound volume of the *Cricket* for 1903. Then for the years through 1905, I realized I could safely limit my attention to "the season," which extended from June into late September or the beginning of

October, concentrating on a column called "Along the Shore." It was slim pickings, mostly social name dropping and gossip about the impending scheduled arrivals of people apparently worth mentioning and their families, and what they had been up to party and travel-wise. There was the occasional sentence long report about a song or music hall recital, an unspecified theatrical performance, a regular Saturday dance or special large hop, a bazaar in the parlor benefitting charity, a sleight of hand exhibition in the Casino, a baseball match between the colored workers against the staff of a hotel in nearby Magnolia, a putting match on the lawn, and so on.

There were also a number of reports of unfortunate auto collisions with buggies, wagons, or even riders on horseback, horses often bearing the brunt of these encounters. The roads could not accommodate much traffic when congestion was defined as several horse-driven teams and a single auto on a narrow street, or three vehicles meeting at a brook. Weather conditions contributed, especially when muddy surfaces led to skidding. The severity of the incidents ranged from those requiring an ambulance to Beverly Hospital to one with the auto owner himself driving the scraped and bruised victim back to her home. The mishaps involved a disproportionate number of chauffeur-driven touring cars, some going at high speed, and in these cases the names of the car owners were often of more interest than the details of the accident.

I spent most of the remaining four hours exploring town. I ventured a couple of blocks into the neighborhoods surrounding the main drags of Central and Union Street, where the regular folk lived and worked before the wealthy from Boston came to play in the summer, building massive cottages on the water or on overlooking bluffs. By the late-nineteenth century the town had transformed itself into a service community for the rich. The big money and old families were still around but out of sight, sheltered off private roads and behind tall laurel hedges and gates.

My self-guided tour of the quintessential New England town did not take me beyond any walls or gates. I killed some time in a burial ground that was dated 1648, reading the headstones that hadn't been windblown into illegibility. I walked down the central aisle of two churches, one Congregational, the other Catholic, strolled through Town Hall, and peeked into the garage of the fire station. There were a couple pharmacies, three grocery stores, and a newsstand shop called Floyds that sold penny candy, a condensed version of an old five and dime. There was also a liquor store, but only one real restaurant as far as I could tell, near the inner harbor and a hardware store. In truth, Manchester-by-the-Sea was not a place where one could kill a lot of time, apart from spending a day at the beach, so I spent a good portion of my afternoon sitting in a leather chair in the library, looking at magazines. It was also one of the few places with an accessible toilet.

After loitering for hours, I was rewarded with a pass to the other side of wrought iron gates and hedges. I arrived at Becca's parents' home entrance at around 5:50 p.m., and found the gate unlocked, as I was told. The entry point to the property was a short way down Masconomo, but because of the foliage, not much of anything was visible from the street. The road had curved slightly and the path to the house was more like a private road than a driveway. First I saw the garages, two of them, each with triple doors, and next to them a two-story guest house that I first mistook for the actual residence. Reaching the main house further along, I realized how disoriented I was. The large, immaculately landscaped front lawn ended at a row of shrubbery and then a drop to sandy beach. Becca's house fronted on Singing Beach and was one of the grand residences we had walked past on our short excursion earlier. She had neglected to point it out.

The main part of the house was like a couple of normal-sized houses jammed together, with peaked sections that suggested Tudor. I wondered if there were a name for the style. I could only relate it to the replica Tudor homes I was familiar with in Old Mission Hills—the swankiest part of Kansas City—so I assumed it was built in the thirties. What came to mind was the Russell Stover mansion, a red brick Tudor easily identified by the awnings over every window with the emblematic "S" on them. I had never been in the Stover house or any of the other stately homes in Old Mission Hills, and didn't know anybody who lived in them, but my parents would sometimes drive out-of-town visitors through those winding, leafy streets as an expression of local pride, showing off the town.

The back deck was enormous, the central portion a rotunda extending out toward the view. Built-in benches occupied all the water-facing sides, and in the middle was a round white wrought iron and glass dining table, bare except for a camp-sized green Coleman ice chest. Inside were several inches of ice supporting two bottles of Heineken beer, a bottle of Blue Nun Liebfraumilch, a bottle of Gordon's gin, and a bottle of tonic. A lime, small knife, two plastic cups, a corkscrew/bottle opener, a bag of Granite State Potato Chips, and a jar of Planters Mixed Nuts were also being chilled, Becca not having bothered to lay them out on the table. I deferred selecting anything until she arrived. If I went for the gin and tonic, was I a sophisticate, or just pretending to prefer gin over a beer?

After a couple of gin and tonics with Becca—dilemma solved when she told me what she was having—I was relaxed and enjoying myself. We eased into comfortable banter, and I would go so far as to describe myself as funny and charming, at least in spurts. I drew from my repertory of droll, self-deprecating anecdotes, not to say that I wasn't initially knocked off stride when Becca apologized for the gauche munchie selection, explaining that the cook along with the rest of the house help had taken off while "the parents" were gone—except for the three time a week tidying up of the house and the landscape and garden work. And admittedly I might have been momentarily slack-jawed when she first appeared from the house wearing a riding jacket, high boots, and jodhpurs.

"Pretty fabulous house," were the first words out of my mouth. The last thing I wanted to do was gush. I just wanted to say something nice and get it over with.

"It's not as impactful if it's all you know," she replied.

We had not conversed long before it was established that I was up for dinner at JP's Harborside, but she had to shower and change out of her riding clothes, and naturally dry her hair, which prolonged things. I could watch Uncle Walter on CBS inside. She led me through the kitchen, fit for a restauranteur, with an enormous work station underneath copper pots hanging from a metal ceiling rack and commercial grade refrigerator and separate free standing freezer. The oven and gas range were hooded by a glimmering copper air vent that was the size and shape of a gigantic window awning. In passing I glimpsed the formal dining and living rooms, real-life photo spreads out of *Architectural Digest,* all custom and coordinated, and appearing unlived-in. She left me in a wood-paneled lounge, a television-viewing area with an oversized caramel-colored leather sofa and matching arm chairs, that was still roomy enough to also accommodate a bar, vintage pool table, and an octagonal card table and chairs. The table looked ancient, wood topped by leather, with ornate carved legs—which is to say, it wasn't a card table in my usual sense, since it couldn't be folded. Becca turned on Walter Cronkite for me and I willingly subjected myself to being swallowed by one of the side chairs.

I had momentarily fretted about dinner, since I only had a couple dollars in my wallet and the return rail ticket. I had no choice but to confess my financial situation up front, which she laughed off. She had the parents' credit card, which she was living on while they were gone, and it was their treat. The owner of the restaurant—a thin mustachioed man with a necktie completely covered in souvenir pins—greeted her like a celebrity and took us to a window table facing the harbor. For me it was a meal of firsts—between our shared orders, I sampled steamers, lobster bisque, fish chowder, fried whole clams, and lobster pie. Our middle-aged waitress, as weather-worn as a lobsterman but sounding to me like a Kennedy—was so tickled at the foreign exchange student's appreciation and enthusiasm for such standard fare that she brought us an order of Indian pudding with vanilla ice cream for dessert, on the house. I hadn't had that before, either, and she stayed at our table to watch me take the first bite, beaming.

It had been nearly dusk when we arrived at the Harborside, and was well into night by the time we finished eating. The commuter rail stop was only a stone's throw distant, the railroad crossing in view from the restaurant entrance. But it was bad manners to let a date walk home alone in the dark, so the old-fashioned Midwestern boy didn't hesitate to head the opposite direction down Beach Street to accompany Becca home. The road toward the beach was dark and deserted, canopied by large and foreboding trees. How could I leave her there by herself? I might as well have left her at one end of

Cambridge Common. By the time we have reached her driveway, and still had a decent walk to her door, I was contemplating the possibility of a goodnight hug, or even a kiss, at her threshold. Thinking past that was so beyond the realm of possibility, that even unleashing a decent fantasy was masochistic.

We had passed the garages and the guesthouse, and were illuminated by motion detected floodlights. Both of us were squinting from the glare.

"How are you getting back?" she asked.

"The train, and the subway back from North Station, same way I came."

"You missed the last train to Boston," she informed me flatly. "It's running on a holiday schedule."

I stopped in my tracks, now squinting more from straining to think than from the harsh light. No words came to mind, so Becca took the reins. Nearly an apt metaphor, since I don't think she actually ever let go of the reins.

"You don't expect me to drive you home at this time of night, do you?" Statement of fact, with no annoyance or belligerence. But what a rookie mistake not to check the train schedule!

I thought I had responded with a resounding "Of course not!" but actually I just shook my head, eyes cast downward, as ashamed and repentant as a chastened first grader. No, I would never do that again, teacher, whatever it was.

I waited for the punishment to come, perhaps staying in from recess or a note home to my parents.

"Well then," said Becca, with a sigh. "I suppose you'll just have to spend the night here."

I nodded in agreement solemnly, suppressing the pounding of my heart.

"And we can finish off the gin," Becca added, as she pulled the house keys from her purse.

Which we did, in the movie set of a manor house living room. I was proud of myself for becoming accustomed to the opulence so quickly; I was now almost casual about my surroundings. Just like home. I had already traveled on my own to and from the powder room a couple of times, peeing, using the bar soap, and wiping my hand dry on the monogrammed guest towels. It was just a very lovely living room to me now, in a lovely and spacious house. The room—and all the other parts of the house I had seen—felt more than comfortable. So homey, in fact, that Becca and I proceeded to get very drunk.

We were both giddy and in good humor as we walked barefoot along the tideline. In my fantasy life we would have been holding hands. Back in the house the Gordon's Gin bottle was empty. Earlier we had moved to the lounge to watch "The Thin Man" on late night TV, but found it silly and made fun of Nick Charles for being a hopeless alcoholic.

"Nick and Nora remind me of the parents," Becca eventually confided, so I dispensed with any further derogatory comments.

Bored after a few minutes, we left the television on as we opted for a diversion of nocturnal sand and surf. My sleeping accommodations for the night had not been discussed as bedtime approached and passed, and I wasn't sure if I'd be staying in a spare bedroom in the main house or in the guest house. I was trying not to obsess over it.

Our shoes and my socks had been left at the top of the beach stairs. The temperature had dropped, and I wished I'd brought a heavy sweater to wear under my polyester-filled jacket. Despite rolling up my khakis as far as they could go, the bottoms were still getting wet from unanticipated rushes of foamy water. My feet were stinging and starting to numb. Becca was oblivious to the chill, wearing a full length black quilted parka that I assumed was Arctic grade and filled with the highest quality goose down. Underneath she wore an unseasonably light violet-colored shift-like dress, short sleeved and with a V-neck. The material was thicker, but otherwise it was like an extended T-shirt, ending just above the knees and clingy in the right places.

We had finished the beach loop and were heading back to the house, cutting across from the shoreline to the access to her property. We hadn't felt the need to speak for a while.

"Want to go in?" she asked.

I thought she was referring to the house, then I realized she meant the ocean. I didn't have time to tell her she was crazy. She had taken off her overcoat and thrown it down on the dune grass by the bottom of the stairs. And then she crossed her arms over one another bending down to grab the bottom of her shift, which she lifted up in one smooth upward body extension. Despite my over-arching anxiety and concern for her well-being, I could momentarily appreciate what Becca Wyatt looked like in her bra and panties, until she tossed her dress down alongside her coat and sprinted toward the water.

I ran after her—it was only in my own personal hero movie that I would have shed my clothes and flung myself into the Atlantic with her—having the foresight to grab her coat to bring with me. By then she was well beyond the wave break, and I stood in the wet sand helplessly, watching the transit of her head bobbing in the deep water, making surface ripples that reflected in the moonlight. I was praying that she wouldn't drown, mainly fearing I would have to rescue her, which would not have gone down well for either of us. But after less than a minute that felt like an hour she stroked toward the shore. Her feet finding bottom, she emerged from the breaking waves in a winter wonderland version of Ursula Andress surfacing from the Caribbean in "Dr. No," except she was fucking freezing. A prolonged cold gust was snapping across the beach, and it felt like snow in the air. Hugging herself tightly, she splashed through the undulating shallows. Shivering, she threw herself into my arms and I wrapped the overcoat over her shoulders.

"Get me warm," she said, her voice quavering.

So I wrapped my arms around the back of the overcoat, and brought her wet body into mine. We swayed together, bear-hugging on Singing Beach. And at some point, while caressing her nearly naked body and transmitting my body heat to her, when her breaths were no longer short and gasping, and her trembling had nearly ceased, she maneuvered her head and kissed me urgently. As I kissed her back and we parted our lips to kiss more deeply and with considerable oomph, I simultaneously became aware that I had a hard on and that I was not likely to be sleeping in the guest house. And then I silently castigated myself for having passed two different pharmacies that very afternoon without even thinking to purchase a pack of condoms. Later my qualms would be expressed hurriedly at an opportune moment and immediately dispelled by the lone sweet nothing whispered into my ear that night.

"I'm on the pill, you dufus," Becca would say, mid-mount.

I'm not sure what Nick Charles was doing when we barged back in to the house in rather a rush, but Becca didn't bother to turn off the TV. The house was darkened and she led me down a hallway unknown to me, the bedroom wing of the house. Through double doors we entered a very large one, unilluminated except for a single night light plugged into a floor outlet, a faintly glowing blue circle. In the shadows I could make out a sitting area and a desk and a King size bed, which could be considered excessive for a nineteen year old. Later, in the afterglow, I would learn that we were in the parents' bedroom.

Becca rested one knee on the bed and reaching across, cleared off a large number of decorative pillows and bolsters haphazardly, like a spoiled child digging into her toy chest for a particular favorite and throwing aside anything in the way. With both feet back on the ground, she flung back the coverlet and blankets with a whoosh, completely on task and not finding conversation necessary. I didn't offer to help with the housekeeping, and thought it imprudent to start taking off my own clothes without some sort of go ahead, much as I had waited to see if she ate her Orange Delight muffin with a fork or her hands.

Ultimately, I allowed myself to be blissfully swept away, but not in the fashion of a cherub floating on some fluffy cloud, hands behind its head. Becca, already in her wet underwear, required only an abbreviated stripping down. By then a frantic quality had taken over, as if some magic misty love potion had wafted through the room. Removal of my clothes was not a choreographic marvel; it had started as my own slow-paced solo, but became a chaotic duet that threatened the costume designer with needing to sew shirt buttons back on. On film, it would have resembled the movie scene where the boyfriend is about to be caught in bed by his lover's husband and jumps up to get dressed, except in reverse. Becca was impatient and ravenous, which is not to imply that I was dispassionate. I was as excited as a Golden Retriever whose master has just returned from a two week vacation to Puerto Vallarta.

I was well aware of the importance of foreplay, since that was all I knew. It had been reinforced, a lesson repeated, like my Spanish language tape playing the same passage over and over again. Foreplay was a prelude that I believed I had a handle on; I was an actor who had memorized his lines and was ready for the performance. But my cue never came, the performance skipped ahead. Becca was straddling me, leaning forward and pinning my wrists to the mattress, an overpowering wrestler on a Sealy Posturepedic. She squeezed my loins with her equestrian-conditioned thighs as if I were Winchester. First she led me slowly down a curvy, rock strewn path, and then into a trot, and finally a full canter. There were a couple of short jumps over a brook in between, and at one of those crossings I had seen fit to ejaculate. Remarkably I kept enough of an erection until Becca had ridden herself out. It had culminated in much grinding and bumping, Winchester an uncontrolled bucking bronco, Becca able to hold on just with her thighs, one of her hands on her own breast, massaging her nipple, and the other manipulating her own crotch, her finger pushing against my penis like two fat people trying to share a small bench.

If the earth had moved for her, it was because she had moved it. Becca collapsed beside me and I held her. We were both slick with sweat, and the sheets underneath me were damp. I knew a little something about refractory periods, and I was wondering how long mine was. I wanted another ride before taking Winchester back to the barn.

I was given my chance and exhausted myself to the point of obtundation. Becca was wide awake and chipper, as if she had been energized by sapping the life force from my body.

"Let's go to the beach and get stoned," she said.

"I think I'm too tired to get dressed."

"We don't need to get dressed."

"It's fucking freezing out."

"The parents have these great fluffy bathrobes." She had grabbed me by the arm and was pulling me out of bed.

"What if they catch us?" I asked, not exactly sure who "they" were. And would it be for being naked on the beach or smoking an illicit drug?

"Don't be such a weenie."

After a trip to the parents' capacious and customized master closet, we were fraternal twins in matching monogrammed, dark gray bathrobes. We traipsed down the hall to a bedroom with only a double bed—Becca's bedroom—where she opened a jewelry box on her dresser and brought out one of several pre-rolled joints. On the way through the kitchen, all the while still leading me by the hand, she stopped in the butler's pantry for a box of kitchen matches.

We walked barefoot across the lawn to the beach access. A few steps down led to a platform, well-hidden by brush and tall beach grass. Becca sat down on the platform facing the ocean and hung her legs over it. I joined her. It was still damn cold, especially barefoot, but at least the foliage provided some wind break. We sat quietly, taking in the expanse and listening to the pounding surf.

"This is my quiet place," she said, taking out a match from the box. She lit the joint and took a long drag.

"You've never smoked before, have you," she asked, knowing the answer like a good prosecutor.

"No. And I never had lobster pie before, either." I had no trepidations about entering the world of weed, even though it was not something I had specifically set upon doing for self-improvement, like learning how to drink black coffee. I took a drag and held the smoke in for as long as I could, suppressing a nasal gagging. I handed it back. I was already feeling something different. Another first.

"Well, you're certainly willing to try new things. Throwing all caution to the wind seems to suit you. Although you didn't quite have it in you to get in the water."

"I would have if you had needed saving," I said.

"How valiant of you! And how would *you* know if I needed saving?" she asked. Assuming it was a rhetorical question, since she placed the emphasis on "you," I didn't respond. The answer was that I probably wouldn't, and that the question didn't have anything to do with water or drowning.

She had taken another hit and handed the joint back to me. I realized I was nodding my head, slowly, in time to the rhythm of the surf.

"And it was your first sex, too, right?"

"It was only my first time the first time," I said.

She laughed. "It's a responsibility, you know, being on the other end."

"What do you mean by that?"

"I'll always be the first one, regardless of how many women you ever have. Your entire life. Tonight will always be a memory wired into your brain cells."

"I think you're being overly dramatic," I lied.

"No I'm not."

The next wave came in and I nodded with it.

"I hope it wasn't too much of a burden for you," I finally said. I thought it a lapse into self-deprecation.

"Mark Levinson . . . are you fishing?" She laughed and then I laughed too. I was too happy to lapse into self-deprecation, but stoned enough to unconsciously fish.

"So are you still afraid of me, Mark Levinson?"

"Not so much," I said.

"Just goes to show what a good lay will do for you," Becca said, taking another hit. "You're a changed man."

It was my turn but I declined. She took a final hit, crushed the end of the remaining joint, and flicked it out toward the sea.

I looked up and saw the stars collapsing on me.

"Fuck, it's snowing," I said.

"Come on," she said, getting up and pulling me up with her. "I have a surprise for you."

She turned off the TV, which was in a test pattern and making static. From there we made a brief stop to her bedroom, where she picked up a book that had been set on the desk. I recognized it immediately, the Harvard Class Album from 1906. How long had she had it there?

"I went over to the big house this afternoon and got this from my grandfather's library. I thought it would be fun to look it over."

"Longneck Cove?"

She nodded. "Julia, who more or less runs the rest of the staff—or as Aunt Lil prefers to say, her 'helpers'—let me in. Normally I'm not much interested in my grandfather's old books."

I nodded. I had pored over the thing in the Archives, but why not again? It was a thoughtful gesture on Becca's part, and I didn't want to appear ungrateful. It was probably three or four in the morning—I didn't want to look—and I was exhausted, all the worse because my thoughts were foggy and swirling from the marijuana. Every time I tried to focus on something, I would seem to lose my place, and would have to start all over again. I desperately wanted to lay back and close my eyes and wait for the world to stop spinning. Becca's eyes were glazed, but her facial expression was one of amusement so I could manage to fluff up enough to look through the book with her.

Back in the parents' bedroom we ditched the robes and I took the book and propped it up on a pillow. We turned on both lamps on the matching nightstands. Things were moving in slow motion. But certainly there were worse things than being stoned with Becca Wyatt, lying naked on a King-sized bed and looking at pictures.

We found the page of Hollis Wyatt's main entry and stared at it for a while.

"We can find him in group pictures if we look at his activities his senior year," I said. I already knew those included the Hasty Pudding Club, the O.K. Club, the Political Club, the Class Day Officers, and Varsity Crew. So we systematically thumbed through to find the group photos that were available. We spent an inordinate amount of time trying to find him in the Hasty Pudding shot, because it was by far the largest group with the smallest faces. The clearest images of Hollis were in the Class Day Officers photograph—he was a First Marshal—and the photograph of the 1906 Varsity Crew. I remembered the photo well from the Archive—particularly the expression on the face of the undersized coxswain lying on the ground in the front of the group, which seemed to announce, "Don't mistake me for some scrawny shrimp of a fellow, I'm the most important man in the boat."

"Are you hungry?" Becca asked me.

"Yep."

"Do you want to get the nuts?"

"Sure. Good idea. Are we done with this?"

"Almost." Becca was fixated on the photograph, trance-like. I imagined she was on her own mental Mobius strip, particularly as she had smoked more of the grass than I had.

The nut jar, still in the lounge, was about half-full, but we had already picked out all of the cashews. I brought what was left back to the bedroom, and hopped into my earlier position on my stomach, propping myself up on my elbows.

Becca browsed the cannister and selected a Brazil nut. "What did your grandfather look like?" she asked.

I told her that I only really remembered him as an old man, and had never seen many pictures of him when young. "He was fairly tall, and I suppose his hair must have been brown. . . but I only knew him as gray-haired. Earlier shots were black and white."

"Any distinguishing features?"

"He had a birthmark, or a mole, rather, right here." I pointed to a spot on my own head, just next to the end of my left eyebrow.

Becca picked out another nut and chewed on it, still apparently transfixed by the picture. I wondered if she was seeing a blur, or actually able to focus on something.

"Like this one?" Becca asked. She had her finger next to the face of one of her grandfather's crewmates. He was second from the right in the back row, and happened to have a small, but definitely visible mark on the left side of his forehead.

I stared at the photograph in disbelief. The small dark spot did not appear to be an imperfection in the print. And it was in the right spot. Holy fuck, could that be Poppa?

I looked at the list of identifying names, but of course I had done this before. Being stoned, I had some trouble hooking up the correct name with the oarsman in the photo. I would go from name to photo, and then start back again at the same place. Back row, front row, it shouldn't have been all that complicated. I was in a loop. But I didn't recognize any of the names beside Hollis Wyatt. Eventually I was able to confirm that the student oarsman in question was named Chauncey B. Porter.

My mind was racing.

"I need to talk to Eleanor . . . I can't say for sure that this is him, but we have to run this by Eleanor . . ."

"It might not be him," said Becca calmly. She offered me a nut.

"Chauncy Porter. That's his name." I looked at her, but she shrugged, her face a blank.

"Wait . . . wait . . ." I flicked the pages to the alphabetical list of portraits of all the members of the senior class. There were a couple of Porters, but no Chauncey.

Becca was watching me, trying to place our thoughts on the same track.

"He wasn't a senior," she said.

"Right," I agreed. "He didn't have to be a senior to be on the varsity crew. I need to talk to Eleanor. Wait . . . wait . . ." I was rubbing my forehead, feeling panicky. "You have to ask your Aunt Lillian again. You only asked her about Michael Levinson. You need to ask her about Chauncey Porter."

"For sure. I can do that. No problem."

"And I really need to talk to Eleanor."

"Right. But you can't talk to her now."

Apparently I had a questioning look on my face, because she felt the need to elaborate.

"It's four in the morning and you're really stoned," she said.

"Okay, okay. But when will your parents be back? And Aunt Lillian?"

"Not until after the New Year."

"Fuck." In three weeks I would be heading back to Kansas City for Christmas break. I spun around and sat on the edge of the bed. I had the Class Album in my hands.

"In the meantime you can talk to Eleanor next week. About Chauncey Porter. On Monday."

"Right." I was trying to calm myself. I didn't like how the marijuana was making me feel. I felt like I was losing my boundaries.

"And when Aunt Lil is back, I'll introduce her to you and you can ask her yourself."

"Thanks," I said. Now Becca was sitting beside me, holding the nut container in her lap.

I had calmed enough to reach for a nut. There was nothing I could do but wait things out. And nothing was for certain. The young man's hair was lighter than I imagined Poppa's to have been. The birthmark could have just been coincidental.

"But see how helpful I can be? Spotting that mole?" Becca turned me toward her. I looked at her face, her blue eyes, her mussed hair, and wondered how anything could have possibly distracted me from her.

"Have another nut," she said, lifting the container from her lap and holding it up between her breasts. I reached in and took a few.

"Enough?" she asked. I nodded and she found the plastic lid on the sheets and secured the top. Then she took the volume from my hands and placed it on her father's desk. A nearby switch on the wall turned off both of the bed stand lights.

"Did anybody ever tell you that you were nutty, Mark Levinson?" She took me by my hands and lifted me up so I was standing facing her. Then she kissed me. This time, there was nothing urgent about it.

Then she moved my hands to her breasts, and slowly moved them up and down exactly twice, which was all that it took to switch on my ignition, whether I could focus or not. For a while, Chauncey Porter was the farthest thing from my mind.

Masconomo House

Manchester-by-the-Sea
Summer, 1904

"Well, you're certainly a presentable young man. How can I help you?"

The young man had knocked on the entry frame, the glass-windowed door being fully open. The man, slight with thinning hair slicked down with a middle part, sat jacketless behind his desk, collar loosened. It was unseasonably hot for the first week of June. He removed his feet from the desktop to sit upright in his desk chair. Several large registers and accounting books were on the desk, one of them open.

"I'd like to ask about summer employment, sir."

"Very good. There are still some hires to make. What's your name?"

"Michael Levinson," he said, "and I'm nineteen."

The man took him for a Harvard student. He was hatless, but the suit jacket and trousers looked expensive, and he wore a high stiff collar. But the clothes were almost too fine for a middle class Harvard boy looking for work, possibly used bargains from Max Keester. Obviously, the truly wealthy school boys had no need or desire to work at all.

The presentable young man had taken the Boston and Maine railroad to the Manchester train station and walked a short way to the Masconomo House. There was considerable activity outside the front entrance, with several wagons in the circular entrance drive. The air smelled of fresh earth, dung, and burning brush. A large steep sided wagon contained soil and manure, which several men with shovels were dumping into large piles. Other men were removing pallets of flowers from a flatbed wagon and arranging them for planting. Still others were trimming bushes and hedges and pushing lawn mowers. The job seeker had been led to the ground floor office of the hotel manager, E. C. Stimson, by one of the workers leaning against an entry pillar, about to take a smoking break. The worker, corralled by an unknown rich kid, swallowed his annoyance at being bothered. Otherwise he would have told him to "sod off," disturbing him like that just as he was about to light a ciggy.

"How did you hear about us?" Stimson asked, as if the grandest hotel on the North Shore were a back alley retail establishment.

"I had a conversation with Hollis Wyatt a while ago," he answered, "and it just came up. That this was a good place to work in the summer."

Moishe had not discussed the Masconomo House with Hollis Wyatt when they had met. Nor was Moishe aware that the Wyatt family estate and summer residence, Longneck Cove—one of the most impressive cottages along the shoreline of Manchester-by-the-Sea—was only a short carriage ride away. He had learned about the Masconomo House from the public library, prompted by the serendipity of finding Stimson's business card in the vest pocket of the clothes Wyatt had given him. And wouldn't it be more pleasant to spend the hot summer at a luxurious hotel, instead of *schvitsing* over O'Rourke's forge all day? Surrounded by the fineries and rich people? All on his own he had decided that he would adopt the given name of "Michael."

"I see," said Stimson, noting a slight strangeness in the kid's manner of speech. He nodded as he tried to piece things together. Not at Harvard, and certainly not part of young Wyatt's society crowd if he needed work. Stimson's best guess was that the young man in front of him was some relation to a member of the staff at the estate.

Levinson was only mildly discomfited by the notion that Wyatt could find him out if the manager were to mention him. He hadn't gone so far as to use Wyatt as a reference. And indirectly, Moishe had learned about the Masconomo House through Wyatt, had he not? And if he were to get a job and encounter Hollis Wyatt, why would it be of concern to him? It was a free country after all.

"I expect to see the Wyatt family dining at the hotel this season," continued

119

Stimson. "They're quite fond of the musical and theatre performances." The manager, for discretion's sake, had no intention of bringing up this kid's name to any of the Wyatts should the occasion arise.

Levinson was quiet, looking at him uncertainly.

"As you must know, this is a very big place. We obviously have a large and varied staff. So what can you do, what work skills do you have?"

Levinson confidently informed him that he was good with horses, that he could be a driver. He also had experience as a blacksmith's assistant and could do farrier work. Stimson raised his eyebrows, pleasantly surprised. Robinson, the staff manager, could place him as he saw fit. The boy had more to offer than being young and strong.

"I'll introduce you to our staff manager and we'll see what he can work out. We have a dormitory to house workers, and we supply uniforms that we will launder. For you that would be black trousers, white shirt and black waistcoat. No collar necessary. That is, of course, if you are facing the public," he added with a slight smile.

Levinson nodded and thanked him.

"We won't need you to start for at least another week. The hotel doesn't open for the season until June 27, and we won't be at full staffing until a few days before. But there's a good amount of preparation work to get us ready for the season and much of it requires some muscle. You might come in handy sooner."

Levinson settled in, but kept to himself. Before the hotel opening, he was mainly unloading crates of sundries and other supplies for the kitchen. Room updates and redecorating required moving and rearranging heavy furniture. Once the guests began to arrive with regularity, he would drive either the wagon or the horse barge to the depot to load up the trunks and other baggage. His coach and stable boss was Owen Brown, a sinewy middle-aged local, assisted by his son Riley, in his mid-twenties. Owen was all-business and taciturn, but generally accommodating and relatively easy-going for a supervisor, especially in comparison with the tempestuous and moody

O'Rourke. Riley had a young wife, who was a waitress, and they both boarded in the coachman's quarters in the basement of the three story annex to the south of the hotel. Riley was a somewhat aloof, and as a married man, didn't seem to think he had much in common with Levinson, so most conversation was shop talk.

Levinson had opted to sleep evenings in a small wooden lean-to off the rear of the stable that had a bed, chair, and an oil lamp. Originally it would have been for the main coach hand, but Riley had better accommodations in the relatively new annex, and Owen lived with his wife in a house on North Street. If he wanted, Levinson could bunk in the helps' quarters, but he relished his privacy, his own room rather than an open dormitory set up. The three teenage colored boys who did the stable muck work and tended to the horses sometimes slept on straw in a corner of the stable, preferring that to the nearby shanties for negroes off Beach Street.

Aside from the stable boys, many of the colored employees were white-gloved servers, some seasoned Memorial Hall Harvard waiters relying on the Masconomo House for summer work. The boiler staff and laundry workers, who operated a twenty horsepower boiler and laundry in the basement of the annex, were also all colored, except for the pot-bellied man in charge. The maids, bellhops, errand boys, and beach cabin caretakers, as well as those assigned to tennis, boating, the casino, dances and other entertainments—everyone else who directly interfaced with the guests—were white. No colored females were employed.

Simple but hardy meals were provided for the staff, self-served from pots and casserole dishes in a dining area in the annex basement below the first floor kitchen. Meals to the two hundred fifty-foot-long main dining hall for guests were transported on covered trays to the staging area at the near end of the main dining hall, an uncovered outside walk of ten paces. Bread and rolls were freshly baked daily but generally didn't find their way to the staff table until day-olds or older. Depending on the wants of the guests, more sumptuous entries and even deserts could be offered if available, hit or miss, and usually a cause for envy if acquired. The tables for eating were segregated by race.

The white male workers stayed in dormitories above the old dance hall, and the women slept above the bowling alley and pool room in an adjacent narrow building. Both utilitarian buildings were shielded from the hotel proper by the famous bandstand, from which music emanated nightly. During daylight hours the band often performed on the roof of the bathhouse, with guests listening from the piazza or sitting on the beach itself. Less expensive guest rooms were outside the hotel building proper, on the second floor of the annex above the kitchen. There were also several well-appointed guest cottages on the grounds, the two nicest Booth properties designated for the orchestra director and his musicians and the actors who were invited to perform in repertory.

Since Owen and Riley drove either the buggy or the carriages to ferry the guests to and from the depot, Levinson had little direct contact with the guests themselves; rarely was there any call to interact with them, his flatbed wagon the equivalent of a baggage car. By the time he had the wagon loaded, the passenger-containing vehicles were well ahead of him. The guests were already being shown to their rooms while he unloaded the luggage by the front portico for the bellhops to sort and deliver later, or in some cases he would put them in the storage room in the annex. Some patrons stayed for a week or two; others would ensconce themselves for most of the season.

Levinson was enthralled by the spectacle of wealth and society. Unless boating, playing tennis, or at the beach, the men were immaculately attired. The women carried parasols and presented a rainbow of parading fashion. Some guests came with their own valets and personal staff. Diplomats with foreign sounding names from the eleven summer embassies in town or from Washington D.C. itself were among the throng. The majority of guests picked up at the Manchester depot had transferred to the Boston and Maine line upon arrival in Boston from far-off locales. Of those guests not coming in by rail, some came in their own carriages from nearer environs, others arrived in chauffeur-driven touring cars or smaller autos they commandeered themselves. Many of the wealthiest Bostonians, of course, had their own cottages in Manchester or nearby Magnolia or Beverly Farms, so they could attend social events as they pleased, without the need for hotel accommodations.

The last train to arrive from Boston was at seven p.m., so unless he was needed for extra duty somewhere, Levinson had most of his evenings free. He would stroll on Singing Beach and even venture into the water on warm evenings. He could walk to the harbor or Masconomo Park. Sometimes he would saddle his favorite horse—he came to know all of them quite well, but was particularly partial to a gelding named Baked Bean—and trek farther afield, up the paths to Smith or Coolidge Points. If feeling less ambitious, he could sit down with a daily paper—many were to be had, abandoned on tables throughout the hotel and stacked in a wooden box on the floor of the staff dining area. Nor was there any lack of good books or magazines for reading— each of the dormitory common rooms had a lending library, collected over the years from reading material abandoned by guests. Before bedtime he would shower behind the men's house. It was as good a life as he could have, Levinson thought, other than by being a guest.

The Importance of Being Earnest, performed in rotation with other theatricals in the concert hall, was Levinson's introduction to a live stage performance. The propriety, demeanor, and manners of the stage characters, enhanced by the well-spoken British accents, seemed appropriate for the Masconomo House audience. The performance was well-attended and the spectators appreciative. Standing in the shadows of the room near the back entry, Levinson's view of the stage was partially obscured by tall folding panels he had set up earlier. On an evening when he had just planned to read anyway, Robinson had assigned him stagehand work. His job was to bring and return the large backdrop screens from the storage room in the annex. Once set in place, he could have chosen to leave and return later, but Levinson would not dare miss an opportunity to see such a show.

The set was makeshift to the extent there was no painted backdrop or fixed back wall, just the panels for the actors to stand behind when off-stage. Most of the stage furnishings were sturdy and stylish, requisitioned from spare hotel furniture, and the costumes were exquisite, brought from the storerooms of the Boston Theater thanks to Agnes Booth Schoeffel's contacts. The cast included two renowned retired players who resided in town on Actor's Row. These elderly gents—the older quite ancient but with a flawless memory for his lines and surprisingly strong projection—were scene stealers, both cast in the female roles of Lady Augusta Bracknell and Miss Letitia Prism. The old pros were hilarious, but Levinson was smitten by Gwendolen Fairfax; he couldn't tear his eyes away from her. She was a tall and full figured red-headed beauty who spoke slowly and precisely, and with a huskiness in her voice. Mesmerized, Levinson lost most of the plot of the story. He had to find a way to see the play again. He would speak to Robinson and offer his services for whatever evening theatrical performances were scheduled. He could make himself available. He'd do anything.

Some weeks later, after another performance of *Earnest*, Gwendolen Fairfax had words for the stagehand. The other actors had dispensed with a coterie of admirers and were heading to their makeshift dressing room in what normally served as a green room for musicians. Gwendolen, trailing behind, watched the stagehand fold up the first of the panels. She had noticed him standing by the back concert hall door for other performances and was curious about him.

"You must be quite the theatre patron," she said in her sultry voice, with her perfect elocution. "I see you standing here for every show."

Levinson wasn't sure how to respond.

"Surely you don't have to wait and stand in the dark," she continued. "You could certainly go off somewhere and come back when the performance is finished to cart away these things. You must have other business to attend to." Her British tone had taken on a certain imperiousness, as if she were being critical of him for admiring the arts. "That you do not do so I must assume you are quite taken with stage performance. A true aficionado. And if that is the case, I'm curious as to whom your favorite player is."

"I've nothing better to do, and I've never been to the theater before," Levinson stammered. "So I suppose my favorite player must be . . . you."

She flicked her parasol and showed no pleasure at hearing the compliment. "Stage door Johnnies are *so* tiresome, but I must say you are one of the more attractive ones I have come across. But if you have acting ambitions, you might want to spend more time watching the other actors, especially Messrs. Evans and Hunter, since they are masters. They have worked with Jefferson and Proctor."

"I don't want to be an actor. I just like to watch and be taken away to somewhere else."

"You're a dear boy," said Gwendolyn, patting her hair. "After you've finished taking back all these screens to wherever you take them, why don't you come to the actor's residence? We will be having our customary little gathering with some alcoholic beverages, a cast party if you will. And I can introduce you to the other players, except for Messrs. Evan and Hunter, since they will be tucked into their own beds at their homes by then."

"Thank you," said Levinson, "That would be . . . a wonderful thing."

She started to walk off, then looked back behind at him, presenting a beautiful face and a full bustle.

"And if you don't move your damn arse taking those bloody things back, there won't be any swill left," said Emma Conghlan in her natural brogue, winking and flashing a flirtatious grin.

"I thought you were English," Levinson confessed.

They had seated themselves on the sofa in the parlor of the cottage known as Actor's House, smaller but more sumptuous than the neighboring Musician's House. After procuring Levinson a beer, Emma had taken him around the room for introductions. It was a relaxed and slightly inebriated after-show wind down for the cast, a transition before they headed to their sleeping quarters in upstairs rooms. All were quite cordial; Levinson in particular had imagined that the Jack Worthing actor would show possessiveness toward Emma, but he seemed more interested in Algernon Moncrieff's attentions. Agnes Booth dropped in to pay her respects and offer her accolades and was in the midst of saying her goodbyes when Emma introduced him. She presented a hand to shake and a smile, and then cast a glance at Emma with one eyebrow theatrically raised. Booth was a somewhat plain woman in her sixties, who sucked all attention to herself like a whirlpool the instant any utterance sprang from her lips.

"It is always such a joy to be with my people," she elocuted with a broad gesture of her arm as she exited. Having deserted high society, if only briefly, to demonstrate her commonality and solidarity with "her people," Booth Schoeffel headed back to the hotel to fulfill business obligations with patrons she exploited more than admired.

"It's called acting," said Emma Conghlan. "It's all a matter of listening carefully and practice. I'm as English as you are. I grew up on Harris Street. Across from St. Stephen's."

"The Catholic Church on Hanover Street?"

She nodded.

"I live on Salem Street, on the other side of Hanover!" Levinson couldn't contain his excitement as well as disbelief.

"I figured you as a Yid from the old neighborhood," said Emma, "or from the West End. Not intending any offense, mind you."

"How did you figure?" Levinson asked.

"Your inflections and your hard "g" to begin with."

"I see," he said softly, looking at the ground.

Emma took a sip of her beer. "How old are you, Michael?"

"I'll be twenty."

"When."

"In a few months. How old are you?"

"For heaven's sake, don't you know it's rude to ask a woman her age, and if she answers you she'd be lying anyway?"

Levinson shrugged. It didn't seem like an unreasonable question, and he was just trying to make pleasant conversation.

"I'm twenty-eight," she answered.

"Are you lying?" he asked.

"Not this time," she replied. "Why would I lie to a Yid?"

"The excess and wealth, it is something to behold . . . but most of all I am taken by the beauty here. Such beauty like I have never seen."

"So you're an aesthete."

"I don't know what that means."

"It means you are someone who appreciates beautiful things."

"It's more than that, but it's hard to describe. It's more than just the beauty."

The beers had conferred an unaccustomed glibness on Levinson, and the salty Irish actress had put him at his ease. Both, in fact, were slightly in their cups. They had deserted the Actor's House after the gathering had broken up and decided on a walk around the grounds. They had ended up at the stables, where Levinson had introduced Emma to Baked Bean. She was stroking the horse gingerly as Levinson held the halter. Emma found herself quite comfortable with the attractive young man, while still mindful of the difference in their ages. He was a young innocent, which admittedly held an appeal for her.

"So you want to be like them?" Emma turned to him sharply, a dramatic stage gesture. "That's what you want out of life? You want to be rich?"

Levinson shook his head with conviction.

"No, but they fascinate me. Everything seems . . . so easy. Servants doing the *dreck* work for them, all the things they don't need to bother with. So they have more time . . . more time for—

"—for what?"

"Other things. I don't know to be exact."

"Spending their money, showing off, perhaps?"

Levinson strained to articulate the complicated feelings he had not yet seriously considered. What did he covet, and why? Perhaps the topic was something that deserved some reflection. Definitely it went beyond the grass is always greener. And surely it was more than simple jealousy and greed, a not so flattering explanation. But for the moment he deflected, unable to hide his defensiveness.

"I don't think it is showing off . . . and so what if it is?"

The look on Emma's face said she wasn't convinced, his argument less than paltry.

"Hell, I know a bunch of poor Irish kids on the block that show off more than they do," he went on, flustered.

Emma rolled her eyes.

"Just ask Mick Flanagan, why don't you? I bloodied his nose once because I couldn't take his showing off any more." Levinson paused. "Plus he called me a sheeney."

"My hero," Emma said as a stage damsel, then laughed. It was the laughing that prompted Levinson to steer the conversation back her way.

"Well, then, what is it that you want, smarty pants?"

She raised her eyebrows, as if the young man's familiarity was boldly taking a liberty, either acclimating to, or ignoring, their age difference. The alternative was a disrespect for his elders. In fact, that was the best Levinson could come up with to be flirty, and he had regretted it immediately.

"I'm going to be a famous actress," she replied honestly, which if anything, sounded as if she herself were regressing in age to make up some of the disparity. "I'm going to strut my behind on that stage of the Tremont, and people are going to clap for me and give me standing ovations. And kiss my arse if I ask them to."

"Seems to me like it is you who wants to show off."

She looked at him deeply, a bit glassy-eyed and straining to focus.

"But you have a lot to show," he qualified immediately, another attempt at flattery masked by an apology.

She ignored both the compliment and the contrition.

"I want to show people that this poor Irish girl can be a serious actress. Is there anything wrong with that? I have a goal. And I'm well on my way, if I have to say so. And what do you want to make of yourself?

Levinson felt like a child belittled by a school master. "I haven't thought about it in that way. I want to read and learn things. I like books . . . and magazines too. I want to experience things that I'm not supposed to experience, that I'm not allowed to experience. I don't want to have restrictions."

"Being poor restricts you."

"It defines me. And so does being a Jew." he said.

"You can't change that," she said, "and I don't think you can change the world either. Would you like to be an actor? You could be an actor, you know that? Such strong features, and these muscles. You can be my younger leading man!" She put a hand on his shoulder and gave a squeeze. A grasp of his shoulder would usually cause Levinson to flinch, but these weren't ordinary circumstances. Instead, he felt his entire body loosen, as if a heavy pack had been lifted from his back.

Levinson shook his head, which had drifted forward. When he looked and met Emma's eyes, he realized something had shifted. She had not removed her hand.

"I think for now . . . I just want to be in a story," he said.

"The story and experience part I can help you with," Emma said, drawing him into her body with both arms. Levinson felt light-headed, his body tingling at her closeness and scent. He closed his eyes. When he opened them, Emma Conghlan was staring into them. Levinson was standing still, awaiting direction. He began stammering, overcome with fear of humiliation as much as desire.

"I'm not so sure . . ." he began, but she shushed him.

"I've decided to call you Moishe," she said.

He nodded. The truth was an intimate thing.

Then she kissed him, and he responded in kind. Transported and in disbelief, Moishe Levinson was about to make love to Gwendolyn Fairfax.

"You'd better put the horse away," said Emma, the silence in the stable broken only by the rustling of her lifting up her skirt.

"What was that really about?" he asked afterwards, shifting in the hay.

"I find you attractive. And you're a boy with real potential. Are you sorry?"

"No. God no." He bristled about being referred to as a boy, but let it pass for a more important response. "Are you?"

"Of course not." She began dressing with business-like efficiency. Levinson watched the pantomime in shadow, captivated by the provocativeness of the ordinary.

"I put you in a story, Moishe. That was something you can appreciate, yes? And for me, a girl has her needs. As for you, you had to grow up some time. Now you can find a girl your own age. Besides, why waste all this hay without a romp in it." She was reciting lines from an unwritten play.

"Are we going to do this again? I mean, would it be all right if we do this again?"

Emma smoothed her hair. "You are such a sweet boy, Moishe. This may be new and special to you, but I'm not all that special, really. Being with you like this might just be the most special I can ever be. So I don't want you to make me more in your head than I really am. I'm old enough to be your mother. Maybe not your mother, but . . . like an older sister. A very overprotective older sister looking out for your well-being."

"You didn't answer my question."

"It's not wise to get too attached, so let's not think about that right now. I've been selfish." She was her brushing hay off her skirt.

"How so?"

Fully dressed, she lay down beside him. "An actress like me spends a lot of time fighting off men. And it's not that they appreciate my acting ability. It's a heavenly change not to need to fight."

"You can't expect men not to find you attractive. You're beautiful."

"It's a nuisance. Last night an old gentlemen guest said he could get me a leading role at the Park Theatre. He wouldn't stop hounding me. It all gets very tiresome. It happens constantly."

"Could he? Get you the leading role?"

"I asked Agnes. She found it all very amusing. And she told me he could get me a job as a teller at his bank, maybe, but not on any stage."

"And what if he could have . . . gotten you a part?" Levinson was wondering how far she would go, how much she would compromise herself, how much she would risk.

"How big is the part?" She laughed and jabbed him in the arm, then swung herself on top of him.

"Agnes would definitely not approve," she said, "but she would understand."

"I appreciate your acting ability," said Levinson. "I appreciate everything about you."

"You certainly don't need any more lessons in wooing a girl," Emma said. "You are the special one, my dear. And I am not Gwendolyn. She's the one you really want." She bent down and kissed him on the cheek. "You're a natural. I don't think there is anything else I can teach you."

"Yes there is," Moishe said quietly. "There is."

Emma tilted her head. She couldn't make out his expression in the darkness. She leaned closer and waited for his response.

"You can teach me how to speak like them," he said.

Tragedy!

High season at the Masconomo was nearing its end. The Actor's Company would be heading back to Boston the beginning of September, some to join regular season players in set companies, others to audition for work or find temporary employment elsewhere to tide things over until a paying opportunity arose. Emma, thanks to Agnes, was already lined up for a minor but highly visible role in an upcoming revival at the Madison Square Theatre on Broadway. She would have an opportunity to be seen, and perhaps even garner review attention in the New York papers.

She had maintained her relationship with Moishe initially as a language coach, meeting up with him in his stable residence during free hours they held in common, ultimately establishing a regular schedule, generally in the evening after a weekend performance. During daylight hours, they pretended not to know one another were they to cross paths, something that Agnes would have suggested had Emma not established the ground rules herself early on. The last thing Emma wanted to do was cause Agnes or her husband John any embarrassment through indiscretions with a young hotel employee. She owed it to Agnes, who would have expected nothing less from her, and besides, she had her own career to think of.

As a text, Emma started with the most suitable script from the repertory, *The Importance of Being Earnest*, since Moishe was already quite attached to it. After general discussions on diction and inflections, he was assigned to read all the male parts. She herself would recite the female parts for continuity and to liven things up. Initially she trained him in a British accent, since he was already familiar with the lines as delivered by the resident actors, a basis for his mimicry. He would change his tone and vocal qualities accordingly. Next, she transitioned him to an assortment of American accents, spending the most time, at his insistence, on learning how to sound like a blue-blood. And despite Moishe having less interest, she acquainted him with a hodge-podge of English, Irish, Scottish, and even French and German accents, which she considered valuable ear-training in general. He was a quick study and an eager learner, with the ultimate goal, she knew, being to not sound like an immigrant Jew. For all his protestations to the contrary, she could have been preparing him for a career on the stage.

The scope of her mentorship expanded. Michael was able to learn certain exemplary manners from stage directions, but those only went so far. On one occasion when he had brought hard boiled eggs and sandwiches to share from the kitchen annex, Emma was stunned to watch him chewing with his mouth open. Could anyone imagine the shock of seeing Algernon chewing with his mouth open and wiping his chin with the back of his hand? And thus began more comprehensive sessions on table manners and dining etiquette, including the proper placement and usage of cutlery. She herself had learned the hard way over time, often embarrassing herself, but had also benefitted by schooling from Agnes, who had recognized Emma's plight and come to her aid only months earlier. Emma had needed her own preparation for dining at the Masconomo gala events when she and her cohorts were thrown in with the distinguished and well-heeled. On those occasions, the actors interfaced as celebrities and curiosities on short term leases, with Agnes taking a proprietary joy in their acting abilities.

Emma decided to relent and bed Moishe regularly after the first couple of sessions as payment in kind. It was pleasurable and fun for the both of them. With their separation from Manchester-by-the-Sea approaching, she could view their assignations as a time-limited summer fling, a mutual recognition of non-permanence being the defining quality of their affair. With Moishe's determination and seriousness over his new studies, Emma allowed herself to believe that his lessons in assimilation had taken priority over their sexual relations, not that he ever showed a lack of interest in her. Still, this appeased earlier concerns she held about causing him heartbreak when they separated. Emma had grown extremely fond of Moishe Levinson and would miss him dearly when they parted. Sometimes she wondered whose heart would really be broken. He had, in fact, become her Pygmalion, a common Jew molded into a man whom she would want to spend her life with, were such a scenario possible. She fought the notion of it. And had he been so common, after all? Perhaps she was taking too much credit.

A Masconomo House employee who was one of the first witnesses to the tragedy sprinted to the hotel and arrived breathless, barging into Mr. Stimson's office with the news. Agnes and John Schoeffel were immediately notified and hurried to the scene in their personal buggy. At the time, the identity of the young man had yet to be determined. The guest had gone for a horseback ride at dusk but had dismounted to pick some flowers, leading the horse by the reins as he bent down upon the roadside. A touring car rounding the corner at Tappan Street and Beach at too great a speed had stuck them both head on. Out of some misplaced notion of decorum, the gunshot that put down the broken and heaving chestnut mare was delayed until the ambulance had arrived to retrieve the limp and bleeding human body and headed to Beverly Hospital.

From the murmurs of the small group of townspeople who had gathered, held back by a handful of officials that had raced to the scene from a meeting at Town Hall, the victim had already preceded the horse in death. The driver of the vehicle, who had been thrown from the auto into the bushes, was dazed but conscious, and being tended to by a few of the bystanders. A second ambulance had been called for at the behest of the mayor as a precautionary gesture, even though the driver's wounds didn't appear serious. Precautionary perhaps, to remove the gentleman from the scene, since it was obvious to everyone he was the reckless person at fault. That he was an out of town guest at the Masconomo was obvious at the sight of his automobile; there were hushed conversations among the onlookers speculating on who he was.

But before the arrival of the first ambulance, a distraught Agnes, feigning composure, was back at the hotel to find the boy's mother, while John had rushed to the stable to order Owen Riley to prepare the landau posthaste and have it waiting at the front entrance. It was the woman's hysterical wails and screaming that kindled the wildfire spreading of the news of the accident. Agnes needed to be aided by Stimson in physically supporting the poor woman as she was led from the Pavilion through the lobby to the front entrance, where only moments earlier she had been sipping Earl Gray. The procession was painfully slow and halting, an interminable stage exit. Guests and staff froze in place, and the Masconomo's Great Hall was silent except for the echoing cries of grief.

Levinson had helped Owen Riley hitch the horses to the Landau. He was startled by John Schoeffel's appearance—the hotel owner was sweating heavily and disheveled when he unexpectedly showed up at the barn. Witnessing his agitation, Levinson knew that the accident was a serious one. And he knew whom it involved. All the horses were stabled save one. Not a half hour earlier Levinson had prepared Buttercup for the guest who had requested a mount, the young man—near his own age or younger—known to him as Mister Porter.

Porter had arrived at the Masconomo House about a month earlier, and had requested a mount in the early evenings on a number of occasions. Michael had not taken much of a liking to him owing to the dismissive manner in which he was treated compounded by the resentment of addressing someone his own age as "mister." Not that he wasn't accustomed to being treated rudely, or at least subservient, but the demeanor of this particular guest rankled him. Porter was well-kept but ordinary in appearance, with an angular face, an upturned nose, and a weak chin. He was roughly Levinson's height but slighter, with a manner of refinement that came across as prissy. Worse, from what he had seen of him in passing, Levinson considered Mister Porter an inveterate mother's boy. But credit where it was due, the *shaygetz* knew his horses. Despite that, Levinson was determined to never allow this particular swell to take his excursions on the back of Baked Bean. And thankful he was for that when he overheard the news from Schoeffel in the stables. He mourned the fate of Buttercup. And things did not bode better for the rider, that was certain.

Outside of their contact at the stables, Michael had seen Porter on the hotel grounds, alone or else in the company of his mother, a slender and attractive matron. She was polite to the staff but kept to herself, seeking no company or society, and dining with no one other than her son. When not in his company she was frequently listening to the orchestra by the bandstand, book or cross-stitch in hand, or taking tea on the Pavilion. Later, when the gossiping among staff had commenced full steam—the most specific details coming to him from Emma, who got them from Agnes—Levinson came to understand what was behind her behavior.

Amelia Porter, the daughter of a country doctor and a school teacher, was from Montana and a widow of several years. Her inheritance resulted from a fortuitous marriage to a hardscrabble and ambitious rancher who had made a fortune both from cattle and mining. With a lifestyle of relative isolation and rural elegance, she tended more toward horse breeding than cotillions. So she had not journeyed to the Masconomo House as part of a social season and cared little for such things, barely hiding her contempt for the women parading their wealth and connections. The socialites were unlikely to embrace her either. No, the sole intent of the month-long stay was to establish her son for his freshman year at Harvard College, which explained why Riley had been called upon so often to transport her and her son in the carriage to the train station and back. Rather than enjoying the diversions of Masconomo House, the Porters would spend entire days in Boston, first procuring a wardrobe for a proper Eastern gentleman, then meticulously selecting accessories and furnishings befitting a college man.

Chauncy Bates Porter, a beneficiary of privileged upbringing and education by private tutors, was nonetheless a country boy, albeit coddled and spoiled. His mother could have sent him to boarding school in the East years earlier, but particularly after her husband's death—with both of her own parents dead and without siblings—the thought of sending away her only child was unthinkable. Still the time had come for him to complete his education in a manner that the West could not offer him. She had trepidations, but was convinced she could manage his absence for the greater part of four years. He would be back to the ranch every summer, and she would make the trek east at least once during every term. But first, it was a mother's job to get him settled and prepared as best she could.

Amelia was determined to make sure that Chauncey would not be looked down upon by Eastern snobs. Simply by being from the Western country, her son faced a variety of hurdles, the worst being iced out despite his status as a gentleman. More inclined to the outdoor life and not well traveled, her son was relatively unsophisticated. And having not attended a New England academy or a prestigious Episcopal boarding school, Chauncey would have no established friendships. Making friends would not be easy; invitations for teas and other social gatherings in Boston's best private homes would not be immediately forthcoming. Not that Amelia Porter sought the Harvard smart set for her son; she simply didn't want him to be isolated and lonely.

There were more mundane and practical concerns. Amelia knew she was disadvantaged in acquiring lodgings for Chauncey, since all the New England boys could scoop up the most desirable accommodations well in advance. The most luxurious private apartments on Mt. Auburn Street would be spoken for, she had been informed, and accommodations at the most exclusive one, Claverly, even if available, could be difficult to lease without the requisite social bona fides. Recording Secretary G.W. Cram—well experienced in the difficulties encountered by the few students matriculating from the West— had confirmed such disadvantages by mail immediately upon Chauncey's acceptance. He would do his best to look after the boy and ease his transition in any way he could.

On the basis of Cram's recommendation, Amelia had secured a large, third floor room at Mrs. Murray's boarding house on Brattle Street, sight unseen, and paid for the first term's lodging and board in advance. Not only was the lodging reportedly in a highly desirable and convenient Cambridge location, but Mrs. Murray was the reputed provider of hearty and nutritious meals, which obviated the need for the food offerings at Memorial Hall or a private dining table. Regarding outfitting, Cram recommended J. August or L.P. Hollander for the current collegiate styles of apparel, and suggested a generous allowance for incidentals; in particular, enough money for excursions into Boston for meals, concerts, and the theater.

The activity prompted by the tragic death was immediate and intense. Amelia had arrived at Beverly Hospital to learn that her son was already dead. Her hysterics required heavy sedation and temporary placement in a hospital room of her own overnight. Bed-ridden and groggy, she allowed the Schoeffels to arrange the embalming of her son at a North Shore funeral home, where they purchased a suitable coffin—paid for by the hotel as a courtesy—and scheduled transport by rail for Mrs. Porter and her son's body. For the first short leg of the trip to Boston, Amelia would have personal use of the private Masconomo House rail car, customarily coupled to the Boston and Maine train only to transport Boston visitors for special events. Agnes had contacted a dressmaker in Beverly and procured ready-made black dresses and hats for Amelia's travels, as she had no mourning apparel and would not even leave the hospital unless dressed appropriately.

Amelia would only spend one final night at the hotel before her departure, aided by Agnes and the head maid, who under Amelia's distracted and sometimes stuporous supervision packed her travel bags and items for the long journey. Amelia remained sedated, although the dosage was reduced from what had been previously required. Slumping despondently in a lady's chair and occasionally dozing while Agnes and the maid scuttled about the rooms, she refused dinner. After Amelia had finally settled into bed, Agnes took occupancy of the chair and stayed overnight. By then, all the other luggage and trunks had been taken by the valets and runners to the front entrance, where Michael Levinson had been instructed to bring the cart for loading. The Schoeffels would drive Amelia to the train station in their own carriage first thing in the morning, and Michael would drive behind with the luggage and manage the unloading with one of the colored stable boys. The funeral home was bringing the coffin from Beverly to meet the party, and would arrive well before the departure of the train at 8 a.m.

Amelia Porter had another breakdown at the station at the sight of her son's coffin being removed from the funeral carriage, collapsing to the ground and being lifted to her feet by Agnes and the funeral director. In the meantime, Levinson and his helper Simon were removing the suitcases and trunks from the cart, which were also to be placed in the railcar. The coffin, along with the luggage, would occupy most of the central aisle of a car which otherwise would only transport Agnes and Amelia as far as North Station. From there, the coffin would be loaded in a hearse for the transfer to South Station, where it would be placed into a baggage car for the trip West. Fortunately, Agnes had arranged with a hire service in Boston for a professional lady's maid to chaperone Amelia for the entirety of her journey and was meeting the retired school mistress at South Station. Amelia had not hesitated at the necessity for such a chaperone or the expense involved, and was too exhausted to allow her pride to decline the service.

At the Manchester-by-the-Sea depot, funeral workers loaded the coffin at the front entrance of the car while Levinson was at the rear, transferring his load through the equivalent of a makeshift servant's entrance. Two suitcases and a trunk remaining on the platform held her son's possessions. Standing on the platform, with the coffin having disappeared into the rail car, Amelia absently glanced to the other end of the car and saw the luggage. She was horrified at the sight of it, the prospect of dealing with her son's belongings too much for her fragile and irrational state of mind.

"NO! NO! NO!" she screamed, running towards Levinson and a stunned Simon. "I CAN'T BEAR IT!" she wailed. She threw herself on the largest trunk and began sobbing anew.

"I NEVER WANT TO SEE THESE THINGS AGAIN!" she bellowed between gasps. "I CAN'T BEAR IT! GIVE IT ALL AWAY! HE'S GONE! MY LOVELY BOY IS GONE!"

Eventually the woman was calmed, but all of Chauncey's things had to be left on the platform and reloaded on the cart by Levinson and Simon.

"We brought back his trunk and suitcases," Levinson informed Emma when they met later, "and put them in the storage room." During the ensuing pause, both spontaneously realized they shared a macabre curiosity.

That evening, in lieu of a dialect lesson, Levinson and Emma thoroughly assessed the abandoned inventory. Aside from an embossed leather satchel with paper, communications and fresh notebooks and writing pads, the trunk contained newly purchased items: an elegant glass and silver inkwell and writing set with a silver fountain pen and mechanical pencil, a silver repousse gentlemen's toiletry kit, and monogramed silver flask, water tumbler, drinking mug, cigar case, and match safe. Framed photographs included a portrait of his mother and several matched photographs of American West scenes, two labeled as Mount Cleveland and Lake McDonald. Neatly folded clothes, clearly expensive and new, including formal attire as well as shoes, stockings, undergarments, and collars, occupied most of the trunk space. The suitcases mostly held attire brought for the stay at the Masconomo House from Montana, as well as more utilitarian toiletry items in a leather bag.

"There's a lot of money here," said Emma, riffling through the stacked clothing. "These are really expensive outfits. Not to mention the silver."

"But we can't just take it, can we?" Moishe asked.

"You told me she didn't want it," said Emma.

It was like stumbling upon a buried treasure. Moishe downplayed the emotions he felt by shrugging. Perhaps Chauncey's mother would change her mind later and ask for it.

The next day Emma advocated to Agnes on his behalf.

"Michael is as much a charity case as anyone," she said. "I'm sure he could use some of the boy's things."

Agnes didn't want to be bothered. The entire episode had just been too sad and traumatic. And certainly, Amelia Porter had been adamant in making her intentions clear.

"He can take whatever he wants," Agnes said with a dismissive wave of her hand. One less thing to worry about. Agnes thought nothing more of it, nor did she ever remember to ask about any remaining items left in the storage room that could be forwarded to the Salvation Army. As it happened there were none. In a week's time Chauncey Porter's suitcases and trunk would make it back to Boston in the cart with all the actors' other properties, dropped off at the Tremont Theatre before being taken to Emma's lodgings with the rest of her things, courtesy of the Masconomo House. Unable to easily move the trunk, Michael Levinson would make several separate trips to Max Keester's establishment in Harvard Square on the streetcar to dispose of many of the clothes for cash and some credit. He packed the remaining items in the suitcases and a large canvas sack, which he took back to his Aunt and Uncle's house.

Moishe had offered to split all the proceeds with Emma, but she declined.

"But I still have the silver things," he protested.

"You keep everything," said Emma, kissing him on the forehead.

Soon she would be leaving for rehearsals for her first acting performance in New York City. Mr. Stimson, impressed by Levinson's abilities and work ethic, offered him one of the few plum off-season positions at the Masconomo House at good wages, with housing and meals included.

Michael Levinson, while appreciating the offer, had declined it. Moishe Levinson went back to stay with his aunt and uncle on Salem Street, with plenty of time to think and dream.

Tea with Eleanor

I called the Archives before my first class on Monday. I knew it didn't open until ten, but I left a message for Eleanor on the answering machine. Could she pull files for me on Chauncey B. Porter, Class of 1908? He was a crewmate of Hollis Wyatt's on the 1906 varsity boat that beat Yale. I would try to stop by the Archives after my last class of the afternoon to check in with her, although I knew it might take her a day or two to retrieve student files from off site.

When I got there at around ten of four, the room was empty except for Eleanor and her bearded colleague Warren, both at work behind the counter. As if Eleanor had been expecting me for dinner and had set up a meal for me, short stacks of old volumes and a file folder were neatly arranged on the table nearest the reference counter.

"How was your weekend?" she asked, smiling at me over the counter. "Productive, I imagine?"

I looked up at her halfway through signing the entry book by the door. Her smile was more than a smile of greeting, she had that twinkle in her eye. No doubt she read my anxious expression and was beginning the calming exercise of a Yoga master. She was nothing if not deliberate and self-contained.

I pulled an ambiguous face of sorts in response, then finished checking the box identifying me as a student, filled the research query line with "Hollis Appleton Wyatt," wrote my research user number which I of course knew my heart, and the time of day. I had looked at my watch upon entering, but nervously checked again and wrote "3:54 p.m."

She had come around the counter and was facing me. Her reading glasses were propped upon her head and she was wearing a blue cardigan sweater over a rather shapeless near ankle-length print dress. On her feet were thick white socks and white low top basketball shoes, specifically Converse Chuck Taylor All-Stars.

"I went to Trask House in Manchester-by-the-Sea and checked old newspaper clippings for references to Emma Conghlan at the Masconomo," I said.

"Didn't find very much, I suspect."

"You're right. Not about Emma, anyway."

"But somehow you came up with the name of Chauncey Bates Porter," she said flatly, but as an inquiry.

"I . . . I was with Becca Wyatt—Hollis Wyatt's granddaughter who is also a freshman here—and she had a copy of the 1906 Class Book. The same one I went through here . . ."

Eleanor had raised her eyebrows at the mention of Becca Wyatt's name.

"We went through it again . . . and it sounds silly, but she noticed a birthmark on the forehead of a member of the Varsity crew, like my grandfather had . . ."

"And you think he could be your grandfather?"

"I know it sounds silly."

"Indeed. It certainly does sound silly," she replied, "but let's have a seat and I can show you what I've got for you."

She led me to a seat at the table and took the chair beside it, moving it closer to me.

"Anything else interesting to be discovered in Manchester-by-the-Sea?" she asked, reaching for the file folder in front of me. I could see the identifying label of Chauncey Bates Porter hand-written on the tab.

I paused, distracted at the sight of the file. "When Becca's great-aunt returns from Europe in the New Year, we'll be able ask her on the off-chance if she knew or remembered him. She didn't remember anyone named Michael Levinson."

"Lillian Wyatt was quite the tennis player," Eleanor replied, gazing at a corner of the ceiling, one of her mini-reveries. "She certainly gave the Curtis sisters a run for their money back in the day."

I wasn't surprised that she knew of Aunt Lillian, and had no idea who the Curtis sisters were, but I had more important matters to discuss.

"That's his file," I said. "How did you get it so quickly from storage?"

"Oh, I managed to get it myself over lunch. Warren held down the fort." Warren, a veritable mountain man with a ponytail in addition to a bushy beard, looked up briefly from his labors and smiled over at us. Eleanor smiled back, then inhaled deeply and set the file down on the table to her left, conspicuously out of my reach. "You see, I quickly checked on things when I got your message. Just the basics, you know, nothing in depth. First, from the Quinquennial Catalogue I saw that Chauncey Bates Porter was not a graduate. Shall we refer to him as Chauncey? Otherwise it's such a mouthful . . ."

I assume I had a blank look on my face, which, smiling once again, she interpreted as my assent.

"Not unusual, of course, not to graduate," she went on. "But it explains his absence from the catalogue, as well as no photograph or bio material as a class member in the Class Album for 1908. Which is right over there." She pointed to a red book in the far second stack. "But as you already know, the yearly course catalogues, in addition to faculty and course listings, include a student list by class, along with addresses. From them I was able to determine that he was indeed a registered student for two years." She pointed to the spine of another red book, at the bottom of a stack of three, that identified itself as the Harvard College Catalogue for 1904.

"Freshman year, 1904-05, Chauncey was residing at 60 Brattle Street." She moved her finger up a volume and up a year on the stack, as if instructing me as to the order in which one chooses a fork. "1905-06, again registered, now living on Shepherd Street, oddly at an address that appears to have been in proximity to the Hemenway Gymnasium." She slid her finger up another volume to the third level. "1906-07, when he should have been a junior, no longer registered."

She waited for a nod from me before moving on.

"Attrition during the second year was not uncommon, particularly for those with academic difficulties, many of whom were privileged slackers. Academic probation—one too many Ds as it were—could ultimately lead to dismissal. Typically, the student would get into academic troubles his first year but would have a chance to remedy matters sophomore year. If things didn't improve, he would be brought before the administrative board and dismissed from the college."

"So you're saying that Chauncey essentially flunked out."

"Actually not. You see, under probation, a student could not participate in extracurricular activities and might even be required to obtain a tutor."

"But Chauncey rowed against Yale in the spring of his sophomore year."

"Precisely. Now there were non-academic reasons—basically bad behavior—for suspension, dismissal, or expulsion that could account for someone leaving the university prematurely. And still other reasons for withdrawal, primarily personal ones, such as finances or ill-health. And a variation on the theme—sometimes students would voluntarily withdraw rather than undergo dismissal. But let's leave that, for the moment, and go to the regatta in May of 1906 . . ."

Eleanor needed to stand to reach and slide over the largest volume on the table, an oversized, bound copy of the *Harvard Crimson* from the second half of the 1905 academic year. With a blue bookmark indicating the particular issue and page, she spread the volume open for me. The article was written just prior to the race and provided a pre-race assessment of the Yale and Harvard crews. It was a long, multi-columned piece. Harvard was favored.

"I can make a photocopy of this article for you later," she said, "but for now just glance at the second and fifth paragraphs of this particular section." Her finger led me to a sub-heading in bold, "Criticism of the University Crew."

I read silently as directed. *"Individually,"* began the second paragraph, *"Captain Wyatt, stroke, has been lately rowing very well. His chief weakness is a tendency to hang at the catch, but he has nearly eradicated that fault. He has a good idea of beat and rhythm and is easy to follow, and benefits from the experience of a prior regatta against Yale."*

I marked my place on the yellowing newsprint and moved it down three paragraphs.

"Porter, number three and only a sophomore, makes his varsity debut as a last minute replacement for Thayer, sidelined by a hamstring strain in practice. A

standout on last year's freshman crew and football teams, Porter is a powerful oarsman with great endurance. He has an unusually long reach and strong drive with his legs and back. He controls his legs well, although at times he has a tendency to hang at the catch and the finish of his stroke can be awkward."

I looked up after finishing. Eleanor closed the volume with a thud and slid it back to its original position. In its place she brought over a stack of two books. The top one was relatively skinny for anything having to do with Harvard; the bottom one I recognized as the Class Album of 1906.

"Moving along," Eleanor said, "I was squeezed for time but some of Chauncey's other activities can be determined by a closer look at the Class Album of 1906. It wouldn't include his freshman or sophomore class activities, and certainly not social club memberships, but it does include clubs and organizations having membership from all classes. For example, it wouldn't record if Chauncey played freshman football, but you could find him listed as a member of something like the *Advocate*, or the *Lampoon*, or the Phillips Brooks House Association, or the Banjo Club. Often there are group photos, and you just need to check the names on the captions, just as you did with the Varsity crew photograph. Club and organization memberships are recorded elsewhere, but let's not get ahead of ourselves . . ."

"Right."

"Definitely what you might call supplemental reading, or extra credit, if this were a course." She took a deep breath. "I don't mean to deprive you of any of your fun, but I couldn't help but briefly look through the Album, and I can tell you with some certainty that it doesn't appear Chauncey wrote for the *Advocate* or the *Lampoon*, nor was he a member of the Phillips Brooks House Association."

I couldn't help but smile. My anxiety had seemed to evaporate as Eleanor had so methodically proceeded with her presentation. I was riveted, but almost relaxed, as if the material were washing over me like flowing warm water.

"I forgive you," I said.

"In that case," she went on quickly, "I may as well tell you that he *was* a member of the Harvard Banjo Club."

At this we both laughed.

She reached over and held the thin volume up as an exhibit, and slid back into her prosecutorial demeanor.

"But where one CAN find listings of an underclassman's activities is in the Secretary's First Class Reports, published two years after graduation. It lists class members, addresses, where the recent graduates are employed. Like the subsequent Reunion Red books, only without the biographies. More pertinently, it lists all the sports teams and scores, along with team and club rosters, etcetera, specific information that doesn't appear in the Senior Class Album."

"Okay."

"But interestingly enough, Chauncey isn't listed, or mentioned in any fashion, in the Secretary's First Report for the Class of 1908." She shook the soft cover volume in her hand like a rattle before setting it back down on the desk.

"But he was a standout member of the freshman crew, and also played football, at least he was according to the *Crimson* article . . ."

"Yes, so they reported."

"And are the freshman crew and football rosters included in the report?"

"Yes, they are."

"That is weird," I said. "Extremely weird."

"King Mongkut of Siam might have referred to it as 'a puzzlement,'" said Eleanor, in a reference that went over my head, "which is why I took it upon myself to walk to the storage facility for his student file. And while there, I checked the Dean's Disciplinary files covering the years 1903 through 1908 and confirmed that there was not an individual file on him. So no evidence of any major disciplinary issues possibly leading to dismissal. The only thing on record was this, Chauncey's student file."

She handed me the file folder, which I set on the table and opened. There were only a handful of documents. First was his application form with the usual personal information, which I skimmed. His residence was in Bozeman, Montana, his father deceased. His early education had been in public schools, but later on he had been tutored privately. The next two pages were letters of recommendation from two of his tutors, which I didn't bother to read. Next, on a half sheet of card stock, were the results of his entrance examination, individual grades written in ink on the pre-printed lined form. He had taken and performed well on "advanced" exams in Greek, Latin, and French. Ink-stamped printing in the lower left corner of the form indicated that he had been "Admitted Clear." Finally, a single sheet of stationery from the office of the Dean of the Faculty, LeBaron Russell Briggs, undated. The Dean had written his signature at the bottom. Aside from that, the correspondence was a concise two words, printed in block lettering in the middle of the sheet: "NEVER MATRICULATED." Period. End.

I turned to Eleanor. "I don't understand."

Eleanor nodded slowly. "Which is exactly why I made a call to the Historical Society in Bozeman not two hours ago and spoke to a very lovely volunteer there. Apparently, they use an index card system, as they used to at the Boston Public Library, so she only had to consult a card catalogue rather than go through old newspapers. She found a file card for him."

"A file card? What kind of file card?"

"An obituary file card," said Eleanor. "It appears that Chauncey Bates Porter was struck by an automobile and died on August 27, 1904 while staying at a New England resort outside of Boston with his mother. The Masconomo House, as it happens."

"Holy shit," I said. I immediately apologized for my colorful language. I was in a library, after all, with a very proper New England librarian.

"No apologies necessary, Mark. I found it pretty fucking amazing myself."

I sat in stunned silence, trying to comprehend what I had just learned. Eleanor stared at me solemnly, like a funeral director overseeing the pallbearers. Neither one of us came out and just said that Poppa had gone to Harvard by assuming a dead student's identity. Instead, after a few seconds, Eleanor asked me if I was all right and I nodded that I was.

"You've found the answer to your grandfather's mystery. It appears he was indeed a Harvard Man, after a fashion."

"And a criminal as well," I said. "I just have so many questions."

Eleanor nodded. "You shouldn't rush to judgment, Mark. As to your questions, to be honest, most will never be answered. But it's still possible to pursue certain things if you care to. From that Secretary's First Report rosters you have a list of teammates who could have been his friends. You can find out who else boarded at 60 Brattle Street his freshman year to learn who his neighbors were. Determining the classes he took and his grades is more problematic, since the individual transcripts were normally kept in the student files."

"But they won't answer the main questions I have."

"No, it isn't likely that they will."

"They're . . . they're just details, strands that don't connect to anything or reveal anything. I want to know why he did it. And what happened. Was he found out? Was he arrested? Did he just decide to leave on his own?"

Eleanor shrugged. "I have some thoughts, some conjectures, if you want to hear them later. But we don't close for another half hour, so if you're up to it . . ."

I nodded.

". . . you can look through the group photos in the 1906 Class Album more closely. Also . . ." She slid another red volume on the table toward me, the only one to which she had not already referred. "This is the Annual Reports of the President and Treasurer of the College from 1905/1906, published in January of 1907. There will be a general report on the College from the Dean of Students at the time, Byron Satterlee Hurlbut. Dry stuff, mainly enrollment statistics and other minutia, but it does include a reference to suspensions, dismissals, and expulsions. No names mentioned, just generalities."

I nodded again.

"After that," she added, pushing herself up from the table, "perhaps you would join me for a cup of tea at the Algiers."

The Algiers was a coffee house and café located in the basement of the Brattle Building, the red brick structure that also housed the Brattle Theatre and the Club Casablanca. I had passed it many times but never ventured in, threatened by its Bohemian ambiance. Through the windows I had seen strong Turkish coffee being poured from copper cezves, which was not a good sign. For an unsophisticated lightweight such as myself—who at the time didn't know what a cezve was—the Algiers seemed an unwelcoming private retreat for graduate students and local artistes engaged in serious conversation, perhaps in a foreign language, and smoking imported cigarettes. The subterranean space was intimate, with closely packed small tables and Middle Eastern décor.

Eleanor was clearly a regular, judging from the warm welcome by the proprietor who showed us to a small window table.

"Your usual tea?" he asked her.

Eleanor looked at me. "A pot for two?"

Not about to ask to look at a menu, I was going for it, whatever it was.

"And baklava," she added.

And thus I was introduced both to the Algiers and Turkish black tea by Eleanor. And baklava. The foreign and intimidating would soon morph into familiar and cool. The barrier broken, I ultimately became a regular at the café, progressing from tea to strong black coffee.

"So what did you find?" she asked, pouring black tea into my tulip-shaped glass from a copper teapot.

"I didn't find him anywhere else except for the Banjo Club. And he's nearly impossible to make out in the group photo."

"Not surprising. Many of the social clubs like the Hasty Pudding and the O.K. Club were for seniors. The major sophomore social organization was the Institute of 1770. Ranking as a top society man would be a far reach for someone from Montana, no matter how wealthy. Still, a banjo playing footballer and Varsity H crewman wasn't doing too bad. And," she added, "I *did* check the sixth catalogue of members of the Institute for his name, anyway, and it wasn't there. But the catalogue was published in 1909, so he could have been scrubbed even if he had made it in at the tail end."

She held up the plate of baklava and I took one for myself.

"And anything interesting from Dean Hurlbut's report?"

To answer her I had to consult my notes. I bent down to pull the loose sheet of paper from my green book bag.

"Four suspensions" I read. "Two for taking unauthorized vacations and two for handing in work not their own. Two dismissed for deliberate cheating and lying, Expulsions for gambling, burglary, attempting to purchase exam questions from a printer, and forgery."

"Doesn't sound much like our Chauncey, does it now?" said Eleanor, bringing the glass to her slips for a careful sip, blue eyes peering at me from above the rim.

"So they didn't catch him?"

"I don't know if they caught him, but one way or another he was found out. Maybe he gave up the game before the hammer came down. Impersonating a dead person for the purposes of fraud is a criminal offence, and he could have been charged if Harvard turned him over to the authorities."

"And you're sure they didn't?" I said, sinking my teeth into my first ever piece of baklava.

"I can't say for certain," replied Eleanor, and you could check the *Cambridge Chronicle* for court notices, but it would be big news and certainly not in Harvard's interests for it to come out. A major embarrassment, to say the least. The press would have had a field day with the story. So instead, they attempted to expunge him. Destroyed his records and pretended he never matriculated. Not exactly airtight, considering his crew photo in the 1906 Class Album, let alone published articles reporting him as rowing for the Varsity crew. There might be other mentions of his name in the local newspapers or the *Crimson*, for all we know."

"Which is why he isn't mentioned in the Secretary's First class report . . . it was published after the fact."

"Exactly, my supposition is that they erased everything they could and hoped for the best. The class catalogues had already been printed, so there was nothing they could do about those. But otherwise, there is no record that Chauncey ever attended Harvard. And we can't determine if they ever caught him without a disciplinary file. Maybe he never had one. Or maybe he did and it was destroyed. No reason to destroy it if he were brought up for indictment."

"So you're saying they covered the whole thing up."

"Indeed, at the highest levels. Harvard Administrations weren't particularly transparent in those days. And why on earth would LeBaron Russell Briggs, Dean of the Faculty, be putting that note in Chauncey's file? That would be in the purview of an admissions officer or recording secretary. Undoubtedly the lower level administrators were in the dark if Briggs took the task on for himself."

At this point I felt the need to contribute my own insights, even if they were things that Eleanor had already figured out.

"Okay." I put down my fork. "Assuming my grandfather worked at the Masconomo House, that represents the source of intersection with Emma and Chauncey."

"Plus Hollis Wyatt lived at Longneck Cove, and could have dined or attended social events at the Masconomo during that summer of 1904, when Emma was performing there. Hollis Wyatt would have completed his sophomore year, and Chauncey was to start his freshman year in the fall."

"And both Emma and Hollis were aware of Poppa's false identity. Hollis addressed his letter to Michael Levinson, so he had to have known, and Emma's inscription on her photograph is a giveaway as well. She made it out to 'C,' and commented that she had to be discreet; namely, I bet, not personalizing it to 'M' or 'Michael.'"

"The rest of the inscription is a giveaway as well," said Eleanor.

I finished chewing the last piece of baklava and recited by memory. "Look how far we have come! An Irish lass and a—"

"Jew!" both of us exclaimed together, perhaps too loudly, as we both instinctively looked around ourselves before breaking into laughter.

"Jinx!" I said sophomorically. Not to make excuses, but at the time I was still only a few months out of high school.

Eleanor was too kind to make me feel like an idiot.

"Jinx!" she repeated, extending a curved pinkie for me to lock hers with mine.

Back at Claverly

"Do you remember me?" The Harvard student, nattily attired in collars, suitcoat and trousers, stood at the threshold of the rooms on the third floor of Claverly. The occupant of the apartment, having opened the door routinely, unprepared, was stunned.

"Why . . . why yes . . . you're that Jew . . ."

"Please invite me in."

"You're not wearing my outfit . . ." was all that Hollis Wyatt could manage to say, an unusual thing to fixate upon, given the circumstances.

"No, I am not," Levinson said, walking into the room past his doubtful host and taking an unoffered seat on the sofa. "I have my own wardrobe now, but please be assured I have not discarded the one you so generously gave me. I considered that it might be inappropriate, or at least beyond the bounds of acceptable irony, if I wore it today. And the name is Chauncey Bates Porter. I'm a freshman here. And it's an honor to call upon an upperclassman."

Hollis ran his hand through his head, adding to a mildly disheveled look, as his collars were already loosened. He cupped his chin in his hand, started to speak, then halted. Why did this alien now sound like someone who had attended St. Mark's? He threw up his hands in controlled exasperation.

"I don't know what to say."

"A gentleman would offer me a drink and a cigar," said Levinson, leaning back into the sofa and crossing one leg over the other.

A number of responses occurred to Hollis, accounting for his pause, the primary one being "How dare you!" but no words came from his lips. His usual deliberateness of speech had crossed the line into a total loss for words, his expression one of sober perplexity. His upheld hands, losing all force of will, collapsed to his sides. He could not fathom the imperiousness coming from this Jew, tricked out like a show pony, and more confounding, his response to him. He cast a hard stare at the intruder, thought to shout "Who the hell do you think you are!" but again said nothing. Spellbound, a continuation of a hard stare was all he could manage.

Levinson responded with what, in retrospect, must be called a somewhat restrained, but unquestionably winning smile.

Hollis, graciously defeated, cracked a smile at the ridiculousness of the situation and went for port and his best smokes. He didn't really know any Jews, but if they were all as intriguing as this one, he might have to expand his social circle. But for the moment, a trial of one was more than enough.

"How did you come up with the alias of Chauncey Bates Porter?" Hollis asked. He was sitting in the Morris chair beside the sofa. The side table between them held a communal hammered copper ashtray and served as the resting place for their glasses. Hollis was working under his initial assumption, as improbable as it was, that Moishe Levinson had applied and been admitted to Harvard using the alias of a man of good family.

"You've no doubt heard of the young Westerner staying at the Masconomo House who was killed by a touring automobile this past summer . . ."

"Of course I had," said Hollis, "but I didn't know that was his name."

Levinson nodded. "And did you know he had been admitted to Harvard?"

Hollis shook his head. An abrupt change in facial expression indicated that the offset cog had abruptly shimmied back into place.

"Mother of God" he cried, bolting forward in his chair. The banjo that had been leaning against the arm of the chair fell to the floor with a clang.

"Hear me out. I was counting on you not knowing his name. That is a good thing."

Hollis leaned back into the chair and reached for his glass. Only after taking a large gulp did he nod his assent for Levinson to continue.

"The story made it into the *Cricket*, but it wasn't something that most Boston papers picked up. And if reported, the account was vague, no names specifically mentioned. Guest at the Masconomo House, from the West, tragically killed, more Talk of the Town gossip than the reporting of news of import. Why do you suppose that was?"

Hollis paused, and availed himself of more port. The heat warmed him, providing relief, but not changing the fact that Levinson expected an answer. An answer Levinson already knew, and Hollis was obliged to confess that he knew more than he had let on.

"I would imagine the papers would be guilty of some impropriety in revealing specifics if the owner and driver of the touring car were a person of prominence."

"Someone you know?"

"Of course I know the family. It would be quite impossible for me not to."

The silence was uncomfortable, Hollis not accustomed to shielding his society peers. He also feared that Levinson would ask him to name the person, in which case he would say that it was not only no one's concern, but was completely irrelevant. Or so he intended, but he was not asked. And would the North Ender have known the name anyway?

"But from what I have heard from . . ." Hollis was trying not to sound defensive, ". . . from people who were on the scene, as well as reliable sources who are quite well acquainted with the person in question and have been privy to direct accounts, it was an entirely unavoidable accident. A tragedy, but no one at fault. No speeding or reckless driving was involved. And certainly no . . . no drinking."

The last was said without conviction, and its inclusion at all was telling beyond Hollis's intentions. Clearly the gossiping old boys at the Somerset knew the score.

Levinson sat silently and let the implication sink in, deeper and deeper until hitting bedrock, before he spoke again.

"'Mister Porter,' as he was known to me, was on the horse path along the park, off the road. The horse—whom I must confess I knew better than Mister Porter—had a name as well, which was Buttercup. But Mister Porter was off his mount and leading Buttercup by the reins, so he could pick flowers for his mother. I have that from reliable sources as well."

Levinson observed that even when deflated and revealing vulnerability, Hollis was still more handsome than pitiable. He was not inclined to twist the knife.

"But no matter," he continued, "all water under the bridge. Had the driver of the car not been so well connected, and had a Westerner not been more or less invisible in certain circles, which is oddly something the two of us had in common, I would not be sitting here with you." Levinson picked up his glass, and showing that there were no hard feelings, smiled disarmingly. Regrettably, it was impossible to remove the knife without twisting it just a bit as it exited.

"So before I go on with my story, shall we both raise a glass to invisible men?"

Hollis, as if manipulated by a puppeteer, found himself reaching forward with his glass.

They clinked.

Hollis was refilling Levinson's glass before he topped up his own.

"I didn't steal his things, you must know that. They were given away, all of his possessions, and I got them. Some of the clothes, and some of the other items that were in his trunk, I sold. But they were all honestly come by. Agnes Booth Schoeffel herself consented to it."

"Except you stole his identity," said Hollis.

"I'm borrowing it. Short term. And I'm not harming anyone."

"And the reason for this . . ."

"I told you before. The first time we met. I want to be a College Man. Or at least see what it feels like."

"You're much more likely to end up learning what a jailbird feels like."

"I'll be circumspect," Levinson replied. "And if anyone is on to me, I can just disappear. Just like that." He snapped his fingers. "Besides, if it weren't meant to be, I wouldn't have taken it this far. And most to the point, it will only be a short excursion."

Levinson explained how the fates, or luck, had been with him at every turn, beginning with his language coaching with a player at the Masconomo House. Even his being at the hotel to begin with was from the serendipity of Stimson's business card in the pocket of the jacket Hollis himself had given him. Finding that card had changed his life, giving a reality to his wildest imaginings. A struggling Jew on Salem Street with few prospects other than a life of backbreaking labor and disrespect was transported from the North End to the North Shore. Though still an outsider, he had become a spectator, and most especially, an onlooker from the inside. He was experiencing first-hand, not from reading magazine stories. The more he saw, the more he wanted to experience for himself a college life he had only read about.

Still he had been cautious, and never fully committed to his plan. When he walked into the Admissions office, prepared to inform Mr. Cram that Chauncey Porter had died and would not be attending, it was obvious that Cram had never seen Porter in person and knew nothing of the tragedy. A well-dressed Levinson had simply walked into his office, said "Chauncey Bates Porter?" in a questioning tone, and the admissions officer had greeted him warmly, extending best wishes to his mother, and offering any help or advice should he need any. He then went on to recommend classes, discussed the procedure for registration, and gave him a number of forms to fill out, a pamphlet on "Rules and Regulations of Harvard College," and a map of campus.

The portly administrator asked if he had been to Hemenway yet to take his physical fitness examination.

"Later today," Levinson said.

"No rush," said Cram, "you can find the location on the map." Finally, in parting, he asked if the accommodations at 60 Brattle Street with Mrs. Murray were suitable. Levinson, who had yet to see the place, responded, "More than suitable."

"I'm sure you're overwhelmed by all this," Cram said, certain that was the explanation for the lad being so taciturn. He would get acclimated in no time.

The next step, similarly anxiety provoking, was introducing himself to Mrs. Murray, and again, as if by Providence, she had never met Porter in person. Evidently, when Mrs. Porter and Chauncey had come to visit—on only one occasion that summer—Mrs. Murray had been vising her sister in

Tewksbury. A niece living in Brookline had been enlisted to let them in to show them the accommodations.

As before, Levinson had greeted the middle-aged woman at the door of 60 Brattle Street with an ambiguous "Chauncey Bates Porter?"

"Pleasure to meet you, Mr. Porter," she had said, and handed him a room key that was lying on the entryway table. "Number seven, third floor, as you know. No pets, I'd like to remind you." She smoothed down her apron. "Keep the noise down, and you'll find you'll have no problems. Meals at seven, noon, and six. I can make some modifications if the need arises and you let me know ahead of time."

"And my account?" Levinson asked.

"All paid up, room and board, for the first term. Deposit for the second term will be due a week before the session starts As I explained to your mother, there are no refunds, so mind yourself not to flunk out!"

Levinson would need to return later to his aunt and uncle's home to retrieve Porter's suitcases as well as his satchel. He had already explained away the new suitcases and his expensive outfit as a bonus from the Masconomo House for his exceptional service over the summer. And he had contrived a cover story to explain his forthcoming absence, telling them that he had taken on work with boilers for the maintenance department at Harvard—a position with potential for advancement—and would be staying in worker accommodations provided by the university. Hiding Porter's treasures had been made easier by no longer sharing the bedroom with Shmuel. His cousin had graduated from Harvard that spring and taken a low level managerial position at a clothing mill in Springfield.

"And you're wearing that outfit for a job as a boiler worker? Uncle Abe had asked that morning. "You look like you're going to a Bar Mitzvah for a Seligman."

"It's Harvard, Uncle, and I'm meeting with a manager. A *macher*. I need to make a good impression. I'll come back for my things."

"A good impression I can understand," said Uncle Abe, "but sometimes I can't understand these *goyim*. To me it seems like putting a bonnet on a brisket."

"So tell me why you're here," Hollis asked. Amazed by the chronicle, he had let things sink in for a few seconds before speaking.

"I'm here to see you," said Levinson, "because you're the only one who can expose me. I don't think any of your friends from the herring incident at the Institute would recognize me. Just you. Unless you agree to keep my secret, everything is off. I can't risk it."

"You know I can't be any part of this subterfuge."

"I'm not asking you to be involved. Just don't tell anyone and don't turn me in."

All that remained of Hollis Wyatt's cigar was a short stump, which he crushed in the ashtray. He then finished off his drink and set the glass on the table with finality.

"I know nothing of this," he said. "Do you understand? I know nothing of this. I'm not so foolhardy to take part in this charade, and I'm certainly not going to risk my neck or reputation for you. Why in the world would I know some Jew named Moishe Levinson in the first place?"

"You wouldn't," said Levinson. "And you don't. But you could possibly meet a freshman from Montana named Chauncey Bates Porter. An outsider to Boston who doesn't have any friends or social connections. Chauncey could use an acquaintance, perhaps, to help him make the adjustment."

"Chauncey might be a gentleman, but is nonetheless a disadvantaged outsider. He is not part of my social circle. And besides, he's a freshman. From whom did you acquire a proper letter of introduction? How could I legitimately make his acquaintance?"

"At Weld boat house, perhaps."

"We have nothing in common."

"You might be correct. For instance, I scored higher than you on Doctor Sargant's physical fitness examination this afternoon. One might say you're not in my league."

Hollis bellowed a laugh. The entire thing was preposterous, but he saw no harm in playing along. He would not stick his neck out of course, but he was curious as to how far Levinson could actually take it. Would he even last the month? Of course, with suitable accommodations and meals for the term . . .

what an item to wager on, if only other people could know!

"All right, Mr. Chauncey Bates Porter. Can I call you Chance? Because you're certainly taking an enormous one, and most in my circle of friends use a nickname."

"See? You've given me good advice already. And people call you . . . ?"

"Hol. Of course, we have no friends or family in common, and you're a freshman, but should I run into you, I'll tip my hat and give you a hearty 'Hallo!' which I suspect is more than you'll get from anyone else. Harvard can be a cold place, you know. And should anyone ask how I've made this strange acquaintance, I met you at the boat house."

Levinson nodded. Everything was in place and he was ready to proceed.

"Yes, but we haven't met at the boat house. I haven't yet gone. For appearances, we will need to meet there. At your earliest convenience. Perhaps sometime tomorrow."

"And why on earth would that be?"

"Quite simply," said Levinson, "because I need someone to teach me how to man a shell. I plan to try out for the freshman crew."

Hollis laughed again. "You're rather presumptuous for a lowly freshman," he said, "but I find your naiveté endearing. And it so happens I can meet you there at four tomorrow, since it's part of my practice schedule."

Levinson smiled, rose to his feet cautiously, and extended his hand. Hollis, who was also tipsy, struggled a bit to get to his feet.

"Unless there's something else I can do for you," he intoned sarcastically, "I'll see you tomorrow. But let's not make a habit of it. I suspect my life would be much easier if I didn't have the misfortune to know Chance Porter at all."

"Now that you mention it," replied Levinson, shrugging his shoulders to get his jacket into place and giving a thoughtful glance to the floor beside the Morris chair. "I wonder if I might borrow your banjo . . ."

A Harvard Man

Hollis took out a two man shell with Chauncey twice that week, instructing and drilling him on the fundamentals of sculling. They were extended and grueling sessions. He already was aware of the young man's strength, but was surprised by his coordination—the first timer was a natural on the water. After those sessions, he rarely saw Chauncey on the college grounds, but often caught sight of him on the Charles, practicing in a single shell. Initially Hollis had feared the foolhardy transgressor would be an albatross around his neck, badgering him for help and increasing his own reluctant involvement in the scheme. Not only did all misgivings dissipate as the weeks passed, but it was evident that the freshman was making a name for himself among his cohorts. That in itself was impressive. Porter was an unknown quantity from the West who had arrived without friends or contacts, making good in an unwelcoming environment. It had been said that for someone in his circumstances, coming to Harvard was the equivalent of arriving in a strange town and living in a hotel.

Chance Porter, from the beginning of the term onwards, was far from lying low and cowering in fear of discovery, anything but invisible. Before the mid-terms, he was already recognized as an athlete as well as an activities man. He had made the freshman football squad despite never having played the game before. The coach, hearing of his spectacularly high fitness score from Dudley Sargent and impressed by his speed and strength at tryouts, had taken a gamble that paid off. There was already talk of recruiting him in the spring for track.

Bobsy Baxter, now a fellow Spee Club member, had a freshman younger brother, so Hollis was able to keep even closer tabs on the goings on in the Class of 1908. He learned that Chauncey had been on the organizing committee for the first freshman smoker, was helping with the management of the Banjo Club pending his actually learning how to play, and had joined the Freshman Debating and the Harvard Memorial Societies. Revealing himself a diligent and serious student, Porter had garnered positive attention from the notoriously prickly professors Barrett Wendell and Charles Eliot Norton, and had even been seen in casual conversation with the universally despised Archibald Coolidge. Geology Professor Nathanial Shaler had suggested he apply for membership in the Natural History Society. And the amiable lecturer Charles Copeland, noting the freshman's weekly attendance at his oratory sessions in Hollis, had reportedly encouraged him to try his hand at writing poetry.

By the time the Christmas holidays had passed, Hollis was no longer seeing the aspirational imposter Jew in Chance Porter—the herring vendor had ceased to exist. But as to be expected, Porter remained a non-entity in society circles. From a family unknown to the matrons seeking eligible men for their daughters, he had not made the list for invitations to at homes, teas, or dances across the river. Had he been from Chicago, Denver, or perhaps even as far afield as San Francisco, his family and financial bona fides might have been obtained and critically evaluated. But investigating a young man from Bozeman, Montana for social appropriateness was too difficult and low-yield for the matrons to bother with. Social tentacles did not penetrate that deeply into the heartland, and for good reason. Digging into earth in which the wells would inevitably be dry was a foolhardy pursuit. Chauncey Porter was predictably overlooked.

Hollis had not intended to introduce Chance into respectable society after the New Year; he simply had the extra theatre ticket from Weatherhill, plus he was curious. It would be a test tempting the fates, since Bobsy Baxter and Teddy Wilcox would be among the usual gang having an early pre-theater dinner at the Parker House, followed by, per custom, the post-show inebriated carousing that typified any number of Sundays during the school year. Was Wyatt subconsciously trying to expose Porter by placing him in close contact with Bobsy and Teddy, who had both witnessed the pickled herring debacle? The moral dilemma was an unusual one—Hollis seldom bothered with moral dilemmas anyway—but he would alleviate any potential ill-willed intentions by informing Chance of the facts beforehand and letting him make the choice as to whether or not to accept the invitation. If he incurred any risk of discovery, it would be his own choice.

Chauncey was startled to open his door to Hollis Wyatt, but recovered as best he could. He wore a heavy winter sweater and casual trousers. An open book and scattered papers on the desk in view behind him, along with rumpled hair, indicated he had been studying.

"Good to see you, chum," he said, "what brings you here?"

"I was hoping an old friend could reciprocate my previous offering of whiskey and a cigar," said Hollis. "Or at least a beer."

Chauncey grabbed his lower lip with his upper teeth, fending off a grimace, and paused to think. "I'm afraid I can offer you nothing more than a cup of tea or a glass of water," he finally answered, motioning Hollis into his suite with an outstretched arm. "Excellent company will have to compensate for the lack. You see," he continued without stammer or indecision, "unfortunately my family has recently encountered a financial reversal, and I am currently a bit short on funds. Frugality reigns supreme."

"I'm sorry to hear that. It happens to the best of us. Excellent company will suffice." Hollis entered, removed his overcoat, and set himself comfortably onto the sofa as if it were a favorite and familiar spot, noting that the large room was more well-appointed than the usual rooming house. Besides the sofa, which only showed mild wear, a bed was tucked into the least obtrusive corner, leaving still enough space for the desk adorned by a brass Harvard lamp and silver desk set, and two side chairs. The lamp, the oriental carpet under foot, and two plaid wool comforters—one hurriedly draped across the desk chair at the sound of the door knocking and the other on the sofa—had been late arrivals to the domicile, along with additional outfits and shirts and accessories from J. Press, earlier purchases unexpectedly delivered in the initial weeks after Chauncey's move-in day. Otherwise, the room was cold, the coal grate empty. Hollis declined the tea, not discerning a way for which it to be easily heated, but accepted a glass of well-chilled water from a large decorative ceramic pitcher. Across the room, in visual counterpoint to the pitcher, Hollis saw his banjo propped in the corner.

"Anything I can do to help?" he asked after taking his first sip of water.

Chauncey shook his head.

"The college office can help you with employment. I'm sure they'd understand your situation."

Chauncey nodded, not revealing he had already made enquires. Uncle Abe had also offered him work at the shop on Sundays, but the logistics were daunting. A trip by streetcar to the North End and transitioning into a delicatessen counter man posed a variety of obvious problems and risked discovery.

"I might sell some more things," he said. "I won't need this carpet to keep my feet warm once Spring comes."

"Well, I'd advise you to stay away from Poco Bennett if you require a loan."

"I'm certain I can find someone less usurious than that old Jew, if it comes to that," Chauncey stated without irony.

This time the thoughtful nod came from Hollis. The moment was awkward, and he questioned his intent to broach the invitation. He had assumed that he would pay Chauncey's costs for the outing, but didn't want his offer to be taken as an act of charity, especially in light of the just revealed situation. He plunged in anyway.

"I come because I have an extra ticket for a Boston show. This Sunday. A group of us are going to dine at Parker's beforehand, and then perhaps have a few drinks afterwards."

While Chauncey gauged his response, Hollis continued. "Baxter and Wilcox, with whom you've made a previous brief acquaintance, will be attending, if that matters to you."

"I don't recall ever having made the acquaintance of either of them," said Chauncey flatly, "but I'm sure that if they are friends of yours, they must be very pleasant chaps. Still, I'm afraid your plans, as entertaining as they sound, are beyond my current means. As you can imagine, I have initiated a very tight budget."

"I'm asking you to be my guest."

"I see."

"And it's not often that a freshman from the Hinderlands is invited for an evening on the town with a group of Institute and Spee Men. Some might consider it an inestimable honor." That he found his own comment amusing came as a surprise and revelation, since he had tried to express himself seriously.

"I'm charmed by what I assume to be a self-deprecating smile," responded Chauncey, who couldn't help but allow his own face to relax in surrender. "I've never been to Parker's," he admitted, more intrigued by the possibility. His nutrition had been exclusively provided by Mrs. Murray, and he was considering removing himself from her table in an effort to economize. "I trust the production is not too much of a somber one."

"I would not think of subjecting my guest to such an indignity," said Hollis. "It's 'An English Beauty.' Have you heard about it?"

"A bit." Chauncey pursed his lips. His decision was made. The costs meant nothing to Wyatt, and pride be damned, here was truly a gift horse if there ever were one.

"The show itself isn't all that noteworthy from what I hear, but the lead actress is the jammiest bit of jam by the name of . . ."

"Emma Conghlan."

"Ah, so you know it . . ."

Hollis was unusually quiet at Parker's. The rather raucous conversation among the other five of them—all junior classmen besides Chauncey—provided the opportunity for studied observation, as if his guest were under a dissecting microscope. Little of academic concern was discussed aside from the usual ridicule of professors and tutors, at which Chauncey had laughed politely without contributing.

Porter's manners were impeccable, his comportment one of ease and self-assuredness. He did not commandeer the conversation or draw attention to himself, but was an earnest listener, thoughtful and serious-minded when he chose to speak, without coming across as stodgy. Hollis recognized that Chance had the advantage of being defined as an athlete, which always commanded respect. But Hollis knew that if Porter were among a crowd of genuine scholars, he could handle any conversation with equal grace and competence. Porter had little to say about parties or teas or women, an aspect of society excluded to him. Not surprisingly he avoided or deflected all talk that could stray to Montana or his upbringing or his family. What others saw as a private person with introvert tendencies, Hollis recognized as deliberate guardedness.

"We're glad you brought Chance along, Hol," Baxter said to Wyatt, who suddenly became aware that he was being addressed. "I know there's a reason I seldom talk to freshman besides my brother, but with this young chap around, I can't remember what it is!" And then, addressing Porter directly, "My brother spoke volumes about how you laid out that Dartmouth tackle on the freshman squad. He still goes on about it."

Porter tapped his lips with his napkin before responding. "It was a square hit," he said. "He should have known better than to lead in with his head." The group reacted with approving laughter to what Porter had merely stated as a fact. He was not inclined to mockery. Upset when his opponent had to be carried off the field, he was more than relieved to learn, upon inquiring, that the injury was not serious.

"There's talk that Coach Farley has his eyes on you as a prospect for the varsity next year," said Wilcox.

"Ha!" said a tall and rather delicate accomplice named Stillman. "Doctor Sargent says it's all in your measurements!"

"Dr. Sargent certainly has his ideas about numbers and proportions," Porter said humbly. "He's designed a specific workout program for me at Hemenway, and unfortunately put me on rather a strict schedule. I'm trying not to disappoint him, but football seems a bit rough and tumble for me. It would be nice to get to leave this place in one piece. I have my sights more on being a varsity oarsman," he continued, catching Wyatt's eye.

"More brutal than football, as far as I'm concerned," opined a lad who had been introduced as Bertie Howe. "Who can take those freezing mornings in a boat on the Charles? You might as well trek to the North Pole! I don't know what you see in it!"

"I think I would find the training table quite satisfying," Porter answered, once more to laughter. Again, he had not intended his comment as a joke. He had been burdened by knowing he was unable to afford Mrs. Murray's boarding house his sophomore year, and finding accommodations he could afford—let alone the funds for meals—would be a problem. He had drawn out budgets and concocted schemes. Were he only able to make the varsity squads in crew as well as football, just as a substitute, at least the meals would be taken care of for much of the year. Thus he found himself gravitating to sports over activities, not from any particular desire, but as a strategy for sustenance. The company of humorous chaps at the *Lampoon* or the literary types hanging around the *Advocate* was certainly more appealing to him than butting heads, but he had to make sacrifices. Accepting scholarship money did not sit right with him.

The group, except for Porter—who had perfected the art of the sip—was well into their alcohol but managed to remain reasonably composed during the production at the Tremont. Afterwards, as was their habit, they meandered to the stage door to catch sight of any attractive young actresses emerging before heading to a bevy of drinking establishments. There was always the possibility of enticing some to join them, since even inebriated Harvard men of obvious wealth held substantial appeal for a class of girls working in theater. But overall pickings were disappointingly slim. 'An English Beauty' was not a musical production with chorus girls, and the cast consisted of a preponderance of males and mature females. Still, the group was rewarded with the appearance of Emma Conghlan herself. Spotting her silhouette in the doorway as she readied herself for an after-show entrance for a group of fans, Hollis Wyatt elbowed his way to the stairsteps and extended his hand to help her down.

"Thank you, but I believe I'm perfectly capable of walking down three steps," she said, nonetheless bestowing a smile of appreciation. Her love of the attention and adoration was not concealed. The Harvard men, while only a portion of the group waiting by exit, were the most vocal and aggressive admirers. Hollis's chums surrounded her with requests for autographs, holding out their programs and patting their jacket pockets for their pens while attempting to ingratiate and distinguish themselves from the herd. It was during this commotion that Emma saw Chauncey Porter at the periphery of her admirers, standing as if frozen by a conjurer's spell. She gave no discernable reaction, but instead reached into her purse for her own pen and began signing autographs, congenially requesting patience and orderly behavior. By this time the doorman along with the stage manager had emerged and come down the stairs, making themselves available as impromptu bodyguards and crowd controllers.

The crowd eventually thinned. Hollis's group remained as hangers on, anticipating that Hollis—the most esteemed and arguably the most charming of the clan—would extend an invitation for the actress to join them for after show drinks. Porter, who had not approached for an autograph, had not moved from where he stood.

"The invitation is most kind of you gentlemen," the actress graciously responded, as if anyone in her position and of sound mind would have strayed off with a bunch of drunk students, "but I must gratefully decline." The stage manager had been aghast upon hearing of the proposition, as he always was— intoxicated Harvard boys were familiar theater patrons and their reputations preceded them—and he noticeably relaxed. But he would stay just in case, to make sure the frisky swells with more money than sense would disperse without argument or additional harassment.

The social circle responded with protestations and moans of disappointment.

"I'm so very sorry," Emma apologized, "but you must understand I'm quite fatigued by the performance and don't have the energy to be entertained by such a large number of eligible bachelors. Just the thought of it makes my head spin terribly!"

They could not help but be placated.

"We will come see the show again!" Baxter shouted jubilantly, his associates in whole-hearted agreement.

"That would be wonderful. But for now, I am in need of a handsome gentleman to escort me home," Emma said, shocking the stage manager, who always pre-arranged for a carriage. "And perhaps just a private drink to calm me down after all this exertion!" She tossed her head back in an overly dramatic gesture, and purposefully sauntered over to Porter. Multiple jaws slackened before dropping.

"Don't think I didn't notice that you were the only one not to ask me for an autograph, whoever you are! You've bruised my feelings terribly!"

Porter allowed his own jaw to slacken. The sudden silence in the alleyway was quickly broken by the sound of hoofbeats from an advancing carriage.

"And what might your name be?" she asked.

"Your carriage is right here, ma'am," the stage manager intervened, motioning the driver closer. Emma ignored him and kept her gaze on her reluctant fan.

"Chauncey Bates Porter," the young man said. "But everyone calls me 'Chance.'"

"Chance? Are you willing to take one?" She grabbed his arm and led him to the carriage, leaving everyone dumbstruck.

Emma whispered instructions to the driver, who had leaned over from his perch to hear them, then extended her arm for Porter to help her enter the carriage door. Without letting go of his hand, she gently pulled him in and down into the seat beside her. The slap of the reins and the cluck of the driver shattered the quiet like a thunderclap. The buggy passed through the side alleyway and had disappeared from view before anyone moved.

"My giddy aunt!" Hollis said to the air, the others still too stunned to articulate anything of substance. Then his recollection: Emma Conghlan had performed at the Masconomo House that previous summer. Gwendolyn Fairfax. And everything rapidly clicked into place—he had discovered Moishe Levinson's tutor, and perhaps his muse! Hats off to him!

"Someone's having a lucky day!" Hollis exclaimed. "Let's go to the Vendome and drink to Porter's off the field pursuits!"

"But he's a FRESHMAN!" moaned Wilcox.

"What? No comments or compliments?" Emma asked him. They had been sitting together, swaying side to side without speaking a word for some time.

Relieved of the burden of keeping their guards up, both were more than comfortable; they were at home with one another.

"Your performance was fabulous," he answered.

"I can only aspire to your own," she replied, "which apparently has been masterful." She pulled back to appraise him. "My, my, my, what a handsome gentleman you are! And now it looks like you're too good for this aging Irish commoner. Just look at you keeping company with the hoity toity. Jazus, Mary and Joseph! I recognized the Wyatt boy!"

"No one's too good for you, Emma."

Emma wrapped her arms around him and kissed him full on the lips.

"You're my leading man," she said. "Did I tarnish your reputation?"

Porter laughed. "I certainly hope so!"

She kissed him again.

"A girl has her needs," said Emma.

"So I've been told."

"And I suppose you'll want an autograph as well . . ."

The amatory adventures of an undergraduate, especially those involving females of the lower classes and especially prostitutes, would not generally recommend a young man to Boston social matrons. Whether denied or the product of willful ignorance, the entire subject was taboo. After all, women in polite society could expect no more from the sons than they could from the fathers. So practically speaking, appropriate decorum only really mattered in the realm of the cotillions and teas; a proper gentleman and a womanizer, at least a discreet one, were never mutually exclusive. Some boys, heaven forbid, exhibited much worse unmentionable and highly illegal behavior. Eligibility for invitations depended upon the proper family background, wealth, and respectful behavior toward their daughters when and where it mattered. No gain was ever achieved in peering, uninvited, behind closed doors.

The specifics of Emma Coghlan's attentions toward Chauncey Porter—whatever actually transpired was only whispered speculation—likely did not make it to the ears of the women across Back Bay who were assembling guest lists. What gossip did emerge, however, was that a freshman from Montana had made a name for himself, garnering respect and admiration from his peers. He was a highly presentable scholar, activities man, and athlete, rumored to be well and favorably known not only among fellow freshman, but prominent upperclassman as well. The tittle-tattle had even penetrated the clubhouse walls of the society and club men, and diffused to earlier generations of alumni, with his name bandied about by the old boys at tables at the Somerset. Was not a potential multi-sport and multi-year Varsity "H" man a worthy topic of conversation? The icing on the social cake was that Porter had been seen in the company of Hollis Wyatt. Under such circumstances, how could Porter's family background and wealth not hold up to scrutiny? Thus came the first invitation to Chauncey Bates Porter for dinner—not afternoon tea—at the Marlborough Street home of the Curtises, a leap in society protocol which shortly thereafter precipitated the avalanche.

Wyatt had not been among the gossip mongers. He not surprisingly received numerous polite inquires and the occasional pestering but remained discreet when asked about the Porter and Emma Conghlan episode. That he had drunk too much and had little recollection about the evening was both a manly and credible response. His chums, however—Baxter, Wilcox, Stillman and the others—felt no such restraints. Sobriety the following morning had not diminished their exhilaration, but enhanced it. Highly animated, they relayed the events to all their friends and club brothers. Hollis observed the effects with growing concern, and was determined to speak to Porter about it.

Porter immediately sensed his raised profile by the chorus of "hallos" of upper classman who strolled past him, including the smartest of the smart set. Of course, they did not stop to introduce themselves or engage in conversation, but more than enough was said by their mere recognition and tossed-off acknowledgements. However, some emboldened peers who shared courses with Porter did broach the topic, and he was prepared for their queries.

"The boys made too much of it," he would laughingly reply. "Miss Conghlan was actually having it on with Baxter and the rest, and she chose me to enable her joke. Believe me, I was hustled out of the carriage as soon as it rounded the corner. But I did manage to get an autographed photograph before that." He stuck to the story, and never mentioned Wyatt's name, as if the group's leader had not been present.

Hollis found Chauncey at his quarters much as he had on his previous visit, wearing the same warm and casual clothes and again interrupted from his studies. This time, however, Chauncey was not surprised to see his visitor, nor to observe that he had come prepared with a bottle of his own whiskey. Hollis took his previous place on the sofa and noted that the banjo was leaning against the back of it—Chance, ever diligent, had been practicing.

"You met Emma Conghlan when she was performing at the Masconomo last summer," Hollis began. He held up his bottle, signaling a request for two glasses.

"You know I'm in the middle of studying . . ."

"Just enough to warm you up," said Hollis. "And so I can take off my coat."

Chauncey used his retrieving of the glasses as an excuse not to answer.

"And she was your tutor and drama coach," Hollis continued, shrugging himself out of his overcoat without standing up.

"Yes. And a damn good one."

"No doubt the capabilities of the student had a lot to do with that." Hollis poured each of them a drink. Chauncey sighed before taking it from him. "Was she more than that?"

"Not you also, Hol," Chauncey snapped, "impugning the reputation of a lady . . ."

"I apologize."

Chauncey took a seat on the sofa beside him and they both sipped in silence.

"I saw several of her performances at the Masconomo House last summer. I went with my parents and sister. We frequently dined there."

"I know," said Chauncey. "I saw you more than once."

Hollis raised his eyebrows.

"I need not remind you that I was an invisible stagehand." Chauncey continued. "But I hid when I saw you, just to make sure."

Hollis shook his head. "I'm afraid now you're becoming awfully visible," he finally said.

"I believed that was the point," Porter retorted. "Were I content to sit at the Jerusalem table in Gore with the other Hebrews as an outsider, I wouldn't have needed Chauncey."

Hollis took a larger sip from his glass. "Well, then . . . I hope you are at least enjoying yourself. Or satisfied. Was the bite of the apple what it's cracked up to be?"

"You do not appreciate what you have," Chauncey said. "And it's not a game for me. I'm not pretending. I'm earning my marks. I give and take my hits on the field. I contribute to the organizations I belong to. I'm valued and judged by my accomplishments. Chauncey just gives me the opportunity."

"Certainly," Hollis said after a thoughtful pause. "And I'd venture to say that no one from the Jerusalem table has ever been invited to dine at the Curtises."

"So you've heard."

"Of course, Bertie mentioned it. Bertie Howe could be a town crier if he were halfway literate. Everyone's heard. At least everyone who matters."

"I plan on declining."

"So at last you find your limit? Discretion being the greater part of valor? Or to put it crudely, a hot case of cold feet?"

"Don't mock me," replied Chauncey. "Actually, I sold my only suitably formal outfit."

"Oh, for pity's sake!" cried Hollis. "I'll lend you one of mine. What are friends for?"

He gulped down what was left in his glass and held it up for a refill. Chauncey obliged, poured a small amount more for himself, then set the bottle back down between them.

As the school term approached its end, Hollis was more and more likely to encounter Chauncey at social events in the city as well as in private Boston homes on Sunday afternoons. He would greet him in a civil manner and engage in brief pleasantries, but otherwise keep his distance, as expected of a prominent soon-to-be rising senior in the presence of a still wet-behind-the-ears freshman. Specifically, he did not include Chauncey with any of his chums on any more city jaunts and unsupervised carousing. Hollis's own associations had been somewhat altered since being invited into the Porcellian Club—a not uncommon progression from the Spee waiting club—ascending from socially rarified air to the summit of the social mountaintop.

Of his close group, only Baxter had also made it to the peak. Although still part of the Club set residing on the Gold Coast, Wilcox had been punched for the A.D. and Stillman was taken by the Fly, small and larger steps respectively from the apex. The Porcellian did not allow any guests, of course, so neither Wilcox nor Stillman could ever cross the threshold and while away inside hours with him and Bobsy. Most of Hollis's time and attentions were focused at the club with his Porcellian brothers, where he took most of his meals, played billiards, drank port and smoked cigars, and did what little studying he did in the club library. His Harvard life had been narrowed by the exclusive and extremely pleasant enclave of the most prestigious of the final clubs, where college men could retire, it had been said, into mutual admiration.

When not comfortably ensconced at the Porcellian, Wyatt was mainly to be found training with the varsity men on the Charles; he was a certain pick to be captain his senior year. And thus his only consistent contact with Porter was at the boathouse. The freshman star oarsman had caught the eye of Coach George Wray, who had discussed the lad's physical abilities with Doctor Sargent and Coach John Farley at length. With some technical help, he could be brought along quickly and possibly serve as a varsity substitute his sophomore year. Wray asked Hollis Wyatt to take the lad under his wing and give him as much attention as he could. The blustery Australian rowing coach would even arrange the schedule so the freshman could manage workouts in the tank. In the meantime, Sargent was concentrating on Porter's overall strength and agility in Hemenway, which included daily workouts with weights and on the rowing machines.

"If we can get this young bloke up to speed for next season," Wray told

Wyatt, "he could potentially lead the crew his junior and senior years. I'm thinking of the future here."

Wyatt nodded absently. Would Chauncey be able to make it back for sophomore year? Even if he weren't found out, how would he be able to continue to pay for his enterprise?

Hollis didn't have to wait long to find out. Ever discreet as to his intentions, Chauncey didn't inform Hollis of his plans or appraise him of any progress. He simply presented his return to the college for sophomore year as a *fait accompli* right before the school year ended. Hollis knew the gist. Chauncey would never accept direct financial aid, but apparently he had finally mentioned his family's financial reversal to someone well-placed in the Administration, who recommended him for work in a Boston law office over the summer. But more importantly, Doctor Sargent would provide free accommodation for his prized physical specimen in a partially cleared out equipment storage room in Hemenway, as well as a stipend for maintaining the exercise machines and helping to administer and record the physical education assessments for undergraduates. While Sargent had ideally wanted him to play football as well as crew, Porter graciously bowed out of the former while agreeing to help manage the exercise workouts for Coach Farley's varsity squad in exchange for a spot at the Memorial Hall training table from the beginning of term. With no need for deal-making, he would rightly assume a position at the crew training table in the Spring, as he had hoped. The room and board financial problem was mitigated.

Chauncey Porter, already a familiar figure at the gym, was given a key to the facility and 24-hour access to the equipment, showers, and toilets, not to mention a small room of his own, beginning directly after Commencement week. The rooming arrangement, an unorthodox one, was known only to Sargent, his assistant, his secretary, the regular janitorial staff, Tom the postman, and Coaches Farley and Wray. The only student who knew, of course, was Hollis Wyatt, whom Chauncey had chosen to inform in confidence once everything had been settled.

"I'll be taking up quarters in Hemenway when the term ends, thanks to the generosity of Doctor Sargent," he told Hollis shortly before the year's big regatta. The news came out of nowhere. They were floating in the middle of the Charles in their two man scull; a rare spring session together since Hollis was usually tied up with spring practices with his teammates in the eight man boat. "And I'll be working in a law firm over the summer," Chauncey quickly added. "So no need to worry about me. Just want to assure you that I'll be back for fall term."

Hollis was incredulous. "You're going to live in Hemenway?"

"It's a very favorable situation, which I can tell you more about sometime," replied Chauncey with nonchalance. "Besides, as you well know, I never entertain in my rooms anyway. So what difference does it make?"

Hollis, who had twisted his body around to directly look at his rowing partner, shook his head in disbelief.

"But keep it under your hat. It's a rather unusual arrangement. I'm not sure if the Administration even knows of it."

Hollis, robbed of his initial chance to respond, could only blink. Chance Porter would never cease to amaze him. "Of course."

"Let's call it a day. You've got the big race coming up and I don't want to wear you out." Chauncey put his oars in position. "However, if you hear any rumors of Hemenway being haunted, please try to dispel them."

"Haunted?"

"You know, reports of eerie sounds of moving chains and such in the middle of the night." He paused to smile. "That will be me on the rowing machine."

Houdini

"I thought you'd never get here!" Chauncey grabbed Hollis's arm as soon as he was visible near the entryway and pulled him roughly from the jostling crowd.

The echoing din as excited students rushed to find seats in a frantic and directionless swarming was a steady assault to the ears, punctuated by the cacophony of wooden seats falling into position. Sanders Theatre was packed, and the exhibition didn't begin for another quarter hour. Quickly glancing upward as Chauncey tugged him toward the front of the auditorium, Hollis saw that nearly all the balcony benches were filled, and students had already abandoned their hopes for a place to sit and were claiming their own standing spots in a line along the upper back wall. On the main floor, a diminishing number of young men were side-stepping through the rows to claim the remaining available seats, while those still stuck in limbo within the aisles craned their necks and desperately searched for gaps. Ultimately the standing room line would be three persons deep in the balcony and deeper on the main floor before the Cambridge Fire Department Inspector put an end to additional occupancy, which was met with a chorus of boos. A disappointed group outside on the Delta by John Harvard's statue lamented, chastising themselves for not arriving earlier and debating alternative plans for the evening.

"I've saved you a seat," shouted Chauncey, still leading Hollis along behind him, as they made their way to the sole unoccupied chair in the center of the front row. Chauncey ripped off the crimson ribbon and "reserved" sign that were draped across it, and guided his friend into the seat with a gentle push.

"You look sharp tonight," Hollis shouted in response. Chauncey was wearing his best non-formal suit and his hair was neatly brillantined into place. Despite his many responsibilities in the final preparations for the event—with the added bother of tending to Hollis Wyatt, who had promised to arrive early—Chauncey was unflappable, a picture of calm amidst the human storm. Hollis noted that Chauncey was not even perspiring, while he—who had only traveled a short distance amidst the throng—already felt urged to tend to an itch under his collar. Nevertheless, sophomore Chauncey Porter, the brainchild and organizer of Harry Houdini's complimentary performance at Harvard in late October 1905, had no time for small talk.

"I only hope you were late because you were practicing your knots," Chauncey said dismissively in parting.

Hollis Wyatt leaned back in his seat, unbuttoned his suit coat, and sighed. He had no idea how Chance had pulled this spectacle off. They had discussed the event briefly a few weeks earlier where they always had their discussions—in the middle of the Charles, in the respite after a series of two hundred meter practice sprints. Chance, as usual, didn't go into details of the arrangement or how he had managed them. Hollis had already heard that the escape artist would be coming to Harvard and seen the flyers posted all over campus, but had no idea that Chance was behind it. People were paying good money and fighting for tickets to see Houdini for his short run at B. F. Mark's Theatre, so why would he give a free performance at Harvard?

Winded from the strenuous row, leaning forward on his oars, Chauncey had panted, "I've organized a performance by Houdini at Sanders Theatre. You must come."

That was the extent of it. As it happened, Chauncey had learned that A. Paul Mark, the assistant general manager of his father's burlesque houses, had been in the Class of 1901. He had taken the initiative to approach the young alumnus directly with his proposition for the exhibition, which he volunteered to organize and manage, and Houdini had agreed to it. Hollis was oblivious to this Houdini-Harvard connection primarily because Paul Mark had not been an Institute man. His father's success in burlesque was not a qualifier for any significant social standing in Wyatt's circle, so recent graduate Paul Mark, as far as the smart set was concerned, was among the faceless hoard of unknowns.

Later, Chauncey had left a long length of thick rope for Hollis at the reception desk of Claverly, accompanied by a note. "You'll be called upon to help secure our special guest with rope," it read, as if the task entailed nothing more than tying up a package with string. The unsigned message concluded: "Might I make a suggestion that you practice your knots?"

As he had sailed since early childhood and had considerable experience crewing on his father's schooner, Hollis was adept with the most common and practical sailing knots—but most of them were hitches and inadequate to the task at hand. So he made a rare visit to Gore Library for a manual and decided to master the double fisherman and gunner's knots, more appropriate for binding a man than rigging a sail or securing a boat to the dock. These he diligently practiced in his parlor, envisioning himself a pirate and holding his roped-in Morris chair captive.

At 7:35 p.m., a poised and confident Chauncey Porter stepped onto the Sanders Theatre stage and held both arms up for the crowd to quiet. It was a motley crew, and he smiled as he scanned the audience. For a moment in time, the aristocracy, the middle class, and the laboring class of Harvard were admixed, the social order obliterated. The great Houdini was going to perform for free, equally for the wealthy as for the financially struggling. The stage was empty except for a curtained box about four feet in height by two in width and depth and a single chair with a straitjacket draped upon it. Porter introduced himself simply by stating his name and class, and gave a short speech thanking Houdini as well as the kind people at B. F. Mark Enterprises who had made the special visit possible and complimentary to all attending. The students cheered. Once again raising his arms for quiet, Porter then introduced the escape artist himself, who burst from the cubicle to the surprise and delight of everyone. The immediate applause was thunderous and lasted over a minute.

Houdini was a short and compact bundle of sinewy muscle, with prominent bulging veins in his arms and legs. His eyes were light and piercing, his nose aquiline, and his wavy brown hair appeared windswept. He wore a black skin-tight strongman's outfit, scoop-necked and sleeveless on top and extending to mid-thigh on the bottom. After making his own gracious remarks in a soft-spoken manner, he explained that he would give a demonstration of three different types of escapes. Then, obviously fed by someone in the know, Houdini apologized for being unable to attempt the most difficult escape of all, which was from Professor Norton's lecture. The crowd roared with laughter. Houdini would have a hard time finding a more appreciative audience. He was glad he decided to throw in the comic line that the Porter fellow had suggested.

The first escapes were from three different types of handcuffs, affixed in succession by invited participants, each entering from offstage with their particular variety of manacle, and each receiving a more spirited reception than the previous. First was the Harvard University Chief of Police, in full uniform for greatest effect, followed by the popular Dean of Students Byron Hurlbut, and for the finale, the bushy-bearded Irishman John Lovett, the beloved Harvard Square fruit vendor and Harvard team mascot commonly known as John the Orangeman. After each "jailer" affixed his cuffs with aplomb and ceremony—John the Orangeman of course hamming it up for the crowd—Houdini crouched behind the curtains of the cubicle and soon emerged, hands free, in less than a minute for each.

For the second escape, Houdini was painstakingly secured in a straitjacket from the Danvers Asylum by Dean of the Faculty Lebaron Russell Briggs. Before doing so, however, the Dean proudly held up the jacket for the audience to see that the words "Academic Probation" had been emblazoned on the apparel of confinement, which caused much laughter. In full view, through a series of trunk convulsions, grinding his shoulder on the floor, unbuckling the strap with his teeth and undoing the strap behind his neck with his sleeve-enclosed hands, Houdini eventually pulled the garment over his head with about five minutes of intense effort. To a chorus of cheers, Houdini rammed his fist upward, straitjacket dangling from it, as if he had vanquished an opponent with a knockout punch.

Houdini walked over to the cubicle and bent down to retrieve a large glass of water that had been set behind it, and then with his free hand slid the chair to center stage, where he sat down and acknowledged the crowd. The noise in the theater had not diminished. At this point Porter walked onstage carrying a long coil of rope.

"While Mister Houdini has a moment to rest," he shouted, then repeated two more times, holding up his free arm for quiet, "we will avail ourselves of the opportunity to tightly secure him with this rope to the chair in which he sits so comfortably. Do you think I have enough? It's only sixty feet!" Porter played to the shouting crowd, shaking the looped cord vigorously. "To aid me in this task, I am calling upon much needed help from our resident expert knotsman, who also happens to be the next Captain of the Varsity Eight . . . Hollis Wyatt!"

While knowing it was coming, Wyatt was still startled by the introduction. He sheepishly stood up amidst cheers of approval, waved at his fellow students, and hopped up on to the front of the stage. After Porter relieved Houdini of his emptied water glass, Porter and Wyatt worked over their bindings, tying Houdini to the chair in every possible way around his chest, neck, arms and legs, cutting the rope into appropriate lengths with a knife, or trimming off excess rope after each individual knot was completed. There was no impatience from the crowd during this painstaking process; rather they reveled in the completion of each knot, shouted out suggestions, and grew in excitement and encouragement as the binding progressed to its completion. The escape artist played along, reacting during his binding with alternating looks of mock apprehension, dismay, and terror. At the end, with unanimous consent from the crowd that the binding was complete and inescapable, Houdini was smiling broadly. Most of the remainder of his body, covered in overlapping stout rope, could not be seen. He was wrapped like a mummy except for the knots protruding around him like random blossoms on a flowering tree.

Ten minutes later, amidst a continual and undulating echoing clamor that reverberated like a full stadium squeezed into a library reading room, Houdini was free and the chair in splinters. The gladiator in the wood-paneled coliseum raised his arms for the crowd and then lowered his head in a bow. So still was he that it appeared he might have nodded off to sleep standing up.

The room seemed to calm down with him. Then abruptly, a disappearing act in full view, he surprised everyone by darting out the stage side exit. Having escaped the theater, he bounded across the Memorial transept, out the south doors—held ajar by Paul Mark—and around to the stairwell to the basement of Memorial Hall, which had been unlocked. For several moments the students still sat in relative silence, wondering if he would be returning or had just left them there. Finally, amidst a crescendo of chairs clattering, twelve hundred enthused Harvard men congealed themselves into a molasses flow to the bottleneck of the two main exits, while on the stage a cluster of undergraduates scrambled for pieces of rope as souvenirs.

"That was wonderful, Mr. Houdini!" Porter gushed the instant he was led into one of the smaller classrooms in the basement of Memorial Hall. Paul Mark had retrieved him and escorted him to the room, where he found himself alone with the escape artist. The door clicked behind him as Mark bowed out from the meeting. He and a couple other well-placed accomplices would continue to roam the transept and the immediate outside environs of Memorial Hall, spreading false rumors as to where Houdini had disappeared. Per prior arrangement, and reasonably certain that the coast would be clear, Houdini would meet a carriage waiting for him on Kirkland Street at 9:30 p.m., which would take him back to the Parker House.

The magician had changed into his street clothes and sat alone at the head of the classroom with his legs elevated and crossed on the desk in front of him. Near the door were two matching valises of slightly different sizes, latched and ready for transport. Porter stood awkwardly at the door, hands clasped. He rubbed them nervously.

"It's such an honor," he effused.

A nod and a smile, but the eyes were piercing. "I asked Mr. Mark to bring you here so I can thank you for the invitation. But also for another reason."

"Yes?" Porter was curious as to what the great performer could want of him.

"Would you like me to autograph a photograph?"

"Of course. Of course I would. I didn't ask because I didn't want to impose."

"Then bring me my bag."

Porter took a step forward and reached down for the closest one, the larger of the two. Suddenly he froze, bent over and arm extended, and looked back at Houdini. The request had been in Yiddish.

"Der klenerer." The smaller one, Houdini clarified.

"I speak German," Porter attempted to cover, and realized how weak and idiotic it sounded.

"Breng es aher aun zits zikh," Houdini said as if were ordering a child. *Bring it here and take a seat.* He removed his legs from the desk, scooted his chair back, and rapped his fist on the table.

Levinson set the valise on the desk where indicated and took the nearest seat.

"The other reason was not to give you my autograph," Houdini went on. "I'm a creature of habit, and misdirection is one of them." He opened the valise and removed a stack of cabinet cards, then carefully untied the thin blue ribbon that bound them. After removing one and setting it down on the desk, he methodically retied the ribbon in a simple bow around the stack and put the cards back from where they had come. Firmly he shut and latched the valise and pushed it away from him on the desk. Levinson watched in silence, his heart in his throat.

"The other reason," Houdini continued, pulling a pen from his coat pocket, "is that being an illusionist, I am always interested in other . . . illusionists."

"Please don't tell anyone," said Levinson.

"Fortunately for you," said the man who was born as Erik Weisz, "illusionists are by necessity masters at keeping secrets. People who try to expose me are such a nuisance. Why would I want to be like them? I simply need to satisfy my own curiosity."

"How did you know?"

Houdini feigned taking affront. "You think I'm just some *zhlob*? I'm the Great Houdini! You think you can fool the Great Houdini?"

"I had never planned on encountering the Great Houdini," Levinson replied, smiling in spite of himself.

"All right, so it is like this. At first your hands when you were tying me. A workman's hands. And you speak just a bit too well, almost staged, which sounded strange to my ears. But occasionally the tell of, just a trace of the Old World lilt. Of course, I am more intuitive and a better listener than the average Harvard man, who is more interested in what he himself has to say. And I have the advantage of knowing Yiddish myself. But you are very good. And I say that as from one illusionist to another."

"Mit der tseyt ken afilu a ber zikh lernen tantsn," Levinson answered. *With time even a bear can learn to dance.* The words in Yiddish felt strange coming from his mouth. But it was a pleasant sensation, almost producing a tangible pleasant aftertaste.

"Geshmak iz der fish fun yenems tish." Tasty is the fish from someone else's table. Houdini sighed. "I hope you have not done harm to anyone."

"I have not. I would not. Of this I can promise."

"Good. Then I only hope you do not harm yourself."

Levinson, looking down, had no words in reply.

"If it makes you feel any better, I always hope the same thing for myself . . . especially when I am underwater." The stunt performer smiled expansively, and Levinson felt his shoulders relax downward, away from his ears.

"What is your real name?"

"Moishe Levinson."

"They called you Moishe?"

"Yes . . . or Moey."

"So we're agreed that you won't call me Erik and I won't call you Moey."

"Yes, sir."

"So explain to me why. To get an education?"

Levinson shook his head. *"Ikh viln tsu zeyne a kolege mentsh."* I want to be a college man.

"And you can't exactly become a *kolege mentsh* at a Yeshiva, I imagine."

"No," answered Levinson, "I'm not that kind of Jew anyway. But a Jew can't be a college man anywhere. Not a real American college man. Like in the stories. Like Dick Merriwell. Like Dink Stover."

Houdini nodded, took the cap off his pen, and began inscribing the photograph. He held it upright in his left hand and blew on it a couple of times, then reached across the desk and held it across to Levinson. During the pause, Levinson had stood up on his own initiative, feeling he had said enough. He feared that if he allowed Moishe out for too long, everything would unravel. He took the small photograph in his left hand, where the inscriber had directed it.

Houdini stood up himself and extended his right hand across the desk for it to be shaken. The handshake was firm, and Houdini made it firmer by bringing his left hand over to envelop Levinson's hand like a clam shell.

"I wish you well, young man," said Harry Houdini, still clasping, "but let me ask you another question, an important one." He squeezed his hands together as if shaping a meatball. "Have you given any thought as to how you will escape?" For a couple of seconds he pressed even harder, modulated not to cause pain, but to manifest his total control. Levinson could not find words; he was even unclear as to which version of himself he would be escaping.

"Give it some consideration," said Houdini, abruptly releasing his grip and pushing both forearms outward in a flourish. The illusionist held the grand gesture for dramatic effect, keeping his hands motionless and separated, as if showing someone the size of a fish.

Moishe Levinson's arm involuntarily dropped to his side, his freed hand slapping against his thigh as if he had been stricken by sudden paralysis.

Hollis Wyatt stared at the cabinet card in wonderment, shaking his head.

"What a treasure," he said. "You must have it framed! This deserves a suitable carved frame!" He glanced up at Porter, whose expression indicated that such an extravagance was not part of his budget.

"Listen, chum," he went on. "Let me take it and have it framed by our man in Boston. It will be my gift to you. I insist."

Porter relented. They were sitting in The Holly Tree having a cup of coffee. The establishment was crowded, many in the audience having headed there after the Houdini event. The room was noisy, most of the patrons in animated conversation about the escapes they had witnessed. Hollis had hurriedly suggested the meeting earlier, whispering in Porter's ear during the confusion after the performance. He avoided being seen alone with Porter publicly, but after their very public joint demonstration, there seemed little rationale for efforts at discretion. Realizing that perhaps the popular haunt was too public for the conversation he had intended, though, he made small talk about the exhibition as the others were doing, and after Porter had drained his cup, suggested that they take a stroll.

"I've been meaning to mention something to you," Hollis began, as soon as the door closed behind them. They began to walk.

"Yes?"

"There's been talk among the Institute men . . . talk about you."

Porter walked for a few paces alongside Hollis before responding.

"Is that so?"

"It is indeed so."

Porter stopped walking and turned to his friend, who stopped with him. "But haven't they selected everyone?"

"There's the final group of ten remaining," explained Hollis, "and I have it on good authority that your name is among that list of ten. I must confess that . . . that I did not see this coming."

"Holding up the rear," said Porter, feigning disappointment. "Please tell me I'm ninety-nine and not the one-hundredth . . ."

"I'm not privy to the gruesome details," Hollis answered with a laugh, "even as a former first pick of the first ten, considered by some Proper Bostonians to be the greatest honor a man can achieve." He topped the sentence off with a wink.

"And well deserved," said Porter, "but they say that if you don't rank within the first forty, you're almost as much of an outsider as a non-society man."

"I am delighted to have discovered a realm in which you are not in my league. You cannot arm wrestle your way into the Social Register." Hollis laughed.

"And here all along I was believing the smart set to be a meritocracy," Porter replied in mock earnestness, "the only predicate to success being the quality of one's pickled herring."

Hollis laughed again, then nodded thoughtfully before speaking. "Chauncey Porter has the stigma of Montana to deal with," he said, "the cross you must bear for him." Then he turned more serious. "There is a logistical issue, of course. You cannot be retrieved from Hemenway . . . that would be impossible. Few even know you are living there."

Porter nodded.

"And not only do you not know that you've been elected, you do not know when they will come for you."

Porter looked at his companion more intently.

"You have a proposal?"

Hollis nodded. "Baxter's younger brother Curtis, your classmate, was elected in the third ten. He's now involved in matters of recruitment and ceremony. I've taken the liberty to let it be known that you are living with me in Claverly."

"Starting when?" Porter asked.

"Starting tomorrow."

"I can't impose on you like that . . ."

Hollis cut him off. "You assume too much. It is no imposition and you overblow my generosity completely. In fact, you need only be my roommate for one night."

The following evening, Hollis Wyatt and Chauncey Porter sat in the window seat in the Claverly sitting room in total darkness. Shortly after midnight they first heard the familiar melody of the Institute song in the distance. Chauncey leaned his forehead against the window so he could make out the points of candlelight snaking around the corner from Dunster to Mt. Auburn Street. A procession of upwards of a hundred men slowly approached, with spectators following at the margins. The men holding candles were all in formal attire. Were they not in such a mood of gaiety and enthusiastically singing, or in formal garb, one might have misconstrued the group as a lynch mob.

"Step back from the window," Hollis said, and Porter did as instructed.

They assembled outside of Claverly in a semicircle, the string of candlelight now a star-filled sky on the pavement. A selected group of ten men passed their candles off to nearby fellows and entered the building. Their footsteps pounded on the stairs as they continued to sing. Soon they were pounding on the door and screaming "PORTER! PORTER! CHAUNCEY BATES PORTER!"

Porter remained immobile a few steps from the window as Hollis ambled toward the door to the bedroom. He turned as he passed through the doorway, and instructed Porter once more.

"Let them in now," he said. "This has nothing to do with me." And he disappeared behind the closing door.

Porter was soon swarmed and helpless, manhandled down the stairs to the street. The crowd was screaming and chanting his name. He was jostled among the revelers, disoriented and staggering, bouncing off bodies and trying his best to stay on his feet. Arms waved and surrounded him, as if he had been thrown into Medusa's scalp. And then the arms and bodies seemed to coordinate, and Porter was lifted off his feet and carried atop his pursuers. They reassembled into a line and began marching away, again singing the Institute song. Porter would be subjected to an evening of drinking and celebration, and when he would awaken the following morning, hung over and bruised, his runnings—a week of hazing and initiation—would begin.

The crowd was jubilant, and once he got his bearings, so was Porter. Bouncing in the air, carried by his new cohort, he realized how much he had to look forward to. The possibilities at Harvard were endless. New intellectually challenging classes would begin, as would crew training. He would perform with the banjo club, he would attend Copeland's Wednesday lectures as well as sports events. He would submit his poetry to the *Advocate*, and perhaps present himself to the *Lampoon*. Established on the guest list for teas and dances, he would meet some of Boston's loveliest and enchanting young ladies. Surely an invitation to the Hasty Pudding would come his senior year, and he could perform in the farces. He might join the O.K. Club, and the Signet.

A waiting club, and even one of the less prestigious final clubs were now possibilities: the Fly, the Delphic, the Fox. He would be burdened with money for dues, of course, but that would be no obstacle; he was certain he could come up with the funds somehow. But for now, he would have access to his own clubhouse, where he could read and play pool and socialize: the Institute of 1770, of all places, where last he had entered carrying a large jar of Uncle Abe's pickled herring. That was where his odyssey had begun. And now he would be a member! Porter tried to focus as he looked ahead and to the side and saw the flickering of the candles. He looked upwards at the flickering stars. The music was hypnotic and filled his ears. He wished he could free up an arm so he could wipe away the tears streaming down his face.

Hollis Wyatt stood alone by his bedroom window in the darkness, watching the procession retreat down Mt. Auburn street, now carrying Chauncey Porter's outstretched body over their heads. Like a football hero being carried off the field. Or perhaps like a thief brought down from the cross.

"Mother of God," Hollis Wyatt heard himself saying. "What has become of this world? Moishe Levinson is an Institute Man!"

Waiting

Before leaving for Christmas break, I had tracked down the short single column article in the *Crimson* announcing the tenth and final "Ten" for the Institute of 1770 for 1905-06. And miraculously, there it was: "C.B. Porter, Bozeman, Montana," the next to last name listed. I blinked, rubbed my eyes, and read again. Between my hours spent studying and the time spent in the in the Archives, I was sleep-deprived and found myself frequently on the verge of tears. In response I had resorted to becoming highly caffeinated, which still didn't combat continuing drowsiness, although definitely contributed to my inability to sleep.

My eyes were burning as I moved my finger along the lines of the brief announcement several times; no fanfare, just the names. I had fully anticipated another dead end, and was only going through the tedium of investigative motions out of compulsion. My time would have been better spent hitting the books—in my case needlessly pummeling them into submission—or even going to the Plough and the Stars to get drunk. But I was restless and couldn't concentrate well, and mindless, fruitless tasks served a purpose. There wasn't much else I could do until after break, when I might get a chance to talk to Aunt Lillian.

"Well, this certainly gilds the lily," Eleanor said when I showed the announcement to her. That his name had not appeared in the 1909 Catalogue of the Officers and Members of the Institute of 1770 substantiated Eleanor's supposition that Harvard undergraduate Porter had been "erased" from the record after the fact. "It appears your grandfather was the first, and only Jew ever to belong to the Institute of 1770."

"That no one will ever know about . . . or admit to," I replied. "It doesn't still exist, does it? The Institute?"

"No, it dissolved and became absorbed by the Hasty Pudding in 1927."

I didn't respond. My initial elation had surrendered to despondency, my thoughts swirling like water lazily draining in a partially clogged sink. I felt fatigue to the point of collapse.

"Well," I finally said, "I suppose this finally gives legitimacy to that 'Chosen People' business . . ."

"Maybe it's time to put an end to this," Eleanor said, a look of concern clouding her face like a thick mist. "What you've discovered is absolutely remarkable. There may not be any further to go."

"I'll just follow up with Aunt Lillian," I said, "and after that I'll stop."

"That sounds like a reasonable plan."

I was holding out hope for the meeting not because I was expecting anything earth-shattering—possibly Aunt Lillian had never even come across Chauncey Porter—but because it gave me another opportunity to have some alone time with Becca. We hadn't seen much of one another after my notable Manchester excursion, and it seemed more and more likely that our sex had been a one-off—the stars aligning with alcohol, drugs, and perhaps a touch of mania—than the beginning of a serious relationship. She was her customary acerbic self, with sarcastic barbs passing for her usual manner rather than contempt. But there was no inkling of a special warmth or intimacy, no recognition or admission that we had crossed any sort of boundary. Would Poppa being an Institute Man somehow make me more eligible?

She was busy, it appeared, with Winchester in Hamilton or listening to her music assignments, or with a study group she had joined with fellow History and Lit majors. I felt calling her to arrange something casual or spur of the moment was invading her privacy, as if I had become a bother. The few times I called a different unrecognizable female voice answered. None of the rooms in North House had individual phone lines; only a common phone on each floor with an inordinately long extension cord. Anyone nearest to the ringing phone would answer and see if the desired party was available, shouting out her name or walking down the hallway to knock on her door. I couldn't be sure, when told that she wasn't around by some anonymous Cliffe neighbor, if I was being given the runaround or not.

I had managed a few times with her that could qualify as "dates": a lunch at the Pamplona—where she introduced me to quiche and Calvados, a movie at the Orson Wells, and the Joni Mitchell concert. The crowning blow, to which I've already alluded, was her informing me after the concert that she had a date with a junior tutor in Lowell House at 11 p.m. My grand plans of another bout of sex were dashed like waves against a rock face. Would she be having sex with the junior tutor, a graduate student in Sociology? On those few occasions when I saw her on campus, she was always accompanied by a preppie-looking male or males. She had already specifically mentioned a "close" friend of hers, who had been a couple classes ahead of her at Milton, who was a Porcellian.

"You probably won't be punched by any of the clubs next year," she told me one afternoon, on one occasion after I had seen her with her coterie of male admirers. Had she been talking to her club suitors about me? Recruiting parties happened sophomore year.

For me the clubs existed more in a theoretical and historical context than anything else, and I had not considered joining one a possibility. But I had never before felt excluded until she pointedly brought it up. On what basis would I not be acceptable to be punched? Why was I an automatic reject?

"I don't think I'm interested, anyway." I said.

"Well, how convenient for you, then."

She informed me that her father was a fourth generation Porcellian, and I wondered if club membership was a prerequisite for a serious relationship with Becca Wyatt. The Wyatts hadn't maintained themselves as Wyatts over the generations by social slumming, after all. I had previously blamed my insecurities on being an untraveled, unsophisticated public school kid from the Midwest. But education and travel and sophistication could be acquired. I was not destined to be a rube forever; Harvard had taught me that. But Harvard had also shown me society was not so easily transcended, and I was naïve in believing a Jewish kid from Kansas could fulfill the expectations of Becca Wyatt or her family. Of course, it never occurred to me that Becca might be struggling against her own payload of expectations.

My relationship with Becca was not something I could discuss with Eleanor. Certainly, she knew the score. She knew we had been working together and seeing each other, and no doubt she sensed how infatuated I had become. She never inquired about Becca, but I suspect she watched me with nervous anticipation, as one would a tightrope walker making his way between high rises without a net, gale force winds in the forecast.

"It's a reasonable plan," Eleanor repeated.

"What is?" I had no idea how long I had been in my reverie, staring off into space.

"Concluding your research after you hear from Lillian Wyatt."

"Yes."

"There always has to be an endpoint to historical research, and it always feels like the endpoint is arbitrary, because in fact, it usually is. You can never learn the complete story. You answered the questions about your grandfather—or at least as much of it is answerable—and discovered a very interesting bit of Harvard history along the way. No mean feat."

"But is it history? I mean, history is past, right? We're presuming things have changed, but have they really?"

"Some things appear to have changed more than they have, because we have insight into them. But what are you getting at, Mark, specifically?"

I took a deep breath.

"Could I ever be a Porcellian?"

"No."

"Why not?"

"It isn't your world. You know that."

"What about other clubs? Will I be invited to join other clubs?"

"Do you want to?"

"Not particularly. I don't think so. But it would be nice to be considered."
I waited for her to answer.

"You're at a disadvantage," she said, "because you're not part of an established social clique. You didn't attend a prep school or a boarding school. You're not from a wealthy or prominent family. You're just not as connected as others are.

Those are just circumstances . . . but they don't diminish your worth. Still, that doesn't mean you couldn't be in a club. That doesn't totally exclude you."

"What about being Jewish?"

Now it was Eleanor who took a deep breath.

"I would be lying if I told you that some clubs might find that as a disqualifier. But not something ever expressed; it's always been more insidious than that. But things are improving. I think the Owl and the Fly may have admitted Jewish students, at least one or two. And the same is happening for African-Americans."

"I'm not naïve," I said. "I understand all this. It's just that I find myself relating to my grandfather in a very real way. Not as extreme, of course, but I feel that to some extent I'm like him. Because all of this is something not totally in the past."

I took another deep breath before going on. "People back home are impressed that I was accepted by Harvard. But I don't think Harvard *accepted* me . . . I think Harvard *admitted* me. Like a visitor. Showing off. 'Here it is. Take a look. But you can't have it.'"

"I think," said Eleanor, "that one day you will see things differently. And you can be anything you want. Perhaps you do have a lot in common with your grandfather. That being said, your grandfather was a great success by any measure."

"Why do I think he never got what he wanted?"

"I bet he got exactly what he wanted," said Eleanor, "and you will too. What you want as opposed to what you think you want."

I was feeling even more tired and vulnerable, and it just came out. "I'm not going to bring up Becca Wyatt," I said. "I promised myself I wouldn't."

Eleanor smiled. "You don't have to," she said, "and please don't anyway. I'm afraid all the resources of Harvard's library system are inadequate to that end, and I am merely a guide. Besides, anything I say as a friend—not a reference librarian—will be ignored, and rightly so."

I nodded. It was time to leave. Were I in a bar instead of the Archives, the person behind the counter would be refusing to sell me another drink and telling me to go home.

"I'll be back after break," I said. "Thanks for all your help, Eleanor. Have a nice holiday."

"And you too, Mark. Get some rest. The break will be good for you. And I'm sure your parents will be so proud about what you've learned. You'll have time to really fill them in on all the details of their hitherto lost family history. How surprised they'll be!"

I had taken my parka off the back of the chair and was putting it on as Eleanor was retrieving my book bag from the cubby behind the counter.

"I haven't told my parents anything. And I won't be," I said definitively. Eleanor arm was suspended, my bag dangling over the counter, her blue eyes focused on my face, searching it for an answer.

There was none to be found there, so I said straight out what I had decided from the beginning.

"If Poppa had wanted my father or anyone else to know, he would have told them," I said. "I'm not about to betray our secret."

Great Aunt Lillian

"What did you say your name was again, young man?"

"Mark Levinson." I nodded thanks to her assistant, who had just poured me a cup of tea after first serving Lillian Wyatt and Becca. She laid the serving tray—which in addition to the silver tea service held a plate of small sandwich squares of white bread and some slices of cake—on the coffee table and unceremoniously exited the parlor. The china was a Victorian-looking floral pattern, and faint lines of crackling indicated that it had been in the family for a while. I picked up the cup with two hands, not completely trusting either the delicate handle or the steadiness of my grip.

Aunt Lillian first blew, then took a sip of tea and held her cup and saucer in her lap. She looked as if she were trying to calculate a math problem in her head.

"And how did you say you are related?"

"His grandson."

"So," she said, having completed the necessary calculations, "if you are Chauncey Porter's grandson, you must be the son of one of his daughters."

"Um, yes, yes I am," I lied. I pointedly turned my head to look at Becca, who was looking back equally pointedly.

"Becca called and asked me if I knew your grandfather, and I said 'yes,' which I suppose is why you are here. It's always a pleasure to meet Becca's friends, regardless of the reason."

I nodded warily, and set my teacup back into its saucer on the table, not trusting my ability to hold it any longer even with both hands. My heart was pounding and I felt light-headed.

"He was a friend of my older brother Hollis and an oarsman on the 1906 crew that defeated Yale," she stated matter-of-factly. "Hollis, naturally, was the captain. And people with whom he was well-acquainted called him 'Chance.'" Was there anything specific you had in mind to ask me?"

Where and how to begin? I hesitated, trying to gather my thoughts. I felt as if a teacher had asked me a question I didn't know the answer to.

Had we been in a classroom, Becca would have thrown up her hand and excitedly waved it, unable to contain her impatience with me.

But Becca only interrupted. "So did YOU call him 'Chance,' Auntie Lil?

Becca had called me out of the blue on Wednesday of that week. I had been fiercely resisting the urge to pester her about exactly when Aunt Lillian would return from Europe and when Becca could get a chance to speak with her. It was now the end of January, and I had been back from Kansas City for a few weeks, trying to concentrate on studying despite being on pins and needles. We were in the middle of reading period before finals, and I hadn't seen or spoken to Becca since my return. Nor had I been back to the Archives and seen Eleanor. I had assumed, correctly, that Becca had been spending most of the free time at her home.

"She remembers him," Becca said as soon as I picked up the phone and said 'hello.' She didn't bother to exchange any pleasantries or even say who was calling, which weren't necessary.

"What else did she say?"

"Nothing."

"What do you mean 'nothing?'" My voice had risen in register by at least an octave.

"I didn't ask. He wasn't *my* grandfather," Becca concluded with an edge of sarcasm. "You'll have to ask her yourself."

"So we don't know if she just remembers his name, or if she really knew him, or how much she remembers, if anything . . ."

"I already told you, Levinson, I didn't ask. Did you want me to spoil it for you? Deprive you of anxiety and suspense?" She paused. "And when it comes right down to it, it just isn't really any of my business."

"Okay, "I said, "I get it. And thank you for asking. Can I meet her?"

"If you want—I guess that's a pretty stupid way of putting it, isn't it? Let me rephrase that. I've arranged a visit on Saturday afternoon for tea at Longneck Cove. And I told her I was bringing a friend. I assume you don't have more pressing plans."

"Of course I can make it. Jesus, yes."

"Take the 1:05 train and I'll pick you up at the station."

"Uh . . . should I wear a coat and tie?" I asked, immediately regretting how stupid I sounded. Would Becca's high school friends from Milton needed to have asked that question?

"I'm wearing a white linen crop top without a bra and a sequined mini-skirt and stiletto heels," Becca chided me. "I don't really give a fuck what you wear, Levinson. It isn't a job interview."

"Okay," I replied sheepishly, determined that I would wear a sport coat and tie. "I'll see you at the depot."

"Right."

"And Becca," I said before she could hang up, "by the way, uh . . . how's everything? How are things going?"

"Everything's fine, Levinson. I'm really busy. But I'm making time for this."

I would have been blown away by Longneck Cove had I not been already experienced Becca's house. It was a much older estate, a shingle style mansion situated at the top of a bluff overlooking the cove of the same name, and beyond, Massachusetts Bay. Unlike the more contemporary abode of "the parents," Longneck Cove was darker not only because of smaller and fewer windows but owing to a more oppressive décor: dark wood paneling, heavy draperies, deeply saturated Oriental rugs, oversized antique furniture, and large old oil paintings with thick gilt frames. The detailing, of course, was fabulous, with embossed ceilings, carved architraves, over-the-top chandeliers, and stained glass. Unfortunately, I was only privy to the impressive entryway and the parlor, the room in which we would have our tea, talk, and cake, and later, briefly the library. But I was struck by the notion that this was the house Hollis Wyatt had grown up in and romped through as a young boy, exploring every nook and cranny, hiding from his nanny. And then there were the grounds, only a portion of which I had managed to see when coming up the long driveway. Contemporaneously, most of my relatives had been living in a shtetl.

Becca had told me that in its heyday Longneck Cove had a full-time staff of twelve, but now there was only a single full time live-in, a woman who served as a personal assistant and prepared light meals, but was a companion more than anything. A cook would come in several times a week to prepare more substantial dinners, and a house cleaner worked exclusively at the house but lived elsewhere. Gardening work was contracted out to a high-end landscaping service catering to historic estates. We had been shown into the room by the assistant whom Becca greeted as Julia, a short but trim mousy woman in an expensive-looking business suit.

Becca and I sat down beside one another on the sofa in front of an Italianate coffee table that was already set up for tea. The sofa was Victorian, heavily hand-carved and covered in a plush but worn blue velvet, which yielded unevenly when we plopped down out of unison. Becca and I started to rise when Aunt Lillian made her entrance, but aborted the effort in response to her quick and rather imperious hand gesture indicating she had no time or desire for such nonsense. She was a tall and elegant octogenarian, not the least bit stooped, and had Becca's beautiful piercing blue eyes. Her face was fully made up, her white hair immaculately styled in a length and tight curls that I would characterize as "rich old lady hair." She wore a double strand of pearls with a relatively casual loose-fitting but clearly expensive dress that fell just below her knees. It was also a flowered, bearing some similarity to the china. The only incongruity to her outfit was what she wore on her feet: thick, heavily cushioned orthopedic shoes that my grandmother also wore, commonly known as "moon shoes."

Lillian walked over to the sofa and bent down to her grandniece, offering a cheek to be kissed. Since Becca, as instructed, didn't stand up but only leaned forward, the result was more the sound of smooching than actual contact. Apparently it was close enough for a blue-blood display of affection. Becca then introduced me and, instructions be damned, I couldn't possibly stay seated for the handshake. But getting up from the deep sofa required a contortion, as I had to push myself up with my left arm, so I never made it to a fully erect position in any case. But I was more than close enough to smell Aunt Lillian's floral old lady perfume, sweet and cloying, but perfectly in keeping with her surroundings.

Aunt Lillian took the straight-backed carved wooden chair at the short end of the coffee table and immediately unfolded the napkin in front of her and placed it in her lap.

"Now isn't this just the nicest way to spend a Saturday afternoon," she said. Then she nodded, and Julia began pouring the tea.

"Yes, dear," Lillian answered Becca, "As it so happens, I *did* call him 'Chance.' Would you like to know anything else, or should we start on the cake?" She was being facetious, her eyes sparking, and I decided that I liked the old gal. "Just promise me that we won't talk about the damn Vietnam war. By the way, Mark, you favor him, you know."

The remark startled me. "I've never seen any pictures of him as a young man," I said, forgetting that I very recently had seen the group shot of the 1906 crew in the Class Album. Had there been a noticeable family resemblance, it hadn't occurred to me. The grainy black and white image was too small for me to appreciate any such thing.

"And that's a compliment, you know," she continued. "Your grandfather was a handsome man."

"Thank you," I said, probably blushing, since my face suddenly felt warm. "He died when I was about ten or eleven."

"I'm sorry to hear that," Lillian said, appearing sincerely and deeply sorry. "But remind me before you leave today and I can show you a photograph of him. I have it in an album in the library and I know exactly where it is."

"You do?" I must have sounded incredulous, which I was, in addition to being very excited. "Was he ever here?"

"Oh, yes," Lillian answered, "on more than one occasion. Ostensibly to visit with Hollis, but I did my best to be involved as much as I could. Little sister hanging around with big brother and his friends. We all went sailing once on 'Angela,' one of our father's sailboats, and picnicked on Misery Island. And I played tennis with him on the court here. I beat him of course. He wasn't much of a tennis player—although he was a strong athlete and very quick—but no match for me. And it wasn't in my competitive nature to let him win." She smiled.

Becca had deferred to my commanding the conversation, but now couldn't contain herself.

"So you knew him quite well, then."

"Yes I did, Becca darling."

"Did you know much about his past, his family?"

"Not too awfully much. He was from Montana, as you know, Mark, and an only child, and had lost his father early on. But his mother had inherited a good deal of wealth, apparently. He didn't talk about his experiences growing up very much. I knew he was very good with horses, which isn't surprising. And he certainly didn't act or sound like he was off the farm or some country yokel, so I assume he had excellent tutors. I had the impression he had left his past behind him."

"But you knew him quite well," Becca repeated, perhaps trying to comprehend how her aunt believed to know him so well, but actually didn't know him at all.

"You have no appreciation for subtlety, Becca, just like your father. So let me spell it out for you. Chance Porter was in love with me. He was courting me. There you have it."

Becca and I were gobsmacked. As one would expect, Becca was the first to regain her composure, and forward enough to pose yet another impertinent question.

"Were you in love with him?" she asked.

"Of course I was," said Lillian. "I was seventeen and he was a handsome Harvard man." She paused and looked at the two of us, both rapt and leaning forward on the sofa, like athletes waiting to be called up from the bench. "And if the both of you are just going to sit there with your mouths hanging open, this might be a good time to pass around the cake. Or at least pass it over to me."

Lillian, who went by Lily in those days, had first met Chauncey Porter at a dinner party at the Curtises. At the time, she had no inkling that the dashing freshman had ever met her brother. Chauncey, of course, immediately knew who she was upon their introduction. The prettiest girl in the room was Hollis's little sister. He had seen her with Hollis and his family at the Masconomo. Later that first evening, when the subject of his participation as an oarsman came up, she asked her new acquaintance if he knew her brother Hollis and was surprised to learn that her sibling had been mentoring the Westerner in rowing.

"It's odd that he's never mentioned you," she remarked.

"Well," said a self-effacing Chauncey Porter, "your brother will be captain of the Varsity Eight next year, and I'm only a freshman."

Their paths would cross several more times at teas and dances before the end of the year. Despite the lack of privacy and social obligations, they cumulatively managed to have private conversations of substantial length and breadth.

"Oh, *do* write me some time, Mr. Porter," said Lily Wyatt on the last gathering before summer break, when the Boston social world would be displaced to the North Shore, Newport, and other warm weather playgrounds. "We'll be in Manchester-by-the-Sea all summer and I do so much want to hear what you're up to."

Chauncey, without reluctance, promised he would. He knew he was playing with fire, but he was smitten. And Lily, since her own brother had been so close mouthed about the eligible Harvard man for Heaven knew why, would remain tight-lipped about the whole thing herself.

"It wasn't until Hol's senior year that he finally brought Chance here to Longneck Cove," Aunt Lillian said, replacing her empty cake plate on the coffee table. "We all went sailing together early that fall, and I recall it was quite chilly when we played tennis, so it must have been around that time. Perhaps the same visit."

"Did Grandpa know that you and Chauncey were corresponding, and that you knew each other . . . fairly well?" Becca asked.

"No he didn't. In fact, the first time Chauncey came over with him, your grandfather introduced us as if we were strangers. And neither of us let on. Strange that. It's not as if I had told Chance not to say anything . . . it was just instinctive on both our parts. Chance must have been aware of how protective of me older brother was."

"But he eventually found out?" Again it was Becca asking the questions.

"Oh dear, yes. But let's not get ahead of ourselves." Lillian poured herself the last bit of tea, emptying the pot. Then she picked up a silver bell from the table—which I had previously not noticed—and gave it a good shaking. Becca and I waited impatiently while Julia entered and took the teapot away for refilling. Both of us shook our heads when she asked if we would like more cake.

"So much was going on that spring, that it all runs together," Lillian began. "Of course, I had found myself running into Chance more frequently at social events in Boston before that. And then Hol was seeing much more of Chance once Coach Wray selected him as a substitute on the Varsity boat. Then Chad Thayer had the injury and Chance took his place on the boat. When they beat Yale it was quite the celebration. Not only did I attend the regatta with Mother and Father, but we all went to the celebration dinner at the Vendome that evening. It was all so exciting . . . and I was so proud of Chance."

She had paused, and was smiling at the memory when Julia re-entered with the tea. Julia poured another cup for Lillian, who continued to look into space as she poured. Again, both Becca and I declined anything more for ourselves. I was paying too much attention to my own stomach churning to think much of what Becca might have been thinking.

"It all becomes so compressed in time," Lillian began again, "that it's hard to keep straight after all these years. But the dinner was soon followed by Class Day and Commencement Week. I had promised Chance that I would meet him at the dance in Memorial Hall after the spread at Beck on Class Day. Somehow I let this slip to Hol and he was furious when he found out. And I mean furious. Trying to downplay things I casually mentioned that Chance and I had exchanged a few letters and Hol was fit to be tied. I suppose he thought the three of us were chums, palling around like the Three Musketeers or something. It hadn't occurred to him that there might have been something more romantic between us."

"Any idea why Grandfather reacted so strongly?" Becca was now leading the witness.

"I suppose it was the shock of it all," she replied after a pause. "Neither Chance nor I had led on to him, so understandably he just must have assumed . . . oh, I don't know. In any event, I became rather emotional myself, and it all seemed to get out of hand. Then Hol apologized, and explained that I was too young, and he was just trying to protect me, and a lot of other things that I didn't find particularly convincing at the time. He asked to see the letters, and I suppose I was so exhausted from crying that I just gave them to him. There were only three or four and they were completely innocent—nothing incriminatory or embarrassing in them—just chatter about classes and crew practice and that sort of thing—but you know, a girl likes to keep her letters private."

"Do you still have them?" I popped out like a champagne cork.

"Oh, no. I never got them back. I suspect Hol threw them out or burned them. But by that time it didn't matter, since things had ended and there was no turning back. Chance disappeared from my life."

"What happened? How did it end?" Becca asked. We were both leaning so far forward on the sofa that we risked falling off.

"I mean that literally, Becca dear. The last time I saw him was at the Victory celebration at the Vendome. He just disappeared. We all went to Class Day, and I waited in Memorial Hall for him to show up for a dance, and he never did. Ironically, I did have a dance or two with Chad Thayer—he was such a bad dancer that his injured leg didn't matter all that much—but my mind was elsewhere. Anyway, I never saw or even heard from him ever again. Chauncey Porter disappeared into thin air." Aunt Lillian took another sip of her tea. "Without another word," she added, setting the half-filled cup into its saucer with a sense of finality. "In today's lingo you might say I was dumped."

"Wait! That's it? You don't know what happened to him?" It was me this time, beyond restraint.

"Well," said Aunt Lillian, a bit taken aback by my outburst, which bordered on a breach of decorum, "I know . . . broadly speaking. And I assume you would know." She looked at me, questioning me with her eyes. "You mean you don't know?"

I shook my head slowly.

"Your grandfather was expelled from Harvard. The shame of it all must have kept him from ever contacting me again. She took another sip of tea. "It mattered to me not one hoot."

"Do you know why?" I asked, trying to compose myself. "Why he was expelled?"

"In fact I *do* know, although I didn't at the time. It's all really rather silly, actually."

Becca and I looked at one another, both obviously thinking the same thing. How could any aspect of this affair be silly? We both looked back at Aunt Lillian, who read the perplexity on our faces.

"I'll let you judge for yourselves," she said, picking up the bell and shaking it to summon Julia.

"Are you done with your tea?" Julia asked as she came into the parlor. "Shall I take it away?"

"Please do. And then, if you don't mind, Julia dear, could you go to the library and bring me the door stop? I know it's heavy, but it's always easier to tell a story with exhibits."

The door clicked quietly with Julia's exit from the room and we sat in silence.

"I suppose I should preface this," Aunt Lillian broke the quiet. "Has either of you heard of the Med. Fac.?"

Still baffled, we shook our heads simultaneously.

The grande dame went on to explain. "It stood for Medical Faculty, but had nothing to do with Medicine or the Faculty. It was a secret society at Harvard, a long-lived and notorious one, dating back to the early nineteenth century. The members were mainly from the Porcellian and the A.D., but some were from other clubs. All well-bred and prominent lads, but the society encouraged their inner rapscallion to come out. All in good fun, usually, but their stunts were surely a vexation to many. The Administration hated them, of course, a real thorn in their side, but there was nothing they could do. They hardly ever caught any of them."

"What do you mean by 'stunts'?" I asked.

"Oh, the usual fraternity boy types of things. Painting the statue of John Harvard, starting bonfires, letting rats or pigeons out in classrooms. They were especially attracted to things that went boom, from firecrackers to more potent explosives. They were the ones responsible for the dynamiting of the Old College Pump a couple of years before Hol and his group matriculated. And about the same time, an explosion that went off in Sanders Theatre during a Beethoven concert. No one was hurt, fortunately. But you catch my drift. I'm not condoning their behavior, but boys will be boys. They likely considered their dare-devilry as 'manly' behavior, if you can believe that."

"Are you saying my grandfather was one of these Med Fac. people?" I asked.

"Oh, no, not at all," replied Aunt Lillian. "But Becca, *your* grandfather was. I didn't know until years later, and he, in fact, wasn't the one who told me." She waited for a response from Becca, but none was forthcoming.

"Hol's friend Bobsy Baxter spilled the beans years later. You remember Bobsy, don't you?"

"Not really," said Becca, rolling her eyes.

"Well, he and his wife Stella were often over here—I was quite good friends with Stella. Anyway, they were my guests for cocktails and dinner one evening—It must have been in the mid-thirties, since Prohibition had ended, I remember that—and Bobsy had been drinking a bit too much, as he had a tendency to do, and inadvertently he let it out. Bobsy was a Med. Fac. as well, you see. That's how he knew."

Julia entered, laboring to carry a narrow, roughly two-foot-long piece of bronze with a bulbous end. She did her best to conceal its weight and the strain carrying it entailed.

"I better just set it down here," she said, clearly out of breath, and unsuccessfully attempted to place it on the floor without a loud thud. "I'll come back later for it. Mind not to trip on it," she warned, taking her leave.

"I remember that door stop," said Becca.

"Yes, dear, but you never knew what it was."

"What is it?"

"It's a bell clapper, dear. The tongue of the bell from Harvard Hall. Your dear grandfather pilfered it in 1906."

"Where are we going with this, Aunt Lillian, and what does it have to do with Chauncey Porter?" The story had dragged on long enough for Becca.

"Bobsy Baxter, that night I was telling you about, noticed it on the floor of the library holding the door open and told me the story of the theft, and along with it the fact that Hol had been a Med. Fac."

"What does this have to do with my grandfather?" I was more anxious than impatient, but regardless couldn't stand any more suspense myself.

"The police thought your grandfather had been the culprit, and arrested him for the prank. He covered for Hollis and took the rap, as they say."

"So my grandfather was expelled for stealing the tongue of a bell."

"Yes, which he didn't do. But it was a noble gesture to protect my brother. This all happened right before Class Day. Noble, but a misplaced gesture, and all very silly, or at least needless."

"And why, exactly, is that?" I asked, trying to mask the irritation that had crept into my voice.

"My dear Mark," said Aunt Lillian, "you can't possibly imagine that Harvard would ever expel Hollis Appleton Wyatt for stealing the tongue of the chapel bell, could you?" She held out her left arm, and with her right hand, slapped the back of her wrist a couple of times. Her meaning was more than clear.

At the end of our visit, Becca offered to drive me back to the station to catch the train, but we were quiet during the short ride. She only spoke when

I had opened the car door in the parking lot and was half-way out.

"Jesus," she said. "At first I figured my grandfather had ratted out your grandfather to keep him clear of Aunt Lillian. But this is much worse."

The Stunt

Chauncey had gotten fairly tipsy during the celebration dinner at the Hotel Vendome—the drinks were free—but not as intoxicated as the rest of the oarsman, who had imbibed with little restraint at the dinner and then migrated to the bar for supplemental refreshment after officials and family had departed the event. Ebullient, each had in his possession a satin red 'H.'" Earlier, Chauncey had little opportunity to speak with Lily privately. With her parents there, as well as a hovering big brother, he was only able to pointedly mention that he would be present at Memorial Hall on Class Day and hoped she would reserve a dance for him. Lily responded with a beaming smile and affirmation of willingness. While Chauncey attempted to contain his excitement and anticipation, Hollis appeared reserved and distracted.

Wyatt and Bobsy Baxter, to Chauncey's surprise, decided to excuse themselves relatively early from the continuing celebration at the bar—it was only approaching 11 p.m. after all—and Chauncey asked if he could return with them to Cambridge in their cab.

"I can get out with you at Claverly and walk back home," he offered, not wanting to impose any further. Baxter clapped him on the shoulder and confirmed that it would be their pleasure.

Dropped off on Mt. Auburn Street, Chauncey had hoped to be invited up to Hollis's rooms, but no invitation was forthcoming. The three well-dressed young men stood outside the Claverly entrance, seemingly at a loss for something to do or somewhere to go. Chauncey soon realized that the two of them were waiting for him to leave.

"I had hoped to have a word with you," he said to Hollis.

Baxter, showing no signs of affront, quickly said, "I'm actually heading to the Porc for a nightcap. Maybe I'll see you soon, Hol?" And with that he headed toward their home-away-from-home quarters at 1324 Massachusetts Ave.

Once Baxter had rounded the corner at Linden Street, Chauncey turned toward his friend, who had been uncharacteristically quiet during the ride. He had sensed something was wrong all evening, and asked Hollis outright.

"Let me put it bluntly," Hollis replied. "You are to stay away from Lily."

Chauncey paused before responding. The smell of liquor on Hollis's breath was mixed with barely contained vitriol. Chauncey didn't want to ask but had no recourse. He felt his stomach churning, a visceral response to the recognition of inevitability.

"Why?"

"You know perfectly well 'why'! I had understood that you were just friends. All the time the three of us spent together at Longneck Cove . . . I thought she was tagging along because of admiration for her big brother. I've come to believe that she is much more admiring of you."

"I'd be lying if I denied being quite fond of her. And I believe she feels the same way."

Hollis covered his mouth and chin with his hand, subconsciously an effort to muzzle himself. He squeezed his chin. He would remain composed even if it required squeezing his mouth shut. "I have never questioned anything you have done up until now. I have not questioned, nor have I criticized or interfered. I could envision no possible harm to anyone but yourself. Your success has been admirable and in many ways beyond my comprehension. But now you are overstepping. Anything beyond the merest acquaintance with my sister is unacceptable. And I forbid it."

"Because I'm a Jew?" Chauncey asked with a threatening edge to his voice.

"No," replied Hollis, "because you're a fraud."

Slammed into a conversational brick wall, Chauncey had to clear his head and reset, a process necessitating a prolonged moment of silence.

"And if I weren't a fraud?" Chauncey pushed.

"There is no need to engage in hypotheticals. You know the situation.

Surely you can't be so self-involved to not understand the situation. Am I to allow my sister to become emotionally involved with an imposter? What kind of future does that bode for her?"

Chauncey looked down. He could say nothing.

"Are you going to continue this charade for the rest of your life? Is that your intention?"

Still, Chauncey could say nothing.

"Have you not given it any thought, man? Hell, where does it end?"

"I don't know." Chauncey's voice was breaking. "It didn't start out like this. I just wanted to show that I was as good, as worthy as anyone else."

"That I will grant you. But keep away from my sister. And after graduation, in one week's time, my involvement with you will end as well."

"Hol, please listen . . ."

"Bobsy is waiting for me at the Porc." Hollis turned his back on Chauncey and headed toward Linden Street.

Porter, dizzy and deep in muddled thoughts, was fighting back tears. He walked aimlessly around Cambridge for nearly half an hour before trudging back to Hemenway. He had not admitted to himself but known all along what Hollis's reaction would be to his relationship with Lily, why else had he tried to downplay things from the very beginning? He had been seduced by his own success and achievements, at times forgetting who he really was. The goalpost had been moved. It was not enough for him to be a College Man; he wanted more time in his newly discovered world. He had almost become more comfortable in the shoes of Chauncey Bates Porter than in his own. But what was the end game? And how did he end up in this bind, a victim of his own success?

Chauncey knew Hollis was right—he had to give up Lily. But wasn't she his real-life Gwendolyn Fairfax? The intensity of his feelings—he could never possibly experience those again or with someone else. He was destined to spend the rest of his life in loneliness. There could never be another like her.

His life as a college man would be inexorably diminished without the woman for whom he yearned. He still had college dreams to fulfil, but he could not continue his life as Chauncey Porter once his alter-ego received his Harvard diploma. He would vanish, go back to his old life as best he could, and make it a starting point for a new one, a life that was uniquely his own. With no useable contacts or recommendations, and no Harvard degree in his own name, he would have to scrape by. But could he ever go back to working for old man O'Rourke as a blacksmith's apprentice? Or worse, peddle Kosher pickles and herring in his uncle's delicatessen? Even going back to Stimson for a job at the Masconomo House was no longer a possibility. And whatever his future had in store, it would be a life without Lily.

By the time he reached Hemenway, Chauncey felt compelled to go back and talk things out with Hollis. He would apologize. And he would swear to abandon his pursuit of Lily. He had to talk to him, he had to explain himself, and it couldn't wait.

Chauncey stayed only long enough in his room to safely tuck his Harvard "H" in the drawer of the small desk. He headed down Massachusetts Avenue from Hemenway, opting to stop at the Porcellian Building before proceeding onward to Claverly. He was uncertain if Hollis was still in the club with Baxter, and there was no way of finding out. The street was mostly empty, it being close to midnight. Chauncey walked back and forth past the entry door of the club a few times, pausing each time to study the window display at Leavitt and Peirce. Despite few people about he felt conspicuous, so he crossed the street to lean against the McKean Gate, where he kept watch for a few more minutes. A couple of Cambridge cops sauntered toward him, and he nodded at them. Dressed as he was, it was obvious that he was a mildly liquored-up Harvard student having a rest and not a loiterer. They nodded back and walked past him without question or ceremony, but Chauncey decided it was time to move on. He would go to Claverly, and if Hollis had not yet returned, he would wait there until he did.

Hollis Wyatt and Bobsy Baxter had shed their jackets, collars, and waistcoats in Hollis's rooms. Both now sat together on the sofa, wearing flat workman's caps and lightweight chore coats. They were nervously sipping from whiskey-filled tumblers, killing time by further bolstering their courage with spirits. Hollis pulled out his pocket watch and once again checked the time, as he had been doing every couple of minutes.

"We should probably go now," he said. "It's almost midnight."

"Let's wait a bit longer," said Bobsy. "We want to make sure Teddy has unlocked the door before we get there. We don't want to be hanging around outside waiting. We need to get in immediately. No telling where the watchmen will be."

Hollis reluctantly nodded in agreement and took another sip from his glass. He set down his timepiece on the table in front of them, case open, so he could watch the progression of the minute hand from where he sat.

They had all agreed that Teddy Wilcox would unlock the entry door to Harvard Hall by midnight. Since Wilcox was a footballer and not a crew man, he wasn't attending the post-regatta dinner and was available for preparatory break-in work; specifically, picking the lock of the door leading to the attic—or whatever else was required—to enable them access to the belfry. He had entered the classroom building through the main entrance at 9:30 p.m., proceeded up the stairs, and hidden in a closet in the northwest recitation room until sometime after 10:30 p.m., when he heard the janitor locking the doors and windows. He had brought with him a bag containing a variety of tools, including a monkey wrench, a hammer, a screwdriver, a chisel, a small bar, and a false key for picking locks. He had matches and a couple of candles in his pocket as well. If all went to plan, Wilcox would have gained access to the attic and possibly into the belfry itself by midnight, when he would unlock the front door for his Med. Fac. Brothers and accomplices, Wyatt and Baxter.

After working for more than an hour, Wilcox had still not been able to pick the lock to the attic door, and decided that his only choice was to force it. With his chisel he began cutting the wood out from around the lock, and eventually was able to pry the door open with the crowbar. By then it was nearly 11:30, and Wilcox was drenched in sweat from his efforts. Once in the attic, another set of stairs on the opposite side of the building led to the tower. From there, Wilcox had been told, a ladder would lead into the belfry itself.

Wilcox, however, had not expected that the scuttle from the attic would be blocked by a sturdy piece of wood, with substantial hinges and two sets of heavy Yale padlocks on opposing sides.

Damnation! Austin Jones, for forty-eight years the bell ringer, had been a Med. Fac. nemesis for decades. The old man was a congenial but stubborn adversary who rather enjoyed the challenge of prankster students hell-bent on thwarting his ringing of the morning bell. There had been many attempts on the clapper, few successful, and even those that were never kept Jones from his appointed duty. Once, when the tongue had been stolen and all access to the belfry closed off, he had resorted to sawing a hole in the attic floor to replace it. For years, he had kept an extra tongue on hand in case of emergencies, after an incident years earlier when he was forced to manually strike the bell with a hammer for several days.

Wilcox's assessment of the situation was dire. He could never pick the locks. He could drill bore holes through the thick wood, but then sawing was risky because of the noise and slow as well. Access to the padlocks would be difficult with his hacksaw, and using a file would take forever, and besides, the file he brought was likely to break. Not being the person in charge, he would have to wait for further instructions from Wyatt and Baxter, since they would clearly have to come up with another plan of attack or else abort the stunt altogether. Wilcox laid down all his tools in a row on the attic floor under the scuttle, and headed back downstairs to unlock the front door. It was almost midnight.

Just about to head toward Claverly from the McKean Gate, Chauncey had spotted them emerging from Holyoke Street and crossing the street to head up Massachusetts Avenue. Despite their attire, he had recognized Hollis and Bobsy immediately. They sauntered with a forced casualness, all the while looking furtively about them, obviously on the watch for patrolmen. The streets were empty except for a few passing carriages and a couple of motor cars, as the street cars had stopped running. But what were they up to, dressed as they were? Chauncey immediately knew it was mischief. Fraternity and Institute initiations were for sophomores, and generally occurred in the first term. Here were two seniors, up to something just before Class Day. It did not take a great leap for Chauncey to realize that Hollis Wyatt had a secret of his own. He, along with Bobsy Baxter, had to be Med. Facs., and they were in the midst of pulling a stunt of some sort.

Hidden within the archway of the gate, Chauncey had not been spotted, but if he followed behind them on the sidewalk, he surely would be seen. Taking a calculated gamble that the pair would continue heading north along Massachusetts Avenue, he turned back into the yard and ran along the outer pathway behind Grays and Matthews Halls. With his shortcut inside the fence, not to mention his sprint compared to their walking pace, he could station himself by Massachusetts Hall near Johnston Gate and see which way they were headed.

Winded, and crouching in the shadows against the building, Chauncey saw the pair come into view through the wrought iron fence bars and watched as they walked a few steps further before turning to pass through the gate. Hollis stopped just outside the entrance to Harvard Hall, while Bobsy continued to walk past the building, where he looked around and took in a full view of the yard. Clearly satisfied that all was clear, Baxter hurried back to Wyatt, and the pair entered Harvard Hall through a front entrance that should have been locked. So there was at least one other accomplice on the inside, Chauncey reasoned, which explained why neither Hollis or Bobsy were carrying tools. Without question, they were after the tongue of the bell, a prank from the old playbook. If he were to stay and watch things unfold— which Chauncey was determined to do—he needed to find a better place to station himself than off the main access to Harvard Yard. So rather furtively himself, he worked his way to the other side of Harvard Hall and stationed himself behind the Old Chapel, crouching in the darkness. It was becoming obvious that this might not be the night he would have a chance to atone to Hollis Wyatt for his transgressions.

"It's impossible," Wilcox whispered to his cohorts. The three conspirators were all in the attic, assessing Austin Jones's formidable security measures.

Until successfully pulling off a stunt they could not obtain full society status as "Doctors," and would remain society "Leeches" in perpetuity.

"We'll have to access the belfry from the roof," said Wyatt.

"How do you intend to do that?" Wilcox asked.

"One of us could cross from the roof of Hollis Hall," Baxter suggested. It was a fairly long leap from the roof of the adjacent dormitory, but possible. "It's been done before, and successfully."

Hollis knew his Society history even better than Baxter, having gone through many of the records himself, and was not enthusiastic. "It was done once, in 1850, and no one's tried it since. Especially since the rooftops weren't slate then, and now they're damn slick."

"Well, maybe we can steal something easy from one of the classrooms as long as we're here. Like a plaster bust, maybe," said Wilcox.

"Or maybe we can use a ladder and access the roof from the second floor porch, from Harvard 5," said Hollis.

"Where are we going to get a ladder?" asked Baxter.

Hollis knocked on the front rail of the ladder leading to the belfry, secured to the side of the scuttle below the wooden lid by only a couple of screws.

"Right here," he said. "Give me that screwdriver."

Ladder removed, the three took it down the stairs to the large recitation room on the second floor, unlatched one of the large windows, and slid the ladder out to the porch as quietly as they could. The porch was fully exposed behind the white wooden balustrade, and they or the ladder would be easily seen if anyone entering Johnston gate happened to look up.

"This will have to be quick," said Hollis, who had taken it upon himself to be the one retrieving the clapper. Unsure if bell ringer Jones had set up any more surprises, Hollis decided he needed to take a wrench, a small hammer, and a small hacksaw with him. "As soon as I'm on the roof, put the ladder back down out of sight from the street and wait inside for my whistle."

Baxter and Wilcox quickly set up the ladder. Not long enough to reach the roof itself, they leaned it against the bricks between two of the windows, the roof overhanging the top rung. Thus positioned, it was a stretch for Hollis to reach back to the snow guard and pull himself up, but he managed, and was crawling along the slate roof to the cupola as his cohorts brought down the ladder and laid it against the building. Reaching the belfry, Hollis pulled himself erect and twisted his body through one of the arched openings of the cupola. He was relieved to discover that rather than being welded, the tongue was fastened to the bell by a swivel. Easily slipping out the key to the swivel, he removed the swivel bolt with a couple taps of his hammer to free up the tongue. The clapper was much heavier than he had anticipated, though, perhaps forty or fifty pounds.

Hollis heard the first shout as he was backing out of the cupola. He had been spotted by someone on the street and heard an outcry for the police or one of the Harvard watchmen. One of the watchmen had been making his rounds across the yard by University Hall, and bounded over to the front of Harvard Hall, shouting for his cohort. Baxter and Wilcox rushed to set up the ladder again for Hollis, then ran back into the building and down a flight of stairs to escape from a lower floor window on the opposite side of the building. Chauncey, from his position behind the Chapel, could see Hollis's actions by the cupola, and soon after the yelling, witnessed Baxter and Wilcox crawling out the window and making a dash for it, all while Hollis was still on the roof holding the bell clapper.

Seeing that the watchmen were about to enter the front of the building, Wyatt knew that he couldn't escape using the ladder. Cradling the tongue to his chest, he slid to the edge of the roof, and planting his feet along the snow guard, bent both his knees and lunged across the gap to the roof of Hollis. He landed hard, sliding on the slate and twisting his ankle, but was able to catch himself. And now he found himself atop a different building, four stories up, with no clear means of escape. From his vantage he could see University Hall and the Old Yard on one side, and on the other, a smaller courtyard with the diminutive Old Chapel and the Phillips Brooks House. And there, in front of the Chapel, was Chauncey Porter, frantically waving his hands at him and shouting for him to throw down his coat and cap.

"Lie down by the big chimney and stay down and I'll draw them off!" he shouted. "But first throw down your damn coat and cap!"

Hollis quickly did as he was told. Chauncey scrambled to pick up the coat and hat and hurriedly put them on. Then he stood in the center of the courtyard, his arms crossed over his body as if he were concealing something. His heart was racing, but he forced himself to stand patiently. The two watchmen were now inside Harvard Hall, fumbling around. One ran to check the upstairs, and the other, realizing that someone had escaped out an open window at the back, shouted to his companion and headed to the rear exit. He opened the door, out of breath, hoping to catch sight of whomever had escaped, fully expecting to be too late. The Harvard watchmen were well accustomed to a lot of chasing but very little catching; usually the most they could hope for was aid in the identification of culprits. But there one stood, in a work coat and cap, holding something against his chest, not more than twenty yards away. Chauncey looked the watchman directly in the eye, motionless, until the watchman overcame his own surprise and made his move. And then Chauncey Bates Porter ran like hell.

The Reckoning

Porter wanted to lose the watchmen, but not too quickly. They were both after him now, and he didn't want them abandoning chase until Hollis had a chance to safely get down from the roof of Hollis Hall. Perhaps one of the skylights was unlocked, and he could exit through the interior of the dormitory, or else he could climb down along a ridgepole, if not to the ground, at least to one of the fire escapes.

Porter had worries of his own, as he envisioned the escape route in his head. He angled across the yard past the northeast side of Holworthy Hall, but instead of leaving the yard enclosure there, crossed toward Emerson Hall and beyond, to exit by the President's house onto Quincy Street. From there he intended to continue past Memorial Hall, and by taking a right on Kirkland, he could go a couple more blocks before turning down Francis Avenue. Once in the leafy neighborhood of the Professors houses, he could lose his pursuers in the maze of cross streets. Eventually he would ditch the jacket and cap, then head back to Massachusetts Avenue and home to Hemenway. As it turns out, the watchmen had given up the chase even before they made it to Emerson. But Porter hadn't counted on pumping right into the two patrolmen at the corner of Broadway and Quincy.

"It was just me, no one else," he said without giving it a thought, assuming the alarm had been sounded and the patrol was out looking for him. Instinctively, encountering a surrendering young man in working clothes, the cops proceeded to place him in handcuffs, encountering no resistance.

Porter was relieved, confident that Hollis would find a way out of the debacle. And now he had successfully covered for him. What a disaster it could have been, had Hollis been caught right before Class Day and been prevented from graduating! But what punishment would Harvard mete out for him? Probation meant that he would not be able to participate in any sports. But crew wouldn't seriously start until the next year's second term. As long as Sargent would allow him to keep staying in Hemenway, he could manage. Surely he would be allowed to continue helping with the physical fitness tests. The most practical concern was having enough money for meals. His thoughts whirling, he was led ahead of the two cops to be taken to the station. In any case, he thought, for Hollis's sake it was all worth it.

At this juncture his musings were interrupted by the larger of the cops, a ruddy-faced Irishman named McNulty.

"So what's this all about, young man?" he asked.

Chauncey spent the night in the Cambridge jail and was thoroughly questioned the following morning, getting an unexpected and unwanted lesson in the criminal justice system. He had anticipated that he would be turned over to Harvard for disciplinary action by Dean Hurlbut, but was blindsided by being told that the assistant district attorney was intending to indict and present his case to a Middlesex county Grand Jury. His bail had been set at an astronomical $250. He couldn't possibly ask Hollis for the money and risk involving him. If there had been an easy way to contact Poco Bennett from jail, perhaps he would have resorted to a loan from the notorious usurer, as costly as that could end up being.

He had told his examiner that the theft of the bell clapper had been a prank. He had conceived of the plan and done it entirely on his own. When asked, he stated he had heard of the Med. Fac. Society but was not a member. As for the bell clapper, he had abandoned it somewhere in the bushes as he was running away. He couldn't remember exactly where, but he had thrown it in bushes against a building. Of course, he was counting on the fact that if it didn't turn up, Hollis had safely sequestered it somewhere. Perhaps Wyatt had thrown the clapper off the roof of Hollis Hall and it was actually somewhere concealed by shrubs.

Dean Hurlbut personally came to the station to speak with him later that same Saturday afternoon. Byron Satterlee Hurlbut, as Dean of the Harvard College, was the official sponsor of the undergraduates and the first port of call in matters of discipline. A popular teacher of English composition and eighteenth century literature, he had spent his entire academic career at Harvard and served as Dean for five years. Having just turned forty, he was rather stout, a clean-shaven, bespectacled, ordinary-looking man. After being led in to speak with Porter, he waited until they were alone before proceeding. His manner was kindly, sympathetic, and non-judgmental.

"It was a foolish thing for me to do," Chauncey confessed, "and I meant no harm by it. Please don't tell my mother. She has a weak heart."

"Let's not get ahead of ourselves, Mr. Porter." Hurlbut naturally knew of the sophomore as a member of the recently victorious Harvard boat. But he had long known that Porter was an honor student and not a troublemaker, two facts alone that had accounted for Hurlbut not previously having had any direct contact with him.

"You did this all on your own?"

"Yes, sir."

"And you're not a Med Fac."

"No, sir. I swear."

"Then let me clarify the situation. It has long been the policy of the university to let the law take care of crimes with a prank motive. But the college itself takes no action. Our current dilemma is how to convince the D.A.'s office not to pursue pressing charges. They seem to be a bit over-zealous. And thus the situation of your bail, which unfortunately it is not our policy to pay. Unless you yourself want to ask family or friends . . ."

"It's my responsibility, and I'll see to it myself," answered Porter.

Hurlbut nodded. "And in the meantime, we'll see what we can do on our end to get the charges dropped."

Chauncey Porter only spent one more night in jail. When informed that he was being released, he asked if the charges had been dropped and was informed they had not been, he was being released because his bail bond had been paid. Chauncey assumed that Hollis had come through, perhaps he had gone about getting some of his chums to pitch in. Or simply written a check for the entire amount himself.

Porter was surprised to be turned over to a bearded older man, impeccably outfitted, a total stranger.

"May I ask whom you are?" Chauncey was completely mystified.

"Not your usual ambulance chaser, I assure you," said the man.

"And you bailed me out?"

"Are you Chauncey Bates Porter?"

Porter nodded and said that he was.

"Then assuredly I did. Magnificent job in the boat on Friday as Number Three."

Confused, Chauncey nonetheless thanked him, more humbly than he might have under other circumstances. Who was this benefactor?

"And you purloined old Austin's clapper from the Harvard Hall belfry?"

Chauncey did not smile when he lied, admitting that he had. He had nothing to be proud of, no accomplishment other than letting himself be caught.

"Well," said his elder, leading him out of the room, "I certainly have to admire you for your sand."

"To what do I owe this honor, Professor?" Hugh Bancroft, Assistant District Attorney for Middlesex County, stood up from his courthouse office desk so rapidly that he bumped his thighs on its underside.

The venerable Civil War veteran and esteemed Harvard Professor of Law extended his hand over the desk to be shaken and bestowed an enigmatic smile, a relaxed and neutral manifestation of good manners. The indeterminate emotive state was a convenient starting point for expansion into pleasure or tightening into resolve. John Chipman Gray was a formidable man, and not easy to read.

"Shall we both sit down?" he asked. "And might I call you Hugh?" The tall man with a full salt and pepper beard and closely cropped hair had already taken one of the two chairs in front of the desk. Instantly the twenty-seven year-old assistant D.A. knew what the visit was about and experienced a sinking feeling. He was at more than a decided disadvantage. The co-founder of the Boston law firm Ropes and Gray was not an easy man to cross.

The eminent man unbuttoned his suitcoat and took a moment to appraise and absorb the entirety of the small office. The chair was so uncomfortable that he hoped he wouldn't have to sit for long. He noted the requisite leather bound law volumes on the single bookshelf, but the furnishings were otherwise in keeping with the armless chair, and could best be described as spartan. What could one expect from a county government office? The old professor tried his best to not condescend; he already harbored a paternal feeling toward the young lawyer. But this was not the time to offer Hugh Bancroft a position at his firm and put him out of his misery.

"Well, this is certainly a nice place for a young man like yourself to start out."

Bancroft had taken the job four years earlier, immediately upon graduation from law school. He had consciously decided not to pursue a job in a private firm, turning down several offers, and until that very moment had not regretted his decision.

"How's your father doing?" Gray began, establishing the requisite social order, and also a chronology for his closing argument. There was a strong resemblance between Hugh and the younger version of his father. Both were good-looking despite strong features, being heavily browed and with fairly broad noses. Both had a chin cleft and prominent philtrum, which the father had come to cover in later years with a large mustache. As befitting a prosecutor, the younger Bancroft was clean-shaven, so the space between nose and upper lip was more apparent.

"Fine. Still up every morning either running or horseback riding. And spending every Saturday at the estate in Groton."

Hugh's father, William Amos Bancroft, currently president of the Boston Elevated Railway, had held a term as Mayor of Cambridge in the mid-nineties, but for Gray, his Harvard credentials were more relevant. Known as "Foxy" during his undergraduate years, the elder Bancroft had been an athlete of renown, a footballer as well as stroke and captain of a succession of winning crews, for which he later had served as coach. Until the previous year, he had served as a Harvard Overseer for two consecutive six-year terms. Still, even the elder Bancroft would find himself deferential to the Royall Professor of Law, who had started his own law firm a year after the Civil War had ended, when the senior Bancroft was only a ten-year old.

"I'm much older than your father, as you know, but I saw him row in Springfield."

Hugh smiled, and started to relax, still fully aware that he was being lulled by old boy talk and social register bonding. They were all members of the same club.

"And in fact, I even saw you row victoriously in—when was it?"

"Ninety-nine," answered Hugh, who couldn't help but feel flattered. "I'm afraid we didn't do so well the next two years, though."

"It's all about the effort," said Gray philosophically. Then, segueing to the practical, he followed with "By the way, did you see the Porter lad row number three against Yale last weekend?"

"I did, in fact," Hugh answered warily.

"Would you like to meet the young man? He's actually waiting for me outside the office."

"I don't think that would be appropriate," said Bancroft, completely unaware that Gray—or someone—had apparently paid the young man's bail.

"You doubtless know you haven't got a case," said Gray, his smile unchanged.

"He confessed."

"Clearly that was before he had a reputable lawyer."

"He literally barreled into the arms of the two Cambridge patrolmen, nearly knocked them both down. They had seen him loitering earlier that evening across from the Porcellian, and had just turned the corner into Quincy Street. They were completely unaware of the theft. Porter just came out with it. It could hardly be considered a coerced confession when the cops were unaware of the crime."

"An unskilled and fortuitous capture. Of course, it would have been better had a Harvard watchman made the grab rather than Cambridge coppers. It never would had made it into your hands and saved us all a lot of bother."

"The Harvard watchmen have a hard time catching a cold," quipped Bancroft. "The officers made the arrest on the spot, which in retrospect—I have to agree with you—was unfortunate. But perfectly legal. And I'm obliged to follow through. A grand jury can decide if there's merit to the case."

"There is no merit, and Harvard can deal with the necessary punishment," said Gray. "As I said, you haven't got a case. The Grand Jury will hand down a 'no bill' before you've finished your argument. You don't have to present it."

"We have a good witness. A watchman can make a positive identification."

"And the stolen clapper? Have you even found it?"

Bancroft was silent, looking down at papers on his desk.

"What? Cat got your tongue?" Gray, who could effectively lash out in a myriad of ways, including in the guise of humor, made matters worse with his hearty laugh.

Bancroft did not find the barb in the form of a pun amusing.

"I fully understand you're trying to make an example of this young man," Gray continued, with a trace of sympathy.

"Even Harvard has had enough of this nonsense," replied Bancroft, "especially after the Old College Pump was blown up. There's little tolerance for these sorts of stunts anymore. Someone's going to get severely injured or killed. Tradition and sentiment are one thing, but times have changed. This is the twentieth century."

"You're never going to stop rambunctious young men from playing practical jokes, but I'll admit that dynamiting the old well went a bit too far. Normally the fraternity boys are just having a good time with their hazing and initiations."

Bancroft gave Gray a skeptical look.

"I think Porter's a Med. Fac.," he said.

"Well, now. Did he say he was?"

"He denied it. Which is exactly what he would do if he were one."

"Well, that's a cogent argument to present to a grand jury. But as regards his possible membership in that ignoble organization, I have no interest or idea." Gray paused for effect. "But perhaps you could ask your father. He might know."

Bancroft felt physically winded from the sucker punch. There had long been rumors that Foxy Bancroft, an Institute and an A.D. man, had also been a Med. Fac. member—even a Society president—during his college years. John Gray knew it to be the case. He also knew, that unlike other prominent Brahmins in the city, Foxy hadn't stayed in the loop as a venerable "former doctor."

"I understand and sympathize with your position," Gray continued. "I'll admit there is less and less tolerance for these shenanigans, which have tended to become more spectacular—and not in a good way—these past few years. The arrest has already been reported, and you don't want it to appear that your office is evidencing any bias in not going through the motions of a prosecution. After all, your father is a Harvard man and former Harvard overseer, you attended Harvard, as did your younger brother Guy, and your younger sister recently married a Harvard man, if I'm not mistaken. You fear being accused of leniency if you don't pursue charges. We Harvard men must all fight against the appearance of privilege and social pull, mustn't we?"

"District Attorney Sanderson would present the case," said Bancroft, "to avoid any possible appearance of bias."

"Well, at least someone has found some use for a Yale man," quipped Gray.

Bancroft, mentally flailing against the ropes, could not manage to come up with a reply of any kind.

"I don't recall Sanderson ever being a student of mine," continued Gray, twisting the knife. Bancroft well knew that Gray was not asking a question to which he didn't already know the answer. But he was helpless and replied needlessly.

"Sanderson did his law at Boston University."

Gray didn't bother to comment further, as his snide questioning only established that Sanderson indeed would not be accused of Harvard bias. Sanderson's academic pedigree spoke volumes to any proper Bostonian, and not favorably. No one would ever dream of accusing District Attorney

Sanderson of a bias toward Harvard. Even so, the Yale man, if he had any brains, would do well to consult Harvard administration before making any sudden moves. His professional bread and butter was in Cambridge, after all, not New Haven.

"I assume you were an A.D. man, like your father," said Gray the Porcellian, a seemingly random diversion that was meant to provide Bancroft with a mental breather, but was also a social place marker. The A.D. had the reputation of taking the top athletes and class leaders, but lacked the mystique of the Porcellian, which boasted a loftier membership. The Boston upper crust, while sticking together against their lessers, did occasionally succumb to rivalries among their own ranks.

"I was," replied Bancroft flatly, not in the mood for a digression. "But consider, sir, there was considerable damage done to Harvard Hall during the break-in. Charges include breaking into a building at night with intent to commit a felony, malicious mischief, destruction of property . . ." Bancroft realized how weak his argument sounded.

"Harvard's problem. If they have to fire an assistant professor to offset the cost of a couple Yale locks and a set of hinges, it's their decision to make. With the advice of a lawyer, if need be. And that lawyer would be me." The legal maven paused. "Prosecute a more suitable depredation. I'm sure many others will come along, you'll have ample opportunity to make your point."

Bancroft had closed his eyes and took in a deep breath. Gray was feeling sorry for him.

"There was no substantial loss, Hugh. Neither the Harvard administration nor faithful alumni will want a Varsity oarsman—who will likely bring glory to the College for the next two years—to be prosecuted. Everyone recognizes it was a prank, and one, I might add, exceptionally well done. And most tellingly, the little incident didn't even stop Austin Jones from ringing the bell the following morning. He had an extra clapper on hand. Had that not been the case, had the morning bell failed to chime for the first time in half a century, then you might have reason to pursue the case. Perhaps even try for the death penalty."

Bancroft, totally defeated, shook his head.

"The press has already reported the theft and arrest. This can't be swept under the rug."

"Your patrolmen arrested the wrong man. There's no shame in admitting that. The press isn't going anywhere with this anyway. If they bother to report anything, it will be a human interest story about Austin Jones, bless the old man's soul. Hell's bells, he was even waking me up for Chapel back when I was an undergraduate. We cursed and loved the man. Assaults on the bell give him something to live for."

The time for Bancroft to argue was over. It didn't take more than a fool to admit to the power of sentiment, even for bad traditions. None of the old boys were inclined to turn on the Med. Fac.; some of the most prominent ones had been members themselves. Gray was addressing a jury of one now.

"Barely a mention in the *Globe* and the *Crimson* so far. The *Crimson* never identifies a student in trouble by name, but even the *Globe* kept him anonymous—probably the stringer who fed the paper the story didn't connect him with the regatta. Or more likely he did. All the news is, and will be, about Class Day and Commencement. Most of the underclassmen are on their way home, so there will be no organized outcry by those undergraduates with a plethora of logic and lack of common sense which are such delightful attributes of youth. The only way this affair draws any attention is if you go to indictment, when your office suffers the humiliation of losing. The alternative to shooting yourself in the foot is shooting yourself in the leg. Let me give you a piece of advice, my boy. Not from a lawyer with more than a modicum of experience but from a wounded Civil War veteran: this is not a battle you should choose to fight."

Gray got up from his armless chair—pressing both palms on the seat to push himself off—and made his move toward the door without waiting for the verdict. He didn't need to.

"It was wonderful to see you, young man. Please give my best to the folks. And if they ever stop treating you well in this place, you just come to me, you hear?"

The assistant district attorney for the county of Middlesex nodded, his eyes heavy, succumbing to a hypnotic trance. Harvard tentacles ran deep, and were usually uplifting. For Hugh Bancroft, this was perhaps the first time he had found himself on the wrong side of privilege.

Gray had pulled the door opened, but turned back for a final word.

"You can expedite the return of the bail bond, correct?" The Harvard Law professor once again didn't wait for an answer. "It came from my own pocket," he said.

Chauncey didn't think that anyone would be in University Hall on a Sunday, and was surprised that Professor Gray escorted him there on foot. The walk from Cambridge City Hall to Harvard took less than five minutes, and the day was cloudless and pleasantly warm.

"I'll leave you here," Gray said after they had both entered the yard and stopped in front of the white limestone building. "Dean Hurlbut is waiting for you in his office. I've fulfilled my assignment." And with that he tipped his hat and walked in the direction of the Law School.

The entrance door to University Hall was unlocked, and Chauncey entered what otherwise appeared to be an empty building until he walked through the open door of Number 4. Not only was Dean Hurlbut behind his desk, but Dean Briggs occupied one of the two upholstered side chairs. The rather frail-appearing Briggs was another Harvard lifer with a background as an English professor, but about a decade older than Hurlbut.

Briggs rose when Chauncey entered—though only to a hunched, semi-upright position—before sitting back down, and nodded for him to take the wooden "student's chair" in front of the desk.

"I thought I might join Dean Hurlbut in the discussion of this matter, Mr. Porter," he said in a clear, high-pitched voice. He had blue eyes and sparse, unruly light hair and a boyish finely wrinkled face. He was not a threatening presence, and his nervous energy and tendency to fidget somehow made him less imposing. Well-thought of among the students, in his earlier role as Hurlbut's predecessor he had a reputation as a student advocate, one known to bend the letter of the law, but not the spirit, to benefit a youth in trouble. Given his reputation and inclinations, his presence was calming, and

Chauncey considered it a good sign that he was there, even though Hurlbut did not have a reputation for heavy-handedness.

"I may have given you the wrong idea when we spoke at the courthouse," said Hurlbut, "but when I discussed the situation with Dean Briggs, we concluded that we had no alternative but to place you on Probation, and in so doing we would have to notify your mother."

Chauncey stiffened, disguising his involuntary movement as an adjustment in his seat.

"Then you have written her?"

"Given the distance, we thought it more expedient to wire. And we were saddened to learn of her suicide several months ago."

Chauncey could not be certain of how much time passed before he responded, but the earth might have stopped moving.

"It was not something I wanted to mention," Chauncey tried to not visibly panic as he searched for his manner of expression. He had not known of Amelia Porter's death. How could he have heard? And he was more than cognizant that only a day earlier he had asked Hurlbut not to contact her. "I have chosen to keep it a secret. There is such a stigma associated with the way she died. And I didn't want to provoke sympathy," he went on, "or make my chums feel uncomfortable."

The atmosphere in the room had become funereal.

"We understand, and we are all very sorry," Hurlbut finally said. "I imagine it's been quite a financial struggle for you, being on your own."

"I've managed," said Chauncey. "There has been a tie-up and some complications with the estate, but I assume they will be sorted in due time."

Hurlbut nodded. Chauncey looked over at Briggs for reassurance. Briggs's facial expression was appropriately solemn. But otherwise, he was silently tapping on the arm of the chair with his right hand, while his left, resting on his knee, absorbed the rapid bouncing of his leg. He stopped his extremity movements to briefly reposition himself in his chair. He leaned forward, then back, and readied himself for entering the conversation, since Hurlbut seemed disinclined to speak further. Perhaps it was a matter of deference, respecting the hierarchy of deans.

"The bigger problem," Briggs finally spoke, "is that in addition to learning of the tragedy of your mother, we also learned that YOU are dead."

With this interchange, one could persuasively make the argument that the earth stood still.

"I can explain," Chauncey eventually said. He had spent the preceding moments slumped forward in his chair, rubbing his forehead as if the massaging could conjure a change in his reality. He was determined not to cry and to preserve his dignity.

"Organize your thoughts, Mr. Porter," said Hurlbut. "And start over."

"Take your time," said Briggs, "we will have no more tolerance for lying."

"Tell us your REAL name, young man," commanded the tall patrician man who had just entered the office, apparently eavesdropping outside of the door and waiting to precisely time his entrance. The right side of his face was defaced by a large irregular stain, as if celebrants had haphazardly swathed part of his face with crimson paint in celebration of a team victory.

Hurlbut, Briggs, and Porter all stood at attention.

"Take my chair, President Eliot," Hurlbut offered, moving out from behind his desk to the unoccupied upholstered armchair in the room.

The seventy-two-year-old Charles William Eliot, who had led the University since 1869, walked around Briggs and plopped down behind the desk with a faint, but discernible groan. Under most circumstances, Hurlbut could put out the student-lit fires without the assistance of the President. But this situation was different, delicate, and likely requiring the pulling of levers that neither Hurlbut nor Briggs could reach. Eliot, after all, had been the one to ask the favor of Professor Gray, whom otherwise he had kept in the dark.

Chauncey Porter didn't wait to be asked again, as it would show disrespect.

"My name is Moishe Levinson," he said.

Eliot cocked his hand behind an ear. "Could you say your given name again?"

"Moishe," he said slowly, enunciating both syllables.

Eliot repeated it, as if rehearsing to get it correctly for a public speech. "And can you explain yourself . . . Moishe." Eliot was all business, no emotion.

Levinson answered the only way he knew how, the way he had explained it to Hollis Wyatt.

"I just wanted to be a College Man, sir," he said.

"I've seen your record," said Eliot. "You could have been admitted easily on your own right. There are a number of poor Jewish students at Harvard."

"I did not want to be treated like a Jewish student, sir."

Eliot bristled. "Let me inform you. There is not one particle of anti-Semitic feeling in this university. Some of the most distinguished of our staff are Jewish, either by descent or by practice. I value them highly. Some of my best friends are of Jewish descent. I value infinitely the liberality of Harvard University."

"With all due respect, sir, you are speaking in theory."

Hurlbut interceded. "It is undeniable that Jewish students have been discriminated against in several of the clubs or fraternities, but . . ."

"One of these frats in particular, I am informed," interrupted Eliot, "elected two members of your race who had represented Harvard victoriously in intercollegiate debating contests. In other instances, I deny that the Jew has been discriminated against solely on account of his religious beliefs. Some might claim that the motive has been personal unpopularity or social undesirability rather than racial prejudice."

Briggs blanched, wriggled in his seat, and cleared his throat.

"What President Eliot is trying to say," he said, "as far as social undesirability is concerned, if I might clarify . . . it could be more on the basis of wealth and social standing, rather than any inherent deficiencies in any particular race of people."

"Chauncey Bates Porter is an Institute man, Dean Briggs," Levinson replied. "Could Moishe Levinson be an Institute Man?"

"Again," persisted Briggs, "that does not necessarily have anything to do with race."

"Which is why there would be no Irish or colored men in the societies as well."

"Nor I. Nor Dean Hurlbut, for that matter," Briggs retorted. "You might not be aware that neither of us were invited to join the Institute as undergraduates. And we must confess ourselves to being neither Irish, Jewish, or colored. We were not, and still are not, part of the Boston society of which that organization for the most part is representative. It is not something that either of us find particularly lamentable; it is merely the truth of the matter. Hebrews are not the sole recipients of this discrimination, if that is what you wish to call it." Briggs was well aware that Eliot, a Boston Brahmin, had been an Institute member. He cast a nervous glance at the university president. As he hoped, Eliot remained silent.

"Then why are none of these races represented on the staffs of the *Crimson*, or the *Advocate*, or the Varsity sports teams? Should those skills and talents be predicated by social standing?"

"There have been notable exceptions of colored students performing very well on the football and baseball squads," Eliot interrupted. "Who was that colored boy who graduated just last year?" he asked, looking at Hurlbut and counting on him to come up with the name he couldn't remember.

"William Clarence Matthews," Hurlbut said softly, looking downward.

"Yes. That's the one," said Eliot, seeming to brighten.

There was an awkward silence.

"Then you continue to deny the antisemitism, President Eliot?" Levinson pressed.

"Don't be impertinent, Mr. Levinson. Your race has suffered nearly two thousand years under grievous forms of persecution, under almost the complete loss of freedom, except the freedom to think and hope. But at last, in this land, you have found a complete intellectual freedom. When I was a student here there were no Jewish students in the college; the same was true of my early years of teaching here. But in the past two decades this has changed—this institution is more hospitable than it was in the beginning, and has become more and more hospitable as time has gone on." He paused. "You must ask yourself, What can you do for the strengthening of your race in this free land? The first object to be pursued is education, the highest possible education for Jewish youth. It is through education that the race can be lifted under freedom. That has been my goal for all students at Harvard. And to achieve that, you do not need to be an imposter . . . and a criminal."

"I did not intend to commit a crime . . . I meant no harm," said Levinson, his voice cracking. "I just wanted to experience what other students have the opportunity to experience. I did not want to be invisible. I did not want to be an outsider."

"And yet in doing so," Eliot spoke more confidently, on his firm philosophical grounds, "you are abandoning your culture, the rituals and traditions of your fathers. That saddens me. It is my belief that kindred races should maintain their own individuality, celebrate racial and ethnic pluralism. The notion of this country being a "melting pot" is a myth; it isn't and never will be. Assimilation or amalgamation of the races is simply non-existent here, and has never been desirable."

"So we should just accept, and be content with, not being able to fully participate in the life of this university?" Levinson asked, having regained his composure and unwilling to concede the argument, even to such an august presence as Eliot.

"You should only be concerned with the freeing power of education," said Eliot. "There are many distinct pathways of experience here. Harvard has and will maintain a rigid policy of religious toleration and admit students without the least regard to the racial qualities of religious or political opinions. But we cannot control the minds and sentiments of the students here, and I am personally unconcerned with what unawakened minds dawdle with. Admittedly there are careless, indifferent, lazy boys who have no bent or intellectual ambitions of any sort here, only social ambitions. The vast majority are students of wealth. And though we might wish that the University did not offer the same contrast between the rich man's mode of life and the poor man's—or that of the Christian and the Jew, for that matter—that the outer world offers, it does, and it is not certain that the presence of this contrast is unwholesome or injurious."

Levinson could think of nothing more to say in his defense. How could he explain that he had never had a desire to attend Harvard for the freedom of education? He could educate himself on his own with books. But as himself would he have fared better than Shmuel, whose Harvard only consisted of a handful of classroom buildings and the Jerusalem table in Gore library? He had only wanted the chance to prove he could be a college man. Which he had certainly accomplished and more, and he didn't regret anything. But everything was over. And what was to become of him?

"I'm sorry, sir," he said to President Eliot.

"Sorry isn't enough, Mr. Levinson."

With the atmosphere now ominous, a storm pending, Hurlbut changed the direction of the conversation, seeking momentary shelter by delaying a decision on how they would proceed. Clearly the young man was gifted and capable, despite the manner in which he exhibited those talents. He and Briggs had admitted to one another a certain admiration for the wayward boy, a feeling they could not express to President Eliot. Both curious as to how Levinson had managed his impersonation, they questioned him regarding his background and how things had transpired. They listened passively, their faces not betraying their astonishment. He had done it all on his own, both his academic and athletic accomplishments. Under other circumstances, he was a Harvard man in whom they could take great pride. President Eliot looked aggrieved throughout the discourse but allowed the Deans to proceed with their queries as if it would make a difference. It would not.

Levinson described his home life before he embarked on the guise, his life and work in his ethnic North End neighborhood. All the men were surprised that his cousin Shmuel had graduated from Harvard with honors three years earlier, though none could specifically remember him. Levinson informed them that Shmuel was now working in a junior managerial position for a clothing manufacturer in Springfield, conveying that it was not an occupation to which he himself aspired. Eliot interjected that although members of his race might not be sought after in the banking and financial realms in Boston and New York, they certainly could avail themselves of opportunities in professional school, Harvard Law and Medical Schools being his preferred examples.

Next Levinson described his job at the Masconomo House, and how that had afforded him the opportunity to acquaint himself with lives of the privileged. That, as well as the linguistic and social lessons taught in *The*

Importance of Being Earnest. He confessed that he had learned his speaking and behavior from none other than Emma Conghlan, whom all, including President Eliot, had seen on stage. He detailed the tragic death of the real-life Porter, and how he had come to acquire his possessions. He explained how at the beginning he had intended only to assume his identity for a short time, but things—precipitated by his success—had gotten out of hand. He emphasized that he had never stolen anything from anyone, and had not attempted to obtain scholarship money from the University. While all three men had assumed Levinson worked fairly closely with Coach Wray, they were unaware of Levinson's mentorship and close relationship with Doctor Sargent, or that he had managed to obtain housing accommodations in Hemenway, the latter being startling news to all of them. Levinson never mentioned that Hollis Wyatt was aware of his true identity.

"So no other students knew of your duplicity," Hurlbut asked.

"No sir," Levinson lied. Under all circumstances he had to protect Hollis.

"And not even your aunt and uncle knew?" prompted Briggs.

"No, sir."

"So only the actress Emma Conghlan knows," Hurlbut reiterated.

"Yes, sir."

"And absolutely no one else? It is most important, crucial, that we determine this," Hurlbut continued.

Levinson paused and took a deep breath. "Actually, only one other person."

"And who might that be?"

"Harry Houdini," answered Moishe Levinson.

All further conversing fell into a sinkhole. Seconds passed before sound returned, in the form of faint foot tapping against the floor. The administrators exchanged looks amongst themselves, sequentially as if stage-directed, as Briggs added finger-rolling to his tattoo.

"I believe he can keep a secret," Levinson finally added, a point of information without intent of irony.

Levinson was asked to leave and sit outside the office while the Deans and the President discussed the situation, which was clearly untenable. For Levinson to stay enrolled as a deceased Montanan was out of the question; and Gray had already confided to Eliot that an indictment for the bell clapper theft from Middlesex county was unlikely to be sought, and if foolishly attempted, would result in a no bill. To publicly reveal the imposture instead would be disastrous, even if the charges resulted in a prison sentence. As far as Harvard disciplinary options were concerned, expulsion would require a majority vote of the faculty at a regularly scheduled, documented meeting. That, too, would require a disclosure of the stolen identity, since the faculty was unlikely to expel a student for a prank. The only option was to pressure Levinson's withdrawal and silence, even though they knew that they had no real leverage over him.

"We must never disclose this," said Eliot, "and neither can he. Prison or no prison, can you imagine what the press would do with this story if he came forward and talked? What a scandal! And throw in the antisemitism nonsense! And the complicity of an actress and escape artist!"

Neither Briggs nor Hurlbut spoke. The President would have to make the call.

"And just before I intended to announce our fundraising campaign!" Eliot lamented. Practically everything came down to his major priority, raising money for increased faculty pay and growth of the university. Harvard, despite being flush relative to other universities in the country, had been running at a deficit for several years and Eliot had no intention of compromising on his ambitious plans.

"Let's just say he doesn't come back," said Hurlbut. "There will be a lot of people asking questions, particularly when next year's crew season approaches."

"He was caught stealing the bell clapper from Harvard Hall and he withdrew," responded Eliot. "It's not as if athletes have never been on probation or gotten into trouble before. Wray won't be happy, but he's had the misfortune of losing oarsmen in the past and managed. People will soon forget. We might perhaps encourage the rumor that Porter was a Med. Fac. No one can confirm it, and no one will dispute it."

"A rumor like that could generate interest among the press, so I wouldn't advise it," said Hurlbut. His thoughts instantly turned to his assistant dean, Edgar Huidekoper Wells, who would have proffered the same advice. Wells would know better than most, being the only current Harvard administrator who had himself been in the Med. Fac.

"You make a good point," said Eliot.

"Let's just hope no enterprising reporter determines that Chauncey Porter had been dead for nearly two years when he rowed in the Varsity boat," said Briggs.

"It's a chance we'll have to take," Eliot replied. "Heaven knows we don't want Yale finding out there was a counterfeit oarsman. This is the first time I've ever wished that Harvard had lost a race." He turned to Briggs, whose judgment he unreservedly trusted. "Well?"

"Officially, at least as far as the records show, it's probably best that there is no evidence that Chauncey Porter ever matriculated, since the real Porter died before his first term even started. There will be traces of his namesake, so to speak, but as you suggest, eventually people will forget. At least there will be nothing to find in the records." Briggs was being practical and it clearly pained him, as it ran against his nature.

"We expunge his records and put Levinson in exile," said Eliot. "Agreed?" He looked first at Hurlbut, who reluctantly nodded, and then back at Briggs.

"But we have to think about the boy . . ." Briggs said, true to his character. "He clearly has talents and intelligence, and it would be a shame to destroy him. He should be given another chance."

"You are talking about an imposter," said Eliot.

"I'm talking about a twenty year old boy who has a life ahead of him," countered Briggs. "And besides, don't you want to give him some incentive for keeping things to himself? Is it in our best interest to make him so desperate he chooses to lash out? If he were to go public, irreparable damage would be incurred by Harvard. Despite all appearances, I have confidence that our Hebrew is a gentleman and a man of his word. But we shouldn't press our luck."

Eliot saw Hurlbut nodding in agreement.

Fittingly, Eliot remembered the exact words he had used to describe Dean Briggs when he had conferred a Doctorate of Laws degree upon him five years earlier, referring to him as "patient, tender, discerning, candid, just and cheering because convinced of the overwhelming predominance of good in the world." Briggs was right, Eliot could not allow his anger to overcome his better angels and better judgment. "And what do you suggest?" he asked.

"Help establish him somewhere. A train ticket west and enough cash to keep him from becoming destitute until he lands on his feet."

"Somewhere far away," added Eliot, although he was convinced in principle. "Ideas?"

Both Deans looked at their President blankly.

Eliot took a deep breath and reflexively covered his right cheek with his left hand. Rather than hide the disfigurement, the gesture made it more prominent, appearing as if he had set his hand into a pool of blood.

"I will give Louis Brandeis a call," he said. "Nothing like asking one extraordinary Jew what to do about another one."

Dean Briggs obtained a passkey to Hemenway from the janitor on duty in the Building Superintendent's office, since the gymnasium closed at 3 p.m. on Sunday afternoons. He waited until after dinner with his wife Mary Frances and their three children before walking to the building as dusk approached. He went empty-handed, knowing from Levinson that there were already two suitcases in his storage room quarters.

Earlier, after Levinson had returned to 4 University Hall, the ultimatum was presented and accepted. The terms were non-negotiable. He was never to speak of his time at Harvard ever, to anyone. He would never communicate in any way with any of his previous classmates, friends, acquaintances, or faculty from the nearly two years he had spent on campus. Chauncey Bates Porter was dead, and had died before ever coming to Harvard. As far as Levinson was to be concerned, Chauncey Porter did not exist and never had. A stern President Eliot assured him that if he were ever to violate his word of honor, Eliot would personally see to it that Moishe Levinson spent the rest of his days in prison. Few men could make such an idle threat sound as convincing as did the distinguished Boston Brahmin and Harvard President Charles William Eliot. He then excused himself and went to his office to make a phone call, offering Levinson a civil "Godspeed."

Levinson would not return to his living quarters in Hemenway, but instead spend the night with his aunt and uncle to inform them that he was leaving town, and had job prospects in the West. Briggs would pack a suitcase of everything that he needed and meet him at South station the next morning at 9 a.m. There he would purchase a train ticket for Levinson for a location to be determined, and provide pocket money to hold him over. Afterwards, Briggs would return to his office and call both Doctor Sargent and Coach Wray, to inform them of the unfortunate but justifiable withdrawal of Chauncey Porter from Harvard College.

Briggs found a janitor mopping the floor within the main exercise area of the gymnasium. He informed the worker of his presence there, not wanting to be mistaken for an intruder, and found the storage room in the basement unlocked. Briggs lit the gas lamp on the desk and assessed the surroundings. He only saw one of the tan leather suitcases, but once opening it, found the smaller one had been placed inside. Briggs had already determined that he would use the larger one for Levinson's clothes and toiletries—all the lad's earthly belongings that would fit—and the smaller one for the papers, notebooks, and other items that identified Chauncey Bates Porter as a Harvard student. These he would take away and personally burn. Dismayed by the monograms on both items of luggage, he dealt with their removal as his first order of business, both by scraping off the leather with his pocket knife and holding a match flame to the area. The larger bag he placed fully open on the cot; the other, similarly opened, he set on the floor beside the small desk.

Chauncey Porter's shirts, collars, undergarments, shoes and socks were on shelves, sharing space with spare medicine balls and a variety of weighted exercise devices and dumbbells. His jackets, trousers, and winter outerwear, including a Harvard scarf, were hung from a waterpipe that traversed a corner of the ceiling. Briggs selected carefully, tossing the few monogramed items, such as several handkerchiefs, into the smaller suitcase. Even excluding all of the bulky winter wear, there was only room for about a third of the Chauncey Porter wardrobe. Levinson had several months before winter, Briggs reasoned, so he could make due for the short term, but for good measure he selected one of several sweaters to include. The remaining clothes would be boxed and transported to Cram, who could disperse the items among the neediest students. Fittingly, many of the clothes would ultimately end up on the backs of Jewish students.

The desktop had four neat stacks of notebooks, exam booklets and loose paper, each stack representing a different course Porter had taken that term. He had already received the self-addressed postcards informing him of the grades received on the final examination and for the entire course, each on top of the appropriate pile, all either "A" or "A minuses." Briggs scooped the piles up without bothering to examine them further and tossed them into the suitcase beside the desk. What was he to do with the expensive silver inkwell and pen and pencil set, all monogrammed with 'CBP'? He hesitated for a moment, contemplating having a jeweler or silversmith disguise or modify the engravings, and deciding against it, tossed them into the small suitcase. He would scrape the monograms off himself and somehow rid himself of the defaced items. If Levinson had inherited other engraved silver items from Porter, he had already sold them.

Besides some pencils, a few blank notepads, and a straightedge, the letter drawer contained a copy of the pamphlet: "Rules and Regulations of Harvard College," with Porter's name in the upper right hand corner, and several letters bound by string. Briggs picked up the stack of correspondence and turned it over. There were nearly a dozen, all of identical size, the stationary belonging to the same person. The back of the visible outside envelope was embossed with the name and image of Longneck Cove; handwritten in pen above the return address was "L. Wyatt." Briggs had already been stunned by Levinson's astounding achievements, and this was just the icing on the cake. It appeared that Chauncey Porter, with Moishe Levinson as his Cyrano, had received the attentions of the Wyatt daughter. Briggs could only assume that he had not revealed his true identity to her, and it was easy enough to confirm by reading the letters. Which he would not do, respecting Moishe Levinson's privacy—they would be burned unread. He tossed the letters, along with the pamphlet, into the suitcase for disposal.

A single deep side drawer of the desk remained. It was nearly full, again with papers, notebooks, and exam books related to courses Porter had previously taken. On top was Chauncey Porter's Varsity "H." It had yet to be sewn on to a sweater, a white one designating crew, since the red "H" of a footballer adorned a black one. Next to it was the Institute of 1770 medallion, threaded with a crimson ribbon, and underneath, at the top of the stack of papers, was his unframed Institute of 1770 shingle, diploma-like confirmation of Chauncey Porter's high ranking social standing among Harvard men. Briggs shook his head. A Hebrew in the Institute of 1770, anonymous and forever unknown, or else Boston Brahmins would be sent into conniptions. At the thought of it, Briggs let out a girlish giggle that morphed into a snort. There was hope for the meritocracy.

Briggs pulled out the drawer and overturned it, dumping its entire contents into the smaller suitcase, all to be destroyed and lost forever. He leveled the pile out with his hands so the suitcase would close, like a child smoothing out sand at the seashore. He shut it firmly and secured both of the leather straps. And then he thought of a young man as an older man, finding comfort in his memories, remembering a regatta victory over Yale. What did it matter? It was only a swatch of cloth after all. So Dean Briggs unlatched the suitcase, fished for the crimson "H," and tucked it into one of Levinson's shoes in the larger suitcase. He closed and strapped both suitcases and carried them out of Hemenway, any traveler coming or going, a solitary figure walking in the dark.

It was after nine that evening when he received the telephone call from President Eliot. His instructions were to write a letter of recommendation for Moishe Levinson, a self-educated polymath who was qualified for, but had been unable to attend Harvard College due to circumstances beyond his control. But it was with the utmost confidence that LeBaron Russell Briggs believed he would qualify for admission to the Law School of the University of Missouri in Columbia and wholeheartedly endorsed him. Eliot then gave him the name and address of the recipient, who happened to be Dean of the Law School.

"Louis Brandeis used to practice in St. Louis, but only for a short time." Eliot explained. "Still, he knows people, of course."

"Shall I say that Louis Brandeis gave us his name?"

"Absolutely," said Eliot. "just, for Heaven's sake, keep MY name out of it."

"Anything else?" asked Briggs.

"On second thought," Eliot replied after a pause, "say his name is 'Michael' Levinson. Let's not borrow trouble."

Briggs wrote the letter in long hand on his personal stationary, and sealed it in, and addressed, the envelope. The next morning he would take the Atlantic Avenue elevated train to South Station and hand it to Moishe Levinson, along with a second envelope with fifty dollars in cash, a single large tan leather suitcase—marred and discolored near the handle—and a one way train ticket to St. Louis, Missouri on the New York Central Line.

"Do you object to being known as Michael?" Briggs asked him.

"Not at all. I went by Michael at the Masconomo House."

Briggs nodded. "Do Harvard proud," he said, clasping Michael Levinson's hand at the train platform. Briggs deservedly had the reputation of being a champion for the underdog. He wiped the corner of his eye, and finding his hand in close proximity, began scratching his forehead. "No student loves Harvard College more adhesively than the man who has been turned out of it. Only keep the love to yourself," he added. "You can do that; do I have your assurances?"

Levinson nodded. He tried to focus his thoughts, but they kept settling on a line from *Earnest*, like a tune he couldn't expunge from his mind.

"You have my word," he replied. "Remember what Algernon said in *The Importance of Being Earnest?*"

Briggs raised a questioning eyebrow.

"'Really, if the lower orders don't set us a good example, what on earth is the use of them?'"

A Wrapped Package

After the meeting with Aunt Lillian, I returned to the Archives on Monday to tell Eleanor what I had learned. She had the relevant volume of the *Crimson* pulled from the files, and set me down at the work desk closest to her, the one at which I always sat and had come to identify as my personal Jerusalem table. I started from the date of the regatta and moved forward. I had previously reviewed the articles when tracking down Porter's association with the Varsity crew. Porter's performance was mentioned in complimentary terms, as was Hollis Wyatt's, but nothing more substantive had been revealed. Two days later, the celebratory dinner at the Vendome was covered in relative detail, including excerpts from congratulatory speeches by both Coach Wray and the man himself, President Eliot. That article I had also seen.

From there, I didn't have to search very far. Two issues later, a small clipping on the second page reported that the tongue to the bell in Harvard Hall had been stolen, and that the Cambridge police had arrested a student, a sophomore, who was being held in custody.

I carried the large volume over to the counter to show Eleanor.

"They don't mention him by name," I said.

"That was newspaper policy. The *Crimson* would generally never specifically identify students who got in trouble. And you might also notice there is no specific mention of the Med. Fac., although many must have speculated that they were responsible."

"Why not?"

"The *Crimson* didn't acknowledge that the Med. Fac. existed. Technically they had no proof of it, and a considerable number of people didn't believe the society was around anymore, at least in its original version. They could explain away the pranks as copycat acts of individual students, or attribute them to fraternity initiations. Also, the University wasn't eager to admit that the Med. Fac. was still around, either. For years some people speculated that Med. Fac. members were never apprehended because the Administration wasn't keen to go after the children of privilege. The old familiar 'social pull' charge."

I looked around the room to confirm we were alone. Warren had left his work station on a retrieval errand.

"So that's it, then. Poppa took the blame for Hollis stealing the bell clapper, and the authorities discovered the ruse."

"Likely the Harvard authorities. Customarily the Dean of Students, which was Hurlbut, would contact the student's father regarding any disciplinary matters. At the very least, notification letters for any student put on probation was the general practice. Similarly, a follow-up letter would be sent when the student satisfied the terms of probation. Copies of these communications would normally have been in the student's file. All of which would have been handled through the Dean's office."

"Hurlbut, not Briggs."

"Exactly. And there's no record of him coming up for dismissal or expulsion in the Meeting of the Faculty minutes."

"So he resigned, or was forced out."

Eleanor nodded. "Voluntary withdrawal. There would be no question that he would have to leave. How could it possibly be managed otherwise? He couldn't continue to impersonate Chauncey, and if the news of his imposture ever came out, there would be hell to pay on many levels. It appears that they cut him a deal, with good reason. In any case, he had a very good run."

Most of the loose ends had been tied together, except for one. "But why did he end up in Missouri?" I asked.

"Did he already have family there?" Eleanor asked.

I shook my head.

"St. Louis, for a city in the Midwest, did have a sizeable Jewish community and . . ."

"And what?"

"And I'm sure that many Bostonians might consider it an appropriate site for exile." She allowed herself a small smile.

"I suppose so, given its proximity to the Land of Oz." Admitting to my home state frequently prompted references to Dorothy and the Wizard. In response, I sometimes told people that I had attended Yellow Brick Road High School, and on more than one occasion I needed to clarify that I was joking. At such times I regretted that my grandparents had ventured beyond New York City or Boston. What would my life had been like had I been raised an urbane Northeasterner rather than a Midwestern rube? Then I would think of Poppa, obliged to start his life in the Pale of Settlement. Who was I to complain?

"It still just seems so . . . so random," I said.

Eleanor considered. "When did your grandfather graduate from the Law School there, do you know?"

"Nineteen oh-nine."

"Then he landed on his feet very quickly. He must have been admitted to the Law School almost immediately after he arrived."

I nodded.

"I would speculate," said Eleanor, "that Briggs had a hand in it. He was a very kind-hearted man. Not the vindictive sort, and always concerned about the student as an individual."

"Even an imposter?"

"I would believe so," said Eleanor, "which would explain the continued success of your grandfather, despite his adventure, or misadventure. The affair didn't appear to set him back professionally, now, did it?" Not a question, but a statement. "Being admitted to Law School nearly immediately was not exactly clawing back from disgrace."

I nodded again.

She continued. "Briggs was more inclined to believe in redemption than Eliot, but Eliot trusted Briggs and might have taken his advice. It can't be denied that attending Harvard gives one certain advantages . . ." Eleanor was smiling fully, and recognizing the look on her face, I expected a zinger.

"There's a saying here," she went on. "At Harvard it isn't who you know." She paused for a couple of beats. "It's WHOM you know . . ."

Harvard had forced me into a transition that wasn't an easy one. The search for the answer to Poppa's secret—to be honest my obsession with it—made things much easier for me. I was compelled to give up my over-studying, to realistically assess my abilities and aspirations. I had a goal to achieve pending others that would emerge after a time of tumult, my identity crisis. I came to love historical research, which from then on would color my life choices. At the beginning of my sophomore year I quit pre-med and declared a concentration in history, which led to parental consternation and strife before eventual acceptance. I also became politically engaged in the anti-war movement, which was equally hard for them to deal with. But acceptance would come in a variety of ways over many different things for the three of us. I abandoned the notion that my life had been indelibly scripted by background and upbringing. And with that my resentments dissipated.

Aaron and Jeff remained my roommates until graduation. As for Eleanor, I continued to see her regularly, especially when the research for my thesis—on Lebaron Russell Briggs and his myriad of influences on higher education in America—again brought me to the Archives. Becca, not surprisingly, faded from my life without explanation, confrontation, or resolution. The latter was the hardest for me to deal with, and occasionally pangs of sorrow and regret would strike me out of nowhere. She was wired into my neuronal pathways, though, and I couldn't always detour around those circuits when particular associations cropped up, like Calvados or quiche or clogs.

As for the remaining three years of my college career, I thought that Poppa would approve of me making the news staff of the *Crimson*, much as he would revel in my participation in a couple of plays at the Loeb and good causes at the Phillips Brooks House. Alas, I could never come close to his physical abilities, and there was no way I could participate in sports at the collegiate level. But in the subsequent springs I would regularly check out a shell from the Weld boat house. Poppa probably would have enjoyed seeing me on the

Charles most of all. I like to think that he was truly at peace with himself on that river, and we shared that. Both of us on the Charles across time, propelling our oars through the water, hypnotized by the sound of our breathing, our bodies folding and unfolding, feeling the chill of the same breeze pushing against our sweat-drenched singlets.

Knowing that I didn't belong in Becca's world, or want to belong, didn't lessen the pain at first. But she could not be faulted for the circumstances of her birth. She was born rich instead of poor or somewhere in the middle, and like everyone else, she had to manage the best she could. Owing to her tutelage, in my subsequent relationships with women I didn't see myself as either a project or an exchange student from South America. After graduation, never really having had a serious college girlfriend, I spent a year traveling in Europe. It was there where I met my future wife Susan, and then returned to enter graduate school in history.

I reflected on these aspects of my personal history on the plane ride home from Boston to Philly, where both Sue and I had established our lives and made our careers in academia at the University of Pennsylvania. I had composed myself enough after the encounter with Becca to delay my flight and participate in one of the following day's reunion activities, the grandiose tented outdoor buffet luncheon in the Radcliffe Quad. I was gratified to reacquaint myself with some old friends and acquaintances, and establish new ones. I didn't see Becca there, but I was glad to reconnect with both of my former roommates, some fellow *Crimson* staffers, and especially my former bodyguard, Fritz Magnussen, who like many former Harvard jocks, was a rich and successful businessman.

I could fit my laptop in the Coop bag that Becca had given me, so I brought my laptop and wrapped package onto the plane as carry on, paranoid that my checked baggage might somehow be lost and never recovered. Whatever she had given me was much too valuable for me to risk losing, if only as a footnote, a missing citation in that early chapter. Not being a patient man, I had phoned Susan before boarding and asked, if possible, that our daughters could join us for dinner. Both daughters, to my great joy and good fortune, had not strayed far from home. Eleanor was in her final year of medical school at U Penn, and Abigail, an English major, was finishing up her senior year as a Penn undergraduate.

"What's the occasion?" Sue asked.

"I have a story that needs to be told. And a surprise."

"Sounds intriguing. See you at the airport."

When I think on it, even I find it remarkable, and perhaps bizarre, that I had never told the true story of my grandfather to my wife or daughters. I had not spoken of it to anyone besides Eleanor and Becca. And even with Eleanor, after our final speculations and summations had been established in the second half of my freshman year, we never spoke of him again. I certainly had every opportunity to make a splash with a *Crimson* exposé once I made the newspaper staff, and with what Harvard was doing in Angola and elsewhere, not to mention their choice of investments, the Institution certainly deserved a spit in the eye. But doing so was unthinkable to me, exploitative and sensational, and most of all disrespectful to the memory of Poppa. And once I had decided to not even confide to my parents, burying his secret and making it my own came easily.

But the time had come to tell it. Both daughters were already in the house when my wife had driven me back from the airport. There had been a delay with the luggage, and by the time we returned, everyone was hungry.

"We already ordered the pizza," Abigail informed us as we entered the kitchen from the garage. "And Eleanor brought ice cream."

"Let's at least have it in the dining room," I said.

Sue hung her handbag over a kitchen chair.

"If you expect a special occasion dinner," she said, "you'll have to give me more notice."

The pizza was delivered, and we had a casual meal in the rarely used dining room, pizza boxes stacked in the middle of the table, dinner plates with no utensils. I opened up a decent bottle of Oregonian Pinot. We made casual conversation, revolving mainly about how things had gone at the reunion, which I reported rather vaguely, but everyone was impatient to hear my news.

I delayed until we were all finished with the pizza and had the table cleared of the dinner plates and boxes. Abigail went to get desert plates and the ice cream, and I went into my office to retrieve a folder from my vintage wooden filing cabinet. It was filed under "Miscellaneous," and contained copies of the documents I had initially obtained from the University of Missouri Archives, plus all the notes and photocopies that had been the product of my investigations with Eleanor. The folder was a relatively thick one, and didn't fold completely flat for an obvious reason.

I returned to the table with another bottle of wine, which I opened while the desert bowls were passed around and the scoops of ice cream dispensed. I refilled everyone's wine glasses from the new bottle amidst a palpable growing impatience. Once everyone had taken their first spoonful of ice cream, I pulled out the reason for the file folder not being completely flat, and held it up in my hand.

"Can anyone guess what this is?" I asked, beginning to relish the moment preceding the upcoming drama.

"What? Is this alphabet time on 'Sesame Street?'" said Abigail, the more irreverent and impatient of our daughters. Time had clearly expired for my being indulged. Mockery and humiliation from both daughters was forthcoming if I didn't cease and desist. I needed to play it straight and get on with it.

"It's a Harvard Varsity "H" for crew. For a Varsity letterman's sweater." I looked first at Abigail, then at Eleanor. "It belonged to your great-grandfather, Michael Levinson."

All sounds associated with eating ceased. Abigail's full spoon had stopped in mid-transit to her gaping mouth. Sue and Eleanor had been prepared to dig into their dishes, but suspended motion, as if just hearing the end of shift whistle at a coal mine. Three pairs of eyes drilled into mine, unblinking. This piece of news did not compute.

It was Abigail's fault, being the wise ass with the "Sesame Street" quip, but I couldn't help but be reminded of the old junior high school joke: "What do you have when you hold one green ball in one hand, and one green ball in the other?"

Kermit the Frog's undivided attention.

And so I began the story, starting with the skinny wait list letter from Harvard. I glossed over the time I spent in Manchester-by-the-Sea with Becca, of course, neglecting to mention the torrid marijuana and booze enabled evening we had spent together. At the time, I only viewed it as my loss of sexual innocence, but it was a prelude to the shedding of illusions of all sorts; more valuable life lessons would be forthcoming. If Poppa helped me to see my life in a different way and proceed accordingly, Becca Appleton Wyatt had dropped me off at school.

The thought occurred to me that Poppa lost his own innocence as I had, but in a more dramatic fashion. I lapsed into a feeling that had first struck me upon learning about Poppa. Compared to him I was soft, coddled, never suffering deprivations as he had. Even his only son, my father, had served in World War II, volunteering to fight the Nazis, risking his life for a cause. What had happened to manhood, to mensch-dom, in two generations? Should I view it simply as good fortune that I had never been tested by daunting challenges? It was enough to propel me into disconsolance. I reminded myself that it was the circumstance of my birth, beyond my control. Just as it was with Rebecca Appleton Wyatt. I should judge neither of us too harshly.

Remarkably, the three main women in my life listened to the entire narrative without interrupting. "And now it's time to open up the package that Becca Wyatt gave me at the reunion."

"You slept with her back in Manchester-by-the-Sea, didn't you," said Susan point-blank. The girls laughed, she along with them. "You always led me to believe it was that Wellesley girl sophomore year," she added.

I rolled my tongue along the inside of my cheek.

"We were expecting the unexpurgated version," said my English major.

"All I can say is I hope Grandfather Levinson got it on with Emma Conghlan as well," Eleanor had to contribute.

"Am I the only one to appreciate a certain symmetry in this narrative?" Abigail opined.

"That's a stretch" countered Eleanor, who lapsed into the sibling rivalry that neither daughter had, or probably never would, outgrow. "It would only be analogous had great-gramps scored with Lillian. Then you have the story of both Jewish boys winning the heart of the uber-shiksa, at least momentarily."

I was beginning to feel that the gravitas of the moment was eroding into a prurient reality show. But was it reasonable to expect that my progeny would react the way that I had? Michael Levinson had just been a name to them, a man they had never met. They knew little of his life other than the fact that he had been a poor immigrant, and then a law professor and civil rights attorney. He was a figure identifiable in old family photographs, but nothing more than that. I never had displayed a picture of him on my desk or the wall of my study, because none of the images reflected the man whom I, and I alone, knew him to be.

"Come on girls," I finally said, a referee breaking up two boxers in a clinch. "This is serious business. To me, anyhow." I considered them suitably chastised as I began unwrapping the parcel. Two flat items were contained, one a framed photograph, and the second something smaller and separately wrapped in brown paper and sealed with tape, likely a photograph also.

I set down the smaller wrapped item and held the framed photograph in front of me. The frame was black and heavily carved, and much too thick and elaborate for the cabinet card—surrounded by a matte of an olive-colored velvet—that it displayed. The photograph was a full length formal portrait of Harry Houdini. I would have recognized him by the face alone, but the giveaway was his outstretched arms, demonstrating three sets of manacles, at and slightly above the wrists, and near the elbow. For the restraints to be exhibited to full effect, his sleeves were rolled up, thick white bands contrasting with the black of his frock coat. His shirt was white and high-collared, the white bow tie of the same brocaded fabric barely discernible from its background. He looked at me with a grave intensity.

"Who is it?"

"Show us."

I turned the picture around and moved it across the table for all to briefly see, like an elementary schoolteacher showing his students the pictures in the book being read to them.

"It's Houdini," I answered, immediately turning it around so I could examine it more closely and read the overlying script at the bottom. "And it's inscribed . . ."

I read it first myself before reading it again aloud.

"For Chauncey Bates Porter, whom I met by 'Chance,'—that's in quotes—Never be afraid of escaping, only be afraid of drowning! And it's signed 'Harry Houdini.' And directly under his name he writes 'C'est Moi! C'est Moi!' And then the date: October 27, 1905."

Sue held her hand out to see it, then passed it on for the girls to examine.

I was shaking my head. "Poppa told me he had met Houdini, along with everything else, and Eleanor confirmed that Houdini had performed at Harvard around that time. I have the *Crimson* and *Boston Globe* articles about it in this stack of papers. This is incredible. It happened."

I waited for Abigail to finish her examination before I opened the other package. She seemed reluctant to give it back.

"Weird inscription," she said.

"I agree," said Eleanor. I looked at Sue, who gave me a non-committal shrug.

"And why is that?"

"Why should anyone be afraid of escaping?" That was Eleanor.

"Exactly," agreed Abigail. "You can't take this at face value. Look for the subtext . . ."

"Come on . . ." I said.

"Emma Conghlan and Hollis Wyatt weren't the only ones who knew Poppa's secret. Houdini did too."

"What makes you say that?" I wanted to move on, but Abigail was persistent.

"Why in the world would Houdini say 'It is I! It is I!?'"

"How about because it WAS him," I answered.

"What was your grandfather's real name in the old country, before it was Anglicized?"

"Moishe."

"Spell it."

"M-O-I-S-H-E."

"And what would it have been shortened to?"

"Moey, I suppose."

"There you go!" Abigail beamed, having apparently made her point. I was dense; it was clear that I didn't get it.

"He's not saying 'It is I!' . . . He's saying 'It is Moey!'" Abigail, seeing the blank look on my face, felt compelled to drive her argument home. "Not Mu-WAH, but MO-ee! He's really giving your Poppa advice, cautioning him, from one Jew to another! He has to know that Chauncey Porter was really Moishe Levinson! It's SO obvious! Jesus, Dad . . ."

I was flabbergasted. But Abigail had to be right. Sue was nodding in agreement, as was Eleanor, giving her sister credit where credit was due. Nevertheless, medical student daughter would have something to say.

"This is HOUDINI we're talking about, Dad, Harry Houdini. You think that dude wouldn't have some pretty sophisticated Jew-dar?"

I readily conceded the point.

The unframed photograph was the one that Aunt Lillian had shown Becca and me before on the day of our visit, from the old photo album in the library. Had Becca pilfered it from her aunt's family photo album for me? It was the original, not a copy, of two handsome young men and a beautiful young woman in her late teens. The photograph had been taken with the three of them—Chauncey, Lillian, and Hollis—sitting on the grassy lawn at Longneck Cove. What style they all had! Both Hollis and his sister wore all white except for their hats—Hollis's was a straw boater with a thick polka dot hat band; Lillian wore a flat-brimmed black hat with luxurious black feathers on one side. Her dress was high-necked, and she held a nosegay of flowers. Had Poppa brought them for her? Poppa wore a short collared white shirt with a long tie. His trouser were white, but his jacket, lightly striped, could have been a grey or beige. He wore a boater of his own, with a thick dark-colored band. They were all looking straight at me.

"This is the only decent photo of a young Michael Levinson I've ever seen," I said, "I'm going to have it framed and it will go in my office."

"Maybe you should hang it in the living room for everyone to see and contemplate," Sue suggested.

"They are all so beautiful," said Eleanor. "What a couple your Poppa and Lillian would have made, although I'm glad it didn't work out for the obvious reason that I wouldn't be here."

"It wouldn't have worked out," I said, "despite the fact that it runs counter to all romantic notions."

"I don't think it would have worked out with you and Becca Wyatt either," said Sue, smiling. "Just saying."

"You're very correct in your assessment."

"What's she like now?"

"Beautiful, vivacious . . . and sad, I think. It's trite to say, but money can't buy you happiness."

"You should thank her for these things."

"I will. I'll drop her a note."

I didn't want to dwell on Becca Wyatt, and changed the topic of the conversation back to Aunt Lillian. "It turns out, according to what Eleanor told me, that Aunt Lillian had a happy and lengthy Boston marriage with a widowed friend. Everyone knew about it."

"So she was a lesbian?" my Eleanor asked.

"It appears that was the case."

"In keeping with NOT countering romantic notions," said Abigail, "I would like to believe that Poppa was her own true love, so she never married, and only discovered an affection for women later in life, knowing that she could never find another man as perfect as Moishe Levinson. At least not anywhere in Boston society. She coveted a borscht and black bread man."

The comment was not meant to provoke a response. Susan entered the discussion again. "I knew you had a special relationship with Eleanor, but this makes it more understandable."

"Is she still alive?" Eleanor asked. She knew the archivist had been her namesake, but little more than that she had been indispensable in helping me with my undergraduate thesis.

"She died about ten years ago," I answered, "and I can say, without hesitation, that present company excluded, she was the most important woman in my life. She made me recognize my value, she taught me how to be an historical researcher, and she eased me out of my innocence. And by that I mean my naiveté about wealth and privilege, about our so-called romantic notions, and even about Harvard."

I looked around and saw they wanted to me expound a bit.

"She saw my infatuation with Becca Wyatt for what it was, and she told me about Lillian's Boston marriage after I had speculated, like you just did, Abigail, that Poppa and Lillian were somehow destined to be together. Both relationships were impossible, and not just because of class differences. And she also dispelled my myths and illusions about Harvard, grounded what had been, I suppose, a sense of awe. Put things in perspective, scuffed up the rose on my rose colored glasses."

"And exactly how did she do that?" Sue asked.

"I don't know, exactly, but she was pretty clear-eyed. I think it came home when I discovered she had been married to a big shot Harvard professor. I didn't find out for a while, but I was particularly impressed. It came up once when we were having tea at the Algiers. Turns out she was wife number two. He left his first wife and married Eleanor when she was first starting out as a librarian at Widener. She was much younger of course. And after ten years of marriage, he dumped her as well for another younger woman. But he was a distinguished professor in anthropology. I never had any courses with him, but he was one of the big men at the time. Up there with Finley and Fitzgerald and Galbraith and William Alfred. One of the revered."

I poured myself a small amount of wine and held up the bottle, inquiring if there were other takers. There were none.

"So," I continued, "when I found out she had been his wife, I started to gush. I mean, he was an illustrious Harvard professor. How could I not be impressed? She told me I shouldn't be. And when I asked why, she simply answered, 'Because he's an idiot.' Lesson learned about misplaced admiration and making assumptions about successful people. Before that, I suppose I was pretty easily impressed. Not so much after that."

"You need to write all this down, you know," said Sue. Both girls agreed, and began a coordinated cajoling.

"It's very personal," I said dismissively.

"Then just chronicle it for the family," she countered.

"There are too many gaps," I said, "too many unknowns that would tie things together." I was expressing the frustration of a historian.

"For Christssake, Dad," said Abigail. "Just use your imagination and fill in the blanks!"

"I'll give it some thought."

"Promise?"

"I promise." I looked at my watch. It was getting late, and the girls needed to get going. We all stood up from the table, Sue told them they didn't need to bother with clearing their plates.

"Thanks for an interesting evening," said Eleanor, emphasizing the sarcasm with her tone.

"Sorry neither of us went to Harvard?" Abigail asked, clearly fishing.

"Not a bit."

Sue and I kissed them at the door.

"You have reason to be proud of your family history," I said. "Even the Pale couldn't keep a good man down. You share Poppa's genes, and his legacy."

"And we'll gloss over the illegal part," quipped Abigail. "And by the way, you also need to frame that Harvard Varsity 'H.'"

"That's a good idea," said Sue. "It doesn't belong in a file drawer."

"I don't think so," Eleanor said. "I'm going to buy you a really expensive white wool sweater and personally suture that little sucker right in the middle. And you should wear it everywhere."

We all laughed and they headed out in the dark to their cars. Sue looked at me and gave me a kiss.

My thoughts turned to Poppa, who never had the opportunity to wear a Varsity crew sweater. He made plenty of other opportunities for himself, though, you had to give him that. I was starting to tear up at the thought of him. I wiped the corner of an eye, composed myself, and managed to yell out while the girls were still within earshot.

"Only around the house, girls! I'll only wear the sweater around the house!"

ACKNOWLEDGMENTS

Most of this book was written during the Covid-19 pandemic, under lockdown in Australia, when I made the best of seclusion. You're living the reclusive lifestyle of a writer, a friend told me, so you might as well write. It is the product of my imagination and self-confinement—I visited no libraries, made no excursions for research, conducted no interviews, consulted no experts. What I was able to do, however, was dig into my computer files. Despite being over ten thousand miles from my beloved Boston, I was fortunate enough to have a trove of research materials from a previous non-fiction book. The bulk of the historical material which I have fictionalized is an outgrowth of that earlier research—a "two-for" if there ever were one—centered on the Harvard of the early twentieth century. For the vast majority of these materials, I am indebted to the Harvard University Archives, with special shout-outs to those with whom I came into contact over a period of several years: Samuel Bauer, Robin Carlaw, Ed Copenhagen, Timothy Driscoll, Virginia A. Hunt, Julliana Kuipers, and Robin G. McElheny.

I am grateful to many readers who contributed more than they probably realize, including Michael Beiriger, Dick Friedman, Sulari Gentill, Robert Gott, Keith Raffel, Robert N. Reeves III, Lawrence Siskind, Caitlin Vincent, and Betsy Wolf. Their advice and encouragement were helpful beyond words. George Putnam helped to fill my knowledge gaps about Manchester-by-the-Sea from the time before I knew it well. And once again, many thanks to Jim Cunningham for his design of the cover.

As always, I've heavily relied on the support of my wife, Sharon Tyers, as a sounding board and editor. Thanks for knowing me well enough, and caring enough, to persist over my obstinacy.

Victoria, Australia
February 2, 2023

IF YOU ENJOYED this novel by L.M. Vincent, you might want to check out some of his other books:

A THEFT OF PRIVILEGE

"Like a latter-day Sherlock Holmes, L.M. Vincent traces the picaresque doings of an elite secret society, from its inception in 1818 to its exorcism in 1905. Over the decades, the Med. Fac.'s daring pranksters tormented the administrators of Harvard College, bedeviled the police forces of Cambridge and Boston, and even hoodwinked a Russian monarch, Tsar Alexander I. Meticulously researched and ably narrated, A Theft of Privilege is an important addition to the annals of collegiate rascality."

—John T. Bethell, editor
emeritus, Harvard Magazine.

"A spirited and cheeky portrait of privilege and the 'smart set' at Harvard at the turn of the last century, complete with snot-nosed scamps and their old boy enablers in all their blue blood glory."

—Marty Kaplan, Founding Director,
The USC Annenberg Norman Lear Center

RECEPTION

"Vincent handles his farcelike plot very capably, as each new doorbell ring sets off a fresh chain of surprises, disasters, or erotic energies . . . A well-engineered farce . . . "

—Kirkus Reviews

261

SAVING DR. BLOCK

"An entertaining coming-of-age story . . . The historical setting provides a rich backdrop to the action, and the spy capers keep the story moving along at a quick pace. Humorous touches and a likeable protagonist make this heartwarming tale a treat."

—Kirkus Reviews

IN SEARCH OF MOTIF NO. 1 (A Non-fiction "Must Read," 2012 Mass Book Awards!)

"Like all good tales it begins with a question and tracks through some pretty interesting turf to get an answer . . . As he [Vincent] unravels the tale, he takes the reader through a delicious amount of local art history populated by some pretty colorful characters . . . It all makes for a quirky, personable read."

—Patricia Harris, BOSTON.COM

PAS DE DEATH

"Pas de Death has wit, intelligence, esoteric information, and a wildly inventive (yet plausible) murder method that is surely unparalleled in all of detective fiction. How much more could anyone want in a mystery?"

—Aaron Elkins

"Great stuff, carefully written and thoughtfully conceived."

—Adam Woog, Seattle Times

". . .the season's most original reason for not telling the police what you know about an unusually clever murder."

—Kirkus Reviews

FINAL DICTATION

"Final Dictation is the most absorbing mystery yet from Seattle's large stable of crime authors."

—The Seattle Times

"Vincent's first novel is a surprisingly ingenious whodunit with a hospital setting and a radiologist hero . . . a wry, well-plotted entry in a pleasantly old-fashioned mode."

—Kirkus Reviews

"Fascinating medical detail, an ingenious plot, and a surprisingly mature style . . . all contribute to a fine whodunit."

—Booklist

ABOUT THE AUTHOR

A native of Kansas City and former editor of the Harvard Lampoon, L.M. Vincent has published both fiction and non-fiction, and his plays have been produced regionally and Off-off Broadway. He and his wife have two grown daughters and live in Melbourne, Australia.

Made in the USA
Monee, IL
06 August 2023

40553710R00163